THE RISK

K. BROMBERG

Worth the Risk
By K. Bromberg

Copyright 2018 K. Bromberg
ISBN: 978-1-942832-13-3

Published by JKB Publishing, LLC

Editing by AW Editing and Help Me Edit
Cover Design by Helen Williams
Cover Photography Nicole Ashley Photography

This is a work of fiction. Names, places, characters, and incidents are the product of the author's imagination and are fictitious. Any resemblance to actual persons, living or dead, events or establishments is solely coincidental.

PRAISE FOR THE NOVELS OF K. BROMBERG

"K. Bromberg always delivers intelligently written, emotionally intense, sensual romance . . ."

—*USA Today*

"This book will have you CUFFED to your chair until the very last page of this high-flying tale."

—*#1 New York Times Bestselling author* Audrey Carlan

A poignant and hauntingly beautiful story of survival, second chances and the healing power of love. An absolute must-read."

—*New York Times Bestselling author* Helena Hunting

"A homerun! The Player is riveting, sexy and pulsing with energy. And I can't wait for The Catch!"

—*#1 New York Times Bestselling author* Lauren Blakely

"An irresistibly hot romance that stays with you long after you finish the book."

—*# 1 New York Times* bestselling author Jennifer L. Armentrout

"Bromberg is a master at turning up the heat!"

—*New York Times* bestselling author Katy Evans

"Supercharged heat and full of heart. Bromberg aces it from the first page to the last."

—*New York Times* bestselling author Kylie Scott

OTHER BOOKS BY K. BROMBERG

never go in search of love,
go in search of life,
and life will find the love you seek
—*Atticus*

Prologue

Sidney

"IT ISN'T WHAT YOU THINK. I PROMISE."

Eyes the same color blue as mine stare at me. Judge me. Scold me. The expanse of a desk is between us, but I can feel my father's fury as if he were sitting beside me.

He pinches the bridge of his nose and gives a sharp shake of his head. "Is there anything you've ever loved besides yourself, Sidney?"

"That isn't fair." Tears burn as I try to swallow over the bitter pill disappointing my father has lodged there.

"Isn't it, though?"

His words cut deep. But I screwed up. *Again.* At least that's the only way he'll ever see it. Frank Thorton is never one to allow room for error.

"Tell me what to do, Dad. Tell me how to make this better." My hands tremble, but I grip the arms of the chair to steady them.

Thortons never show that they are intimidated.

"I've let your mom protect you for too long. I've let her persuade me to give you chance after chance when you continually prove to me that you don't deserve it."

"Dad . . ."

"This is a business. This is *my* business. This is how I've provided you with those chances to do all the nonsense that you do. I love you, Sid, with all my heart, but if you worked for any other company, you would have been fired many times over."

"All I did was—" All I did was rush to Zoey's aid when she called me. I bite my tongue and stop myself from saying more. Excuses aren't allowed. Even if they were, I could have called. I could have let him know something happened so that someone else could cover for me.

But I didn't.

"How do you think my employees feel about you? Would they call you hard working and innovative or would they think you're spoiled and get to keep your job strictly because of your last name?"

"I told you, it isn't what you think."

"Then what should I think?"

My mind flickers back to the frantic phone call from Zoey. The bruises starting to mar her skin when I arrived, my rage over how a man could treat a woman that way, and her pleas for me not to tell anyone. As much as I know it would save my ass if I explained to my father why I didn't show up for the interview with the fashion-designer-turned-whistleblower Wendy Whitaker, I can't. I gave her my word and it wouldn't matter to him.

His impatience radiates around us, and I know from experience that it's best if I just keep quiet. The last word always has to be his, but I speak anyway.

"I know you won't believe me when I tell you someone needed me and I went. I lost track of everything dealing with the situation, and when I realized what time it was, it was too late. All I can tell you is that it was for a valid reason."

"And that reason was?"

I stumble over how to explain. "I can't say." My words are soft, my resolve a mixture of defeat and defiance.

He just purses his lips and stares at me over his steepled fingers.

"I screwed up. No excuses."

"Thank you. You know how I feel about petty excuses."

"I do, and I also know you love this company. I do, too. Journalism and editing are my passion, and overseeing a magazine is everything to me."

He eyes me with skepticism. "Are they, or is this just a passing fancy on the Sidney Thorton express until you find the next who-knows-what at the next stop?"

"That isn't fair," I say even though I know I haven't done anything to prove his theory incorrect. My last-minute trips and changing obsessions. My habit of picking up a new hobby or fad, only to put it down when something new comes along.

"If you could pick your dream job within the company, what would it be?"

His question throws me momentarily. "What do you mean?"

"We own ten magazines. If you could pick the magazine and the position, what would it be?"

Is this a trick question?

"Why?" I stand and move to the wall of windows that overlook the San Francisco skyline and valley below.

"Just humor me." His chair squeaks, and I know he's turned to watch me. "If I know your goals, then maybe I can help you attain them."

"The editor-in-chief of *Haute*. No question." I think back to the years I've spent imagining what I would do with the magazine. The original ideas. The new twists on the tried-and-true stories that have been published time and again. How I would put a fresher face on an industry standard that is slowly fading amid the tapering-off printed editions.

"Why?"

"It combines my two loves—fashion and talking about fashion with people who love it just as much as I do." I turn to face him, needing him to see I'm serious. "Add that to getting to oversee the perfected delivery of such stories . . . I mean, it's everything I could ask for."

He holds my gaze, gauging whether he believes me or not. I deserve his quiet scrutiny—I know I do. That doesn't make it any easier to stand here and not squirm.

"What would be your least favorable position?"

Tread lightly, Sid. He's up to something here.

"As long as I'm learning new things to gain experience to one day earn me that editor-in-chief job, I would be happy anywhere in the industry."

"That's a line your mother would fall for. Too scripted. Too perfect. Don't bullshit me, Sidney." Again, he steeples his fingers and leans back in his chair, as is his habit when he's deep in thought. "I'm in a quandary here over several things."

Quandaries are never a good thing when it comes to my father.

"What type of things?" Why is it I'm twenty-eight and my father can still make me nervous?

"First off, I'm mad at myself for giving you the leeway to think that silver spoon you were born with gets to stay in your mouth without you having to earn it." My gulp is followed by his sigh. "You do great work when you apply yourself. Incredible work, actually. Your eye for what will resonate with readers is instinctive, your ideas innovative, your take on stories fresh."

"But . . ."

"But you're missing the big picture, and that's my fault."

I shake my head, trying to follow his line of thought, but he holds up his hand to tell me there is more to come. "You know you're my pride and joy. But I've done you a disservice. I've let you think working here is a given. That you don't have to act responsibly when your last name is Thorton."

"I know that. I've never assumed—"

"You've never assumed, and yet, you've never had to get a job outside of Thorton Publishing. So, answer my question. If you had to pick a magazine that would be your least favorite to work on, which one would it be?"

Crap.

"C'mon, Dad, you know me."

"So . . . what? No kids. No family stuff?"

"Just no domesticity," I finish for him, and he chuckles.

"Ah, yes, I forgot. The woman who plans on jet-setting her whole life and never being strapped down with a child."

"You make that sound harsh. It isn't a bad thing to know what you want and not conform to societal standards about what a woman should or shouldn't want."

"Only the fashionably acceptable for you. And domesticity is not that, right?"

"That isn't what I meant. It's just . . . I don't know those things—motherhood and children—they're nowhere near my radar, so that would make it hard for me to contribute to a magazine that is focused on them. "

He chews on the inside of his cheek for a moment. "The board and I have been talking about eliminating two or three magazines from our portfolio."

"But why?"

"Decreased circulation."

"Isn't there decreased circulation across the board in this digital age?"

"There is." He nods resolutely. "But these also have a decline in online subscriptions and viewership. Of the three titles, there's one in particular I want to save. It is one of my first magazines, and it holds sentimental value to me."

"Okay . . ." The different titles of Thorton Publishing's magazines run through my head, and I try to pinpoint which one he's referring to but can only draw a guess.

"In order to save it, I need to beef up its online visibility. I need more hits to it, more buzz about it . . . more social media draw. With a fresh take that can reel in new readers, I can net more advertising."

"Okay," I repeat, a little quieter now.

"I think you're just the person for the job."

"What do you mean?"

Really, I'm more intelligent than I sound, but hell if I'm not standing here and staring at my dad as if it's judgment day. If it's a magazine with decreased circulation, it's most definitely one I'm not keen on.

I just screwed myself, didn't I?

He takes one look at my expression and reminds me, "If you really want that job at *Haute*, you'd do anything to get it, right?"

"Of course."

"Even figure out a way to save *Modern Family* and prove you're worthy of the job?"

"*Modern Family*? As in 'what's for dinner,' and 'how to get your kid to behave,' or 'silly summer crafts'?" I sound calm while I'm cringing on the inside at what feels like a major demotion.

"As in domesticity." His grin is wide and unforgiving.

This *is* a test.

He's watching me closely, waiting for the immediate rejection I refuse to give. Domesticity—motherhood, parenting, kids in general—is the one subject I know almost nothing about. Strike that. I know plenty about those things, but they are so far removed from my current life that it makes the notion hard to swallow. I can fake it with the best of them, but stepping in and working side by side with the people at the magazine and pulling it off? Now, that might be hard to do.

But editor-in-chief of *Haute*?

Holy shit.

"I can't just walk in and run a whole magazine."

"Rejecting the idea of hard work already, are you?"

"That's not what I mean." I sigh in frustration. "I mean, to step in without any footing and—"

"Relax, Sid." He chuckles when I don't find his little joke amusing at all. "I don't expect you to step in and take over. *Modern Family* has its own very capable and *tough* editor-in-chief, Rissa Patel."

"Great," I mutter through my forced smile. I can already see her finding ways to make my life hell.

"It will be. She can teach you a lot, but your main focus will be to elevate the magazine's online component. There are a million different and innovative ways to capture new readers and improve advertising. It's your job to figure out what that way is and how to implement it.

Whatever you do, I need to see an increase."

I think of the offices for *Modern Family* in Sunnyville, the town where I grew up. I think of leaving my very sleek apartment in my high-rise overlooking downtown San Francisco. I think of my best friend, Zoey, and having to leave her after everything that just happened. Sure, she says she's fine now. Of course, she'll say it again when I tell her I have to leave. But hell if I'm not going to worry about her or that prick she swears she'll never see again while I'm gone.

And I think of having to leave it all behind for a while to satisfy my dad with the lesson he is trying to teach me.

My resolve wavers. "I know nothing about—"

"And before you answer, I should preface this offer by saying it isn't an automatic. You don't do this and then step into the editor's shoes at *Haute*. Veronica will be retiring at the end of next year. That will give you six months to turn *Modern Family* around and then another six months to a year to learn what you need to do the job. Then and only then—with her blessing—will I promote you to your dream position."

"So, if I can prove myself to you and Veronica, the position is mine, correct?

"Correct."

"Should I assume that you're expecting me to leave soon?"

His tight smile already has me canceling my plans to head to Santa Barbara at the end of the month. The trip I've looked forward to for weeks. "Of course. Time is money." He glances at his calendar and then back to me. "Take your trip with your friends, but know this . . . you will be working on it every day until then from here on out, and the day after you return, you will be in Sunnyville, hands-on. You should be able to accomplish plenty in the month, so when you arrive there, you can hit the ground running."

"Okay." I fight the sudden swell of tears that burn. Are they because I know he's showing me a glimpse of mercy now only to be merciless on me later? Or is it because he's my dad and I hate that I've let him down?

"I'm not messing around here, Sid."

"I know." The words barely come out.

"And don't expect a warm welcome." I swear amusement flashes through the blue of his eyes. "They'll think you're there to spy on them and report back to me. They're already on edge over rumors about the magazine being yanked and their jobs taken away."

"Lovely." And then a thought hits. "What about the current staff? Isn't there someone there already qualified? Won't they be mad at me for taking a position from them?"

"That will be your first test in management. How to handle people with kindness and tact and earn their respect."

"Oh." Excitement flutters in my belly. The kind that flushes across your skin and puts thoughts in your head that you want to hope are real but fear aren't.

"Sid?"

I snap my eyes up to meet my father's and realize he's looking for a response.

"Deal."

"No hesitation? No, 'no, I don't want to move from the city'? No, 'oh my God, there are no malls in Sunnyville'?"

Don't, he's just being a jerk.

"No hesitation."

"Don't let me down."

"I won't."

One

Sidney

"**H**AS IT REALLY BEEN A WHOLE MONTH SINCE I'VE SEEN you?"

Memories of martinis by the poolside and dancing till closing time in Santa Barbara flicker and fade into a subtle homesickness. "Five weeks actually."

"Ugh. It feels like forever."

"That's only because you've been off playing in Seattle with your newest flavor of the month for the past few weeks."

"I like this flavor." She laughs that coquettish sound of hers that tells me she's having way too much fun while I've been here busting my ass to no end. "So, how's the new place?"

The new place is a tiny cottage I rented on the outskirts of Sunnyville. It's cozy and homey and nothing like the sleek lines and rich colors of my condo in San Francisco.

"It's . . ."

"It isn't *you*," Zoey says through her laugh, most likely from where she's overlooking the view of the city I've temporarily left behind.

"No, it definitely is not me." Not the uneven floorboards that creek when I walk on them. Not the hot water that lasts maybe a whole five minutes before turning bone-chillingly cold. Not the nosy neighbors who I've found peering over the top of the backyard fence to see what I'm up to. And definitely not the dog that barks incessantly at all hours of the night.

"Wine country and the headquarters for a magazine on motherhood seem serendipitous to me."

"Either that or a perfect complement. Maybe all those mommies need wine after a long day with the kid." I laugh at her logic that rings true. "Regardless, you left me to go back to your old stomping grounds."

"I was too young to stomp on these grounds. It's more like sleepy suburbia where teenagers go crazy and can't wait to leave."

She grunts. Her displeasure for anything that isn't the hustle and bustle of the city mimics mine. And, yet, the town's different from what I remember while still somehow the exact same. Hot air balloons float high in the sky, the view from their baskets affording the influx of tourists here for the harvest a visual of the mesmerizing rows of grapevines that pattern the hills around us. They look majestic but, years ago I thought they were annoying. Main Street is longer now, with boutique upon boutique of kitschy items ripe to attract tourists' wallets. I used to look at the street and see prison walls confining me, but this time around there is a quaintness to it all. An attractiveness that pulls out-of-towners here for weekend getaways or for wine tasting tours.

"Yeah, well, you left and now you're back."

"Not by choice . . . but what my dad wants, my dad gets."

"And what he wants is for you to prove you can save this magazine."

"Exactly," I say because she makes it seem as if that's an easy feat when I know it's far from it.

"Well, I think you're onto something with this contest idea."

"Who knew dads were such a hot topic?"

"If a man is hot, he's hot. And sometimes being a dad makes him even sexier."

"Uh—yeah, right." I roll my eyes. "It was your comment about how hot you think a bare-chested man holding a newborn baby looks that gave me the idea."

"Mm-mmm. Muscles and sweetness. You can't beat that."

"You need help." I laugh.

"Maybe I do, but you have to admit that there's definitely something sexy about a man who knows how to take care of a child."

"Whatever you say." Not on my radar. Too much baggage. Too much foreign territory.

"I swear to God there's something wrong with you. Either that or you haven't found a dad hot enough to make you see the error of your ways."

"I'll own that there's something wrong with me," I murmur as I approach an intersection and follow instructions as my GPS tells me to take a right, "so long as this contest is a success."

"From what you said, so far it is. Question is whether your editor is still being a hard-ass or not?"

Rissa Patel. I shake my head at the very thought of her. "She's a tough one to figure out."

"Just charm her like you do everyone else."

"She has a serious bullshit meter. Charm isn't something I can use to slide by her."

"Well, your dad did say they thought you were there to spy on them and report back about how everything is running there."

"The funny thing is I feel like it's the opposite. That Rissa is the one doing the reporting to my father."

"I doubt it."

"With my father? You do know who we are talking about, don't you? The control freak."

"Then put your foot down and assert that you're a Thorton. That you run the place." Her laugh is laden with sarcasm. "That'll get everyone gunning for you."

"Ha. Funny. That's exactly the problem. They all think I don't know a thing and am there to shut them down."

"That sucks." And there's something about the way she says it that eats at me. The privileged air of not having to care about where your next paycheck comes from, perhaps. But I fit in the same category, so I push the thought away just like I have tried to with the sneaking looks of annoyance the employees at *Modern Family* give me when they think I'm not paying attention.

"Tell me about it." I know the turns of this town by heart, but I listen to the GPS anyway, noticing new buildings here and there. The elementary school I went to has a fresh coat of paint and new playground equipment. Daisy's flower stand has expanded to take up the whole corner. Little bits of my past viewed through the eyes of someone who couldn't wait to escape and has now come back.

"So, the best way to show them you know your shit is to make this contest successful. And by the looks of what you've pulled together in two months' time, it seems that you do."

"Thanks for the vote of confidence."

"So, what's next with it? You just finished your second round of voting?"

"Yep." A right at Lulu's Diner. A left at the cinema that only has one screen. "We started with five hundred applicants, and I had interns narrow down that field to one hundred. With the second round of voting just ending, we have now narrowed the contestant field down to the top twenty." And lucky for me, calling in a few favors allowed me to get the word out about the contest and the ball rolling faster than I expected.

Nothing is more motivating than getting to return to the city, my life, and the carrot my father dangled in front of my face.

"Oh, twenty delectable daddies to swoon over."

"Let's just hope everyone feels that way, because those hot dads just might be my saving grace."

"More like your *Haute ticket*."

"Very clever."

She makes a noncommittal sound, which is punctuated by the clicking of keys on her keyboard in the background. "Who is it you're headed to see right now?"

"My last one, Grayson Malone."

"Last one. You say that so casually, like you haven't been drooling over nineteen fine-looking men for the past week."

"I haven't. I've only gotten to Skype with nine of them. Rissa took the other half."

"Wait. Hard-ass Rissa is helping you? I thought she was resentful of you being there. Why would she help you?"

"Because my being here and succeeding also means she gets to keep her job, so . . . she wants to help."

"What you mean is that she wants to keep you under her thumb and micromanage everything you do so you don't mess up."

"Maybe. Maybe not."

"At least she's helping some, resentment or no resentment. Just tell me that you're the one who's responsible for all the men and for rubbing down all the beefcakes. Oiling them up. Vetting their, uh, sexiness credentials?" Leave it to Zoey to think about that.

"Technically, we've split everything. The men and the workload. She's responsible for the copy and the website, and I'm in charge of garnering more advertising and press releases to get more attention." I pass the fire station and give more than a passing glance to the men washing the engine. "Once we finish informing them they are officially finalists, get a new photo, have them write a more personal blurb for the site, what have you, then we can move on to the next round of voting.

"You're talking to me here, Sid. That's way too much technicality. Can we just get straight to the more pictures part? Do you need a fluffer to come on set and keep them, er, occupied?"

"You aren't fluffing anything, and most of them are married."

"Damn. All jokes aside, have any had serious potential?"

I shrug. "Are they handsome? Of course. But there hasn't been one that has that *holy shit* appeal I'm looking for. The Mr. All American that will reel women in, with a little bit of rough edge to him that will keep them intrigued, and some kind of heart-wrenching story that will make women want to help fix him and make him all better."

"You mean what every woman is looking for? Good luck with that."

"I mean . . ." I struggle to put words to my explanation. "You know when you see a man who makes you stop in your tracks and just stare?"

"You're a picky bitch, so that rarely happens."

I ignore her comment and continue. "Exactly. If I can find a man who can stop me and make me stare and who has a good story—widowed, champion for kids' rights, something that will tug on heartstrings—then I know I'll be able to use him as the face of the contest."

"You want a man who women can't help but want to fix and then fuck."

"Eloquent as always," I say through a laugh.

"Just have them take their shirts off. That will get some attention. A hot body that makes women clench their thighs—or imagine his face between them—will win out over a sappy story any day," she adds.

"Yeah, yeah." I laugh. "But remember, this is mostly a magazine for moms."

"Moms like sex, too. How else did they become moms?"

"Okay, so I'm looking for a hot man who will make your thighs clench and who breaks your heart. What else?"

"The total package."

"The total package," I repeat in a heavily sarcastic tone. "You say it as if it's the easiest thing in the world to find."

"There's always this Grayson you're off to meet."

I want to tack the word "again" on to her statement because I know Grayson Malone from Sunnyville High School. Or, should I say that I used to kind of know him? Quiet. Resigned. Into academics. A lot on the scrawny side. Or maybe that was one of his two brothers? I try to put a face with his name but fall short.

"True." It's the best I can come up with.

More clicking of her keyboard. "What's with his picture?" She must have gone to the contest site. "How has he been voted into the top twenty? The picture is taken from such a distance you can barely see him. He's in a flight suit while all the other guys are shirtless. He has a helmet and goggles covering his face and everyone else is smiling big. Where's the skin? Where are the abs?"

"Yeah. Well. Flight suit? Nothing says sexy like a rescue pilot. I guess the lack of a visual leaves it all up to the imagination, and that's what some women like."

"*Rescue pilot* may say sexy to some. I'm sure the dad part says hell-to-the-no to you."

"I'm not that bad," I muse as I turn down a tree-lined street, the perfect picture of suburbia with manicured lawns and bikes on driveways. I don't think this neighborhood was built when I left, but then again, I was very limited in the places I ventured back then.

"Ha!" She exaggerates the sound. "A man tells you he has a kid and you leave smoke tracks trying to get away from him."

"Whatever. You're lucky I love you, or else I wouldn't put up with this crap from you."

"You do love me." The line falls silent, and I wait for her to say whatever she has to say. "Look, I know you're there because of me. I know you missed the interview because you were taking care of me instead of taking care of yourself. Thank you."

"No need to say it, Zo. As long as you promise me to never see that bastard again, then I'm okay."

"Done. Lesson learned. Moved on."

"You good, though?" I ask, knowing full well how bruises fade on the skin but not on the mind.

"Yeah, I'm good."

"Love you," I say.

"Love you more."

"Look, I'm almost there."

"Let's hope he has the *je ne sais quoi* you're looking for."

"Doubt it. I'm a hard woman to please."

"Like I said . . . you're a picky bitch."

I pull up to the curb and park, a sigh falling from my lips. "You're right. I am being a bitch. I feel like I've been going a hundred miles an hour since my dad gave me this assignment. I miss you. I miss home. I miss my bed—"

"Your bed *is* amazing."

"I have no roadmap here. I work in an office with a bunch of people who aren't sure if they should help me or hate me, and the only thing I know is that I can't let my dad down. We've gained some publicity for the magazine with this contest, but it's nowhere near where I need it to be . . . so yeah, I'm just exhausted and bitchy." I laugh because I really do sound like a prima donna.

"Well, fingers crossed this Grayson guy will be the one."

"Thanks."

"Good luck, and may your thighs be sore from clenching them together by the time you leave."

I end the call and stare at the address on my GPS and then back to the same numbers on the front of the house. The structure sits back from the road. Its stone veneer is various colors of brown, and the veranda spans its length with a big porch swing to the left. The grass is green, the beds are full of blooming flowers, and a bike ramp of some sort sits along the side of the house. A pickup truck is in the driveway, and a basketball hoop is off to the left of it.

I take one more long look at suburbia run amuck and wonder what will be on the other side of the door when it opens. What will Grayson be like? His wife? His son? Will he remember me?

As I make my way up the front path, laughter floats through the air, and the distinct sound of pots and pans comes through the open windows. I hesitate for some reason, and then I knock.

A voice inside yells, "*Dad!*" More dishes clink. Then there is the vibration of footsteps across the floor.

The door swings open.

My first thought: *what the hell*? I'm met with an oversize silver colander sitting on the head of whoever is opening the front door. No face, just the rough cut of a jaw, the stubble on his chin, and silver holes hiding everything beneath it.

My second thought: *holy shit.* He is wearing a plain white T-shirt that is a little too tight and stretches around biceps that aren't too big and aren't too small, the fabric between just snug enough to showcase every toned, cut inch of what lies beneath. Broad shoulders. A tapered waist.

Please . . . pretty please let this colander-wearing stranger be Grayson Malone because, *hello*? He just stopped me in my tracks. This is what I've been looking for. This is *who* I've been looking for.

A jaw-dropping guy you want to tear your eyes away from because you know you are staring but can't help yourself.

Let the thigh-clenching commence.

And I haven't even seen his face yet.

Is it asking too much of the universe for him to be some kind of tortured hero to boot?

Too much? Thought so.

"Can I help you?" His voice is deep and gravelly and scrapes over my skin in a way that makes me want to stand there and wait for him to speak some more.

For the first time, I have chills just from speaking to one of my finalists. Or is that a tingling hot flash? I'm not sure, but the one thing I am certain of is that he's exactly what I've been looking for. Let's hope that when he hears the news, he's still the nice guy I vaguely remember him to be and that he'll be thrilled to be a finalist . . . and maybe the Hot Dad poster child I'm already making him out to be in my mind.

"Um. Yes." I force my eyes off his torso and back up to the colander, where I can just see the curve of his bottom lip as it turns up into a smile.

"Dad!" a voice calls from somewhere in the house, right before footsteps pound down a hallway and then abruptly stop. "Oh my gosh. You're so embarrassing." A belly laugh. "Take that off." A slink of two small arms around Colander Man's torso.

"Sorry." The man turns to face his son and removes the colander. "But I am your father, Luke," he says in his best Darth Vader impersonation.

The little boy laughs, and I feel like such an outsider standing on the porch as the man ruffles the little boy's hair I can't quite see yet.

I clear my throat, and by the way Colander Man whips his head in my direction, it's as if he had forgotten I was there. I'm struck immediately by the man looking back at me. Light eyes. Messed-up brown hair. A grin that is wide and inviting.

Yep. He definitely has the "it" factor.

When our eyes connect and recognition fires in his expression, that smile that could warm your insides slowly falls, bit by sexy bit.

Oh crap.

"What are *you* doing here?"

The bite in his voice says it all. *He remembers.*

"Hi, Grayson. Sidney Thorton."

"I know who you are."

For the briefest of seconds, I get a glimpse of the little boy as he tries to step out from behind his father. He's the perfect mini-me of Grayson—olive complexion, brown eyes, lopsided smile.

And I hate how Grayson pushes his son behind him, almost as if he's protecting him from me.

"It's been a while, hasn't it?" I infuse cheer to bolster my waning bravado.

"Did something happen?" Confusion fleets across his expression. "Is there a reason you've come down from your castle on the hill, Princess?"

"What do you mean?"

Memories flash and fade. High school idiosyncrasies every teenager endures. The popular crowd and the wannabes. The cool kids who ran together and the kids on the outside who never were allowed in. Grayson working at Lulu's diner, kind and courteous but left to pick up after the mess I'm sure we made. Overhearing us planning our next party or get-together but never being invited. The friends who I thought were my world but who I never spoke to after leaving.

Is that what he's referring to?

"Look, that was a long time ago. We should—"

"What do you want?" He holds his hands up as if to tell me he doesn't want to talk about it, and it takes me a second to switch mental gears.

"I came to congratulate you on making the top twenty."

"Top twenty of what?"

"In *Modern Family* magazine's contest."

The laughter he emits is long and rich. The shake of his head is one of disbelief. The little boy peers at me between the crack of Grayson's body and the doorframe. "I have no clue what you're talking about. I'm not the type to enter a contest."

"It was a *hot dad* contest." Why is it when I say it this time—to him—I blush considerably when it hasn't bothered me at all with the others? Probably because I didn't know any of the others before the contest.

"*Hot dad?*" He shakes his head as if I'm out of my mind. "Nice try but, uh, pageantry isn't my thing."

"It isn't a pageant—you're the one who entered—there's a prize."

"I don't need anything from you. Not a prize. Not a hand up in life. Nothing." He turns away from me and then turns back around, his brow furrowed. He seems just as confused as I am but for completely different reasons. "Is this about Mercy-Life?"

"Mercy-Life? As in the air ambulance? Huh?"

"You're with a magazine, right? Are you trying to ply me with some fake contest so you can try to dig up some dirt that isn't there and create some bullshit story about my grounding? Slow news day, huh?" He stares at me, head to the side, eyes boring into mine, and the muscle in his jaw ticking.

What the hell is he talking about? "I work for *Modern Family*. It's a magazine on *family*. I don't know what you're talking about. You're a finalist and—"

"Nice try to get your foot in the door, but whatever it is you're selling, I'm not buying."

"I'm being serious." Why is he playing coy when *he* entered the contest?

"And so am I when I say that I'm not interested."

He goes to shut the front door, and for some reason, I have my hand out in a flash to stop it. "I just need a minute of your time."

"And I don't have any time to give you." His eyes meet mine. The intensity in them mixes with his disdain. "Have a nice trip back up to your tower on the hill."

The door shuts with a resounding *thud*.

From behind it, there's a whoop from the little boy right before he yells for Grayson to put him down. Those are the sounds of normalcy. Sounds of affection. Sounds I have no interest in, and yet, here I stand, staring at the front door, uncertain of why I'm not heading back to my car.

Thortons don't get intimidated. Or flustered. Or walk away without getting what they want.

Then why did he make me feel both, and why am I doing the last without the result I came here for?

It's the goddamn thigh clench. That's why. Zoey jinxed me. My thighs clenched at the sight of him, and then my head turned to mush.

But he's the one. The total package. Grayson Malone is the missing piece.

Problem is how do I get him to cooperate when he's clearly changed his mind about participating in the contest?

Because I need him.

This much I know for sure.

Two

Grayson

"GO PICK UP YOUR MESS AND THEN YOU CAN GO PLAY out back," I say absently to Luke as I set the colander on the kitchen counter and stare out the window. My eyes are drawn to a very nice ass highlighted by a black pencil skirt and high heels walking down my path.

Sidney goddamn Thorton.

I must be going out of my mind.

I grit my teeth as she climbs into a white Range Rover that has windows tinted so dark I can barely make out her golden brown hair.

Untouchable now, just like she was back then.

I run a hand through my hair. Did I really just accuse her of trying to write an article on a nonexistent story? Paranoid much, Gray?

Sure, her dad owns the goddamn magazine world, but I doubt she's had to lift one of her perfectly manicured fingers a day in her life.

Contest, my ass.

Logically, I know that she was here for a reason, so if the contest is a sham, what does she really want?

I stare at her car a little longer, waiting for her to pull away.

Modern Family? As in the offices off Main Street *Modern Family*? I hadn't known she was even back in town let alone working there.

Not expecting much, I grab my phone and type in the two words and am surprised when the magazine's glossy website pops up on my screen.

Jesus Christ. That's my first and only thought when I see the headline at the top of the page: "Coming Soon: Hot Dad Contest—Next Round of Voting."

I never entered any contest. If I had, why would self-absorbed, can't-break-a-nail, my-daddy-owns-the-world Sidney Thorton be knocking on my door when she made it more than clear so many damn years ago that I wasn't worth her time.

People change.

I snort. Not her kind of people.

So, what was she doing here?

"All done," Luke yells right before the back door slams. There's the clatter of him rifling through the bin on the patio for his helmet, his aimless chatter to himself. The noises come in from outside, but I'm too busy staring at everything I despise—privilege, silver spoons, and conceit—to wonder what exactly he's doing.

Sidney Thorton is just like Claire.

Too good for anyone but herself.

Should I expect any less, considering they were inseparable back then, before Sidney left town?

Anger fires anew when I look outside and spot the little boy I made with Claire. The little boy who is my whole fucking world. That anger only gets hotter when I think of how selfish she was to walk away. How heartless she is to hurt him each and every day with her absence.

Stop thinking about Claire. She isn't worth the wasted time.

Stop thinking about Sidney sitting there at the curb. She isn't worth the energy, either.

Two privileged peas in a pod I'd rather not think about.

Who likes peas, anyway?

But when I pass the front window again, she's still sitting in her car at the curb, head down, hands texting.

A contest. *Really*? What the hell?

She still has you staring, Gray. Still wondering. Just fucking ignore her.

She starts her car, and I force myself to look away. To turn toward the hundred things I have to do before I head out.

The distraction even works for a few minutes. I get lost in the chores. In thoughts about whether I should hunker down and pay bills or wait another day. In the next load of laundry. In wondering if I have enough to put Luke's lunch together or if I have to go to the store later.

Normalcy.

"Dad! Dad!" Luke's excited, and when I hear the front door slam shut, I'm immediately irritated.

"Luke? We've been through this a hundred times. You don't go out in the front yard without telling me!"

"But, Dad, listen. I had to get my bike. I had to—the woman . . . Sidney? She said you were going to win a contest. And it has a huge prize!"

If I weren't already agitated, I would be. Use my kid to get to me? Tempt him with prizes? I grit my teeth and try to remain stern. I grab Luke's shoulders and turn him to face me. "Did you hear what I said?"

His brown eyes look up to meet mine, and I immediately regret letting my irritation with Sidney get the better of me. "I'm sorry, Dad. I just wanted to get my bike so I could ride in the back, and she said you are going to win, and one of the prizes is a trip. A trip! We've never been on a trip . . . and I shouldn't have talked to strangers."

Guilt. The one constant of parenthood weighs heavily on me as I pull Luke into my arms and hold tight to him. "You're my everything, bud. I just want you to be safe." I nuzzle my nose in that spot beneath his neck where he smells like little boy and sweat and makes every regrettable decision I've ever made seem just perfect because they all led to having him.

He indulges me with the bear hug a little longer than normal because he knows he's in trouble, but even then, eight-year-old boys only let hugs last so long before they wiggle out of them. When he does, his eyes look up to mine and widen.

"You're a finalist in a contest, Dad!" His excitement lights up his face. "How cool is that?"

"I didn't enter any contest, though."

"But Miss Sidney said that you did, and out of hundreds of people, you are one of the top twenty. How cool is that?"

I attempt to ignore the twinge of annoyance over Luke knowing her name. I try to pretend that I'm not mad she just used my son to get to me. But the best I can do is keep it out of my expression.

"And she said she knew you in high school. Is it true? She's awfully pretty. Like, wife pretty. Maybe you should ask her out on a date—"

"Whoa, tiger!" I put my hands up in surrender and laugh despite his desire for a mother breaking my heart in two.

Again . . . *guilt*.

"Is it true?"

"Is what true?"

"Did you know her in high school?"

I think back to our brief interaction back then. To how I was definitely not a part of her crowd, nor did I want to be after how I watched them treat people.

"Vaguely."

"What does vaguely mean?"

"It means I barely knew her."

"Oh."

"Is the other part true?"

"Which part is that?" I ask as I turn back to his Star Wars lunch box and reevaluate what I've put in there so far for the trashcan ratio—what he will actually eat and what he will throw away so I will think he ate it.

"The pretty part."

I clear my throat. I can't deny those high-school angles she had have developed into grown-woman curves. "She's pretty." *Gorgeous.*

"So, should we ask her out on a date?"

"*We?*" I laugh and turn around, grab him, and flip him upside down. Anything to clear the thoughts I can already see him forming in his head. No way, no how will Sidney Thorton and I become an item.

She's too much like his mother.

The thought stumbles into my mind and sticks there knowing I'd never take the risk of him being hurt again. "No. I'm not asking her out. I don't even know why she was here since she doesn't live in Sunnyville anymore."

"I told you why she was here, and she is living here," he says as I set him on his feet, only for him to flop onto his back in the middle of the kitchen floor so he can look up at me. "You are going to win a contest. You were—"

"Son of a bitch." I smack the counter as realization dawns on me. Within seconds, I have my cell to my ear and am calling my brother.

"Some of us work for a living. Maybe you should try it," he answers.

"Grady," I sneer. It makes both perfect sense and no sense all at the same time.

"That's my name, pushing your buttons is my game."

"You didn't happen to enter me in any contests, did you?" I think back to a few months ago, to him and my older brother Grant snickering. Their comments about how they were going to get me pussy for miles.

He snorts as he fights back a laugh. "Now, why would we do that?"

We. Not *I.*

Goddammit.

"He's a finalist!" Luke yells and then shrieks as I swat playfully at him.

"A finalist, huh?" Grady sounds so damn proud of himself, and I'm not amused in the least.

"What did you do, Grady?"

More laughter. Then he clears his throat. "There was this hot dad contest."

"*Christ.*"

"We thought you fit the bill—"

"This isn't funny, Grady—"

"Hot dads are in demand to service hot moms, and we figured, what better way to find you a hot mom?"

"I get plenty of service, thank you," I say as Luke eyes me from his spot on the floor, ears tuned in to try to make sense of this contest that Sidney got him all fired up about.

"No, you don't. You get to cherry pick your pies when you're hungry. Quiet pieces of pie so as not to upset Luke and let him hope your just-for-the-time-being is going to be his mom . . . but you never really have someone to share shit with. So . . . fucking sue us if you want, but Grant and I entered you into the contest."

"I don't need a contest to get—er, serviced." I glance at Luke and then turn my back to him as if he won't be able to hear me.

"No one said you did. But it sure as hell isn't going to hurt." He chuckles, and there's chatter from the scanner he leaves on in the background. "Plus, there are prizes."

"I don't need any prizes."

"Money. A trip. Other shit."

"I don't need any money. Or a trip. Or other shit." Luke groans behind me.

"Ha. We all need money; it makes the world go 'round, brother." I can hear his smile through the line. "Besides, you could use the distraction while you're grounded."

"I'm going to hang up now."

"No, you aren't because you're a finalist and you know your ego secretly loves that you've still got it in the looks department."

I roll my eyes and shake my head. "You're an ass."

"And you're a *hot dad*, or so the voters think."

"I'm really hanging up now."

He says something else, but I'm already ending the call before I can hear it all.

Well . . . *shit*.

Bracing my hands against the kitchen counter, I look out the window to the hills beyond. To the greens and the browns nestled around this city I was born and raised in and really have no desire to leave.

There's no way I'm doing this.

Not a chance in hell.

"Dad, what does 'getting serviced' mean?"

Christ. And the beat goes on.

"It means when you go to the car place and you get your oil changed."

"You mean that dipstick thing?"

"Yes, and right now, that dipstick is Uncle Grady."

Three

Sidney

"THE WALL ISN'T GOING ANYWHERE, YOU KNOW, IN CASE you're trying to move it telekinetically."

I look over to Rissa through our communal office space near the back of the building and level her with a glare. Her dark hair is pulled back in a perfect chignon, her flawless skin is the prettiest shade of caramel, and those eyes of hers are sharp and unforgiving.

"You never know until you try, right?"

She lifts her brows and shrugs absently as she tries hard not to let her resentment surface.

She thinks I want her job.

No worries there, Rissa. Modern is one thing I like. Family is not.

"So, do we need to go over your task list again?" she asks with that motherly tone that insinuates if she doesn't remind me, I'm too careless to remember.

"You mean the one I completed last night? That list?" She stares at me for a beat, trying to gauge whether I'm telling the truth while my eyes silently warn her to back off. "I appreciate your concern, as always, but I've been here, . . . what, five weeks? And almost nine in total working on this project? In that time, I haven't dropped the ball once. I've completed every task you've put in front of me—no matter how big or how small or even if it is something completely different from what I've been sent here to do. If you've been testing me to prove my worth, I think I have. If you think I'm here to take your job, I'm not. And if my father has charged you with reporting back to him whether I'm being hands-on or not, then I can't see how you could tell him otherwise. Maybe we should have cleared the air earlier. Maybe not. But can we just drop this petty bullshit and just focus on what we're supposed to be doing, so both our lives are easier?"

Our eyes hold, her expression a mixture of stoicism, not wanting to give a reaction, and irritation at being called out. "Nine weeks is a blip on the radar in the scheme of things, Sidney. While you may have succeeded thus far, you still have a lot to learn. And I don't care what your last name is, I care what you can produce, and right now, you're sitting on a job only a quarter of the way finished. You've yet to hit any snafus, so in my eyes, you still have to prove your worth to me and everyone in this office. Understood?"

I nod out of reflex, the scolding sounding like practiced mother-ly perfection, while inside I want to scream that I've already proven myself.

If there's a reason she runs this place, she just demonstrated it.

"I can handle anything that comes my way."

She gives a measured dip of her chin. "Good to hear."

I take a deep breath. "Any luck with your finalists?" I ask, trying to calm the waters as my mind falls back to my one thought all after-noon: Grayson Malone. I can already see the pictures I'll have taken of him. The staging. The exploitation. Flight suit unzipped, aviator sun-glasses over his eyes. Then some with the glasses off so readers can see how crystal clear those eyes of his are.

I'm obsessing. Usually, it's over fashion. This time, it's over a man.

It must be this fresh country air finally getting to me. Maybe that and the fact that it's been a while since I've had sex, so the first man who makes me clench my thighs now owns my thoughts.

"I've met my ten, and America picked well. They all have serious sex appeal, but I have one who I think will be the winner. Defined.

Dedicated. And Delicious." She licks her lips and grins, the tension in the room suddenly dissipating.

"Is that so?"

"Mm-hmm. I put my money on Braden Johnson to win. Check him out."

She turns her computer screen my way, and I murmur a sound of approval. Dark skin that stretches taut over muscled perfection. Kind, brown eyes that hold a unique combination of sincerity and amusement. A smile that lights up his features and matches the one the little girl next to him is wearing. She's adorable and so are her pigtails.

"He's hot. I'll definitely give you that." I stare a bit longer, noting the way her whole hand is gripping his index finger. It still isn't enough to get Grayson out of my head. "But I'll take your money and raise the ante because the guy I went to see, the Grayson Malone guy—"

"The hometown boy, right?"

"Yep." I meet her smile for smile. "Not only is he the one who is going to win, but also he is going to put a face to this contest *and* give us the publicity we need to bring it to the next level. He's the total package."

Her laughter fills the shared office space. "That's a pretty bold statement about the flyboy we don't have a clear picture of."

"I'm telling you." I turn my chair to face hers. "We put him on the cover, and we'll not only sell print but also increase our online presence. Step up the promotions—I've already been able to secure BuzzFeed, TMZ, Perez. If they'll talk about him, we could get a rally behind him."

"That's pretty biased, don't you think?" she says, pursing her lips as she leans back in her chair and studies me. "Readers are supposed to pick the winners. Not us."

"I believe you already had your pom-poms out for Braden."

"Agreed. But you're the one in control. Pulling the strings. You could easily sway readers to vote for your man over mine."

"First, he isn't my man. And second, if it comes down to these two finalists, we could always have a cover contest. The most votes land the winner on a cover, or something like that. Let the readers feel involved."

"Could work." Her gaze doesn't relent, and I know she still isn't one hundred percent behind my turning her little parenting magazine into a hot man show. Skin sells. Let's hope that's true for my sake, anyway. "Let's get a look at the new images you got of him and the new bio you have written up."

All that bravado I just spewed is about to be shot to shit, but I fake it anyway. "I don't have them *yet*."

"Don't have them *yet*?" she asks as a smile toys at the corners of her mouth. "I'm confused—wait a minute. He's the only one who's local, who we can meet face-to-face, and you couldn't get a shot of him? Braden's from Kentucky." She points to the picture of him on the screen for emphasis. "And I was able to get plenty of new images of him. Last night he emailed about five to me. So . . ."

"It's complicated." Telling her he shut the door in my face doesn't really make me seem like manager material.

"Okay." She draws the word out with an impatient expression that says I'm a novice and don't know what the hell I'm doing. "Then how do you plan to exploit this guy—because, let's face it, that's what you will be doing—if you don't have pictures to show?"

"Like I said, it's complicated."

"You also said every single task was completed . . . and this was one of them." I grit my teeth at the holier-than-thou look on her face but don't say a word. "Listen, you're talented. Damn talented. But that pretty little ego and stubborn streak of yours doesn't allow you to take direction well. I'm here to help you. To teach you. Of course, I'm supposed to give reports to your father, but I know that's a double-edged sword for me in my position. So here's the thing—I'm tough, but fair. I can go toe-to-toe with you one minute and then brush it aside and get down to business without a grudge the next. But the question is, can you, Sidney? Your success only helps me in the long run, so we can either work together and I can teach you some things while you're here or we can go day to day, questioning the other's motives."

My spine stiffens. I want to reject her words on principal and accept everything she's said all at the same time. "Okay." I swallow over the myriad of other things I want to say because she's right. We need to work together.

"Good." All that's missing is her dusting off her hands to demonstrate this topic is over. "So, where were we? Grayson Malone. No new pictures or bio for next round. Why not?"

And just like that, she flips the switch in a way most women can't.

"I'm working on it. He isn't exactly enthusiastic about being a finalist."

"What do you mean?"

"He's either a really good actor or someone else entered him without him knowing it."

"Oh, even better." She rubs her hands together. "A reluctant hero. Those are always the sexiest ones."

"Sexy and then some," I murmur as I absently run an antibacterial wipe over my keyboard. When I look up, she's watching me with her brows raised as if to say I'm being ridiculous when it comes to germs. "You're from around here. Don't you know who he is?"

Her laugh is amused annoyance. "I'm a single mom with three kids all under the age of twelve. I don't have time to breathe or take a pee without being interrupted, let alone meet other people or follow their lives."

Her chastisement of my life—single and what I'm certain she feels is vapid and empty—rings loud and clear. "Oh." Not many people leave me at a loss for words, and yet, on the heels of her "you're-either-with-me-or-against-me" comments, I am. Her statement highlights the stark differences in our lives.

"I know of his family. His dad was the chief of police or something . . . but I've never met them. I live in Riverville and commute in to the office so . . ." Her words fade off as if to tell me that I should know this.

"I didn't know."

"Of course you didn't. You never asked." She straightens her papers with a sharp rap against the desk before she continues. "Was his wife okay with this?"

It takes me a second to respond, my mind still on her subtle rebuke of me never once really interacting with the staff here. "Wife? I didn't see anyone else there other than Grayson and his son."

"Ah, a single *and* hot dad. Even better for marketing. All we need is his backstory—preferably something good and emotional—and he's golden. Tell me we have that."

"I was just telling my friend the same thing, but—"

"But like the pictures you don't have a new bio."

"Right and honestly, I don't know for sure that he isn't married."

"Let me check." There are fingers on keys and murmurs from her as I wait. "The registration form doesn't say. That question wasn't answered."

I walk over to her desk and peer at the screen. "It also doesn't say who entered him."

"Maybe he signed up thinking nothing would come of it, and now he's embarrassed and doesn't want to claim it."

I twist my lips before saying, "Nah. From his reaction, I don't think he entered. He doesn't seem like the type."

"Can't you use some of your history growing up here to connect with him? Woo him or whatever you need to do to convince him he should do this?"

"Our history is a detriment."

She jogs her head and looks my way. "What's that supposed to mean?"

"It means I was a snotty bitch in high school who used to hang out at the diner where he used to work—Lulu's—and I don't think my friends or I were the kindest of people back then."

"The privileged kids too good for the middle-class ones who should be the hired help."

"Something like that," I muse, not too thrilled with the label despite knowing it's deserved.

She nods. "Good on you for owning it. And just think, this is the perfect way to make amends for it."

"What?" I ask through a laugh.

"Get Grayson to participate. Help get him some big-man-on-campus points for being a hot dad. And then reward him with the prizes if he wins. Maybe throw a party as a way of saying sorry for being a dick when we were younger while you're at it."

"Uh-huh."

"No, I'm serious. That's your new task. Get Grayson on board by the end of next week. He's definite eye candy, which will no doubt help with publicity, and that benefits both our jobs."

"You're serious?" I don't know why I ask that when I know it to be fact.

"As a heart attack." That smug smile of hers is back. "Figure out how to soothe his ego and make him your cover boy. My report to your father will be dependent on it." She turns her chair and faces her computer. "And if you can't, I've got Braden over here whose horn I want to toot."

"I'm sure you do."

"Can't blame a girl for fantasizing."

"You definitely can't."

Four

Grayson

"I HEAR CONGRATULATIONS ARE IN ORDER." MY MOM'S SMILE grows wider with each passing second as she stares at me.

"For what?" I look to Luke, whose grin mysteriously matches hers.

"Luke told me all about being a finalist in—"

"It isn't happening, Mom. It's most likely some marketing gimmick to save the whales or something and—"

"And you have something against saving the whales?" Her hands are on her hips, and Luke's snickering because that usually means someone's in trouble.

"She said she thinks Dad has a real chance at winning," Luke says excitedly.

"She?" My mom's ears prick up and every part of me bristles as she bends over and puts her hands on her knees to be eye level with Luke. "Who is she?"

"Miss Sidney," he continues. "She's really pretty and nice and—"

"No one." I push Luke gently on one shoulder as my mom puts her hand on his other and holds him in place.

"He was just filling me in on things you won't," she says with a lift of her eyebrows and that look that tells me even if we don't discuss this now, she'll get it out of him the minute I leave.

Just what I need.

"Why don't you go play with Moose," I say, referring to my parents' mammoth of a dog.

"There's a vacation and money if he wins. A vacation, Nana! Maybe we could go to Disneyland!"

"How fun," she says and smiles. He looks from me to her, shrugs, and then takes off down the hallway.

"No running in the house!" my mom calls out, and his feet slow to a hurried clomp before there's a quick thumping of a tail. The behemoth of a dog winds up in excitement over seeing his most favorite human, and Luke's laughter is loud as it carries into the kitchen.

"Who was this lady?"

"It doesn't matter who she is because I'm not doing the contest." I open the refrigerator and grab a bottle of water before sitting on one of the barstools that gives me a view of the backyard. "Thanks for taking Luke for a bit."

When I turn to look at her, her hands are on her hips and an expression that tells me she isn't buying a word of what I'm saying. "You should do the contest, and who is the lady?"

"I'm not doing the contest, and the lady is Sidney Thorton, as in Claire's close friend in high school, Sidney Thorton. You happy?"

"Oh." I take another sip and push around the unopened mail on the counter out of habit as she figures out what to say next. Recognition flickers in her eyes. I know she knows who Sidney is. "That shouldn't stop you from participating. It might be fun."

"Fun? No thanks. I have my reasons. Subject over."

She stares at me, completely dissatisfied with my response but aware that our staring contest isn't going to get her anywhere. I may be the peacekeeper in the family when it comes to others, but when it comes to my own personal matters, no one tells me how to handle them.

"Well, then," she says as she grabs the sponge and starts wiping down the already clean counters to busy herself. It's also her way to staunch the hurt I've just caused by not letting her mother me more. "So, uh, anything fun you're headed off to do?"

I can't help but laugh. After all that, of course, she reverts back to the classic Betsy Malone staple of conversation. When I don't respond, she turns my way to let me know she's already conjuring up stories about how I'm headed off to have a secret rendezvous with some mysterious woman.

"You already have a grandchild from me, and there sure as hell isn't going to be another marriage in my future, so the things I'm headed off to do won't interest you," I say and wink to cut her and her constant quest for more Malones off at the pass.

"A mother can wish, can't she?"

"You've had two weddings and added two more grandkids in the last three years. I think Grady and Grant are holding down the fort just fine for me."

"And now I don't need to worry about your brothers and can focus all my help on you. I heard you were out with what's-her-name not too long back?"

She's relentless, and I don't need or want her help, but I humor her.

"What's-her-name? She can't be too important if you don't even remember her name." I chew on a smile, knowing I'm frustrating her.

"Anna Metz."

"That was like three months ago."

"Well, was there something wrong with her? Why'd you cut it off?"

I glance over to where Luke is playing in the backyard with Moose before leveling her with a stare.

"I'm not seeing anyone right now. I never am."

"So, you just sleep with them, then? That's no way to find a woman to settle down with."

"No one said I was trying to settle down. Remember? I already tried that once. We both know how that turned out." There's bitterness in my tone that she doesn't deserve.

But then again, I didn't deserve what happened, either. To have the perfect life I swore we were headed toward blow up in my face all because of outside influence. *And affluence.* I'll never put myself in that position again. I'll never allow myself to strive for a happily ever after because that means I'd have to depend on someone else to get it.

"Not all women are like Claire, Gray." Her hand is on my arm, her voice softens.

"Feels like I'm fucking surrounded by them these days," I mutter.

"What?"

"Nothing. I know they aren't, Mom. I know all women don't walk away from a son when he's a couple of months old and then go through the legal proceedings to terminate all parental rights. And most kids don't ask every night if they're ever going to have a mom and look for one in every woman their father talks to. I know settling down might be good for me, but I can't put Luke through the false hope every damn time."

"Having a woman around might be good for him."

"We've been over this. You've seen it with your own eyes. Any woman I bring into my life, Luke becomes attached to. I can't risk him being crushed when we call it off. He's had more heartbreak than most kids should ever have to go through. So I get it, Mom. I appreciate that you're trying to tell me to have a life outside of being a parent . . . but not right now. Not when he's this young. Not when trust is an issue for him as much as it is for me."

"The only way to combat a lack of trust is to invite someone into your life and show him how to trust."

"You don't think I know that? You don't think I would love for him to have a mother who could take him to the million school activities that all the other moms are at, so he doesn't feel left out? I do, but I'm not there yet."

"I'll go with him. Any time. You just tell me when."

My sigh is heavy and is matched by Luke's laughter outside. I stare at him, at this perfect piece of me, and hate that he suffers because I couldn't make Claire happy enough to stay.

Then again, I don't think anything was more important to her *than her*.

"I know you will, and I appreciate it. But it isn't the same."

"I know." Her hand rests on my arm as we both watch him roll around while Moose tries to lick every inch of his face. "Then, you go with him to those mother functions. You're as much his mother as you are his father."

"That's comical."

"I'm being serious."

"I know you are. It's just . . ."

"It's hard balancing being a parent and being a person, being a single man. You aren't alone, though. There are tons of single parents—men and women—who face the same exact thing as you are, and they don't give up. They can't. It's their mini-me beside them who's looking up to them and preventing them from giving up."

I meet her eyes and see the compassion there. I know she means well, but some conversations are better not had with your mother. Like ones about sex and how casual it is or isn't. "I have a lot of shit on my plate right now, Mom. A lot. The last thing I need to do is get involved with someone."

"You'll be back to work before you know it."

"I shouldn't be suspended from flying to begin with."

"You always were one to take risks." Her eyes meet mine, and I can tell she wishes she could take this all away for me, but I'd do it again in a heartbeat if I had to.

"In my job, I have to. That's how I save lives."

"You took off when you were told not to, Gray. You disobeyed orders."

"Are you siding with them now? *Christ.*" I shove a hand through my hair and pinch the bridge of my nose.

"No. I'm a cop's wife," she says and winks as if I didn't know it. "I understand that sometimes the line needs to be blurred. But I also know there are supervisors for a reason."

Silence settles between us, and I push out a deep breath. There is no reason for me to be upset with her because, like before, I know she's right. "How did we get on this topic?"

"Because you're trying to find a reason why you aren't dating. You'll always have an excuse. Quit closing yourself off. Look at your brothers. They both found happiness when they were least expecting it. Love will come to you, too."

"I have to get going."

"That was a subtle way to change the topic," she says, and her smile is back and genuine.

"You caught that, did you?" I head toward the front door.

"Do the contest."

And my only response is to shut the front door behind me.

The base smells like cinnamon when I walk in, and that means Cochran must be here. There's a half-played game of chess on the table. A bowl of pistachio shells sits beside it, and two half-empty bottles of water next to that. Chairs are askew. The television is still on. The scanner and its constant chatter is a low hum of background noise from the corner.

Time has stood still.

Someone, somewhere needed the three-man crew to help save their life. Their injuries undoubtedly too serious to wait for an ambulance to take them to the hospital when our helicopters can do it in half the time.

I feel like a fish out of water—a bystander looking at my life that has been put on hold. I itch to get up in the air again. I'm antsy to do what I've spent years training for—to save people who need to be rescued.

And I can't.

I've been handcuffed by politics and red tape and a simple risk I took that cost someone their life.

A risk that was needed.

Feeling out of place and almost like I'm snooping by just being here, I move over to the schedule board. Extra shifts and overtime, each person having to pick up a bit of the slack my absence has created.

"Spiderman!" Cochran's raspy voice calls as he heads my way— the call sign Luke unknowingly made for me a few years back when he saw my red and black helmet during his Spiderman phase.

"How's it going?"

"Same ol', same ol'." He shrugs and crosses his arms over his chest as he leans a shoulder against the doorjamb. He looks at the schedule and back to me as if he already knows what I'm going to say before the words clear my lips.

"Looks to me like you are paying a shit-ton on overtime here. Overworking your staff. Take me off desk duty over at dispatch and let me fly. It'll help alleviate some of the pressure on them and give me back my sanity."

His expression turns solemn. "You know I can't do that, man."

"How long are you going to keep my wings clipped?" Irritation creeps into my voice, and I clench a fist in silent protest.

"Until Internal Affairs concludes its findings."

"Fucking Christ. I'm spinning my wheels sitting at a desk."

"I know, but you broke the rules."

"You're goddamn right I did. And I'd do it again in a heartbeat if I had to."

"And that's exactly why you're grounded. You take too many risks. First bucking protocol by flying. Then by switching hospitals en route. Someone died because of your decision."

"She was going to die whether I switched destinations or not."

"We have rules for a reason. That's why you're riding a desk at dispatch—so you understand the chaos on our end and why we need those rules and that protocol. That's a five-million-dollar helicopter you're taking chances with."

"And my job is to save lives with it. What good does it do if I'm told I can't do that?"

"The rules are there to keep everyone on the team alive, and you know it. If the team is compromised because one man can't follow the rules, then people die."

I rake a hand through my hair. Frustration and guilt and humility strobe inside me.

"Deep breath, Malone. It will all be over soon."

"Not soon enough." I blow out an exaggerated sigh as the scanner goes off and reminds me of the adrenaline rush I've been without for the past month. It's the way Cochran's brown eyes bore into mine that has me asking the question. "Do you believe I did the right thing?"

"We've been over this." He sounds just as exasperated as I feel.

"And you've never answered."

"Gray . . ."

"We've been over this with other people present. Now it's just you and me. Do you think I fucked up?"

"It was risky."

"I always take risks. I wouldn't be good at my job if I didn't. The question is whether we'd even be having this conversation if the patient had lived? Would the risk have been worth it? Ask yourself that one, and when you have an answer, you'll know I did the right thing. End of goddamn story."

"I have your back." It's all he says, but when our eyes meet, his are a silent mess of contradictions that I can't read and don't leave me any steadier than his words did.

"Then let me get back up in the air and do my job." With a shake of my head and one last look at the schedule that doesn't have my name on it, I walk away from everything that is comforting to me.

I drive aimlessly. I have a list a mile long of shit to do—groceries, new cleats for Luke, stop in to dispatch to get my schedule—but I don't do any of it.

Right now, I just need a fucking breather. No son. No thoughts. No goddamn gray cloud looming over my head.

As I hit the highway, I look over toward Miner's Airfield and see a helicopter lifting up. Fucking Christ. Why not throw what I'm missing right in my face? I jerk the wheel to the side of the road and just watch it.

My job saved me back then. After Claire left, when my mind was in the constant loop asking how she could walk away. And it was a curse. My twenty-four-hour shifts pulled me away from Luke and had me worried the whole time that he thought I'd abandoned him, too.

Of course, a five-month-old wouldn't think that, but it fucked with my head during the downtime while I sat in that room I'd just left and waited for another call to come in. The next emergency.

Strangely enough, each life we saved, saved me a bit, too.

I could still rescue people.

I could still be the best damn father I could be.

Her leaving us couldn't rob me of that.

Five

Sidney

"GRAYSON MALONE."

His groan is louder than the chatter of the patrons as I slide into the open spot at the bar beside his stool. "Quit stalking me." He keeps his head straight ahead and doesn't glance my way.

"I'm not stalking you at all." I glance around and smile. The place is large, dimly lit, and has a good-size crowd. A line of taps sits to my right, and a shelf full of half-filled glass bottles sits to my left. Three bartenders are behind the wooden top, joking with customers as they fill one order after another.

"Doesn't seem that way."

"Bars are popular places on Friday nights. It's a Friday night, and lucky for me, I was sitting right over there, minding my own business, when you walked in the door." More like saw him striding across the street and then heading into the bar when I was driving home and thought it might be the perfect opportunity to hit him up again about the contest.

"Lucky you." He lifts his beer and takes a long drink of it. There's something about the visual that pulls on me. His profile. His lips against the rim of the bottle. The way his Adam's apple bobs as he swallows.

And makes me clench my thighs.

"Mr. Talkative, huh?"

"Not when it comes to you."

"C'mon, I'm not that bad." He lifts an eyebrow in question but still keeps his focus straight ahead. Silence stretches between us as the chatter of the after-work crowd buzzes around us.

"Ha. I find that hard to believe." He turns and stares at me for a beat, his eyes glancing to where my hands are clasped on the bar and then back to me. "What? Is it too blue collar in here for your white-collar hands to touch? You think it will rub off on you?"

His comment throws me for a loop and leaves me sputtering to respond. "No. I'm kind of a freak about germs. I don't like—I'm not—it doesn't matter," I correct and shake my head. "I'm here to talk about—"

"The goddamn contest."

"Yes. It's real. I promise. We've had over seven hundred thousand votes come in for the first two rounds alone, and we're hoping to double that for the next one."

He snorts. "Great. Stellar. I don't need your magazine or its attention. It seems you ran the contest so far without my knowledge or participation, and it's done just fine. Keep doing what you're doing, and we'll both be happy."

"You're going to win, but only if I can get your help. All I need are a few photos of you and a short bio—anything about yourself, really. The next round of voting starts at the end of next week, and I need your help to save the magazine." I prattle on even though he doesn't react. "Your son is adorable. He can be in the photos, too."

"Absolutely not."

There's a bite in his tone that makes the bartender glance our way and leaves me staring at him. "Then your wife. We can include her in the photos, too, if you want."

He winces. "No wife." Those two words come out like a curse.

"I'm sorry for assuming—"

He stands abruptly and faces me so that our bodies are

inches apart. His eyes bore into mine, a combination of confusion and defiance.

"What is it you want from me, Thorton?" There's anger in his voice I hadn't been expecting.

It takes me a minute to find my voice, to remember I'm here to convince him to participate, when all I can concentrate on is the scent of his cologne—clean—and the heat of his body as he stands so very close to me.

Speak, Sid.

"To put water under the bridge."

Of course, I say nothing about the contest. The reason I'm here. There's something about him and the unfiltered intensity in his eyes amid the dim bar light that makes this quiet man seem a little edgy and a whole lot dangerous.

I swallow over the sudden lump in my throat as I wait for his response.

"Fine. The hatchet is buried." He leans closer so that his lips are by my ear, and the warmth of his breath sends chills down my spine. "Hope it doesn't hurt your reputation to be seen with me like it did back then. That would be a travesty." And with that, he waltzes away from me without saying another word.

I stand there for the briefest of moments, slack-jawed and surprised by his animosity when I shouldn't be. What I should be doing is trying to make amends, maybe say I'm sorry, secure him for the contest—and I scramble toward the exit after him.

The cool night air is welcome as it washes over me after the stuffy heat of the bar. I take a few steps into the darkened alley and look for Grayson, but I don't see anyone.

Hugging my arms around myself, I head toward the edge of the building. There's nothing there but a few dumpsters against a chain link fence.

It's when I turn to head back into the bar that I startle.

"Hey, there." The man's hair is disheveled, his belt buckle shines off what little light is back here, and his eyes are laced with a suggestion that makes my skin crawl.

My hands grab the strap of my purse where it rests against my chest, but I stare him squarely in the eyes and nod a greeting I'd rather not give.

He takes a stumbling step toward me. "You're a sweet little thang, you know that? I bet you'd feel *real* good."

My first thought is that his grammar sucks. My second is, why in the hell am I focusing on his grammar when I'm alone in an alley with a drunk man?

Because I'm nervous.

I shouldn't be. The door to the bar is right there, and there is probably at least one other person somewhere close. Yet, even knowing that, fear slowly coats my skin.

When I take a step to my right to put more distance between us, he mirrors the movement and emits a soft chuckle.

Get a grip, Sid. You're fine.

"You're looking mighty sexy. Love them heels with that skirt." A deep, guttural groan suggests what he's thinking about wanting to do to me.

He takes a step toward me.

I take one back.

My pulse thunders in my ears when it shouldn't. I've dealt with plenty of assholes like this in San Francisco. Drunk guys who've had a few too many beers and let their buzz exacerbate their machismo. Only, we aren't in San Francisco where people are constantly milling around. We're in Sunnyville in the back alleyway of a bar where the music is so loud inside that even if I scream, I don't think anyone would be able to hear me.

Another step.

Another one in retreat.

"My friend just ran to his car. He'll be right back." The lie comes out effortlessly, but the lopsided smile he gives me and the way his eyes run up and down every inch of my body tells me he doesn't believe a word of it.

"C'mon, sweetheart, just a little dance in the moonlight with me won't do you any harm."

"No thanks. I have other plans," I say. The only way out of here is to pass him, but I won't be able to do that without him grabbing me.

My pulse pounds in my ears.

With my head up, I keep my eyes on his, hoping my direct eye contact might deter him from escalating this situation.

My palms are sweaty.

"Can you please step out of my way?"

My throat is dry.

"Now why would I shy away from a pretty little thang like you?" He slurs a few words, and his gait is unsteady as he sways side to side.

I'm not sure if I should feel relieved or worried that he's drunk. It's when I try to skirt past him—just when I think I'm free and clear— that he lunges and has a hold of my bicep.

A laugh falls from his mouth at the same time a shriek escapes mine.

"I don't mean no harm . . . just want a little kiss." He fumbles over the words as the stench of alcohol on his breath assaults me.

I yank my arm away, but he holds tight. "Get off me." I grit out between clenched teeth.

He only pulls me closer. The undertone of cologne. The scrape of his denim against my bare legs. The sting of his fingernails digging into my skin.

Panic. Fear. Anger. All three riot around inside me.

"I just wanna dance. Let's dance." He tries to sway to some kind of rhythm as he hums.

My stomach roils, and I freeze when every part of me screams to fight him. Kick him in the nuts. Gouge his eyes out.

Seconds pass. My synapses fire.

"Get away from me!" I shout and shove him off me as hard as I can at the same time I hear, "Get your hands off her."

Grayson?

Grayson.

It's a split second between the man letting go of my arm and Grayson pinning him to the wall, using his forearm to crush the guy's windpipe.

"Sorry, man, I was just trying to have a little fun," the drunk guy slurs.

"Yeah, and she didn't want any." Grayson fists his hand in the guy's shirt and yanks him off the wall.

"I didn't—I wasn't . . ." The guy stumbles, almost falling before he rights himself. "God, I'm fucking drunk."

"Get the hell out of here, before I call the cops so they can help you sober up." Grayson shoves the man toward the other side of the alleyway. The man looks back, almost as if he's been shocked sober and isn't sure what's going on. "Keep walking."

I stare at Grayson's back, my adrenaline fading. My panic shifting to shame. My fear morphing into embarrassment that I couldn't handle myself.

I was handling myself.

I think.

Then why do my knees feel like rubber and my eyes burn with tears?

Right when I feel like I'm going to give in to my moment of weakness, Grayson turns around and faces me.

For one short moment, I allow myself to feel relief, to feel safe. Then the shock of what just happened—of Grayson being the one to render help—has me straightening my spine.

There's a look in his eye—controlled rage warring with complete concern—that pins me motionless, allowing me to feel every thump of my heartbeat as the adrenaline races through my body. A small part of me wonders if it's because of the man who just ran away or because of the man who's standing before me, looking just as dangerous to me but in a completely different way.

Vulnerability is not something that suits me, and yet I feel exposed when the threat is no longer near.

Or is it?

"Christ, Sidney." His eyes flicker over every part of me. Checking for bruises. Looking for tears. Waiting for a meltdown. "I forgot to pay my tab. I was coming back to—how stupid can you be?"

"Excuse me?" If he wanted to give my emotions whiplash, then he just accomplished it.

"What woman walks into a dark alley behind a bar by herself?"

"You're blaming this on me?"

"Damn straight, I am. Are you too coddled to have common sense?"

Asshole. "I was looking for *you*," I say between clenched teeth as I glare at him.

Our eyes hold for the briefest of moments before he turns and paces from one side of the alley to the other. His hands are on the back of his head when he blows out an exaggerated breath as if he's trying to rein in his temper. When he stops in front of me and holds his hands out to his sides, it's obvious his attempt is unsuccessful.

"Looking for me? Why? To *save* your magazine? Save it your goddamn self." There must be something in my expression—call it blanket confusion—that has a smirk coming to his lips. "Ah . . . you didn't realize you said that, did you? A little slip of the tongue while you were fumbling through your sales pitch inside?"

Did I really say that? Crap. Crap. Crap.

"You know, a real gentleman would ask if I'm okay."

"No," he says and takes a step closer. "A real gentleman would step in to save you like I did, and a real lady would say thank you for doing so . . . but it's you, right? You want something from everyone but refuse to give anything to anyone, so a thank you is off the table."

"That isn't fair."

"Save it, Princess; life's not fair." There's a bite to his tone as he takes in my trembling hands and shivering body, but he never utters the words his eyes say—are you okay?—before they turn cold again. The brief glimpse of compassion is gone. "And it seems to me you're just fine, so playing the damsel-in-distress thing doesn't work for me, and it sure as hell isn't going to get me to sign on as the poster boy for your stupid contest."

"The last thing I need is a man to swoop in and save the day."

"Huh. And I thought all princesses were helpless and liked to be saved."

"I am not a princess."

"You just stomped your foot like you were." He shakes his head before looking to the edge of the alley and then back at me. "Are we done here? Because if so, I'll just take off, and you can stay here and find someone to take my place in your contest."

"You're an asshole, you know that?"

His chuckle reverberates off the brick walls of the bar's exterior and back to me, causing every part of me to bristle. "You're not the first to call me that, and you sure as hell won't be the last."

His words grate on my nerves and have my thoughts misfiring so I can't actually form words. All I manage to get out is, "Grayson." My mouth opens and closes several times but nothing else comes out.

"What's that?" he asks as he holds a hand up to his ear. "It seems that you're having a hard time thinking of what to say, so I'll help. The words you're looking for are 'thank you.' Then again, I shouldn't expect it from you now since you never knew how to say them before. I'm old enough to know that people don't change."

"That's not—"

"Fair. I know," he says nonchalantly. "Are we going to stand here and wait for Mick to come back or what?"

"Mick?"

"Harmless drunk guy. Oh . . . wait. Is this all a set-up to see who would take the bait? Should I go so Mick can come back and you can wrangle some other sap from inside to rush out and save you, so you can put him in your contest?"

"This wasn't a setup. I'm not that conniving or desperate to pull a stunt like that."

"You sure about that?"

"Screw you."

"No thanks, I haven't had enough to drink yet."

I grit my teeth and fist my hands as every part of me rejects him. At the same time, I hate myself for watching the flex of his bicep as he runs his hand through his hair in frustration, as I remember the heat and feel of his body against mine earlier.

"Such an ass," I mutter as I stalk past him with fury in my veins.

"So that means no thank you then?" he asks above the click of my heels on the uneven pavement only serving to make me step a little harder.

And then falter.

Fuck.

I stop and hang my head. What in the hell am I doing? I'm standing in a dank alley with the neon from the sign at the front of the bar projecting an eerie glow around me and letting my temper get the better of me.

Is he being a prick? Yes. Is he baiting me so that I hate him and will leave him alone? Hell, yes.

And I walked right into it.

Crap. Crap. Crap.

"Look, I'm sorry." My words are quiet, but I know he hears every word because his steps slow and then stop. "Thank you for your help."

When I lift my head, he's staring at me, head angled, eyes unrelenting, bottom lip worrying between his teeth. "No thanks needed. A gentleman doesn't step in for those . . . but it's amazing what sincerity and humility can do to a person's appeal. You should try it more often."

Don't take the bait.

"What's your problem, Malone?"

"You." He's so matter-of-fact it startles me.

"Me?"

"Yep." This time with a definitive nod.

"Hold grudges long?"

"Nope. Just smart enough to know that people don't change and too busy to give a rat's ass if they do."

We stand there and stare at each other across the dim light as our wills battle.

"You're infuriating."

"Good. Then maybe you'll drop this contest nonsense and stop stalking me to try to win me over." He lifts his eyebrows as he waits for a response.

"That's what this is all about?" I laugh in disbelief. "You're pissed off because you entered a contest and now you don't want to be a part of it?"

"First, I didn't enter any contest—my brothers entered me. And second, my opinion of you has nothing to do with my saying no to the contest. It's your holier-than-thou attitude that has me saying no." He retreats a step, the parking lot of cars at his back now, and then takes a look at my hands and smiles smugly. "Make sure to wash that blue-collar off you. It doesn't suit you too well."

With that, he walks over to a truck parked across the street, climbs in, sends one final glare my way, and then pulls a U-turn and drives off.

For some reason, I walk to the corner of the street and stare at his taillights as they glow at the stoplight, willing him good riddance while at the same time fighting the urge to chase him down so I can get the last word in.

It's probably best he left when he did. I chuckle, clearly hearing the lunacy edging its sound as I wonder how in the hell I'm going to undo all of that. How am I going to step this back so that I can accomplish the one thing Rissa tasked me with?

"Sidney Thorton? Is that you?"

I startle at the high-pitched shriek of someone who obviously recognizes me, and there is only one person who has that kind of voice—chatty Cathy Clementine.

"Cathy? Oh my God, hi," I say the minute I turn and see that I'm right. "It's been forever."

"Over ten years." She laughs as she moves in for a quick hug. It's so unexpected that it leaves me momentarily stunned before I reciprocate it so I don't look like I'm being a bitch. "And you look no worse for the wear."

"And neither do you!"

"Oh, honey, no need to lie. I've gotten rounder and softer, and you've gotten skinnier and hotter."

I blush, feeling neither of those things after everything that just happened.

"Was that Grayson Malone you were just chatting with? Or should I say having a lover's spat with? Things looked a little tense."

She hasn't changed one bit. Always wanting to know everything about everyone.

"No. We're not—he isn't . . ." I pause to collect my thoughts, which are on the far side of chaotic. "He just helped me with something."

"Whew. Thank goodness, or there would be hearts breaking all over Sunnyville tonight."

"Why's that?"

"He's a hard one to compete for, and you're a hard one to compete against."

"Oh, stop. You're too nice to my ego," I say and put my hand on her arm.

"What brings you back to good ol' Sunnyville anyway?"

"I'm just in town to help revive a magazine. Nothing permanent. How are you doing?"

"I'm good. Teaching second grade over at the elementary school. Nothing too exciting compared to the glamorous life I'm sure you're living," she says and laughs in a self-deprecating way that makes me sad. "But enough about me. Tell me more about you."

"There's, uh, nothing really to . . ." For some reason, I glance in the direction Grayson's truck went, and when I look back at her, she has her head angled to the side, studying me with a knowing smile on her lips.

"Those Malone boys really know how to make you squeeze your Kegels, don't they?"

"Jesus." I all but laugh.

"Are you going to tell me I'm wrong?" A lift of her eyebrows. A playful punch to my shoulder. "They are one hot trifecta."

"Since Grayson's the only brother I've seen since I've been back in town, I can't agree or disagree." I figure I'll play it safe with that response because if Cathy is still the same as she was in high school, anything I say can and will be used against me in the court of local gossip.

"Agree. Just flat-out agree because, let me tell you, those men were not created equal."

"Fine, I'll agree, but I have a feeling their wives might take offense to your strengthening your Kegels while thinking about them."

She purses her lips before they spread into a wide grin. "Emerson and Dylan are cool. I'm sure they'd be okay with it for the greater good of man."

"Who? What are you talking about?" I ask, more than aware that chatty Cathy Clementine has not changed a bit—talking in nonstop circles that are sometimes hard to decipher.

"Their wives. Grant, who's a cop now, is married to Emerson Reeves. And Grady is married to Dylan McCoy, who you've probably heard on the radio," she says, and I nod because I do, in fact, know who Dylan McCoy is.

"And then there's Grayson," I murmur, thinking about the colander on his head and the way his body just felt against mine.

"Single as a Pringle." She laughs at her own joke. "And a man who knows how to reel the women in but kick them out of bed before the sheets get too warm if you know what I mean."

"Really?"

"'Player' isn't exactly fair. How about . . . discreet? He has a line of women a mile long who are all willing to be his plaything, but he keeps any relationship—if you can call it that—on the down low because of his son . . . *or so they say.*"

"Who are *they*?"

"The women in line waiting before and after me for a chance at him, who may or may not have friends with firsthand knowledge if you catch my drift." She winks and then startles when her phone texts an alert.

She pulls it from her purse and looks down at it before meeting my eyes again. "I'm so sorry, but that's my friend I'm meeting, and she's wondering where I am. I've gotta run and catch her . . . but we should go for drinks sometime and catch up. I could fill you in on all the town gossip—heavy on the Malone part if you're thinking of stepping in line with the rest of us."

That's ten years' worth of gossip that no doubt Cathy has memorized and is ready to repeat.

"Catching up would be great. I'd like that." My smile is genuine despite her offer being a blatant reminder of why I steered clear of her in high school—her knack for gossip. The fact that everyone knew everyone else's business was one of the main things I couldn't stand growing up here. So why is it now that I'm kind of looking forward to meeting up with her again?

Maybe it's because she doesn't seem to judge me by my past like so many others in town have.

Either way, I have to take friends where I can get them these days.

Six

Grayson

I STARE AT THE LIGHTS THAT ARE ON IN THE OLD KRAFT HOUSE ON Olympic Street and debate whether to go knock on the door or not.

She deserves an apology.

I was in a shitty mood after leaving the station and seeing everything I'm being shut out of. Then she pushed my buttons when all I wanted to do was sit at the bar and enjoy my goddamn beer before going home to a quiet house. I don't want to be part of her contest, let alone be the goddamn poster boy for it. I don't want her friendship. I don't want an apology for the inconsideration she showed me in high school.

But I stood there in that bar with her body so goddamn close to mine, and all I wanted to do was kiss her. How is that possible? How can I despise her . . . not want anything to do with her, yet, have to force myself to walk away just so I wouldn't kiss her?

Then there was fucking Mick. Regardless of how harmless the drunk bastard typically is, he only served to complicate the matter. Forced me to be near her when I purposely made myself walk away. Of course, it wasn't all her fault. Any sane man knows that, but the way she acted—the way she lifted her chin in defiance—or superiority—just like she used to do, and fuck, if my buttons weren't pressed.

Hell if I didn't cling to that reaction to push her the fuck away when the adrenaline coursing through my body was begging for it to be my hands on her instead of Mick's.

Christ.

It's a bad sign when you want to fuck the person you have determined you hate. When you're sitting outside her house second-guessing your reaction.

But here I am.

It only took a few calls to find out where she was staying. The Kraft house is a good choice; although, it's probably far from the high life I'm sure she's used to outside of town.

My intentions were to march up there, knock on the door, and apologize for being a dick. For accusing her of setting the whole situation up. And to let her know that I will not be her trophy to put on display to save her magazine. If it's Sidney Thorton, then there has to be something in this for her. The girl I used to know did nothing unless she got something in return.

But I haven't done shit. Instead, I'm sitting here realizing the excuse I made to myself—to make sure she'd made it home okay—has been surpassed by my need to apologize for all of the above.

Fucking manners.

I'd make Luke apologize. That would be the right thing to do.

So why am I hesitating?

Her silhouette moves across the window and holds my attention. Her hair is down and falling over her shoulders. I stare at the shadow and hate that I'm picturing her from earlier. Those shocked brown eyes. Those parted lips. The heat in her cheeks. The undeniable shape of her body.

I hate myself for staring at her. I despise that I'm wondering what those lips feel like and how those nails of hers would feel raking down my back.

Sitting here and thinking these thoughts makes me no better than Mick.

And that's why I start my car without knocking on her door . . .

because fuck dropping myself to Mick's level. Fuck Sidney Thorton. Fuck the girl who used to push my buttons as a teenager and who is hitting a whole hell of a lot more as a grown woman.

She's the type of woman I steer clear of. Materialistic. Shallow. Selfish.

It doesn't make me want her any less.

I pound my fist against the steering wheel because that isn't fair. That's the teenager she used to be. I have no clue what she's like now.

Goddamn gorgeous is what she is.

Shit. I've changed leaps and bounds since then. A lovestruck twenty-year-old who was so busy with himself and the day-to-day he missed every sign that the mother of his son wasn't planning to stick around.

How fair would it be for someone to judge me as that man for the rest of my life when now I know it's the little things you have to pay attention to? The frustrated sighs. The lack of responses. The back facing me every night in bed when it used to be lips nuzzled against my neck and fingers linked with mine.

Christ. My hands grip the steering wheel as I hit the red light.

People change, Grayson Malone. Look at yourself.

So why am I having such a hard time believing Sidney can, too?

Because she's trouble with a capital T.

That's a fucking fact.

The light turns green, and I rev the engine a little harder than I should. So much for apologizing.

And so much for not thinking about her, either.

Seven

Grayson

THE RAIN WHIPS VICIOUSLY AGAINST THE WINDSHIELD.

Cochran's voice fills my head. "Goddammit, Malone. It's too dangerous to fly in this storm."

The *thwack, thwack, thwack* of the blades overhead is like a metronome to the sights and sounds.

Ignoring Cochran, I turn to my crew. "Who's with me? You don't have to fly, but I can't leave them out there to die." The concerned looks on the faces of my crew as I give them the option while dispatch frantically sounds off in the background.

Drunk driver in head-on collision. Four patients in serious condition. One more a trauma alert.

"You aren't going anywhere."

"Bullshit. They need us. I'll fly on my own if I have to."

The ambulance's lights cut through the darkness of the night. Red flashes over and over as precious seconds tick down, each one another moment less to save the patient we're about to transport.

"ETA Spiderman to Sunnyville General?" Dispatch's voice crackles in my ear as I watch the ambulance doors open and my lone flight nurse help pull the stretcher out of the bus. A medic is straddling the patient, hands occupied somehow trying to save the life as they move across the grassy field. Their progress is hindered by the mud, but they push on. The rain is thick, the air is cold, and it's frigid as fuck.

"We should be airborne in about five minutes."

"Be careful, Malone. There's an aircraft advisory."

"I'm aware." I squint to see through the rain.

"You shouldn't be fly—"

"Our ETA is roughly thirty minutes out."

"Ten-four. Keep us apprised. Staff will be on standby."

"Will do."

The doors open on the chopper and a burst of cold wind whips inside as the crew yells codes to each other above the roar of the rotors. I look back to Alyssa, my flight nurse, who looks wary as she glances at the weather whipping around us before looking at the patient that she's helping to load. She meets my eyes briefly, and the subtle shake of her head tells me that the patient is worse than she thought. The medic from the ambulance doesn't move from astride the patient as the stretcher is secured, and I overhear something about fingers holding the femoral artery.

The doors close as more codes fly between the crew in a symphony of chaos we all understand.

I look back, and for a split second, the crew parts, revealing the face of our patient. Fucking Christ. Blood covers every part of her except for a small section of her face, a face I know. Her petrified eyes are wide open and unresponsive.

Reese Dillinger.

I clench my jaw and turn forward, my hands gripped on the cyclic stick so I can take off as soon as everyone is clear.

Precious seconds tick by as I jog my knee and wait. This hits way too goddamn close to home.

Holy shit.

C'mon.

Tick.

C'mon.

Tick.

C'mon.

Tick.

I get the all clear, and with a deep breath, lift the bird up into the swirling wind. We're jolted violently to the left by a pocket of air when we clear the trees, and Alyssa yelps in reflex, but there's fear in her tone.

"Hold on," I murmur to myself, with a quiet will to make this flight as quick and safe as possible to give Reese the biggest chance of survival.

I think to our interaction over the years. Elementary school with her hair in pigtails. Middle school with braces on her teeth. High school when she was suspended for helping steal our rival's mascot. Hanging out at the mall. Birthday parties. She was a part of my memories growing up, even if she wasn't front and center. A child of privilege and little responsibility but good, nonetheless.

The sounds of vitals and the determination of my flight crew sound off in my headset, spiking my adrenaline so high my hands start to shake.

She doesn't have time.

Reese and her date, part of my circle of friends in the limo on the way to prom.

The ride is rough. We're pitched every which way as my copilot and I battle for an equilibrium of sorts.

Reese strutting her stuff in her cheer uniform during a pep rally.

We pass over the highway. We skirt around a small aircraft that has even less business being out in this weather than we do.

Reese showing up to see if she could do anything to help me after Claire up and left. My pushing her the hell away because I didn't need anything or anyone. I was too scared. Too angry. Too everything.

"She's coding. Christ. Levi, grab it tighter!" I hear from the back, and I can only assume Levi is the paramedic whose fingers are currently somewhere in Reese's leg, pinching her artery closed.

She's just a patient. A faceless patient.

But she isn't. *She's Reese.*

I'm too damn close.

"She needs Melville," I hear one of them shout to the other, referring to the only Level-I trauma unit in our area.

"Heads-up, Malone." I look over at Charles, my copilot, and then track to where he's pointing to the transponder and then back up to something I can barely make out through the storm. It looks like another small aircraft is directly in our flight path and near Sunnyville General.

"C'mon, Reese. Stay with us," my flight nurse urges her.

"She needs MT," I murmur to myself as I eye the small aircraft again and know that's going to delay us when we have no time to waste.

"Dispatch, this is Spiderman in Mercy 445."

"Mercy 445 this is dispatch, go ahead."

"Change of plans. We're headed to Melville."

"Mercy 445, Sunnyville General is waiting for you."

"No go. She needs a trauma unit."

"Understood, but General is closer."

"By ten minutes. Ten minutes where they'll decide she should have gone to Melville because they don't have the equipment to handle her injuries."

"Mercy 445, dispatch is in disagreement."

The radio crackles. The squelch squawks.

"Malone, this is Cochran. Your route is for Sunnyville General. Do not deviate from the plan. I need that bird and my crew on the ground ASAP. That is a *direct* order."

I glance over to Charles, but he keeps his eyes straight ahead without saying a word. The muscle in his jaw pulses. I check the transponder and see the blip representing the small aircraft is no longer there, giving us a clear shot to Sunnyville.

I clear my throat. "Dispatch, there is a small aircraft in the flight pattern. It's preventing us from having a swift delivery to General. We're rerouting to Melville Trauma. Please inform them of our impending arrival."

"Goddammit, Malone! Land that chopper."

In my periphery, I see Charles do a double take my way, but I give him the same response he gave me. The less I acknowledge or involve him the better.

She needs the trauma unit.

That's her only chance.

"Daddy." Charles is tapping my shoulder.

"That's an order, Malone!" It's Cochran barking at me again.

"Daddy." Another tap I choose to ignore. "*Daddy.*"

I startle awake.

The moon lightens the room—clear sky, not rain, and I'm in my bed, not in the cockpit.

"Luke? You okay, buddy?"

I scrub a hand over my face and try to clear the dream from my mind as he rubs his eyes and nods.

"I had a bad dream." His voice is soft, almost embarrassed that he's in here when he's a whole eight years old.

I pull back the covers and pat beside me. "C'mon in. I was having one, too. Thank you for waking me up from it." Too bad I can't wake up from the reality of its aftereffects.

It takes him a second to climb onto the mattress beside me. He takes his time setting himself up in his favorite sleeping position— head atop of my bicep so my arm can curl around him with my hand on his belly and both of his feet propped up on my thigh.

"You good?" I murmur and press a kiss to the top of his head. Somehow, he can push away everything that bugs me, just like that. "Wanna tell me about your dream?"

He gives a soft shake of his head. "Too scary." His voice is drugged with sleep.

"Okay, then think of the one thing that would make you the happiest in the world and focus on that."

"If all the superheroes in the world could bring me a new mommy . . ."

Cue a knife going straight into my heart and twisting. Over. And over.

I pull him in tighter and press another kiss to the top of his head. "I know, buddy. You do have a mommy who loves you." I perpetuate the lie I've always told him. "She just . . ." She was just too selfish to want to stay.

His soft snores fill the room, saving me from having to finish the sentence.

First my dream.

And then his wish.

Christ. Can I do anything right these days?

Eight

Sidney

"THAT'S ALL, EVERYONE. GREAT JOB. I THINK NEXT month's issue is going to be a great one." The five contributing editors of the magazine begin to shuffle immediately. Papers rap against the conference table. Murmurs break out as the managing editor asks for a quick meeting with the opinion editor. The staff outside of the conference room window behind Rissa's back scurry to their desks like they've been working this whole time.

I begin to collect my visuals—mock-ups of graphics with logos and ad copy, a detailed breakdown of the social media campaign that will begin with the next round of voting, a brainstorm of different outlets to try to channel support from as well as the ever-important numbers my contest has affected. Advertising intake and search engine statistics and website hits. All the stuff that makes my head spin but is the exact barometer of my success.

"Your numbers are solid," Rissa says as the last person leaves the conference room, her pseudo-praise surprising.

"They could be better."

"They could be," she says as her fingers click over the keyboard of her laptop. "I did some digging on your Grayson guy."

"You did?" I ask with a glance her way, wondering if she came up with the same run-of-the-mill information I did last night. And secondly, why is she digging anything up on him when he's my task to figure out? But then again, I failed that part miserably if judged by our last interaction.

"Mm-hmm." She narrows her eyes and purses her lips but keeps her attention focused on her laptop.

"And?"

"And from the pictures I could find—Mercy-Life staff photos and whatnot . . . you know, the kind we can't exactly use for our purposes—yeah, he's pretty damn hot."

"Told you."

She lifts her eyes to meet mine for the first time. "Telling me he's hot is one thing. Telling me you convinced him to be an active participant is a whole other ball game."

"He's single," I blurt out for no other reason than to try to let her know I did in fact find out something new about him. The minute I say it though, I feel stupid, and the laugh that Rissa fights to emit tells me it sounds equally as ridiculous to her.

"You're going to have to do better than that, Thorton . . . like tell me he's agreed to give you new pictures?"

"We're in talks."

This time, she can't win the battle, and a laugh falls from her mouth, drawing heads to pop up like meerkats over the tops of cubicles to see what is so funny. "You're in talks? That means you don't have anything, and it most definitely means this." Her smile widens as she reaches out to a mock-up of one of my advertisements and slides a picture of Braden over the center where I'd planned to put Grayson.

"Uh-uh." I shake my head. "That's Grayson's."

"Well, until you get a picture of Grayson, it's Braden's spot." She winks as she throws down the challenge. "You're pretty sure of yourself for a woman who can't convince a man to be part of a contest."

I give her a sideways glance to let her know I hear her but don't want to talk about it. Grayson made his feelings more than clear last night. Now it's on me to eat some crow all the while figuring out what it would take to convince him to change his mind.

"Did you know he's known for being quite the hero around these parts?"

"What do you mean?" I think of those kind eyes of his and try to imagine him in the role. Then I think of last night and how he stepped in and don't doubt it for a second.

"There was an article I found buried a few pages in when I searched his name. Do you remember that rescue in the High Sierras that hit national news earlier this year? A rough snowstorm, high altitudes, those stranded hikers missing for almost a week?"

"I think I saw something about that on *CNN*. Didn't a civilian fly into the storm to try to find them? Something about how he calculated they had gone the opposite direction the authorities thought—"

"That's the one."

"The guy who flew directly into the blizzard, found them, saved them, and flew them out. Holy shit . . ." My words trail off as realization dawns.

"He took the risk to save them. Yeah. That's our Grayson." She purses her lips.

"Then how come I didn't find that when I looked him up?"

"That article and others never mentioned the pilot by name, but I was curious as to why it came up in my search. It couldn't just be because he's a pilot. So, I dug deeper and looked at more accounts of the rescue, and one of the comments on, like, the tenth article mentioned the rescuer's name, one Grayson Malone. Then I called a friend in the know at the airfield, and he confirmed it. He said people around here have respected Grayson's wish for privacy and leave the subject alone. He also directed me to the only interview Grayson gave on the situation. He wasn't identified in it, but he said him finding the hikers had been a matter of circumstances. He had access to the right equipment and had the right skills and that anyone would have stepped in to save them if they could. That he didn't consider himself a hero, and that no thank-yous were needed because he didn't do anything out of the ordinary."

"Huh."

What is it with this man? How can he make me feel like a complete heel even when he isn't around? *No thank-yous were needed*? He can risk his life flying in high altitudes to save random strangers from certain death, while I'm the asshole who was so annoyed with him and his arrogance that a simple thank you was a struggle to say.

Mr. Stoic definitely played me.

"It seems Mr. Malone is not fond of the spotlight or any of the accolades being a hero brings with it."

"So it seems."

"Well, you know what they say about heroes. A real hero doesn't save to get attention; they save because it's the right thing to do. It seems Grayson makes a habit of taking risks, though."

"What do you mean?"

"That same friend told me Grayson's been suspended from flying. I guess he bucked orders to ground his flight in a thunderstorm and tried to save an accident victim anyway. She grew up here. Reese Diller—"

"Dillinger," I correct as my heart drops and I think of the bright eyes and infectious smile of my childhood acquaintance.

"Yes. Dillinger. Did you know her?"

"We were more acquaintances than anything. She was a few grades below me, but yeah . . . I knew her. She was a sweet girl."

"I'm sorry."

It's then I realize Grayson would have known her more, might have even been close with her. It must have been hard on him not being able to save her. Then it hits me. "What company does he work for again?"

"Mercy-Life."

"Mercy," I murmur. The first time I'd spoken to him, he thought I was there to try to get a story out of him. I lean back in my chair and mull over her words as his staunch rejections of this contest rattle around inside my brain and dots start to connect. I'm a Thorton. My last name is synonymous with newspapers and magazines.

Exploitation for headlines. People digging for a hot story. Perhaps he thinks I'm using the contest as a means to get an interview with him about Reese. No wonder Grayson wants nothing to do with me.

"Earth to Sidney?"

"Sorry. Yes." I shake my head and refocus on the here and now. "How did you manage to get all this information when I have come up with nothing?"

"I have my ways."

"Your ways?"

"Yep. I used to work for the *Washington Post*."

She could have told me she used to be an astronaut, and I would have been less shocked.

"Are you serious?" She just looks at me with her arms crossed over her chest and her eyebrows raised. "Oh my God, you *are* serious."

"I was an investigative journalist with WaPo."

"Seriously?"

"Yep. I had a long list of sources that helped me do a lot of digging. Don't act so surprised."

"I'm not. I am." I shake my head. "Why would you ever leave that job?"

"I got married. Had kids. Ended up moving here for a slower life for them. Then we divorced, and I had to go back to work so"—she shrugs—"I ended up here."

"But why not go back?"

"When you have mouths to feed and want as much time with your kids as possible, sometimes you take less to get more out of life in other ways." She leans back in her chair and looks out the window to the world beyond before looking my way. "Would I love to be an editor-in-chief of a big glossy magazine? Of course. Anyone in this industry strives for that . . . but, sometimes, you take what you can get, make the best of it, and figure it out from there. Right now, I'm figuring it out from there."

"Huh. I would have never known."

An awkward silence falls over our small corner of the office. I turn to my computer and stare at the screen for a beat as inadequacy washes over me. Rissa has way more experience than I do. It's no wonder she held a bit of resentment toward me coming here.

"So, uh, those sources. If you contacted them about this, can we make sure your ways don't spread rumors that we're digging up info on him? The last thing I need is for Grayson to be more pissed off at me than he already is."

"My source isn't going to tell anyone. Not unless he wants to be kicked out of my bed permanently, if you know what I mean."

I cough out a laugh in surprise and blush, her comment so unexpected. "On that note . . ." I chuckle. "I'll just be getting back to figuring out how to get more advertising while not thinking about you coaxing information about Grayson out of your lover."

"I'm good at coaxing." She lifts her brow and shrugs without any shame. I just smile and shake my head as I close my laptop so I can bring all my stuff back to my desk. "You should try it . . . you never know what information you might get out of it."

"I've kept to myself for the most part since I've been back." Not that I've been a hermit, but outside of the cautious wave and nod as I pass people, I haven't interacted much with anyone, let alone considered . . . coaxing someone.

See? It's easy to lie to myself and completely dismiss all the thigh clenching I do around the man in question.

"Girl, that's no way to live. All work and no play. Coax, Sidney, coax." Another smile. Another shake of her shoulders in laughter. "Something else my expert coaxing skills netted me—"

"You're making me want to cover my ears." I blush and roll my eyes

"That Grayson's wife, girlfriend, whatever she was to him—Luke's mom . . . up and left when he was a baby."

"Really?"

"You have your heartbreak right there." She nods for emphasis as my eyes widen and his bitterness makes maybe a little more sense. "Add his story with Braden being a widow . . . pit them against each other to win women's hearts and—"

"It would be a marketing gold mine," I whisper.

"Bingo."

"A healthy competition between the two highest-vote-getting con-testants..." My words trail off as I picture the ad campaign. The graph-ics. The interviews. The #TeamBraden versus #TeamGrayson tweets and shares.

"That's the only way it'll work. We've already announced the top twenty, and the other finalists are married..."

"I'm sure if Grayson balks, we could handpick another person who fits the bill."

Her laugh carries again, but this time the sarcasm rings the loud-est. "But that's not what I asked of you, is it? I told you I want you to deliver on Grayson. I want you to prove to me you can problem-solve this and make it work." I stare at her, afraid to tell her what happened last night. Her sigh resonates. "You want help, but don't know how to ask, right?"

I take her lead and run with it. "I do need help. How would you handle Grayson? A man who doesn't like you and wants zero attention? How would you convince him to actively participate, when the last time you saw him, he all but told you to go to hell?"

Or did he in fact tell me that? I'm sure he might have.

"Why would he tell you that? In the meeting, you mentioned that you met up with him again . . . want to tell me what happened?" Her stare is unrelenting as she tries to read me.

"Nothing happened." I pinch the bridge of my nose, but I know my response doesn't ring true. "That's the problem."

"Child, the mother in me knows a lie when she sees one . . . so spill it." She leans back in her chair, and all I see is a woman determined to get an answer out of me.

Is it sad that I want to share it with someone? That I want someone to agree with me that he was arrogant and a prick when all she's been doing is singing his heroic praises for the last ten minutes?

I emit an exaggerated sigh. "I was out running errands and saw him head into a bar. I conveniently had the urge for a drink so I sat beside him and then proceeded to badger him about the contest until he stalked out. I followed again—"

"Now, there's your first problem right there." She laughs. "Never let a man know you're following them. They like hard-to-get. They like thinking they're calling the shots."

"If I wanted to sleep with him, that caveat would work. But I don't." At least I wouldn't. *Would I?* The look she gives me says she's thinking the same thought and doesn't buy my response. "As I was saying, I followed him out to the back alley and ended up alone in the dark with a drunk guy who was a little handsy."

"How little is little? Did he touch you?" I can see the momma bear in her come out.

"He had my arm, but—"

"Oh my God. How scary!"

"I could have handled myself." It's the same lie I told myself as I stared at the ceiling last night while very creepy variations of how the situation could have played out kept me up. "But Grayson forgot to pay and was coming back in and saw us . . . and, of course, he—"

"Stepped in to save the day?"

"I wouldn't be quite that dramatic, but yeah."

"I told you he was hero material."

"Don't, Rissa—"

"Gold. Mine. Marketing," she says, emphasizing each word.

I glare at her. "He was a jerk."

"Because he saved you?"

"No because . . ." Because he found out I was going to use him to save the magazine and was pissed? Because he demanded a thank-you? Both make me look like the ass. Again.

"Because *why*?"

"It's the attention thing. He doesn't want any part of it."

"Then make him want it. It's your butt on the line here. I'd think that would be enough motivation for you."

"Easier said than done," I murmur.

"Isn't everything?"

Nine

Grayson

"Sunnyville native, Grayson Malone, has been credited with rescuing a woman Friday night. Here on a work assignment, Sidney Thorton, daughter of media tycoon Frank Thorton, was cornered in the darkened alley behind Hooligan's pub by an armed thug. Without thought to his own safety, Malone came to her aid, disarming the assailant and ushering Ms. Thorton to safety.

This isn't Mr. Malone's first brush with being a hero. He's been credited with piloting rescue flights in the past but has neither confirmed nor denied these claims.

As a medevac pilot for Mercy-Life, Malone—"

"That's enough."

"C'mon. I want to read more about how my baby brother saved a woman from an *armed* thug," Grant says as he peers at me over the newspaper.

"He wasn't armed."

"No shit, Sherlock. Or else you would have reported him."

"And I'm far from being a fucking hero."

"That isn't what this says." When he starts to read aloud again, I rip the newspaper from his hands, throw it on the table in front of him, and walk to the kitchen for a beer.

"I said that's enough." I'm pissed. Irritated. Why in the hell would she offer up that story?

"Testy. Testy."

"Knock it off, will you?" He knows how to get under my skin and is doing a damn fine job of it. I grab a beer from the fridge and look out back to where Luke is playing in the fort we'd built out of sheets and two-by-fours.

"Let me see. Hot woman. You to the rescue. Why are you here being so pissy when you could be with her, getting laid?"

I set my beer down, brace my hands on the sink, and watch Luke as I ignore my brother. Is that why I'm in such a goddamn foul mood? Because I can't stop thinking about her when I want to? Because I had a dream about her last night and woke up rock hard?

Christ.

I must be fucking desperate.

No. I'm just fucking dumb. I've done this song and dance before. Claire, meet Sidney; Sidney, meet Claire. Except one of them is in the forefront of my mind.

I scrub a hand through my hair. "It's all a ploy."

"A ploy?"

"And it's your fucking fault."

"My fault?"

"Quit repeating what I'm saying!"

"What are you saying?"

"*Grant.*" His name is a warning, and one I almost want to be tested on.

"What?" A chuckle. A lean back so he can prop his feet on my coffee table. Anything to annoy me.

"Sidney's the one in charge of the damn contest you signed me up for."

"Save-me-Sidney is?" He chuckles. "No shit. Do I know her?"

"Dude, we went to high school with her."

"Ahhh, *that* Sidney."

"Yeah, *that* Sidney," I mutter. "And the article isn't a coincidence. You signed me up for this stupid contest, and I told her I didn't want any part of it. Now, I have to deal with this, and it's your fault."

"How is your wanting to get funky with Sidney Thorton my fault?"

"Who said I want to fuck her?"

"You didn't have to. It's written in everything you are *not* saying."

"Back off. I don't—"

He bursts out laughing. "Nice use of terms."

I ignore him and keep going. "I don't want her, I just want her to leave me alone. I want my brothers not to sign me up for a stupid contest. I want someone not to spread false bullshit rumors about me—"

"You sure have a lot of wants with a side of a lot of whines."

"I'm starting not to like you right now."

"Think of her as a distraction. Think of the contest as something to do with your free time. And hell, better those kind of rumors than the other kind," he says softly and then purses his lips as our eyes hold.

And, goddammit, he's right. I've lived through more rumor mills than I care to count. Grayson Malone, the man Claire Hoskin went slumming with. Was it true that her inheritance was threatened if she stayed with him? Were her parents to blame for her walking away, or did Grayson cheat on her?

Those fucking rumors ran my life for years. The lies her parents spread to cover how shallow and selfish they were and how they didn't want their daughter associated with the blue-collar Malones. The payoff Claire gladly accepted because money and promises and freedom were so much more appealing than diapers and spit-up and forevers.

I clench my teeth and force myself to shove it all away. I push it deep into the abyss where I bury it most days so it doesn't eat me whole.

"Don't go there, Gray." When I look up, Grant's studying me. He knows where my thoughts went. "It's been done and gone a long time. Don't drag yourself down that damn rabbit hole again."

"Fuck, man." I plop onto the couch across from him and lean my head back and close my eyes. "I just want my life to get back to normal. Work. Luke. A—"

"—little piece of Sidney's ass on the side."

I crack an eyelid open and glare at him. "You're just jealous that's an option for me."

"No, I'm not." He holds his hand up so his wedding ring is in plain sight. "No complaints here, but I'll spare you the details that will make you jealous about how fan-*fucking*-tastic my wife is."

"I definitely don't need details on the *fucking* part." Leave it to Grant to get me to laugh.

"So, is Sidney still hot? I mean, from what I remember from high school she was. Pretty but untouchable. Snobby but nice."

"Annoying but . . ."

"Hot."

"Gorgeous." The word comes out automatically. There's no denying it, even though I'd prefer to.

"And the problem with this is, what?"

"There is no problem with that. The problem I have is that there is an article in the newspaper about a situation only three of us knew about."

"And we all know how much you *love* attention."

I raise my middle finger to combat his sarcasm. "You know the why behind it, so don't be an asshole."

"Which why is that? How the Hoskins wrote Luke off and you fear anything on you may give them some kind of insight into Luke's life? Or the how you are just the most selfless son of a bitch I've ever known and for some reason, you never want to reap the rewards for being a damn fine human being like every other person on the face of the earth would?"

"It wasn't me who told the newspaper about the incident, and it sure as hell wasn't Mick."

"Mick?"

"The unarmed thug." Being a cop, his eyes fire with recognition as my cell rings for what feels like the hundredth time today. People asking about the newspaper article. Attaboys about saving someone, even though I'm on desk duty for doing the exact same thing.

I switch the ringer off and shake my head.

"You really think she planted this story? Why would she do that?"

"Hell if I know. I even fucking accused her of setting it up, then dumbass me bought it when she said she's not that conniving."

"One bat of those lashes and shift of those thighs and poor Grayson's blood leaves one head for another and impairs his thinking."

"You're being a dick."

"And you got played." He tsks. "The woman's got balls."

"Let's hope not." I laugh as I remember the heat of her body against mine last night.

"You know what I mean." He leans forward so his elbows rest on his knees, and he levels me with a stare.

"Like I said, it's all a ploy. The article. The hero thing. All of it."

"If it's a ploy to get you thinking about her, she's doing a damn fine job of it."

"Jesus," I mutter.

"What's the big deal about the contest, Gray? I mean seriously? Do the damn thing. Let Luke revel in the attention for a bit, let him think he has a famous dad. Win the damn thing and take him to Disney World like you've wanted to do for years. Let yourself relax for a bit instead of pacing back and forth, wearing a hole in the floor as you wait out this fucking stupid flight suspension. Like I said, your participating doesn't give any information to the Hoskins that they couldn't find by asking around town. And if it does, if it tells them that you're better off without Claire, then good. Again, what's it going to hurt?"

Of course, he has to throw Luke in there to get me to really hear him.

"She reminds me of everything Claire was . . . and the contest reminds me of everything I hate."

"It isn't one of Claire's damn beauty pageants."

"Close enough."

"Bullshit. I bet your ass there is no crown in this contest, or high heels to prance around in. If there is, I'm front row to take blackmail pictures of you."

"Very funny."

"And Sidney isn't Claire. Sure, they both lived on the hill when we were in school. Sure, they were inseparable and their friends were assholes to you where you worked in the diner, but hell, I'm an asshole to you sometimes, too."

"You're my brother. That's different."

"You're missing the point. Just because she was best friends with Claire, it doesn't mean she's like Claire. They most definitely had a shit-ton more money than we did growing up, but having similar backgrounds doesn't make them the same."

"That's supposition."

"And that's you being a stubborn ass. Besides, what does any of this have to do with Sidney in the first place? So what? She's running the contest. That's it. Big whoop."

"She doesn't deserve my help."

"*Help*? What in the hell are you talking about?"

"Last night. The alley. I walked out, and she followed because she slipped and said she was going to use me to help save her magazine."

"Save her magazine?"

I shrug. "That's what she said."

"Look at that. You could be a hero again."

"Stop the hero crap."

"I'm serious. Help the contest and in turn save jobs."

He's right and I hate it and refuse to acknowledge it. Yes, I'm acting like Luke would, but the woman is frustrating as all hell. "She doesn't deserve my help."

"Ahhh, so that's what this is all about." He runs a hand through his hair and chuckles. "You're exhausting. All of that to get to the point."

"The point?"

"Yeah. At first, you played it off as you not wanting the attention because of Luke, but dude . . . you're projecting Claire onto Sidney in some fucked-up way, like participating would be you somehow giving in to what she did to you."

"That's such bullshit." At least that's what I tell him, but hell if he isn't somewhat right.

"Uh-huh." He draws the word out, and the sound grates on my nerves. "If that's not true, then do the damn contest. Take a few photos. Give them the bio they want. Then step back and let whatever happens, happen. What would it hurt other than maybe pad your bank account if you win?"

"God, you sound just like Dad with all this wisdom." I shake my head and laugh.

"Not quite. I don't have all of his perfect sayings down yet—but I'll get there."

"Lord, help us." I sigh and glance at Luke as he slams the door and runs up the stairs as he has some kind of mock battle between the Minecraft figures in each of his hands.

"What about him?" Grant asks as he lifts his chin to where Luke just disappeared.

"What do you mean, what about Luke? What would me going along with this teach him?

"That his dad is cool as fuck. That it's okay to take pride in yourself. That it's okay to step outside your comfort zone and do something you normally wouldn't. How's that for a lesson?"

"He's eight. He doesn't care about that shit." The lie rolls off my tongue, and I hate that my brother's words resonate deeper than I want them to. "Plus, you know what a hard time he's been going through with the not having a mom thing."

"Not having a mom. Dad being in a contest." He holds his hands out as if he's weighing both on a scale. "They have nothing to do with each other. So sorry, try again."

"Just drop it, Grant."

"No. You're being ridiculous and stubborn, so I'll say it again. The contest. It has nothing to do with Claire. The Hoskins—fuck them—won't get any info on Luke. Sidney is not Claire. You might get some serious ass as a side benefit. And Luke—"

"That isn't teaching him anything."

"Stop thinking about what it's teaching Luke, and start thinking about what it will be teaching you."

Ten

Sidney

THE FLOOR CREAKS AS I PACE FROM ONE END OF THE ROOM TO another. Papers blanket the table and chairs, the aftermath of the spreadsheet I was making for my father of advertising dollars. The heat is stifling. My cell is stuck to my ear as I wait for her to pick up.

There's no way he's going to think I didn't set the whole thing up now.

No way in hell.

"What did you do, Rissa?"

"Whatever do you mean?" Her voice comes through loud and clear across the phone connection. Kids play in the background, the wind rustles against the speaker of her cell, and her voice sounds *guilty* as hell.

"I just hung up with the who-knows-what-number reporter about an article that was written in the *Sunnyville Gazette* about one Grayson Malone."

"What about him?"

"Oh, I don't know. How about how he saved me from a knife-wielding thug?"

"Huh."

"Huh? That's all you're going to say?"

"What do you want me to say?" There's amusement in her voice.

I walk past the front window, glancing outside to see if the reporter for the local news is still there. The one who'd knocked on the door earlier and asked for an interview and photo.

"How about why you called the *Gazette* and told them about the other night?"

"Who said that I did?"

"Let's call it an educated guess." I put my hand on my hip and look back at the article sitting on my computer screen.

"It must be a slow news day for the *Gazette* to run a front-page article about the hometown hero rescuing damsels in distress, don't ya think? It's about time something other than the damn Harvest Festival has graced its cover. It isn't as if they need to advertise. The whole town shows up, regardless."

"It says the source was anonymous. That wouldn't be your middle name would it?"

"Rissa Anonymous Patel." Her laugh is immediate. "Has a nice ring to it, and it would be cool-ass initials, but nope, not it."

"Rissa," I say, trying to be serious, "what are you trying to accomplish?" *And why are you trying to help me?*

"Did you notice the comments online? It sure seems like local-boy Grayson Malone is getting all kinds of love from the people of Sunnyville."

"Great. Good for him." I sit and start scrolling through the comments. One after another. Praise heaped upon praise.

"It's almost as if they've all been waiting to pay tribute to him for the other rescue he won't talk about, so everyone is heaping it on now as a surrogate."

"You're sneaky." And I damn well underestimated Rissa, mom of three.

"If it were to be known that Grayson was one of the top twenty in our contest, I'd think this would be the perfect time to rally support around him for the vote next week."

I fight my grin as if I don't agree with her, when she's actually goddamn brilliant. So why do I hesitate? Maybe because I don't want to reinforce Grayson's belief that I'm a manipulative bitch. This one stunt confirmed everything I've tried to tell him I'm not.

But since when do I care what other people think of me?

Since I need him in order to be successful at my job in Rissa's eyes. The same Rissa who is trying to help, but who might just have undermined me, nonetheless.

Grayson's eyes flash in my mind. The disdain. The distrust. The intensity.

"Where are you going with this?"

"Do you still think he's the one who can make a face for this contest?"

"Without a doubt."

"Then don't question the means, just worry about what's going to happen when he says yes."

"Dare I ask what else you have up your sleeve?"

"It's hot out today. I'm wearing a tank top, so how could anything be up my sleeve?"

"Rissa . . ." I laugh.

"Let's just say that every hero needs a celebration. Get your party dress ready."

Eleven

Sidney

"SIDNEY THORTON, HOW MAY I HELP YOU?"

"This has got to stop."

"Excuse me? Who is this?" I draw eyes from some of the staff as I step into the conference room and shut the door behind me. They're still leery of me, and I'm sure my answering the phone with the panicked annoyance like I just did isn't going to do me any favors.

"The man you're putting articles in the newspaper about to convince him to participate in your silly contest." Irritation mixed with impatience rakes through his voice.

"It's hard to catch your attention. Should I gather it's working now?" I bite the bullet and take ownership of Rissa's tactics with little guilt. He hadn't returned a single one of my calls, texts, or emails, and then Rissa plants a story, and voila, he calls. I'll take progress any way I can at this point, even if it's underhanded and makes me feel a tad slimy.

His sigh is heavy. "It worked the first time. There was no need to do today's article as well."

Today's article? There's another one? What am I missing? I scramble to log into my laptop, but it has to power up. "What did

I do now?"

"Don't be coy."

Outside the conference room glass, Rissa is holding her fist to her mouth and fighting back a laugh. Dear God, I'm scared to know what she did this time.

"I'm not. I'm just simply trying to do my job."

"The innocent thing doesn't work for you any more than the damsel-in-distress thing did. And by the way, I fell for it. For your shaking knees and trembling hands and blatant lies that this wasn't a setup . . . so just stop while you're ahead. Stop denying. I know you're the one behind these anonymous articles. I know you're the one funding the goddamn party."

"What party?" I cough and squeeze my eyes closed, praying that she did not do what I think she did.

"The one you set up at Hooligan's to thank me for saving you."

"I did no such thing!"

"Save it, Princess. I've already tried to get out of it, but this damn town has caught wind of it, and there's no way they're letting me bow out. If I have to suffer through the damn thing, then so do you."

The call ends, and I lean back against the wall as Rissa peeks her head through the doorway with a cat-ate-the-canary grin on her face.

"A party? Are you kidding me?"

"No one said we had to play fair." She gives me a wink. "I've got the man where you want him. Now it's your turn to close the deal."

"I don't understand why you're doing this when you made it clear that it was my job to—"

"Part of my job is to teach you how to do things. How to check those boxes. I wouldn't be a good boss if I didn't." She shrugs. "And because after seeing Braden's new shots, it isn't fair to all of the other men left for him not to have any competition. Can you say washboard and hung?"

"Jesus." I choke over the word and the lift of her eyebrows. "Do you have no shame?"

"None, but you knew that already." She looks at her watch

abruptly. "Look at the time, I have to go pick up my kids. It's Friday fun day at my house. See you at the pub tomorrow at seven o'clock."

I stare after her as she walks out and I realize I thoroughly underestimated her.

Thank God she's on my side.

Twelve

Sidney

"CAN I HAVE YOUR ATTENTION, PLEASE?"

A man climbs onto the bar top and spreads his arms wide, and just in case I had any doubts about how genetically gifted Grayson was, this man commanding the bar's attention just wiped them away. He has brown hair, aqua-colored eyes that are almost clear, and a wedding ring on that left hand that glints against the lights. He's definitely related to Grayson—someway, somehow—and my money is on him being his brother.

Chants of "Grady! Grady! Grady!" fill the room as he waves his hands to hush everyone. It feels like half of Sunnyville is here to celebrate Grayson and his heroic "rescue" of me. Either that or they'll take any little reason to celebrate.

Rissa is on one side of me, Cathy on the other, and in the thirty minutes since I've been here, I haven't been able to move much farther into the room because it is definitely at maximum capacity. Regardless, I feel out of place in my designer clothes in this working-class bar. People glance at me sideways, trying to figure out why I look familiar, but after ten years, memories fade and looks change, so they just can't quite place me anymore.

It's probably for the better. But at the same time, there's something about the camaraderie among the citizens that is like nothing I've ever experienced before. Neighbors who have known each other since pre-school tap the necks of their bottles together. People hug each other as if they are long lost relatives, when in reality, it's probably only been a week or two since they last saw each other.

It's a fascinating dynamic, and as I stand here and take it all in while the crowd quiets, I realize that Rissa gets this. Rissa understood that this dynamic was all it was going to take to force Grayson to show up.

"In case some of you didn't know, my brother, Grayson Malone, has fallen into the hero status as of late." Hoots and hollers sound off around the bar. I glance over to Rissa, whose smile is smug and brown eyes are alive with mischief, and I shake my head. "Ladies, it seems that if you need saving—or maybe even a little mouth-to-mouth—or to be taken to new heights in his mile-high club"—Grady grins as the crowd shouts another round of comments—"he's your man."

"Save me! I need some mouth-to-mouth," a woman shouts, and laughter rings out in response.

"I hear there's a long line, Linda, but Gray's an equal opportunity kind of guy," Grady says. Someone tosses something at him, and he catches it. "Not only is my brother going around saving damsels in distress—keep the fainting to a minimum, ladies—he has also been named one of *Modern Family's* top twenty hottest dads!"

The crowd erupts in whistles and catcalls as Grady shrugs as if it's no big deal, and Rissa's smile turns knowing. Yeah, she has something else up her sleeve—I know it.

Grady takes a sip of the beer in his hand and then brings his finger to his lips to quiet the crowd again. "But we aren't satisfied with him just being in the top twenty, are we?" Disapproving noises reverberate through the crowd, and from where we stand in the back of the bar, there is what looks like an orchestrated shaking of heads in disagreement. "If anyone deserves to be voted to the top, it's my brother—the hero." He laughs out the word and shakes his head like this is all a joke. Because it is. I mean, a hero's party for nothing? "When voting goes live this coming Wednesday, we're going to vote him into the number one spot, aren't we?"

The place goes crazy, and the shouts vibrate in my chest. It's as if I'm watching a pep rally for the championship game or something.

"Grayson. Grayson. Grayson." His name rumbles, each syllable punctuated by a clapping of hands.

"Without further ado, ladies and gentlemen, please welcome the hero himself, my brother, Grayson Malone!"

If I thought the noise was deafening before, I was wrong, because it almost doubles in volume. A cacophony of cheers and whistles sound off as heads turn to where Grayson must be standing.

I edge up on my tiptoes, every part of me wanting to see him.

Every part of me wanting to be seen by him.

I see a hand rise. I see Grady trying to coax him to join him on the bar. Then the chants of "speech" begin.

With Grayson's affinity for downplaying his hero status, I guarantee he wants to kill me about now.

It's so very silly that, as I see a hand clasp on to Grayson's and help to pull him up onto the bar, I suck in my breath.

He's breathtaking. It's sad that's my first thought when he comes into view. He has on a pair of dark blue jeans and a black button-up shirt, and his hair is styled in a messy disarray, which is similar to his brother's. His cheeks are flushed pink, and that only adds to his appeal. Clearly, he is not a fan of this attention.

He smiles as he shakes his head at the ruckus. "This really is ridiculous." He looks around, and somehow his eyes lock on to mine. They hold, and then that grin stalls momentarily before widening as he shakes his head. "I'm far from a hero. I just did what any of you would have done, but it seems someone in particular wants to make a big show of this. And that one person, I'd love to thank for all of this unwanted attention." He points in my direction. "Ms. Sidney Thorton, ladies and gents."

The people turn their attention my way, and a roar goes through the room as I quietly curse him and wish I could blend in with the wall at my back. "If it weren't for her, we wouldn't have this chance to all get together, drink a few beers, and have a good time—so, do me a favor," he says as his mischievous smile grows wider and his eyes spark with trouble, "make sure you give her a hug tonight and welcome her back to Sunnyville. Or a shot will do. That's the least you can do to help me thank her."

The smug bastard.

It's the only thought I can process before hands start patting me on the back as people close in around me. Nice people. Kind people. Oblivious people who have no idea just how unnerving it is for me to have them all be so close.

I lose sight of Grayson, but he isn't far from my mind as I curse him at length under my breath for his shitty little retaliation.

His underhanded way of telling me I'm a snob. That I think I'm too good to shake hands with—or give hugs to—the blue-collared people who make up this town.

I look for Rissa, hoping she'll save me. She's standing just outside the circle of people who look partially familiar, taking a sip of her margarita on the rocks as if she's a regular here when she isn't.

Damn, she's good.

Thirteen

Grayson

"WELL, SHIT, LOOK AT THAT. UPTOWN SIDNEY IS settling in just fine with us little people."

My immediate response is to defend her. To tell Grant to lay off her and protect her as if she were a friend.

What the fuck's my problem? I'm in this damn predicament because of her and her influence and I'm going to help her?

Not a chance in hell.

I look to where she's standing, her back against the wall, a drink in her hand. Her heels are high, her skirt is fitted, and goddamn those legs of hers call my eyes every chance they get. The curve of her calves and the hint of her cleavage in the V of her shirt are both subtle but so in my face it's as if she's calling to me. My phone has been turned off, battery removed, number disconnected.

And, yet, it still rings.

"*That's* Sidney Thorton?" Grady chimes in, following the question with a low whistle.

"Yep." I tip the bottle of beer to my lips without looking back at her.

"Well, damn. She's all grown up," Grady says it with a swear. Maybe I should remind him of his wife, who would likely have some creative payback for him checking out someone else.

Not that I can blame him. I've been looking her way a lot more than I want to admit. Especially with Grant's words from the other day rattling around in my mind. The "she's nothing like Claire," and the "even if I participate, I'm the one who has something to gain, not her."

I still don't buy it.

She's standing there just like everyone else, and yet, there is this air about her that sets her apart. The way she holds her head high, her back straight, her eyes sharp with a distrust that makes no sense. Then someone comes up to give her a hug, and I laugh, knowing how much she probably wants to fucking kill me.

Turnabout's fair play, sweetheart.

I expect her to frown, to be rude and refuse the greeting, but then she smiles. She smiles, and fuck if I can't take my eyes off her as her expression turns genuine, her laugh rings out, and the people around her hang on her every word. It's hard to despise someone when, with each look, with each drink, you want to walk across the room and go talk to them.

An elbow hits my arm and jerks my attention from her. "You're turning her down, *why*?" Grady asks as he looks over to his wife and shakes his head before looking back at me.

"You make it sound as if she asked me out on a date and I said no." I laugh and take a sip of who knows what number beer I've had. "She asked me to be in a contest, not have a night of hot sex with her. That's all."

Hot sex. With Sidney?

I could probably compartmentalize my feelings for a bit and take that on.

Jesus. What am I thinking? Too much beer. Too much bullshit. Too much of a buzz to think straight.

"If she were to ask you out, would you go?" Dylan asks, and I'm already shaking my head no. Grady's wife should know better.

Asking someone out and having sex with someone are two

completely different roads.

"She hasn't asked."

"What about a night of hot sex, then?"

Damn it.

"Dylan," I warn.

"That isn't a no." She throws her hands up and laughs as Grady rests an arm over her shoulders, pulls her in closer, and presses a kiss to her temple.

"No," I murmur.

"That's such crap," Grant throws in. "Like utter bullshit. Since when would you say no to *that*?" He tips his beer in Sidney's direction and lifts his eyebrows.

I wouldn't. That's the plain and simple answer.

"I've got a hundred on him sleeping with her," Grady says to Grant.

"Not taking that bet because I'd lose in a heartbeat." They high five across the table.

Bastards.

"She's too much like Claire." Another soft response, more to myself than to them. Déjà vu takes me back to another place, another time when I was young and stupid and really thought it didn't matter where you came from or what you did so long as you were in love.

I've learned.

"Again, I call bullshit." Grady snorts.

"The type who'll reel you in with her looks . . ." I glance her way when her laugh sounds off in perfect timing with my comment. She's halfway across the bar, but fuck if I can't hear her as if she were standing right next to me. "Then leave you high and dry because she's so damn selfish she doesn't think of anyone but herself."

And goddamn it if pretty boy Vince Garda didn't just walk up to her and hand her a drink. She smiles, but it's the look on his face—the one that says he's a man determined to leave here with her tonight—that has me gritting my teeth and slipping up on what I just said.

"Whoa. Wait." Grant throws his arms out in front of him

animatedly as his wife, Emerson, tilts her head back and laughs. "Hold up. I thought we were talking about you getting laid. One night. Maybe a few nights—"

"*High and dry* means you want more than a few nights with her," Grady finishes for him. I hate when my brothers are in perfect sync like this—reading each other's minds and finishing each other's thoughts. I hate it exponentially more when it's aimed at picking on me. "And honestly, bro, with her, I think you'd prefer *low and wet*, if you get my drift?"

"Christ," I swear as I stand from my seat and the room spins slightly. "You two are a bunch of little old ladies."

"Leave him alone," Dylan pipes in. "It isn't his fault the woman going to such great lengths to get him to participate in her contest is drop-fucking-dead gorgeous with legs for days and boobs I'd kill to have."

"I, for one, like your boobs and legs," Grady says before kissing her soundly. I roll my eyes.

"You two are sickening. Both sets of you. Christ, can't a guy just drink in peace without having to watch you make googly eyes at each other?"

"We only make googly eyes because we know we're getting laid when we get home tonight." Grady glances in Sidney's direction and then looks back to me. "The question is, are you? Because you're sitting here making googly eyes at her."

I point to the shot of tequila next to my beer and make a show of picking it up and downing it in one fell swoop.

"Ah, yes. You want to drink in peace," Grant says and laughs. "Go right ahead and keep drinking in peace because that woman over there manipulated you into a corner that I kind of think you enjoy being shoved into."

I glare at Grant and his snarky smile.

"I can think of where else he wants her to shove him," Emerson delivers with a look of complete innocence that has me breaking a smile and laughing.

"Christ, Em."

She shrugs. "Well, it's true, right? Hell, if I were a man, I'd want her. Looks like someone may beat you to it, though." She nods toward Sidney, and we all turn to find that Vince's hand is on Sidney's arm. My fist clenches at the sight. My jaw ticks. Jealousy I don't want to feel rages.

The table falls silent, but I don't notice until I turn my attention back to the four pairs of knowing eyes staring back at me. "I change my bet. A hundred bucks says Gray leaves here tonight with her and gets laid," Grady says as he slowly slides a hundred-dollar bill across the table as if I can't see it.

"He doesn't move that fast. He has anger issues," Grant says with a wink. "You're on."

"I am *not* sleeping with her tonight. Not ever."

"Yes, you are." Grady sits back in his seat.

"If you aren't sleeping with her, then what's it hurt to head over there and talk to her. You haven't said a word to her all night, but you sure as hell have been staring at her." Grant shrugs.

It's true, but who says I want to go talk to her? It's so much easier to be mad at her than to admit she's played me well. If I keep my distance, then I can't get myself in trouble . . . .. But, goddamn, how good trouble sounds right now.

"Fuck it." I reach across the table and steal Grady's shot sitting there. I don't back down from his stare as I down it, welcome the burn, and know that it won't be the only thing that burns tonight.

When I slam the empty glass back down, he finally protests as I grab his hundred-dollar bill and shove it into my pocket. I wave him off and then make my way across the bar.

I've already spoken to almost everyone, shaken their hands, had a laugh with them over how ludicrous it is that we are celebrating a guy being decent when it should be the norm. I've explained how this whole situation was blown out of proportion and that there was no weapon, but no one seems to listen. I've played down the damn contest, which everyone but me seems to care about me winning.

A few people stop me, say hi, ask about my parents, who opted to stay home and hang with Luke, but my eyes are on Sidney. And Vince—or rather, Vince's hands and how they are continually touching a woman I have no claim on.

A woman I want no claim on.

Then why do I fucking care?

But by the time I reach her, my blood boils with irrationality spurred on by too much alcohol.

"Can I have a moment?" I ask as I walk up to her and grab her elbow, pushing her down the darkened hallway.

"What is your problem?" She hisses as she fights me every step of the way.

We get looks. I get looks. I don't care because all I keep seeing is Vince's hands on her arm. His eyes on her tits. His bullshit game I can spot a mile away.

I find the closest door down the hallway leading to the bathrooms, and it opens. I push her through it, barely noticing that it's an office of sorts before the door is shut, her back is up against it, and my mouth is covering hers.

Take.

Goddammit. That's my only thought as I fit my lips to hers and take out my anger on her mouth with tongue and teeth and every fucking lick and nip in between.

"What—"

"I'm so pissed at you."

It's all I say. It's the only chance I give her to come up for air before my lips are back on hers. Before my tongue wars with hers. Before my body admits it would beg, borrow, and steal in order to taste every other part of her.

Groan.

I swallow the tiny sound she makes in our kiss as my hands hold her neck still and my lips wage an all-out assault. She hesitates—just a split second—before she reacts. Before her body bows into me, and her mouth argues back.

Fist.

Her hand in my shirt. Her other hand at the back of my neck as our bodies meet—pressed knee to chest. Her perfume in my nose. Her hair tickling my cheeks. The feel of her tits against my chest.

Give.

I can't get enough.

I'm mad at her.

I want her.

I don't want to want her.

Christ, do I want her.

"Gray." A murmured protest.

I tear my lips from hers, shove off the door I have her pressed against, and stride to the other side of the room.

"You are . . . you just . . ." It's as if I can barely breathe. Christ, I'm mad at you."

She stands there, lips parted, chest heaving, and golden brown curls messed from my hands, but her eyes look hurt. A hurt I don't want to see but can't deny.

"Why?"

"You did this," I accuse as I try to manage the anger that's waging a war against my desire.

"Did what?" Her eyes narrow. Her hand goes to press against her chest.

"Made me want you."

It's her laugh that incites me now. That, and the taste of her kiss and the feel of her skin and the sound she made in the back of her throat and the goddamn ownership in her touch. Things I didn't want from anyone. Things she makes me want from her.

Over and over.

Fourteen

Sidney

He's a caged tiger.

That's all I can think when I look at him and his broad shoulders, clenched fists, and anger. Waves of anger are rolling off him.

I stare at him with so much to say in my mind, but every part of my body is stunned by the kisses he just numbed me with.

"Are you happy, Sidney? Isn't this what you wanted?" His voice thunders in the small space but is drowned out by the buzz of the bar on the other side of the door. "Manipulate me? Paint me into a corner so I have to say yes or risk looking like a goddamn fool? So, I'll say yes. *Yes.* I have no other choice. You win. You fucking took the cake. You made me want you when I didn't want to want you. Bet you didn't count on that with your little game, huh?" He takes a step toward me, his lips back on mine without preamble. He tastes of beer and anger, and just as quickly as my body reacts to him, he breaks from the kiss. "What are you going to do about that now?"

He leans back, one hand possessive on the nape of my neck as his eyes bore into mine. Searching. Asking. Wanting. Not wanting to admit.

Then, as soon as I see the fear that glances through his eyes, his hands are off me. He yanks the door open, shunting me forward, and he slams it closed behind him, leaving me in the dimly lit office.

"Well, shit." I laugh; its nervous sound echoes in the empty office as I bring my fingertips to my lips and try to figure out what in the world just happened.

My hands tremble, and I stand there in shocked indecision. Did he really just do that? Did he really just blame me for making him want me and then kiss me senseless?

My first thought is to be pissed at him. No man gets to take without asking. No man gets to kiss me and put the blame on me.

My second thought is . . . the man can have anything he wants if he kisses like that.

Get a grip, Sid.

What the hell am I supposed to do now? This? This, I did not see coming. I may have gone along with Rissa's plan to manipulate him into a corner, I may have just gotten him to participate, but apparently, I'd gotten a whole hell of a lot more from Grayson Malone than a few pictures and a short bio.

With my back against the door, I try to figure out how I should feel and what I should do.

I should be mad at him, shouldn't I? But then I shift my feet and feel the ache between my thighs. For a girl always sure of herself, he just threw me into water that was way over my head and told me I needed to figure out how to swim.

Sure, he just gave me what I wanted—secured my job by saying he'll be an active participant in the contest—but at what cost?

I should walk out into the bar, say goodbye to Rissa, and head home. Walk away from the moment, calm down, and figure it out later when I'm by myself and can process it all without everything about him clouding my senses.

I take a deep breath and yank the door open with every intention of doing just that.

But when I exit the hallway into the main bar area, he's across the way, arm slung over another woman's shoulder, his head thrown back in laughter, and one of the tails of his shirt untucked from where my hands ripped it from his waistband. He may look calm as can be, but I can sense the edge beneath. I still taste it on my tongue.

Go home, Sidney.

I've had too much to drink, and I don't want to do anything stupid. I need to walk my pretty little heels out that door and shake this all off.

It's then that he looks up and meets my stare. It's the subtle lift of his chin. The arrogance in his slight smirk.

And my temper lights.

I stalk over to him, the sound of my heels punctuating every step I take. My pulse pounds in my ears. My anger spins an eddy of discord.

The bar takes notice as people part to make room for me without asking.

With each step closer, his smirk grows smugger.

Bastard.

When I reach him, he unloops his arm from around the woman's neck and takes a step toward me. The cocksure look on his face slowly falls.

Without a word, I step into him and grab the back of his neck, pulling his face down toward mine.

And then I kiss him.

A no-holds-barred, greedy, take-what-I-want kind of kiss that both dizzies me and lights every part of me with the desire he stoked moments ago.

He's stunned at first. At least, I think he is, because I'm so busy giving him the revenge kiss to rival all revenge kisses that I don't even pay attention.

Then his lips are moving.

His tongue is reacting.

His body goes from tense to pliant.

When the outside world seeps through my anger, when the hoots and the hollers break through my thoughts and yank my attention from the devastation of his kiss, I jolt back a step.

A thousand comments race through my mind as I stare at him.

I didn't manipulate you.

I want you, too.

You don't get to walk away without a fight.

I say none of them. I stand there with my chest heaving and the crowd staring and begin to feel like a complete idiot.

"Gotta admire a woman who'll go to extremes to get what she wants." His voice is a quiet rumble against the noise of the bar, and yet, I hear every single word.

"That kiss had nothing to do with the contest."

"What did it have to do with, then?"

"Don't tell me you didn't have a choice. You always have a choice," I finally say through gritted teeth as heat flushes my cheeks. "And don't ever do that to me again."

He takes a step forward. My breath hitches. My eyes close. My body anticipates his touch.

"Then don't choose me," he murmurs, but his words hold so much weight that I swear he's talking about more than the damn contest.

I open my mouth to speak and then close it. The people around us are watching, and I don't want to fuel the rumor mill that I just unthinkingly kicked into high gear. So, without another word, I turn on my heel and walk out of Hooligan's.

Fifteen

Grayson

LAST NIGHT IS A HAZE.

A goddamn haze in which I'm pretty sure I kissed Sidney. Then she kissed me back. And somewhere along the line, I agreed to be a willing participant in her whole contest.

"Then don't choose me."

"Christ." I run a hand through my hair and sigh.

"You really shouldn't say that." I startle at his voice but shouldn't expect any less. Luke and his habit of standing at the side of the bed and staring until I wake up. "You told me I wasn't allowed to say that word, so I don't think it's fair if you do."

I prop myself up on one elbow and look his way as I scrub a hand through my hair.

Shit, it's bright in here.

Can't say that aloud, either, or the bad-word police is going to get on me again.

"Can I say it?"

"No." My voice sounds like I drank a fifth of Jack and smoked a pack of cigarettes. The drinking part was possible . . . I don't quite remember.

"Give me one sec, buddy." I shove up from the bed—slowly, just in case my stomach wants to retaliate—and then make my way to the bathroom to brush my teeth and take a piss. When I come back out, Luke has moved into my space on the bed, his black Star Wars pajamas stark against the white sheets.

"Are you stealing my spot?" I ask as I lie beside him. His belly laugh is instant, and he tries to squirm away from my fingers that tickle his sides and poke at his tummy.

"Just keeping it warm," he says through his laughter.

He clings to me so I'll stop tickling, and after a few more for good measure, I stop and hug him against me. When will he be too old to do this? When will he fight against hugs and tickling? When will he be too cool for his dad?

I close my eyes and breathe him in. The scent of his shampoo. The way his hair tickles my face. The way he tucks his hands between our chests instead of hugging me back.

And I know it's going to kill me when that day comes.

"Did you have fun last night?" he asks. "Nana said you were out with a bunch of friends celebrating. What did you do?"

I nod as the fuzzy images clear some. "We, uh, just talked some with friends."

"We? Were you with a girl?"

"A woman? No. Just friends."

"Were there girls there?"

"Women," I correct again. "There were a lot of women there, yes."

"Did you find me a mom?"

I freeze. "No," I say through a chuckle, "I didn't find you a mom."

"But there were a lot of women there. Did you not like any of their vaginas?"

If I had been drinking water, I would have accidentally just spit it all over the bed. "What?" I cough out the word as I push him away from me. No doubt I must have a crazy expression on my face as I try to control my laughter. "Did I what?" I finally manage.

"Their vaginas." He says it so very casually, and I know I've gone so very wrong somewhere in the equation. "Did you not like them?"

I must open and close my mouth ten times as I follow his eight-year-old train of thought. "Where did you hear that?"

"At school, Sam said that when men like a woman's vagina, they marry them." Stupid Sam Hamner and his parents who don't filter anything from him.

Jesus Christ. I didn't have a dry mouth a minute ago, but it feels like I just swallowed a bag of cotton balls.

"Do you know what a vagina is?" I finally utter the word. I must turn a thousand shades of red when I do.

He tries to lean back so he can see me, but shit, I can't look him in the eyes or he's going to see right through me.

I can tell a woman her pussy feels like heaven. I can dirty talk with the best of them (or so I've been told). But having to ask my son if he knows what a vagina is makes me feel like I'm sixteen and fumbling in the dark as I try to figure out what exactly to do with one.

"I heard Sam at school saying women have vaginas and that's why men marry them."

"He's right, girls have vaginas. But a man marries a woman because he loves her and trusts her . . . not because she has a vagina."

"What does it do?"

I blink several times and realize this is a serious detriment to raising a kid on your own. You think you have it handled and then, *wham*, you realize you neglected a serious part of it.

"Well, just like boys have penises, girls have vaginas." *Let that be enough of a response that it ends this conversation.*

"How are they different? What do they do with them? What are they for?" He leans back and looks me dead in the eyes, innocence shrouded in curiosity.

I clear my throat. And lie. "They are different because boys and girls have to have different parts for the different things they need them for later in life."

Brilliant explanation, Gray.

I could win parent of the year with that comment.

"Like what kind of different things?"

"Just different things."

"Huh. Cool," he says as if I made perfect sense. "Is there an innie or an outie?"

Another sputtering cough from me. "What?"

"Like belly buttons. Some kids have an innie and others have an outie. Do penises and vaginas have innies and outies?"

"Yep. Sure do."

He angles his head and stares at me for a beat. I can see his mind turning this over, and I swear I've said the word vagina more times in this five-minute conversation than I have in years. I should be good for another five.

"Cool." He shrugs and climbs off the bed.

"Cool?"

"Yep. To the Death Star!" he shouts and takes off down the hallway.

That's the best part about kids. Their curiosity goes just as quickly as it comes, and they are satisfied with half-truths all parents feel relieved getting away with.

My phone alerts me to a text. It sounds off somewhere in the room, and it takes me a moment to find it on the floor in the back pocket of the pants I had on last night.

"Yeah, yeah," I say as it sounds off again.

And then I sigh.

Sidney: Photo shoot is set up for Tuesday at 3 p.m. Let me know if that doesn't work for you.

"So, I'll say yes. Yes. I have no other choice. You win. You fucking took the cake."

My words come back to me as I look at the address she sends me next.

Of course, that doesn't work for me. It's three in the frickin' afternoon, which is when school gets out. And Luke has baseball practice. Why would Sidney Thorton think of that? That maybe I had plans already that didn't involve her.

"Christ," I groan, repeating what seems to be my word of the morning, run a hand through my hair, and drop my phone onto the bed.

It's hard to be pissed at someone and want them all at the same time. I keep seeing her last night, looking like the sexy librarian in every man's fantasy. Pencil skirt, high heels, shirt unbuttoned some, and golden hair piled on top of her head, itching for me to take it down.

I can pretend my dick flying at half-mast is simply morning wood, but I know damn well it's because of the visual of Sidney. It's because I know how her lips taste. It's because I know what her body feels like against mine.

This is not good. So not fucking good.

I pick my phone back up, knowing I can get my mom or Dylan to watch Luke for me so I can get this torture over with and leave Sidney far fucking behind.

Me: Yeah. Sure. I'll be there.

Short. Sweet. And no need for her to reply.

"Dad! Hey, Dad!"

I sit on the bed and yank a pillow over my lap. We've already had a talk about innies and outies. I don't want to have to explain why my underwear is tenting.

"Yeah, Luke. What's up?"

He walks down the hall, fingers fidgeting and a question written all over his face. *Please, no more questions about vaginas.*

"Last night at your hero party—"

"It wasn't a hero party, bud. Just a party for some of my and your uncles' friends to get together—"

"Whatever," he murmurs and averts his eyes. *Oh, shit.* "Was *my* mom there?"

His voice is barely a whisper, but it throws me. Like, knocks the fucking wind out of me and squeezes a vise around my heart. He's never asked something like that. He's never wondered about her aloud.

"Luke?" It's all I can manage with a lump the size of Texas lodged in my throat. I soften my voice. "Why would you ask that?"

"I just thought . . . never mind."

"No! Wait!" I reach out to him and put my hand on his shoulder to keep him from running away. I squat in front of him so we're eye to eye. "You just thought what, buddy?"

He stares at his fingers as he twists them together. "I just thought that maybe she would come back because she was proud of you and celebrate." He pauses, and I can see his internal struggle, which makes every part of me hurt for him. "And there's the mother-son picnic coming up soon, and I thought that maybe she would . . ." His words fade and tighten that vise so tight my chest burns.

"You thought she might take you to it?"

He nods but never meets my eyes as a tear slides down his cheek. "No, buddy. She wasn't at the party. And I'm so sorry but she's not taking you to the picnic . . . but Nana is, and you know how much fun she makes everything."

"Yeah. Okay. Fine." He tries to step back and break my hold on his shoulder, wanting to turn around and end the conversation, but for the life of me, I can't let him go just yet. When he finally looks back up at me, his shaggy hair hangs over his forehead and there's a gravity no kid should have in his stare. His bottom lip quivers, a short-lived moment of vulnerability before he shakes his head abruptly. "Never mind. It's not a big deal."

I could play all the baseball in the world with him. Tickle him and hug him endlessly. Build an infinite number of Minecraft worlds with him. Beat every Marvel superhero game there is. None of it would matter because I'd never be able to fill that hole Claire left him with.

Fuck you, Claire.

Fuck.

You.

That isn't saying a goddamn thing about the hatred I feel for her because of what she did to me.

"Hey," I call after him, but he doesn't stop. He doesn't look back. He just keeps walking down the hall.

Fuck you again, Claire. Seven ways from Sunday.

Sixteen

Sidney

"MY GOD," I MUTTER AS I PRESS MY FINGERS TO MY eyes for a second.

You'd think it would be simple. A click and drag here. A justification of the text there. A change in font size there. But I've been trying to master Rissa's little challenge of the day—how to do a print layout of a magazine—and failing miserably.

Well, not miserably. Rather it's just taking about ten times longer to do the print design than it takes the normal staff to do one. As in, my light is the only one still on in the office and everyone else is long gone home and the rest of my to-do list is left sitting there with nothing else checked off on it.

I jump when my cell rings.

"Sidney."

"Dad? This is quite the surprise."

"I was just calling to see what you were doing."

"That's code for you were calling to check on me."

"Perhaps." His chuckle fills the line, and it's silly that a part of me wants to crawl into the phone and go back home with him. Back to the life that I hadn't realized I'd missed until now.

Back to the beautiful view of the bay where there weren't men who frustrated me to no end one minute and then kissed me breathless the next. Back to my friends and my bed and familiarity instead of this office where my light is the only one left on most nights and the stray cat that comes into my backyard is the only thing I really speak to once I get home.

"Figures." I shouldn't be surprised.

"Did you expect any less from me? How's it going?" He asks the question, but I know he already has the facts and figures and web traffic at his fingertips. He just wants to make sure I know my stuff and that I'm not relying on others to do the work for me. I've seen him do this in meetings too many times before.

I figure I'll drive him a little crazy first.

"I'm good. I told you I'm staying in the Kraft house, didn't I? You remember the Krafts, don't you?" When he begins to answer, I just talk right over him. "He was the grouchy old guy who used to complain about everyone at the farmers' market. Well, he passed a while back, and his kids decided to rent the house he was restoring as a vacation home for those interested in the vineyards. Oh, and I know I just talked to mom the other day but tell her—"

"Sidney."

That lasted longer than I expected it to. "Yes?"

"Skip the runaround and get to the facts."

I laugh. "Couldn't you have at least let me get to the part about the next-door neighbors and how they are so very loud at night when they leave their bedroom windows open?"

His laugh is full and rich and makes me smile. The hard-ass who sometimes shows he has a heart. "Great. Good for them. Now if you're done trying to annoy me, we could get to the reason I called, other than to say hi to my daughter."

"You think I don't know what's going on, don't you? You think I have interns doing the legwork while I'm out at wine tastings."

"I never said that."

"You didn't have to." I clear my throat, offended but not surprised. I hadn't really given him reason to think differently before. "You'll be happy to know that I haven't handed anything off. We're all set to start the third round of voting," I lie, knowing Grayson's pictures and bio are the main things holding us up from being one hundred percent ready. I glance down to my sad attempt at writing his bio in case he fails to come through, and the only line I have on there, which is actually scratched out, "Grayson Malone is a man who can kiss the breath out of you."

Not exactly the type of bio Rissa is looking for.

"And the third round will cut the field to . . ."

"Ten."

"Advertising?"

"I've pulled in double the advertising than what we normally do. Possibly because I've opened the option to advertising more male-oriented products—"

"Why?"

"Because women are looking at this contest side by side with the products. They assume that these men use them, and it tempts them to click and buy."

"Okay." The word comes out in murmured consent.

"And according to the hits on the site and for each link, it seems to be working. We've had a fifteen-percent increase for the advertisers' links, and overall, the website has seen a twenty-percent increase in traffic."

He makes a noncommittal sound, but I know it's because he's writing all this down. The man loves his numbers. "How do you plan to sustain this?"

"Why are you asking? I've never seen you this involved in the day to day of your other magazines. Don't you have a set of managers who would love to ask me all of this?" I tease, knowing he would likely double-check their work too.

"Yeah, well, it isn't every day I have my daughter doing such great work." Is it sad that a part of me sags in relief over not having let him down and the other stands tall from his praise? "So . . ."

"So?"

"How do you plan to maintain this level of interest?"

"I'm working on that. I've sent out press releases, have a social media marketing plan in place when the next round of voting begins, and—"

"I was pleased to see the numbers on my report. I was more than happy to know you were applying yourself. Rissa has reassured me that she's given you a few challenges to deal with and she's confident that you won't let her down. Let's see that you don't, because her word is what will either earn or lose you the position at *Haute*."

"I won't."

"So then why are you letting me down?"

"*What?*" I hate the sudden jolt of my heart in my chest at his words.

"I placed a call to an old friend down there, and the first thing she talks about is how you are in today's newspaper, kissing one Grayson Malone. That doesn't happen to be the same Grayson Malone who is on *Modern Family's* website as a contestant, is it?"

Words fail me as I fumble with the keys on my computer to bring up the *Sunnyville Gazette*. I scroll through the home page of the local newspaper, and right there in the Tuesday gossip column is a picture of Grayson and me. Or more specifically a picture of the kiss I planted on his lips in the middle of the bar. Both of my hands are on the sides of his cheeks, and my lips are more than slanted over his.

"I can explain that picture. It isn't what you think."

"Hmm." I hate that sound. "It is you in that picture, right?"

"Yes." My voice is barely a whisper. The high from getting his praise moments ago comes crashing down with the sudden disappointment heavy in his voice. Feeling like a reprimanded child, I try to explain. "He helped me with a situation, and there was a party, and I was thanking him—"

"Whether you are sleeping with him or playing Yahtzee with him . . . how exactly do you think it looks to have the person running the contest for my magazine also mentioned in a newspaper gossip column as dating him? Because, from my vantage point, it would seem a little fishy if, say, said contestant ended up winning the ten-thou-sand-dollar purse."

"But I have nothing to do with the voting whatsoever."

"Do you think the public will believe that? Do you think they care? All they see is bias."

"Dad . . . it isn't as if this is some formal election . . . it's a fun contest."

"For you maybe, but for some of these guys, the prize money is a handsome amount. It isn't their next reservation on a private jet, it's how they are going to pay off their credit card bills or put a down payment on a house."

I sigh. There's nothing else I can do to get him to see my side of things. And sadly, while he has a point about voter perception, it's all quite ridiculous to be so serious about the whole thing.

"Dad. I assure you—"

"I assure you that this isn't something the editor-in-chief of *Haute* would be caught dead doing."

And there it is. The final slap on the cheek to let me know what's at stake, as if I don't already know.

"You know what a small town Sunnyville is, Dad. You know how rumors fly. I've worked my ass off to do what you asked. To make this newsworthy and gossip worthy and trend worthy. All of them. And I'm still pushing for it, so if you want to be mad at me for gossip in the rumor mill, then so be it."

"I know what I see, and I know what it looks like."

"Is it too blue-collar in here for your white-collar hands to touch?"

Grayson's words come back to me, and I hate that I'm hearing them in my dad's words when I've never heard him imply anything of the sort. I hate that I'm wondering if he's more worked up because of the picture and the implication of bias to readers or because I'm kissing Grayson Malone of the Sunnyville Malones.

"And your perception is wrong," I say, knowing that he sees what he wants to see, and once he does, there is no changing his mind. He calls it the privilege of being older. I call it close-minded crap.

"I should have known you'd somehow make this story, this situation, this contest, about you. It's what you do best, isn't it?" The remark is sharp and cuts to my marrow. Does he really see me the same way that Grayson does? Selfish and self-centered?

I clear my throat again as I stare at all of my hard work on the layout on my screen that I'm not even here to do but that I'm trying to learn anyway, and school my voice into neutrality. "It's late. I'm still at the office and need to close up."

"You're still there?"

"Yeah." It's where I am every night.

"Fix this, Sidney. You were doing great right up until now."

The line goes dead, and I lean my head back against the chair and close my eyes as I process everything he just said to me. The accusations. The implications. The bullshit.

When I open my eyes, the picture from the weekly gossip column is right before me on my laptop screen. I sigh and scroll down a bit so I can read whatever nonsense they decided to publish with the picture.

In other news, it seems being a hero in Sunnyville comes with perks these days. Our very own hot dad in the *Modern Family* contest, Grayson Malone, seems to be spending a lot of time with here-then, gone-then, back-in-town-again Sidney Thorton. At a local party to celebrate Malone's heroics from last week, they were seen getting reacquainted with each other. New couple alert. (picture right).

Thank you, small-town rumor mill.

I groan. Now I really do miss home and the anonymity of living in the big city. I was never noticed there unless I chose to be—show up at the right restaurant with the perfect guy so that I know our picture will be taken, only to play coy about it later.

But this is Sunnyville, not San Francisco. This is small-town journalism, not money-hungry paparazzi.

This is Grayson Malone, not my flavor of the month.

Without thinking, I pick up my cell and dial. "Sidney, is that you?"

When I hear Rissa's kids in the background I regret it immediately. "I'm sorry. I shouldn't have called."

"Let me guess, you finally left the office and saw the *Gazette*."

"Nah. I'm still here and finally saw the Gazette," I say.

"If it's any consolation, the gossip column only comes out once a week, so they can't write any more until next Tuesday."

"Thanks for the warning," I part-joke, part-complain. "At least I'll have a week for my dad to chill out before something else is printed."

"When I told you to problem-solve getting Grayson on board, kissing him wasn't exactly what I had in mind." When I don't laugh at her joke, she continues, "Was your dad pissed?"

"It's really none of his business." I glance back to the photo and article for a minute. "He does have a point about perceived bias, though." It almost kills me to say that.

"I'll call him now and tell him I orchestrated all of this. It's my fault and—"

"Those aren't your lips sitting squarely on Grayson's." I laugh and am more than surprised she'd take the blame for me. "Thank you for the offer, but it isn't necessary."

"Well, just think about what they are going to say when people catch wind of the photo shoot you're doing tomorrow." My shoulders sag in exhaustion. "Maybe you should be the one to oil him up—all hands on pec, er, I mean on deck kind of thing."

"You really are trying to get me into trouble, aren't you?"

"Who me?" she asks. "Never."

When I look back to the computer, I know the person who's going to get me into trouble is in the picture in front of me.

I'm not sure how.

I'm not sure when.

But I definitely know he will, because I'm thinking about him way too much, and it has nothing to do with this contest and everything to do with his kiss.

Seventeen

Grayson

"WHO PUT YOU GUYS UP TO THIS?" I LAUGH AS I glance around the dispatch room, where everyone has their heads bowed at their stations, trying to fight the grins on their faces. "Bueller? Bueller?"

I take a step closer to my desk and just shake my head. There are copies of the *Gazette's* gossip column everywhere. There's Sidney kissing me on the lips taped to my chair, to my monitor, to my headset, to my bulletin board. To every fucking place imaginable. The words "hot dad" are on a banner stretched over all of it.

Christ.

I look around again and this time everyone is looking my way and they all bust up laughing. "You guys are assholes." I start taking down the papers.

"Oh, flyboy, come and give me mouth-to-mouth!" McArthur mocks.

"Mount me, Malone." That one was Vin.

"Way to date a rich girl!" Uley says, and his words stop me in my tracks. I know he means nothing by it, but every part of me rejects his comment, and it takes me a second to clear my head. To bring my mind back from the bullshit it brought up.

"Dating? Sorry, Uley, but not this man. How's a guy supposed to work with all this crap in the way?"

"You could always roll it up and spank her with it," someone at my back tosses out, and the whole room busts up laughing.

"She isn't a dog, and it's just gossip."

"Gossip, my ass," Uley says. "Looks to me like she has you right where she wants you."

I look over to him as his words hit, but his head is already down, and his fingers are flying across his keyboard. Then I look back down to the picture of Sidney kissing me. The same damn one my brothers had already given me shit for.

I was letting myself believe it was a coincidence—that I was the one who started the chain reaction by kissing her—but as I look at the photo I realize it's the second time she's made me look like a fool. It's the second time she's manipulated me into her publicity-fueled fire.

It's the second time she's used me.

Maybe that's why I've yet to hit send on the bio she wants. Maybe that's why I've gone to text her ten times already to cancel the photo shoot.

I try to shrug off the notion that her kiss was nothing but a publicity stunt, but it sticks in a way that makes me want to bail from work, from this office that's a kicker of a punishment on top of grounding me.

And I hate that for a second time with a similar woman, I've let my guard down.

Eighteen

Sidney

"It's Grayson."

"Hi. What's up?" The smile is automatic when I hear his voice. I look over to the photographer, who is setting up her reflectors and staging out shots, and then down at my watch. "Where are you?"

"I can't make it."

"What?" It's a half-laugh, half-panicked sound.

"I can't make it," he repeats matter-of-factly.

"The vote is in less than twenty-four hours. I need to get these shots of you, so I can put them up on the site." Desperation edges my tone. I've pushed this deadline as far as I can and still be able to get the magazine to the printer on time. I have no more wiggle room. The website is more forgiving of the time constraints, but not the print side.

"Are you giving everyone else the same personal attention you're giving me?" His question throws me.

"No. Why? They're turning in their own photos."

"Then do the same for me. I'm sure there are plenty of photos from the other night you can use." There's a bite to his words that has my head startling. "No doubt you had photographers staged throughout the pub to snap the perfect picture."

"What's that supposed to mean?"

"Nothing. Never mind." He sighs as I look at everyone around me. They are all trying not to be obvious about eavesdropping, curious who I'm talking to as they wait for Grayson to arrive.

"Grayson?"

He grunts. "Find a picture from the other night. It's that simple."

"It isn't the same." I make the comment and then cringe because it is the same. It should be the same, but it isn't. Photographs from the hero party are not what Rissa is expecting. Grayson's biography forged by me, even less so. The spots I've worked tirelessly to secure with *E! News Daily* and *Entertainment Tonight* are expecting professional pictures, not *Sunnyville Gazette* cast-offs.

"Make it the same. This isn't my thing. You've forced my hand enough, and I'm done when it comes to you."

The rejection is instantaneous, and panic has me responding without thinking. "I should've known you were full of crap when you agreed to do this. Do you know how this screws me up?"

"Fucking typical." His chuckle is full of derision. "Regardless of what you might think, not everything is about you, Princess."

"Fine. Great." I think of the photographer I'm going to have to pay for lost time. I think of my promise to Rissa, and my conversation with my dad.

I blink my welling tears away and tell myself that they're there because I don't want to let people down and not because I feel personally rejected.

Or used.

He said he wanted me.

How was I not supposed to think about that? How was I not supposed to obsess over those words to the point I slipped my fingers under the waistband of my panties and put them to work while I thought of him last night.

It was just a kiss, Sidney. He didn't reject you. He didn't anything you, so stop overthinking. Don't fall off the estrogen-edged deep end thinking this is about you when he's simply talking about participating in the contest.

"Not all of us get to come and go on a whim like you. I don't have time for this in my life. Not in the least."

"Time for what? What do you mean?"

"*This.* The photo and the goddamn contest. *Us.* The kiss. *Me wanting you.* It was a huge mistake, and your response a few seconds ago just made it more than clear why it was."

"Grayson, I—"

"I've gotta go."

The call ends, and I'm left standing in the middle of a photo shoot that isn't going to take place. I stare at my cell phone, not really knowing what the hell just happened, and eventually come to the realization that I never really knew I wanted there to be an *us* until the door shut in my damn face.

Talk about screwing myself on all fronts. *And not in the good way.*

Shit.

What am I going to do now?

If there is any silver lining in my day, it's that when I walk out of the *Sunnyville Gazette*'s office an hour later, I have a thumb-drive full of photos of Grayson I can possibly use for our site. No, they aren't of him in his flight suit with the front unzipped like I'd planned. Yes, I had to deal with the searching comments from the gossip columnist about whether I really needed the pictures just for the contest.

But I have them.

At least there's that.

Nineteen

Grayson

MEET HIM STARE FOR STARE. HIS EYES HOLD SO MUCH DEPTH, BUT the angry red mark on his cheekbone stands out bright against his olive complexion.

"Fighting isn't the way to solve a problem," I say to Luke. On the inside, a part of me wants to give him a high five for doing it, and another part of me wants to pull him against me to protect him from the cruelty of other kids. "Do you want to tell me what happened?" It's the same question I've asked three other times. In the school's office. In the car. In the driveway once we were home.

"No."

"Mr. Malone, there's been an incident here at school. You need to come and get Luke."

"What's wrong?"

"He's been in a fight."

My laugh filled the line. "You're kidding, right? My Luke?"

"I'm sad to say I'm not kidding. We have a zero-tolerance policy for fights."

"I'm on my way."

"Luke, buddy, I can't help you if you don't tell me what happened. You've sat here for the past two hours, now it's time to talk."

"Nothing happened." He spits the words out at me, but his bottom lip quivers.

"Hi. What's up?" Sidney's voice filled the line and aggravated every single part of me—good and bad. "Where are you?"

"I can't make it."

"What?" The superior tone in her voice sliced open my temper, the intonation implying no one ever cancels on her and she didn't quite know how to handle it.

"I can't make it." Deal with it.

I think back to what a day it's been so far, and hell if I'm not sitting here at seven o'clock at night, trying to coax my eight-year-old to explain what happened. All I got out of the principal was that it had to do with that goddamn photo in the paper, some teasing, and then Luke threw the first punch.

I try again.

"Something happened, or you wouldn't have hit him."

"I told you, nothing happened."

Christ. I shove a hand through my hair and walk to one end of the room and back. This is something Grant should be doing. He's the cop. Skilled at interrogations. I should call him to come do the dirty work for me—play bad cop so I can be good cop—because this parenting shit is for the birds.

"Fine. Then nothing is going to happen for you, either. No baseball this weekend. No sleepover at George's house. No—"

"He asked me if the lady you were kissing in the paper was my mom." His voice is so quiet I can barely hear him.

"What?" I ask, even though I heard him perfectly well.

"I told him no. I didn't know what picture he was talking about. He laughed and said you weren't going to get married, and it was because of me. How could she want to be my mom when my own didn't love me enough to stick around? Is that what you wanted to know?" He shoves the chair back so hard it falls to the floor, making a sickening *thud*.

Angry tears well in his eyes. His little body shakes with anger, and his fists are clenched so tightly his fingers are turning bloodless. All I can do is stare at him—my heart broken, my head more than fucked up.

"That's a lie." No parenting award for that one, but it's all I can muster as I sit and watch my little man.

"Then where is she?" he screams at me as the first tear slips down his cheek. "If she loves me like you say she does, then how come she never comes home? How come she never calls me? How come all the other kids' moms love them and do things with them and mine doesn't? How come she doesn't want me?"

I catch him as he tries to run past me. I take a hit to my shoulder and kick to my thigh as I pick him up and hold him to me as tightly as I can. The agony I feel as a parent is a hundred times more painful than any hit or kick of his ever could be, so I squeeze him with every ounce of love I have until his struggles turn to sobs and his hands fist in my shirt. His tears are hot through the fabric.

I was warned this phase would come, by the psychologist I talked to after Claire left. By the friends I've met whose husbands stepped out of their children's lives during their infancy. The rage and the hurt and the sense of unworthiness. No amount of warning could have prepared me for hitting this head-on.

All the hate, all the hurt, all the everything Claire made me feel when she left . . . it's like someone took a truckload of dynamite and detonated it, with all of the debris falling and landing on Luke.

There's no way in hell I can protect him from it.

No fucking way.

"You know that isn't true." I will repeat the lie as long as I can to make my son feel better about himself. It won't work much longer, and every time I mutter it, I feel like more and more of a complete asshole.

"Did you know the day you were born was the best day of my

life?" I murmur into the crown of his head as he hiccups with sobs. "Your mom was eating a piece of chocolate cake, and all of a sudden, you let her know you were ready to meet us."

"But she finished eating her cake first." His voice is muffled, but he's calmed some.

This is our routine. A set of memories to let him know he came into this world being loved. With parents who wanted him.

"Yes. She loved chocolate cake."

"Just like I do."

"Mm-hmm." I think back to the panic. The excitement. The wonder of that day. "We ran around excited, getting everything together and getting to the hospital. Then, a few hours later, you were crying so loud when they put you in your momma's arms."

"And you were crying, too."

"I was." Looking back, I can see the panic on her face and the uncertainty that I thought was a normal thing because I felt it, too. We were responsible for this perfect little human. We were his smiles, his reassurance, his everything. How was I to know that look was a sign of what was to come? "And even though we'd only officially met you a whole five minutes before, we both knew we'd never loved anything as much as we loved you."

Silence lingers as the story I've told countless times replays in both of our minds in completely different ways.

"If she loved me, why did she leave?" His whisper wavers.

"She still loves you, Luke. She loves you with all her heart, but sometimes, people are afraid they aren't going to be enough for their child. They think that being around will hurt their kid more than help them."

"If she loved me, she'd know that leaving was going to hurt me more than her being here."

I sigh, knowing his words are true but needing to reinforce the narrative I've created over the years so he doesn't feel unworthy.

"I know, but as a parent, you have to make hard decisions. Decisions that feel wrong but are for the right reason. That's why she sends you birthday presents. She wants you to know she's thinking of you and loves you. She wants to make sure you know how much you mean to her."

I can't look him in the eyes when he looks up. He'll see the lie there. He'll know it's me sending him the gifts. That it's me making him feel like a normal little boy with a mom who loves him instead of one who abandoned him because God for-fucking-bid the precious Hoskins' bloodline be tainted by a blue-collar worker like me. It's me working my ass off to sell the lie because telling him his mother was more worried about her inheritance and taking her parents' yacht to Cannes than being a mom.

We shift some so that he sits cradled in my lap and his head rests against my chest. His breath still hitches, but I can tell the tears are done for now.

"Who was the woman in the photo?" he asks, circling back to the newspaper article.

"Just a friend." I don't tell him it's Sidney. He's met her. He's asked about her. Telling him who it was will only make him more curious when there is nothing there for him to be curious about.

"Why were you kissing her?"

"It was her way of thanking me for something. In other countries, that's how you do it." *And the award for Liar of the Year goes to Grayson Malone.* "You kiss both sides of their cheeks."

"Oh." His voice falls. "It was just the cheek? He didn't say that."

"Yes, just her cheek." I'm going to hell. Plain and simple. Especially when I've thought about that kiss more than I should have.

"So, she isn't going to be my new mom?"

I chuckle to try to add some levity. "No, buddy. We've been over this before. A kiss doesn't mean someone marries someone. It doesn't even mean they love someone—I mean it does—but . . . just hear me out." I fumble, my own head fucked-up over seeing the pain in his eyes. "Sometimes people like each other and they are lonely and need a friend. They go on dates to do things together."

"They kiss."

"Yes, they sometimes kiss. But that doesn't mean they're going to get married. Marriage is something you go into knowing you want to spend the rest of your life with that person. It isn't something you do after a date or two."

"Is that why you and mom weren't married? Did you know she wasn't going to be here forever?"

Of course, from all I said, he picked up on that. "Mom and I weren't married because of other reasons."

"But you loved her, right?"

"Very much." I barely get the words out, the animosity almost making me choke on them. "We were planning on getting married . . . but in our case . . . our case was just different."

He plucks at his pants with his fingers, his eyes downcast. "Do you miss my mom?"

No. I hate her more each and every day for doing this to you. For being too selfish to see how incredible you are. For not fighting for you. For not choosing you.

"You always have a choice."

Sidney's words are right there in my ears, and I hate them as much as I need to hear them.

"Of course I do. I miss her mostly because I think she'd love to see how awesome you are."

"I wish I knew her."

When he looks at me this time, I meet his gaze head-on. My lips want to tell him she doesn't deserve to meet him and know how incredible he is. She doesn't warrant the time I take to write cards to him with different penmanship so he thinks they are from her. She doesn't merit a goddamn thing when it comes to my son.

"You do know her. She's a part of you, just like I am. No matter how far away she is, that will never change." I press a kiss to the top of his head and pick another memory to tell him about, when, really, I need to address him punching someone today. "There was this one time when you were a baby . . ."

So, we sit there, letting the evening fade to night as I retell Luke stories about memories he'll never remember on his own. Stories that every kid should know about their life. Stories that let him know how much he is loved even though his mom isn't here.

When his giggles subside and his soft snores fill the room, I sit with him for a while and can't help but despise Claire even more when I thought I hated her enough. Then I carry him upstairs, forgo the brushing of his teeth, and put him into my bed.

Then I watch him sleep.

I take in the red mark on the cheekbone that has the same line as his mother's, the subtle dent in his chin that resembles my father, and the freckles over his nose that somehow make him seem more innocent.

I know that I may be doing the complete wrong thing when it comes to him and the memory of his mother. I may be screwing him up more than I'm helping him with these stories and lies and that someday, he may hate me because of it. But if him hating me is the price I am going to have to pay for giving him these small moments of peace, then I'll pay it. They make him feel whole and loved and worthy of that love, so fuck anyone who tells me I'm in the wrong.

Parenting is a succession of brutal decisions, each one tougher than the last, with the only goal being not to fuck up your kid any more than you already have.

It's much later, after I've had a couple of beers and sat on the porch swing alone, that I crawl into bed beside my son with the knowledge that no matter what Claire did or didn't do, I have one thing to be thankful to her for.

Luke.

He's the reason I keep fighting.

Twenty

Sidney

"YOU SHOULD TAKE THE REST OF THE DAY OFF, RISSA. I'LL cover the office."

She looks at me as if I've grown two heads. "Why?"

"Because the third round of voting is a go. We've already had more traffic in the first few hours than we did in the first week of last round's vote. And because . . . because it's sunny outside. Do we need another reason?"

"Maybe because you're trying to get me out of here so I don't call you on the carpet and ask why Grayson's bio is the same one I saw you working on in longhand and the photo is from the party?" She lifts her eyebrows and meets my gaze. "Perhaps?"

"Perhaps, but it was simply a matter of circumstance. We didn't get him on board until too late and"—the look she gives me stops me in my tracks—"and I'll stop my excuse about now." She gives a measured nod. "I can't control someone else. All I can do is cajole and persuade and inform and do my best. So, while I try to get all that to work, I'm busy trying to master all the other things you've told me are important to know."

She crosses her arms over her chest and leans back in her chair. "Such as?"

"Edie is showing me the process by which she goes through editing content. Fran has put together a little tutorial on graphics and re-sizing because I struggle there, and in turn, I'm explaining how I track my progress through the statistics, so she understands. Then there's—"

"Point made, Sidney." She shakes her head. "On that note, I'm heading home."

She doesn't waste any time grabbing her stuff and heading to the door before something happens that I can't handle and change my mind.

For the rest of the afternoon, I sit and watch the numbers the first day of voting brings in. I stay and make sure that nothing goes wrong with the site—no glitches or missing links or whatever else could go wrong. By the time I'm happy that we've had a successful launch and am ready to leave, I realize I don't want to go home to an empty house. An empty house means I'll end up working. Working means I'll think of Grayson.

And Grayson is . . . who knows what Grayson is, other than a jerk for what he said to me yesterday.

Normally after a great day, Zoey and I would live it up some. Go out for drinks and a night on the town. Dance with some men, and maybe end up with one when closing time came.

I may not have Zoey by my side, and I may have no interest in taking some random guy home with me, but that doesn't mean I can't go out and have a drink, right?

I force myself to leave, if only because I refuse to spend the night at the office doing the exact thing I'm worried I'd do alone at my house.

As I drive through downtown Sunnyville, with its rustic store-fronts where the word "wine" can be seen somewhere in every window display, I realize my night on the town most definitely is not going to happen here. But I park the car under the big banner advertising the upcoming Harvest Festival and get out to walk around like the many tourists milling about. I poke my head into a few stores, buy some handmade soap, get a bouquet of flowers, and pick up a cute bracelet to send Zoey for her birthday.

A few people smile knowingly at me, as if they are asking with their eyes if the gossip column is true, but I feign that I don't see them so I don't have to acknowledge the question.

"Sidney!" I turn to find Cathy stepping out from the nail salon I just passed.

"Hey."

"We need to stop meeting like this on the street." She laughs as she glances to her freshly painted toes, which still have twisted paper towels between them so her polish doesn't smudge. "Or else gossip around town is going to be that we're streetwalkers." Her eyes widen as she waits for me to get the joke, and then she laughs even louder when I just shake my head.

"Cute, but more rumors are the last thing I need."

"Sometimes they're good for the soul."

Moving on . . .

"How are you?"

"I'm good. I'm good." Someone across the street calls out to her, and she waves before turning back to me. "But not as good as you're doing, I see."

Yeah, I should have known better than to think she would drop it. "The newspaper."

"*The newspaper.*" She nods. "You made a lot of ladies in that line awfully pissed that a newcomer snagged the last Malone and not one of us." I opt to ignore the "newcomer" comment since she knows I did, in fact, grow up here, and her distinctive laugh sounds off. People walking by turn their heads at its cadence, and I duck my head slightly.

"I didn't snag him. It really was just a picture taken at the right time, and—"

"Oh, honey, you don't have to make excuses to me. This whole town is abuzz with the news." She pats my arm. "How did you think I knew you were out here? Ol' Patsy from the soap shop said something to Kira as she was walking by, and then Kira came into the nail salon. It's like the grown-up game of telephone in these parts."

"It's comforting to know my whereabouts are being tracked so diligently," I say teasingly as we both step back out of the middle of the sidewalk so people can pass. "I can assure you that everything was taken out of context. The hero thing. The party. The kiss."

"At least Grayson is having some fun for a change," she says, talking right over my explanation as if I didn't utter a word. "He had a rough go of it when Claire left town."

"Claire?" Wait. *What*? "As in Claire Hoskin, Claire?"

"Mm-hmm. Didn't you know she's Luke's mother?"

"No. I didn't." My mind stumbles over the information. The beauty queen of Sunnyville and one of my closest friends back in high school. Claire is Luke's mom? Claire was with Grayson? She's the one who walked out on them?

I try to hide my shock as I look over at a group of teenagers who are sitting outside of the convenience store at the end of the street. They screech playfully, and I can almost picture us there, doing the same thing, when we were that age.

Claire. Gorgeous. Conceited . . . but couldn't the same things have been said about me?

Realization strikes. The kind that makes your jaw fall lax and forces you to blink to make sure you're right.

Grayson sees me as Claire. A "walks like a duck and talks like a duck" type of thing. No wonder he hates me.

When the thoughts settle, I'm left with Cathy staring at me with her brow furrowed and her smile frozen as if she just said something she shouldn't but can't wait to say more.

"I had no idea he was with Claire. I left Sunnyville after graduation and never looked back."

"Yeah, it's a long story, which the majority of us around here don't know the half of, I'm sure. You know how money can keep lips from getting loose, don't you?" She waves a hand my way as if the story is inconsequential. "Anyhoo, I'm sure he'll tell you when the time's right in your relationship."

"I told you, we aren't—"

"Like I said, if any man deserves a break and something more than a little mindless twisting of his sheets, it would be Grayson "Make Me Moan" Malone. First his suspension from flying at work, when we all know he's a hero and then everything with Luke yesterday . . . The guy can sure use a little Sidney sunshine in his life."

"What do you mean? What happened with Luke yesterday?"

"Oh my, you don't know?"

"Don't go clutching your pearls on me, Cathy," I say when she lifts a hand to her chest. "What happened?"

"He was in a fight at school."

"About?"

She looks around as if she's about to get in trouble for talking, and the simple action has dread dropping into my stomach. "Well, someone teased him about that picture in the paper—the one of you two—and one thing led to another about his mom not wanting him, and *boom*, he threw the first punch."

"Regardless of what you might think, not everything is about you, Princess."

Grayson had been trying to tell me he wasn't canceling because of something I had done or said. I was just too wrapped up in myself to listen.

God, maybe I am every bit as selfish as everyone keeps implying. As Grayson keeps saying without coming right out and throwing it in my face.

"Little boy is just like his father. Willing to fight for love. How does it feel having two men—Grayson and Luke—love you at the same time?"

Her words snap me from my thoughts, and I mumble some kind of generic response. Even if I refute her, she will argue with me. I take a step backward. "It was good seeing you again, Cathy, but I have to run. Drinks next time?"

"You know I'm definitely in."

I head toward my car, my mind a confused mess.

That damn picture.

It only serves to prove my dad right. That I act before I think, without taking anyone else around me into consideration.

The heat from my dad over the photo was just another reprimand in a long line of them. It's water off my back.

The pang of remorse I feel when it comes to Luke, though, is a whole different ballgame that I'm not sure how to process.

My actions caused him to be bullied and teased. To throw a punch in defense. He's hurting, and it's all because I acted in haste without thought to anyone else who might be affected.

Feeling like shit is putting it mildly.

Twenty-One

Sidney

I DON'T KNOW WHY I'M HERE.

It's because I want to apologize to Luke.

I don't know why I've sat staring at the front of his house.

It's because I really want to see Grayson.

I don't know why I've spent the last thirty minutes watching the porch swing move ever so subtly under the influence of the intermittent soft breeze. Why I keep glancing at the blue BMX bike lying on its side in the driveway or the baseball bat propped beside the front door.

Even more, I don't know why I keep staring at the lights in the windows and wondering what's going on inside.

I should start my car and drive away.

But I can't.

Something happened to a little boy yesterday, and it was because of me. My dad may say I'm heartless and only think of myself, but no matter how many times I told myself to stay home, I couldn't. And then as I told myself I was just going out for a drive to clear my mind, my hands kept turning the wheel to navigate the streets until I ended up here.

With a deep breath, I climb from the car and make my way up the front steps. The house is quiet except for the undertones of the television coming out from the open window.

I hold my breath when I knock, letting my hand fall to my side as my heart pounds in my ears and nerves jitter in my stomach.

Last time I stood on this porch, I told myself that it was just Grayson. He was just some guy from high school I hardly knew.

This time it's so much more. This time, I get that. It's Grayson. It's Luke. It's a whole different dynamic from what I'm used to.

"I got it." The television is clicked off. The door opens.

Grayson seems shocked to see me standing on his porch. He's in athletic pants, a plain blue T-shirt that looks like an old favorite, and a baseball hat pulled low on his brow.

He isn't trying to be as handsome as he is, which makes him simply stunning as he stands there—irritated expression and distrustful eyes included.

"What are you doing here?"

"I heard about Luke."

"Heard what about Luke?"

"The fight. The picture. The—"

"Goddamn small-town bullshit," he mutters under his breath.

"Is it true?

He glances over his shoulder before crossing his arms over his chest and shrugging. "What does that have to do with you?"

I open my mouth to say *everything* and then stop myself. That's exactly what he expects me to say. That's exactly who he has painted me to be.

I try again.

"I heard it started because—"

"And like I said yesterday, the world doesn't revolve around you." A shift of his feet. A huff of a sigh. Impatience that radiates off him.

"I know it doesn't." His snort is one of complete derision. It's one that I deserve, but I'm here trying to make things right, and the sound frustrates me. "Just once, can you be nice to me? Why is that so hard for you?"

"You tell me why I should be?" Grayson gets the words out

seconds before I see something fly by my head. I yelp and flinch.

"Nerf wars!" Luke shouts at the top of his lungs before another foam dart hits me squarely in the chest.

"Luke!" Grayson warns just as he skids to a stop beside his dad. His left eye is a bluish-purplish color, and there's a scratch on his cheek that makes me feel horrible, but the smile on his face widens when he recognizes me. "Miss Sidney? Why are you here? Are you here to go on a date with my dad?"

I sputter out a laugh that sounds like I'm choking on air and shake my head violently, more than shocked by his question.

"No. I'm not here to go on a date with your dad." I glance to Grayson, who's standing beside his son. His eyes are narrowed, and I know he's trying to figure out what I'm really doing here.

Get in line, because I don't know what I'm doing here, either.

"In fact, I came to see you."

Both of them jerk ever so slightly in response. "You did?" Luke asks.

"Yep. I had kind of a weird day, and I thought you might be able to help cheer me up."

"Why was it weird?" He angles his head to the side. I keep my eyes on his, not looking over to Grayson, because I don't want to see his response.

"Just work stuff. What about you? It seems to me you got into a fight with a Creeper." Thank God for the conversation between a mom and her little boy in the soap store earlier, otherwise I would have no idea what a Creeper even was.

His eyes widen and then narrow. "You play Minecraft?"

"No." I laugh. "But I know Creepers can be pretty vicious. So, who won? You or the Creeper?"

"Well . . . uh . . ."

"I bet it was a hard fight, but that you were victorious." I resist the urge to reach out and touch him and then am startled by the want to.

"Can we help you?" Grayson places his hand protectively on Luke's shoulder as he speaks. The warning to leave is loud and clear.

I look at him, see the confusion in his expression, and can only hope he doesn't see how hard I'm working at talking to a little boy when I have zero to no experience in doing so.

"Dad, she came to see me." Luke rolls his eyes and reaches out to grab my hand. It takes everything I have not to think of the millions of germs on his little fingers and let him take hold of it. "Let me show you my Minecraft collection."

"Luke, I don't think Sidney really cares about your Minecraft figures." Grayson grabs on to my opposite arm and holds me steady in the doorway. His eyes search mine, demanding answers as to why I'm here and telling me I'm not welcome, all in the same look. "Give us a sec, bud. She'll be right in," he says to Luke but never takes his eyes off me.

"'Kay."

The minute Luke's feet pound on the stairs, I try to yank my arm from Grayson's grip, but he just holds tighter and pulls me in to him. "Don't think for one second that I'll let you use my son to get to me," he says, voice near a growl.

I should have a witty comeback. I should tell him to go to hell and that I'm not here to manipulate anyone . . . but, for that split second, with the mint of his breath in my face and his hard, lean body against mine, my synapses misfire. My words falter.

"I—Cathy Clementine told me about the fight. That it was started because of the picture. I didn't mean for him to see—"

"He doesn't know it was you in the picture." He spits the words out almost as if they are a challenge. Will I bail now that I know Luke doesn't know it was me, or am I still going to stick around?

"Oh."

"Exactly. *Oh.*" His fingers dig deeper into my arm. "Since your conscience is clear, you can take off the jeans and tank top you wore to let me know you're just like us," he says with sarcasm dripping from every word, "put back on your skirt and red-soled shoes, and stop pretending you care."

"That isn't fair," I argue and hate that he saw right through me.

The attempt to dress down and not be *so* . . . Sidney.

"You and your fair bullshit. I'll tell you the same thing I said before. No one said life's fair."

"I promised him I'd see his Minecraft—"

"Like you really care."

"It doesn't matter if I care or not, Grayson." I grit the words out. "It only matters if he thinks I do, so—"

"Miss Sidney, are you ready to see *all* of them? There are tons," Luke calls from behind Grayson, and his words are followed by the distinct sound of things being dumped all over what I can presume is the table.

I look at Grayson and shrug as I step past him and into the living room. At first glance, I'm surprised by how put together the house is. I know that sounds stupid, but maybe I expected a single dad to have a house that's a mess, with clutter everywhere. Grayson's house is the exact opposite. It's dark wood with blues and grays. There's a television on one wall and an inset den across from it with shelves lined with books. The kitchen is small but homey, a butcher-block island in its center. Luke is sitting at the dining room table and has a heap of miniature figures in front of him.

I take the seat next to him, my grin matching his as I say, "I have no clue what any of those are, but I have a feeling you're about to teach me."

And he does. For the next hour, Luke goes through each character, explaining their significance in the game. Figure after figure. There are so many that I wouldn't even be able to remember the names if I tried (like I would want to), and yet, his nonstop enthusiastic chatter tells me whoever designed this game hit the nail on the head marketing to their demographic.

Grayson sits in a chair across the room, alternating between his iPad and a magazine. I catch him staring at us every so often, and I know he's quietly enjoying this display of my complete incompetence with Luke. I forget the characters' names immediately. I use the wrong terminology, which earns me Luke's exasperated but secretly-happy-he-has-an-audience sighs. Regardless of my flaws in knowing how to relate to him, there is something about this little boy that captivates me. Maybe it's his willingness to listen or his eagerness to share. Maybe it's the subtle way he asks every so often if I'm sure I'm not here for his dad. Maybe it's that shy little smile he gives me as he bumps his shoulder against mine when he shows me a character he deems as "really cool" that has me actually enjoying my time with him.

"C'mon, Luke-ster. That's long enough. It's time for bed." Luke's protests fill the room as Grayson rises from his chair and takes a few steps toward us. He meets my gaze, and I hate that I can't read what his says, but it definitely says something.

"Aw, Dad. But I don't have to go to school tomorrow. Can't I stay up a little later?" Luke walks the few steps to face his dad, and I smile because they both have the same stance as they stare each other down.

"You don't have to go to school tomorrow because you can't. You were suspended for getting into a fight."

"But I didn't—"

"A fight is a fight, Luke. And staying up is a privilege, and privileges aren't given when you use your fists to solve a problem."

Luke huffs loudly and looks to me. "Are you going to the Harvest Festival?" he asks me, his eyebrows raised and hope in his voice that makes me say yes just so I don't let him down again.

"Yes. Doesn't everyone go?"

"See you there," he says and then squeals as Grayson moves swiftly to pick him up and throw him over his shoulder.

"Let's go, monster. Tell Miss Sidney good night," Grayson says and already has a foot on the first step of the stairs.

"Good." Luke giggles as Grayson tickles his ribs. "Night." Another bout of laughter floats down the stairs.

I sit there and stare at where they just were, my mind frozen on how damn sexy the sight of Grayson carrying Luke off to bed is.

They must have spiked my bottle of water.

That can be the only reason those foreign thoughts are filling my head. Kids are not cute. Dads are not sexy. Up is not down. So why am I still sitting here, slowly swiping dozens of Minecraft figures into a big tub while the sounds of Grayson putting Luke to bed upstairs fill the space around me?

Why am I still here? Is it because my place is so quiet and here I was able to listen to Luke talk nonstop? Or is it because now that I've seen Grayson, I feel the need to prove to him I'm not who he thinks I am . . . even when I'm still struggling with proving that to myself.

The problem is now that we're going to be alone, I have no clue what it is I need to say.

Twenty-Two

Grayson

GODDAMMIT.

I stand on the bottom step and watch her. Watch the woman who showed up looking nothing like the Sidney I know and exactly like the one I would want to know. She's wearing blue jeans and a yellow tank top. Her hair is pulled up in a messy ponytail. She looks like she belongs in our neighborhood—in this house—drinking beer from a bottle instead of wine from crystal in the palace she comes from.

Even worse, I want her.

I've sat here all night long, begging myself to hate her, when all I can think about is how much I fucking want her.

Doesn't that make me the asshole?

This is on her. Every single fucking part of it.

She staged the kiss. She planted the picture. She's here to sweet talk me into doing the damn photo shoot for her. She's here to ease her own goddamn guilt because her manipulations hurt my son.

She. She. She. She. Can't say it surprises me.

Well, screw that.

Isn't that the problem, though? That's what I want.

Christ. I'm doing nothing but running myself in circles. I rake a hand through my hair and remind myself I've walked down this road before. I paid the price. Luke is still paying the price for it.

Still, what I can't quite wrap my mind around is why she didn't bail? She really sounded like she cared about Creepers and Villagers and Steve Blocks when I thought she'd be out the goddamn door the minute I told her Luke didn't know the picture in the paper was of her.

I study her as she cleans up the figures and hate that she looks like she belongs here. In my house. At my table. The normalcy of the moment. It's a blatant slap in the face of what exactly I'm missing in my life . . . what I'm making Luke miss out on, and it erodes the desire eating away at me.

When I clear my throat, she drops the last handful into the bucket and turns my way—lips parted, cheeks pink, eyes surprised.

"You can stop pretending you like him now. Your guilt can be absolved. You can go."

"But I do like him." She rises from her seat and takes a few steps toward me.

"Cut the act, Princess."

"What's your problem, Malone? I came here because I heard about Luke and I felt bad that something I did hurt him."

"You mean the photo you staged and the article you planted to save your ass."

"I did no such thing. You kissed me. You said things that made my head spin, and then you ran out."

"And then you followed me out and kissed me again."

"You're blaming this on me?" she shrieks.

"Shoe fits?" I take a step closer to her.

Her laugh grates on my nerves. "My bad. Only the man is allowed to initiate a kiss? How foolish of me to think otherwise."

I disregard her logic, too blinded by my own anger to hear her. "You knew there were photographers there."

"So did you," she grits between her clenched teeth as we stare at each other, our tempers thickening the air around us.

"The difference is that I did what I did behind a closed door. You did it to set me up."

She rolls her eyes and has me clenching my teeth. "That's bullshit. But you keep thinking what you want to think, Grayson. I didn't make you kiss me, and I didn't set up photographers. I didn't plant a story."

"No, but you manipulated this whole goddamn town into making me be in this contest when I don't want to."

"It sounds to me like your own brothers did that to you by entering you, so maybe you should take it up with them."

Her smart-ass comment tees me off. "What the fuck more do you want from me? You've already gotten what you wanted. I told you I'd participate, and you've made certain with the little party that I can't back out . . . so I'll ask you again, why did you come here tonight? What more do you want from me?" My body vibrates with anger as I stare at her and wait for an answer.

"I didn't know the photo was taken. I wasn't thinking."

"You're goddamn right you weren't."

She grits her teeth again and takes a second before she speaks. "I kissed you because I wanted to. I kissed you because you left me in that office and the only thing I wanted was more. I was so angry about what you said, that I just acted." She clears her throat, and I want to believe her. I want to see sincerity in those brown eyes of hers. And I want to ignore every part of my libido that's listening to her tell me she wants more. "I should have remembered there were cameras. I should have realized this place is nothing but one giant gossip mill. I should have thought about Luke and how he would feel if he found out about it. Hurting him was not my intention, and I'm sorry for not thinking."

"Yeah, well, women like you never think about anyone but themselves. I know that firsthand." It's out of my mouth before I can take it back—a swipe at Claire when it's Sidney standing before me. And before I can force the apology from my lips she speaks.

"Screw you, Grayson."

There's hurt in her eyes I can't ignore this time. The desire to kiss her is so overwhelming that I hate myself for it.

Is she telling the truth? I don't know.

All I know is she's standing before me not afraid to go toe-to-toe with me, which makes me think she's telling me the truth. If this were only about her and her wants, then why is she still here fighting with me? Wouldn't she have bolted at the first sign of conflict?

Back away, Gray.

I take a step toward her.

"We can't do this," I murmur as I reach out and tuck her hair behind her ear. Wanting to touch her. Needing to. Hating myself for giving in to her.

"Whoever hurt you, she really did a number on you, didn't she?" I shake my head to reject her words. "I'm not her, Grayson. I'm not Claire." Her voice is soft—tentative and yet somehow resolute. But my face must reflect my surprise. "I ran into Cathy Clementine today. She's the one who told me about the fight and Luke, and she gave me the gist of what Claire did to you and Luke, and there's nothing more I can say about it other than I'm sorry . . . but I'm not her."

I hear her. I know she's right. Yet, I don't trust myself to believe it just yet. "I know."

Our eyes hold in that suspended state just before a kiss when you know you're going to do it but know you shouldn't.

When I brush my lips against hers, it's so different from the kisses we shared the other day. There's no anger. There's no retribution. There's just my need to connect with someone—with her. There's my need to feel like a man she wants rather than a man to fix her problems.

Her lips are soft. Her tongue is warm. And after her initial hesitation, when she moves into me, I know I'm so fucking screwed it isn't even funny.

She tastes like heaven and hell. Like want and need. Like deception and desire.

My hands cup her cheeks, hold her head steady as I sip and take and taste in a slow and silent seduction of senses. Every part of me wants more in this dangerous hand of poker I know I can't win.

But hell if I don't want to go all in.

"Dad?" Luke's voice calls from the top of the stairs. We freeze. My hands on her cheeks. My forehead resting against hers. Our breaths held. Cold water on a fire just lit.

I clear my throat. "Be right there."

But we don't move. It's almost as if it's the first time we haven't been at odds and we don't want to ruin it.

Either that or it's regret dropping like a lead weight between us.

"We can't do this." It's her that whispers it this time. It's her telling me we need to take a step back. But neither of us moves. "This has to stop before it starts."

This time she says the words and takes a step back. Her eyes well with tears I don't understand, and her fingertips reach up to touch her lips.

Seconds tick.

Pass.

Stretch.

And then she skirts around me and walks out the door.

"This has to stop before it starts."

I watch her back as she jogs down the steps and know that she misspoke.

It has already started.

Twenty-Three

Sidney

"I FORGOT HOW CRAZY THIS TOWN GETS OVER THE HARVEST Festival," I murmur to Rissa as I stare out our office window. Main Street has been transformed. There are two rows of booths lining the middle of the street, and strings of lights zigzag between the buildings with a small carnival for the kids set up at the far end of the street. It has a big slide. A maze made out of hay bales. Some rides that were brought in from San Francisco.

There was a palpable electricity in the atmosphere as I walked from the parking lot into the office. The hum of a community coming together to celebrate. The knowledge that everything would be closed tonight so everyone could participate in the only thing in this town that I remember loving doing.

"Crazy is an understatement." She chuckles. "And to think the Chamber of Commerce has put up a booth down there promoting the contest . . . and one Grayson Malone."

Is it sad that my heart beats a bit faster at the statement, and I can't fight the grin on my face? "I'm sure he's going to love that."

"It doesn't hurt that rumors are still flying about the two of you." She chuckles. "I may be good at *coaxing* but, girl, you landed that kiss right on his lips with the whole town watching, and it's the kiss that keeps on giving to us here." I keep my eyes focused on the preparations outside and try not to be irritated by her supposition that I manipulated the situation. Just like Grayson's. "You may not have delivered the photos like I asked for this round, but you roped him in with the town behind him, and now he can't say no. Job well done."

"Thanks."

A truck pulls up and when the back gate rolls up, I smile at the bundles of balloons inside.

"There goes six bucks of my money," Rissa says. "My kids love those damn balloons. Are you going?"

"Of course!" My mind veers to Grayson. To the kiss I can't seem to forget. To telling him we can't do this when every single part of me wants to.

To the possibility of getting to see him tonight.

"That surprises me," she says pulling me to look her way.

"Why? Who doesn't love a festival? It used to be one of the only things I loved about this place when I was a kid."

"And now?"

I turn back to the view of the street laid out in front of us. To the dance floor area off to the left and the food vendors setting up tables and chairs over to the right. I take in the hills around us and their rich greens and light browns. "It isn't as bad as I remember."

"I knew we'd wear you down." Her laugh rumbles across the space as I turn back to my laptop. "Well, get ready to fall more in love with us in a few hours. We always cut loose early on Harvest Day."

"Really?"

"Didn't anyone tell you?"

"No."

"I told the crew as soon as we get the layout finished, we can bail. It may be Harvest Festival time here in Sunnyville, but it's deadline day for us to submit to Thorton Publishing."

"Sounds like a plan."

We turn back to our work. My calls are endless, my press releases about the contest's third round of voting emailed, and between everything I do, my eyes find their way to the preparations outside to watch a festival come to life. Bit by bit. Piece by piece. The staff outside our open office door buzzes with anticipation over one of the biggest nights of the year.

"Rissa, we have a problem."

Those words pull my attention from my spreadsheet. Before Rissa even has a chance to respond to Lilah, I notice all the staff standing in various places of the large conference room, looking our way with defeat etching the lines of their faces.

"What's wrong?"

"Something happened with the software program. The file got infected."

"Did we lose it?"

"We aren't sure. A portion perhaps. We need to go back through each contributing file and try to piece it back together and . . ."

"And that's going to take hours," Rissa finishes for her.

You could hear a pin drop in here. All eyes are on Rissa as her shoulders sag and the festivities spark to life out on the street.

"I'll stay and piece the files back together." I think I shock everyone with my comment. Heads whip my way. Eyebrows raise.

"I couldn't ask you to do that," Rissa says while everyone remains listening with bated breath.

"No. It's fine," I lie, swallowing over the lump forming in my own throat. "I don't have kids or friends out there waiting for me to show up. I have it."

Rissa locks eyes with mine, and there's so much gratitude in them it makes me feel uncomfortable. "Sidney . . ."

"Just go." I plaster a smile on my lips. "I sat with Lilah earlier this week and passed her little quiz. For the most part, I've done this before at my other job . . . I can do it."

"I'll keep my cell on me," Lilah says.

"Just go. I have it handled."

"Knock. Knock."

"Ohmygod." I startle and slam my knee on the underside of the desk as I jump up, but I don't think the racing of my heart has anything to do with being surprised. It has everything to do with the man standing with his shoulder resting against the doorjamb, hands shoved into his jean pockets and eyes finding their way up and down the length of my body.

"Sorry. I didn't mean to scare you."

"It's okay. It's just—I didn't hear the door."

"You were kind of lost in your own world." Silence settles between us as our eyes hold and ask and answer things I don't think we're ready to say aloud.

"I was. I didn't expect anyone—yes." Why am I suddenly so nervous? *Maybe it's because of how I left things with him last time and now I wish I could take those words back?*

"I saw Rissa outside with her kids. She said you were up here. Are you not going to join in the festivities?"

"There was an issue with the layout, and we're on deadline, so I offered to stay and fix it."

"Why?"

Nervous energy has me stepping back and then yelping when I bump into a leaf of the fern behind me. The intrigued expression on his face softens as he smiles at my clumsiness.

"Because I don't have a family or kids who were waiting for me to take them, like most of the staff did. I don't have anyone looking forward to me being there." I shrug as something flashes through the blue of his eyes that I can't quite read. "So, I told them I'd stay and fix things to meet the deadline."

"I was looking forward to you being there." The deep tenor of his voice is a seduction all in its own right.

"Oh." My breath hitches at his comment, and I hate that for a girl who never gets tongue-tied over a man, I'm doing a damn fine job of pretending I am. Next thing I know, I'm going to forget that I know how to walk in heels and accidentally trip and fall into his arms. That's how ridiculously dorky I feel right now.

He takes a step toward me.

"What else did Rissa say?" I ask for the sole reason of needing something to say.

"She thanked me for agreeing to do the contest." He angles his head and stares at me for a beat, and I'm suddenly so very aware how dark the main office space is . . . and how very alone we are. "Why did you say the magazine needs to be saved?"

His question takes me off guard and also gives me a small reprieve from the sexual tension that eats up the oxygen in the room.

"It has failing viewership. I was brought on staff to elevate the numbers and help save it."

"The contest."

"The contest."

"And where do I fit in all of this?"

He takes another step closer, and everything about him seems to consume the small space. The width of his shoulders. The outdoorsy scent of his cologne. The soft sound he makes when his tongue darts out to lick his bottom lip. The dark shadow of stubble starting to show on his jaw.

"You're going to be the winner." The minute I say the words, I feel like such an ass.

His smile widens in a slow, steady slide as he nods. "Flattery will get you everywhere." He chuckles.

"That's not what I meant. I meant that—"

"It doesn't matter. Rissa explained it all to me outside."

"Oh." Panic strikes. Did she really tell him our plan to play up his background to sell more magazines?

"Mm-hmm." My breath hitches as he reaches out and places his hands on the sides of my neck, his thumb brushing ever so slightly over my lips. "If I stay in the contest, do your dog and pony show, you don't lose your job."

"That's right." I nod while breathing a silent sigh of relief. That's all Rissa explained to him and not the exploitation of his backstory. "What do you want in return?"

His grin is lightning quick as I realize what I just implied, and he laughs before stepping closer, so every time I inhale, my chest brushes ever so softly against his. The sensation is subtle but damaging as hell to the dryness of my panties.

"No more games, Sidney." I nod in blind agreement when I have absolutely no clue what he means by that. "No more planted articles. No more manipulated photos. And you keep Luke out of everything."

"Okay."

He leans forward, and I close my eyes in anticipation of his kiss, but the heat of his breath on my ear is just as arousing when he speaks. "After you finish, I'd like for you to come on out to the party."

"I don't think that's a good idea." This isn't even a good idea because anyone could walk in here right now and see us. The thought is fleeting because when Grayson leans back, his lips are a whisper from mine, and his thumb is rubbing back and forth over the dent in my collarbone.

"Why not?" His breath hits my lips and taunts me to lean forward and taste his.

"Because I've already been warned about the impropriety of us being seen together."

"So?"

"If you win, there could be a case that you did because of bias."

Kiss me.

"I don't care what people think. I haven't for a long time."

Kiss me.

"I know, but keeping my job is kind of important."

His eyes are unrelenting as desire swims in them plain as day, and he nods in acknowledgment.

Kiss me.

"For the record, Princess. It is a bad idea . . . but it doesn't make me want you any less."

Then take me.

But all I do is gasp a quick intake of breath as his hands leave my skin.

He takes a step back.

"Figure out how you're going to hide what's between us in this nosy little town."

And he turns on his heel and walks out, leaving me staring after him and wanting him so bad it hurts.

Twenty-Four

Grayson

"**IS THERE A REASON YOU KEEP LOOKING UP TO THAT WINDOW,**" Grant asks as he lifts his beer toward the offices of *Modern Family.*

"No reason." I shrug off the comment with a long tug on my beer.

The air is thick with the scents of hay and cotton candy and fried food. Main Street is so crowded you can barely move, and thank fuck Grady found the three of us a table to sit at while the women took the kids to the carnival end for a bit.

"Then where'd you disappear to?" Grady asks with a smirk that tells me he damn well knows. Considering he was the one standing next to me when Rissa told me Sidney was still up there working, I would have thought it was obvious anyway.

"To the john."

"I have a feeling you were whipping your dick out, all right, but it wasn't to take a piss," Grady continues.

"Do you ever shut the fuck up?" I ask. His shit-eating grin is enough for me to want to punch him just to knock it off his lips.

"Not a chance in hell. Oh look," he says and lifts his chin to two ladies standing on the outskirts of the seating area, "another set of ladies trolling by to see if you're going to take their bait." I roll my eyes at him. "When I was at the bar buying your beer, Uley said they're getting, like, fifty calls a day at dispatch from women looking for you."

"Pussy for days," Grant says, trying not to laugh but unable to quite hold it back.

"You should thank us," Grady says. "We did that for you."

"Jesus." I shake my head and take another sip of my beer.

"I don't think he cares about the bait, Grady. Not here. Not there. Not anywhere," he mocks, prompting me to hold up my middle finger. "I think he has his eye on someone else."

Images of Sidney in that tight black shirt she had on with a silky little camisole fill my mind. High heels and long legs. Hitched breaths and hard nipples.

I shift in my seat. "I care, all right," I murmur.

I should have kissed her. There's no doubt about that. The problem is that there would have been no stopping me once I started. Luke was waiting, and she said no, and fuck if the timing wasn't right, so I didn't.

But that didn't mean I didn't want to.

"Seems to me like someone isn't bitching about being in the contest anymore . . . Now, why would that be?" I eye Grant across the table and know where he's going with this and refuse to give him the ammunition to prove his point.

"And?" I draw the word out.

"And nothing, just glad to see you not worrying about . . . everything."

"I'm not thrilled with the attention," I say with a shrug.

"C'mon . . . you don't like the life-size poster of you over in the Chamber of Commerce booth or the flyers all over the tables saying #TeamMalone?" Grady chuckles as he holds one up before tossing it over his shoulder.

"No. I don't."

"Hey, Grant? How many of these women do you think are going to take these pictures home and have some fun while staring at it later tonight?"

"Dude . . . I seriously think Mom dropped you on your head when you were little. There's something wrong with you." I push Grady's shoulder, and he swipes my beer and downs the rest of it.

"You want another?" Grady asks as he stands, and Grant and I both nod. I shove some money into his hand since it's my round to buy and then lean back in my chair.

"Luke told Mom that Sidney came over to your house the other day," Grant says, getting to the topic he really wants to talk about.

Leave it to Luke to spill the beans. All Luke has done is talk non-stop about Sidney since she came over, which isn't a good thing, so I knew it was only a matter of time before Mom started nosing around. I can see in Luke's eyes how much he hopes she and I are dating. That this woman who paid particular attention to him is more than just a random friend.

That maybe I'll like her vagina and we'll get married.

I snort a laugh, and Grant looks at me like I've lost my mind. Maybe I have. The fact that any of this runs through my head is proof of it.

"So, was she?"

"Christ. Just what I need is Mom on my back about marriage when she knows that will never happen again."

"Famous last words," he says, and I crumple up a flyer with my face on it and throw it at him.

"Fine. She came over to apologize to Luke about the picture in the paper, which was the reason he got into his fight, which . . . who the fuck knows." I scrub a hand through my hair and then close my eyes and lean back against the chair I'm sitting in.

"Which led to her coming over, playing nice with Luke, and then landing in your bed and you not sealing the deal?" Grant makes the comment with humor in his voice, but it's his eyes that tell me he wants to know the truth. That he's worried about me.

That it's none of his damn business.

"She played with Luke's Creepers." I'm not sure why I say that, but it really was the last thing I expected her to do, so it's stuck in my mind.

Well, that and her kiss.

"Wait a minute," he says. "You mean Uptown Sidney came over and played Minecraft stuff with Luke?" The confusion on his face mirrors exactly how I felt when I saw her at the table with Luke.

"Yep." I nod.

"Shit, that isn't the Uptown Sidney I remember," he says. "Doesn't watching her do that with Luke make you want Uptown Sidney to go downtown on Grayson?"

"Very funny."

Grady better come back soon because I need another beer STAT.

"You like her." His simple statement is the first thing in this whole conversation that I don't have a quick comeback to. Because I do. I don't want to, because liking her scares the shit out of me, but fuck . . . I do. I just meet his eyes and don't utter a single word. "So I take it you're over the whole Sidney is like Claire thing?" he presses.

"No." It's the truth. But it's a truth on shaky legs, considering that she's up there instead of down here having a good time. Claire never would have given up her party time for the sake of everyone else. She never would have given up any part of herself, because her needs and wants came first. Always.

And Sidney is up there right now, proving that hers don't.

"But I'm working on it."

"Good." He gives a measured nod as he finishes the last of his beer, and I glance again at the light on in the second story window. "She scares you because she's different from your usual, but that also excites you. She showed up at your house, slid into a seat at your table, and entertained Luke. She reminded you of a reality you want but don't want to admit to."

"Fuck," I mutter under my breath. He's too damn right when all I want him to be is wrong.

"You gotta admire the woman for beating you at your own game."

"How's that?" I ask but already know.

"The hero bullshit in the newspaper. Getting the townspeople to back the contest so you can't say no. Charming Luke when you thought she'd be petrified of him. From where I'm sitting, it looks like the ball's in your court. You want her? You don't want her? I don't fucking care. You need to quit being a pussy and decide one way or another." I look at Grant across from me, one arm resting across the back of the chair next to him, the other holding his beer while his eyes issue the challenge his words just gave. "If she owns your mind—and your moods—like she has, don't you think she just might be worth the risk?"

"Mercy-Life pilot Grayson Malone is a hero." I turn instantly at the sound of Grady's voice, my conversation with Grant on instant hold but still owning my mind. Grady has three bottles held against his chest with one arm while holding up the flyer with his other to read. "Whether it's risking his life to save others trapped in the High Sierras' snow, or on a daily basis transporting trauma patients to save their lives, he knows how to put others first."

"Stop," I say, hating that he's reading it loudly enough to draw looks from those around us.

That fucking bio.

The one I refused to give her because I swore I was going to bail from the contest. The bio I forgot to finish because every time I started it, I got sidetracked thinking about her.

Fuck.

"Grayson's biggest role as a hero, though, is to his eight-year-old son, who thinks he hung not only the moon but also all the stars in the sky around it. Sexy and single, Grayson has a charming smile, a quick wit, and biceps any woman would want to be hugged by." He gives a long, low whistle. "You write that bio yourself, Gray?"

"Will you shut the fuck up?" I growl under my breath as he takes a seat, and my cheeks burn bright from the attention.

"'Cause if you didn't write that, then that means Sidney did, and hell, it sounds like she just might more than like you." Grant's shit-eating grin is in full effect to taunt me. "You need to get a better picture, because, dude, chicks love abs. They love uniforms. They eat that shit up."

"You're an asshole."

"Payback's a bitch, isn't it?" Grady says and sets my beer in front of me with a chuckle.

"Hey, I'm the nice one," I argue. "The one who keeps everything fair. There is no ganging up on me."

The two of them look at each other and burst out laughing. "Like hell there isn't. You're fair game, little brother," Grant says as he tilts the top of his beer toward the window above and shrugs. "Just think about what I said. It's your call, Gray."

Is she worth the risk? His words loop through my head on repeat.

"If the answer's yes, then you know what to do."

Twenty-Five

Sidney

CAN SPOT HIM FROM A MILE AWAY.

The dark jeans. The perfectly fitted shirt. The appeal that would be impossible to miss.

My nerves jitter and my mind continues to spin as it has since he left the office earlier. Since he left me with unspoken promises and a libido in overdrive thinking and wondering and wanting.

But there was also worrying.

Was he playing my own game back on me? Or rather, the game he thought I had played on him?

His turnabout seemed too easy.

Then came my second-guessing. That I'm crazy. That I'm thinking too much. That I just need to see him to know for sure what the answer is.

So, I head toward him. The click of my heels on the sidewalk is drowned out by the music still floating from the speakers and the white noise of a whole town celebrating together.

And then when I'm close enough that the sound of his laugh carries over the crowd, and the anticipation of what I've already acknowledged is going to happen between us sparks to life, the crowd of women around him shifts. His arms are hooked over one woman's shoulder. Her hair is a strawberry blonde, and everything about her is stunning. Like, you want to stare and be jealous kind of stunning. There is a familiarity between them—in the way he leans in to whisper in her ear and the ease with which he responds to her despite everyone around him vying for attention.

I've seen her before, but I can't quite place where.

And then it hits me.

She was at Hooligan's the night of his party. I remember he was laughing with her at the bar. Then she was standing near him when I walked up and kissed him.

Is she one of his regulars? One of the women he sleeps with on the side?

The sharp pang of unfounded jealousy hits harder than I expect as I take a few steps back and try to process this all.

I created this scene. The women around him all vying for his attention. The women engaged and wanting more. The women so charmed by him they'll vote.

The flyers with his image on them that are scattered all over the street are a testament to it.

I just never imagined it would be me standing on the outside wanting the attention from him.

With one last look, I tear my eyes from the sight and head to my car.

Twenty-Six

Sidney

"**P**AIN IN THE ASS," I MUTTER AS I SPRAY THE MUD OFF THE front of my Range Rover . . . again. The street is nothing but mud due to my neighbor's landscape project. Broken sprinkler heads and truckloads of dirt don't make for a pretty road to drive on.

"Hey."

I yelp at the sound and whirl around to find Grayson standing there, sweaty, out of breath, and looking far more sexy than I want to admit.

"What are you doing here?"

"Running. I was out for a jog."

"Great." I try to sound unfazed. Like I haven't rerun the other night in my head a million times to try to figure out if I read too much into what he said. To try to figure out if I overreacted to the situation on the street.

I don't get like this about a guy, never have, said I never would, and so it's driving me absolutely crazy. "Have a good rest of your jog."

"Sid?" He sounds surprised when he shouldn't be. "Is something wrong?"

"Nope. I'm fine. Just fine." I turn my back to him and start spraying my tires again. It's so much easier focusing on them than the incredibly sexy sight of him that I don't want to acknowledge. The visual that immediately clouds the way I felt the other night.

"You're fine? That's universal woman code for I'm pissed at you." His chuckle scrapes over my nerves as he reaches out to take the hose from me, and I yank it away.

"Don't!" I spin around to face him and, of course, he's way too close. The nozzle I aim at him is the only thing between us, and my car is at my back.

"You care to share what I did wrong?"

"No."

"Okay." He draws the word out. "I waited around for you at the festival the other night."

The side that wants to believe the words he said in the office melts while the skeptical one who saw him with the strawberry-blonde snorts.

"What? You don't believe me?"

Did I really just snort out loud?

"No, I don't. I saw you." I jab the hose nozzle in his direction, and a smirk tugs at the corner of his mouth, which only serves to infuriate me further. "I saw you and that woman—"

"What woman?" he laughs.

"The pretty one with the strawberry-blonde hair." He snorts, and I jab the hose in his direction, suddenly on the defensive and more than aware that I think I'm going to look like an ass here. That all my overthinking was for nothing. "Don't mock me."

"I'm not mocking shit." He puts his hands up, but his smile remains. "That was my sister-in-law, Grant's wife. Her name is Emerson."

Oh. Shit.

"I was playing the part you want me to play. Chatting up the ladies asking about the contest, urging them to go online." Embarrassment flushes every ounce of my body. "I was whispering to Emerson how ridiculous it was, and she was there to laugh at it all with me."

"Oh." As in, *Oh shit, I look like the craziest hormonal bitch ever.*

All I want to do is crawl under this car and hide when his grin widens to epic proportions. "Am I forgiven?"

"No."

His laughter rings out, and I hate that I love the sound of it. "Okay. What else do you need from me?"

His words throw me. Words no man has ever spoken to me during a fight. It's usually, "Can we get this over with?" or "Are we done yet?" or "Can we have make-up sex?"

Make-up sex.

The idea sticks but only because he's sweaty and sexy and so damn close that my every nerve is already attuned to him.

Like they needed any help.

"Sidney?" he prompts when I don't respond. His gaze moves. A slow, languorous slide from my head to my toes that makes me feel as if he's undressing each and every inch of me.

"Yeah?"

"You have some"—he reaches out and runs a hand over the curve of my chest just above my tank top—"dirt right there."

I swear my breath hitches. I know my nipples harden. I react when I swore I wasn't going to. *Damn him.* He showed up here with those eyes and those muscles, and hell, even I have to admit that I'm in trouble. I'm down the rabbit hole when it comes to him, when I don't want to be.

And when he leans in and brushes his lips against mine, my mind fogs, and my body tenses and—

"Argh!" I accidentally spray him with the ice-cold water square in the chest, and he jumps back.

"Oh my God." I can barely get the words out as I laugh hysterically. "I didn't mean to—I'm sorry." Tears pool at the corners of my eyes.

He shakes his arms so the water flies off them as his gaze lands on mine. "Turnabout's fair game, Thorton." His brows lift in a taunt. His fingers twitch as if he's itching to touch.

He takes a step toward me.

"It was an accident. I swear."

Another step.

"Uh-huh."

Closer.

I can't resist. The playful look on his face. The desire unrivaled between us. The relief that I acted like an irrational female and he took it with a complete grain of salt.

I tighten my finger on the trigger of the nozzle, sending a stream of water straight to his chest. He tries to jump out of the way, but he's too close to avoid it.

"Oopsie." I shrug and smile coyly.

"That wasn't a very smart move." There's a roughness to his voice that electrifies the air as it telegraphs where his thoughts are. What it is he wants.

And I hope to God I'm right in thinking that it's me.

"What are you going to do about it?" This time, I'm the one who taunts. I'm the one who teases. I'm the one who wants to finish what we've almost started a few times but had too much damn common sense to finish.

Another step.

I can smell the soap on his skin. I can see the beads of water on his neck and arms. I can hear the hitch of his breath. "There are a whole lot of things I could think to do about it, but I'm not sure which of them we'd regret the most once they were done."

I squirt the hose again. This time, he flinches. This time, a laugh falls from his lips. This time, he lunges after me to grab the hose, and I dodge away from him, my fingers pulling the trigger so that I completely soak the front of his body.

The air fills with our shrieks and threats as I hit him and then run. As he dodges and then chases.

Around my car. Another stream of water. My sides hurt from laughing so hard, and I'm not paying attention as Grayson takes the hose lying on the ground and yanks on it, pulling the nozzle from my hands. I turn to run but realize I'm out of real estate. My back is against the fence, and Grayson is standing in front of me, nozzle pointed my way and a smirk playing at the corners of his lips.

"You wouldn't dare," I say, hoping for an ounce of mercy when I showed him none.

I yelp when the cold stream of water hits me in the stomach. "Oopsie," he mimics me, and all I want to do is strangle him as the water slides down the denim of my shorts and over my thighs.

"Grayson." It's a plea. It's a warning. It's an oh my God does he look gorgeous with his hair plastered to his forehead, the lighthearted grin on his face, and his shirt clinging to every cut inch of him.

"You know what they say about paybacks, right?"

"Yes. That a gentleman like you would never retaliate on a poor, helpless female like me." And then I shriek as another spurt of water hits me.

"Oopsie." His laugh rings louder than mine. "Nice try, but you've made it clear you're no damsel in distress, so that doesn't fly with me, Princess."

Crap.

And that's the only thought I get to have before I'm hit full-on with a longer stream of water. "Stop. No. Grayson."

I rush him. I try to yank the nozzle from his hands, and when I do, I throw it to the ground and run. Through the gate. Into the back-yard. Around the flowerbeds.

I make the fatal error of thinking I can run past him on my way back to the front yard, and before I know it, Grayson hooks an arm around my waist, and we both fall laughing onto the grass.

The fall knocks the breath out of us, but within seconds, I'm wrig-gling to get away from him.

Then I'm not.

My body freezes, fully aware of every long, lean inch of his body flanking mine. Of that instant burn in my belly and ache in my thighs when I stop moving only to find his face in front of mine. His eyes on me. His lips inches away. His body wet and warm all at the same time. His dick hard and pressed against my thigh, telling me his thoughts align with mine.

"Grayson . . ." This is a bad idea.

Kiss me.

This is such a bad idea.

Why isn't he kissing me?

And then he does. A soft brush of his lips against mine. And then another. Sips and sighs of a kiss as we lie on the ground in my backyard with the birds overhead and a lawnmower sounding off elsewhere . . . but my entire world is focused on him.

On the rough brush of stubble against my chin. On the drops of water falling off his hair and onto mine. On the softness of his lips, the flex of his muscles, and the hints of restraint being tested.

There's a tenderness in his touch, his kiss, but there's the underlying edge laced with riotous desire that I can taste on his tongue and feel as he touches me.

Every part of me warms. Heats. Wants more when I fear it might only bring the agony of wanting more again.

His hand runs down my rib cage and slides under my shirt. I gasp as his wet palm brings a chill to my skin while his lips bring warmth to every other part of me. He finds my nipple over the wet lace of my bra and squeezes it ever so gently between his fingertips. The sensation is like a mainline to the delta of my thighs. Between his touch, the adeptness of his kiss, and the feel of him getting harder against my thigh, every part of me aches for more from him.

I lose myself in this world. The grass beneath us. The taste on his tongue. The groan of desire vibrating in the back of his throat.

The slowness begins to slip into want.

The tenderness builds into greed.

The desire morphs into need.

"Grayson."

"Inside," he murmurs against my lips between kisses.

"Yes."

But neither of us moves. Neither of us wants to ruin the perfection of the moment. The calm before the storm.

"Inside," he says again.

"Neighbors," I murmur as the dog next door barks.

He pushes himself to his feet and then takes my hand to help me up. We don't speak. We only lose eye contact when I walk ahead of him. His hands frame my hips as I take the steps up. His dick is hard against my backside as I fumble with the doorknob that always sticks.

I giggle as nerves take over, when I'm not one to normally giggle. Nerves I shouldn't feel because I'm a grown woman. He's a grown man.

I shouldn't be nervous about this, but I am.

Grayson Malone makes me nervous.

He presses a kiss to my shoulder. "Let me," he says as his hand closes over mine and we turn the knob together.

The door opens. We step inside, the silence bathing us, making me hesitate as the jitters wage a war inside me.

"Sidney." That voice . . . *his* voice, which is all scratch of gravel and grit of restraint, has me turning slowly to face him.

Our eyes meet and hold, questioning what we're about to do and simultaneously saying to hell with it.

The snap of desire whips and cracks and takes over. Within a heartbeat, his lips are back on mine. Our kisses greedier than before. The tender sips of lips turn to nips and a fight for possession. The soft dance of my fingertips up his spine becomes a fist in his hair.

Wet clothes become frustrating as we pull and shimmy and yank them off, our thirst for each other's skin so much more important than the barriers between us.

The minute we're naked, we're back in each other's arms again. No time to admire the other. No need to when the desire is already at a fever pitch from what feels like weeks of foreplay bringing us to the crescendo of this moment.

We bump into a wall and laugh.

"Bedroom," he says.

I stumble some as he moves me backward, his hand squeezing my ass and the feel of his dick, rock-hard and ready for me is enough of a distraction that I forget how to make my way through my own house.

"We need a bed. *Now.*"

I slide my hand down his chest and abdomen, needing to feel him. My fingers circle around his cock; my palm strokes him ever so gently as my lips and tongue toy with his. His hands tense. His groan grows louder. His body stills as his mouth breaks from mine, and his head falls back as if to welcome the sensation.

He's incredible to look at. The broad shoulders and tapered waist. The strong thighs and the definition of his abs. The bump of his Adam's apple and the tendons straining in his neck. The girth of his shaft and how it bounces in reaction as I use my hands to please him.

As desperate as I am to have him, I take my time because there's something intoxicating about watching the way he reacts to my touch. I spread the precum over his tip and work the length of him again, over and over until his hands grip my arms and every part of him begins to tense.

I'm doing this to him.

I'm making him hard.

I'm making him groan my name.

"Christ, woman. You are going to be my undoing." The second he utters the words, he yanks my hand away from him and crashes his mouth to mine. It's a take-no-prisoners kiss that has me digging my fingernails into his shoulders and losing all sense of my surroundings.

When the backs of my legs hit my bed, we tumble onto it, and the full desirous assault begins anew.

His lips are on my breast.

His hands slip between my thighs, fingers whispering over flesh begging to be parted, touched, pleased.

My mouth parts. My moan fills the room.

His teeth tug gently on my nipple. Bites of pain followed by licks of pleasure make every part of me ache with that slow burn of desire that urges him to rush and begs him to take his time.

My back arches.

The heated breath of his chuckle touches my skin, leaving warmth even after the sound has faded. Chills chase the adrenaline that courses through my veins.

His fingers run the line of my sex and find my clit. Electricity sparks against my every nerve as he adds friction with his touch. Harder. Faster.

Come on. Writhe. *Come on.* Buck. *Come on.* Bow.

His chuckle is in my ear. "Not yet, Princess. Not without me in you."

I groan in frustration and then sigh in ecstasy at the onslaught of sensations when Grayson slides his finger down my seam and circles my entrance. My thighs widen.

"Christ, Sidney." The groan that follows as he slips a finger into me is probably the sexiest sound I've ever heard. Not that I can think about it long because he starts fucking me with his finger. Over and over. He adds a second and curves them within so they hit every hot button he needs to which has me spiraling again. Then a third finger.

His biceps bulge and flex with each plunge in and pull out. His gaze switches back and forth between my eyes and where his hand works its magic. His teeth sink into his bottom lip as he adds a rub over my clit with his thumb on each withdrawal.

My eyes close as I slip beneath the veil of bliss, the surge beginning to build. Bit by bit. The pleasure. The friction. The slide. Each one brings a new wash of ecstasy.

It's almost too fast, too intense, and I don't try to control it as my orgasm slams into me without any restraint. My fingernails dig into his forearms as I beg him to keep going and silently wanting him to draw this out as long as he can. I can't decide which I want more, and he doesn't let me as he runs his tongue up the line of my neck to my ear. My breath shudders, and my heart pounds as my body slowly recovers from the onslaught of pleasure.

"I don't have any protection," he murmurs into my ear.

"Top drawer," I say as I let my body come down from the high.

The bed dips. The foil rips.

"Sidney." His hands are on my thighs, his legs beneath them.

I chuckle. "I'm out of breath, and we haven't even gotten to the good part yet."

"It's good, all right," he murmurs as he runs the tip of his cock up and down my slit, coating it with my arousal. It's almost too much to bear on my hypersensitive flesh. "That I can promise you."

"You're a cocky bastard." One that looks like a damn Adonis.

"You have no idea."

And with that one phrase, he thrusts into me. I cry out in shock. In pleasure. From every sensation under the sun that feels like white lightning and molten lava rolling through my body all at the same time. He starts slow, a barely-there rock of his hips, a tease and a question and an invitation for me to move with him. As we fall into the rhythm, he picks up the pace. Thrust after thrust. Claim after claim. Pleasure after pleasure.

A squeeze of his hand on my thighs.

Right there.

A shift of my hips up.

Oh God.

The slap of his skin against mine as he bottoms out inside me, his crest rubbing over my bundle of nerves within.

Grayson.

A grind of his hips. A slow withdraw inch by glorious inch, allowing me to feel every single sensation he evokes from me.

I'm gonna come.

And then another orgasm slams into me. This time, a little stronger. This time, in a different way. While the last one was high heat and a sharp punch of arousal, this one is like a rolling wave of bliss. It surges and ebbs so right when I remember to breathe, it comes back again stronger than the wave before. My thighs are locked around his hips, my hands fisted in the sheets as he rocks his hips into mine and lets me ride it out.

Just as I resurface from its haze, Grayson's groan fills the room as his body tenses, his hips still, and his head falls back as he loses himself to his own climax.

I'm not sure how long we stay like that, first absorbing and then coming down from our orgasmic high, but eventually, he collapses onto the bed beside me. Time passes in slowing heartbeats and calming breaths.

Our fingers intertwine, but we don't say anything. I relive the past forty minutes. I think of the wet clothes somewhere in the family room. The hose still on, water probably trickling out of the nozzle. The neighbors probably wondering what all the shrieking was about.

Then I laugh uncontrollably. I can't stop. There's something about the push and the pull, the hero and the damsel, the contest and the judge, and everything that's happened between us that makes me find humor in the situation.

"I know," he says as his thumb brushes over mine in the simplest of ways but one that has my heart melting without my permission. "This shouldn't have happened."

"No, it should have. It definitely should have." I pant the words.

"Shh, let's not tell the *Gazette,* though."

Or my father.

Rather than take offense as most would, I just laugh harder. "I guess it's finally true. They can all claim I'm biased now. And damn, am I biased."

He shifts onto his side, props his head on his hand, and leans over so he can brush a tender and unexpected kiss to my lips. "No one has to know," he murmurs, the tenor of his voice already has that ache simmering again.

"No one can know," I correct as I trace a line over a pleat in the sheet between us, realizing suddenly how much that notion bugs me. Not that I normally go around wearing a sandwich board announcing who I slept with the night before, but something about hiding the fact that I've been with him upsets me.

Or maybe, in a petty way, it's more like I want women to know he's been with me, since jealousy obviously doesn't suit me well.

"On the down low. Just how I like it," he murmurs playfully and winks.

"Says the man who has a line waiting in town for him."

"You and that damn line." He rolls his eyes and leans forward.

"Ow!" His teeth nip my shoulder, and it's my turn to shift onto my side so my position mirrors his. "Mr. Malone, how is it that you have willing women taking numbers to wait for you—"

"It's been some time since a number was pulled," he says and taps a finger on the tip of my nose as I lift my eyebrows with this little tidbit of knowledge.

"That's none of my business," I say but obviously am pleased with the spontaneous explanation, "but your son never knows."

"I have a secret," he says, his grin in full effect as he leans forward and whispers, "I'm a ninja."

There's something about serious Grayson Malone being playful like this that makes his comment funnier and more endearing than it should be. I can't stop from laughing or smiling. "A sex ninja?"

"A *pussy* ninja."

"Oh my God." I fall onto my back when my laughter doesn't stop. "You didn't really just say that, did you?"

"Sure did." His fingers reach my ribs and start tickling me until I'm squirming away from him, laughing so hard my sides hurt. "I'm stealthy. Sneaking around keeping my pussy pursuits under wraps."

He kisses the place under my jaw, turning my laughter into a soft moan. "You know this is not right, right? You talking about being a pussy ninja after just having sex with me?"

"I've obviously had sex before," he says, pressing one more kiss to my collarbone before leaning back and looking at me. "I do have Luke for proof."

Now there's a look in his eyes that shifts the mood from playful to serious to I'm not sure what, but I ask the question that flickers into my mind, even if it isn't the right time to do so.

"Why is it that the ladies around town know who you're seeing, but Luke never does?"

His eyes narrow and a sigh escapes from his lips as he falls back onto his back once again. "It's hard to explain."

"Try me."

"Luke gets attached to women too easily. He wants every woman who enters my life—even if it's the mail carrier—to be my wife. *And his mom*."

"Poor guy." My heart breaks.

"You don't know the half of it." His chuckle is edged with sadness. "I'll do anything I can to protect him from getting his hopes up and then having them crushed." He rises suddenly from the bed in all his naked glory and stares at me.

"What are—"

"This isn't exactly what you're supposed to be talking about after I've rocked your world."

I yelp as he leans forward, grabs my ankles, and pulls me to the edge of the bed. When he leans over, his dick rubs against my thighs as he drugs me with a slow, mesmerizing kiss. "That leads me to believe you need it to be rocked again. Shall we?"

And slowly but surely, Grayson has his way with me.

Not that I put up much resistance.

Twenty-Seven

Grayson

"**G**RAYSON MALONE. I KNEW YOU COULDN'T STAY AWAY from me for this long," Devon says. "Come here and give me a kiss." Before I can back away, he grabs my head and plants a big, loud kiss on my cheek that has me shoving him away.

"Hell, you're the reason I've been staying away." I laugh, but then we hook thumbs and clasp our hands together and give each other a man-pat.

"How's dispatch?" he asks, but the smirk on his lips and shake of his head tells me he already knows.

"Like Hell on Earth."

"No adrenaline. No high. No—"

"No chicks asking to see how big your stick is," Alyssa says as she walks into the room with a laugh and a quick hug. "Christ. Please tell us you're here because you've been reinstated. All this overtime means momma ain't getting any."

"First off, my stick is still big, just not getting any use," I say.

"That isn't what we hear," rings out from Christian before going back to talking on his phone.

"Whatever." I roll my eyes. "You need to get some because we all know how cranky you get during a dry spell." I dodge as Alyssa swats at me. "And shit, I don't know what to tell you. I'm still waiting for Cochran to tell me he loves me more and is going to put me up on that board." I lift my chin in the direction of the schedule.

"The only one happy you aren't here is Christian over there," Alyssa says as Christian raises his middle finger. "With you gone, he's getting all the faint-hearted women giving him the googly eyes instead of you."

I laugh, knowing Christian is horribly shy and utterly devoted to his wife. "I'm sure he loves that."

"So, it's really that bad over at dispatch, huh?"

"Not bad. Just same ol' day in and day out. I'm bored to fucking tears." I miss flying. I miss my crew. Being here just reinforces both of those things more than I want to acknowledge.

"But I'm sure Luke is loving that you're home."

"He is." I shrug. "But I'm going stir crazy."

"I bet you are," she says with a knowing smile.

"What?"

She purses her lips and raises her eyebrows. "We all know what Daddy's been doing while Luke's at school."

I just shake my head as Devon stands behind her, pretending as if he's slapping an invisible ass. They all burst out laughing. "You guys are jerks."

"So? Is it true? Are you hitting that hottie who was kissing you at the pub?" Jen asks.

"They're doing a lot more than kissing," Christian yells from his corner.

"Since when have you ever known the *Gazette* gossip column to be accurate? Last year, they had Devon pegged as dating Dixie."

"You're an ass." Devon laughs.

"And Dixie was a pig." I think back to how much we harassed the shit out of Dev when the column came out. And when the subsequent correction was published the next day. Needless to say, someone overheard Dev mention how he couldn't wait for his date with Dixie and misinterpreted it as a literal date. Too bad he meant his appointment to pick the piglet up for his mom and take her to the family farm. The town laughed for weeks over it.

"And you're avoiding answering our question," Dev says.

"Why do I come here for this abuse?" I ask, but I know full well that the abuse is deserved. What I don't like is how the simple question about a certain golden brown-haired woman sends my thoughts straight back to Sidney and what happened and how I can't stop thinking about it. Or her.

"Because you love us." Jen shrugs and heads over to where she's doing one of her thousand-piece jigsaw puzzles—there's sometimes a lot of time between calls.

"Sometimes."

"What's this crap I hear about people thinking you're a hot dad, anyway?" Devon says, but then he holds up a hand. "Wait, let me guess—you signed yourself up for the contest because you weren't getting enough attention 'round these parts."

"That's exactly right," I say as I shake my head no. "My damn brothers signed me up, and now I'm stuck in it."

"You're stuck in something, all right. I hope she is at least worth the pain."

My middle finger is raised back at him as I make my way down the hall toward Cochran's office.

"Don't worry, I'll vote for you!" Jen calls to me.

"At least someone loves me," I say as I stop at Cochran's office door. His head is down, his fingers are typing furiously. I knock on the jamb.

He startles, but a smile spreads when he sees me. "Malone." He nods. "I thought that was your voice out here."

"Sir. Just checking in to see if you've heard anything yet."

"I've heard, all right." He chuckles, and it confuses me. "Getting a lot of phone calls at the station from women asking if you're available to give mouth-to-mouth."

"There's no accounting for taste," I say with a self-deprecating laugh. "Sorry about that."

He shrugs and looks relaxed, when he's typically anything but. "At least you're being productive in your time off. Maybe your next photo should include one of the helos. Get us some added advertising with all this newfound publicity of yours."

"You're shameless, you know that?"

"Yeah, well, with High-Life setting up shop across town, we could use every little added bit of visibility." He's referring to the new medevac company currently encroaching on our turf.

"It's taking that much out of our business?"

"Not the emergency side of it, no. But the medical transport side, yes."

"That sucks." And it does, because now my mind is full of worries about layoffs. If they needed to let people go, the guy who's grounded would be the first one on the block. "Maybe it's because you're missing your star pilot."

There is no shame in reminding him how much money I make him.

"That's exactly why," he says through his laugh. "They want you before the board in a week or two and plan to reinstate you by the end of the month. You just need to make them all the promises they want to hear."

I lift my eyebrows. "I've learned so much about why we have rules while having desk duty in dispatch. I won't take chances. I won't save lives if risks are involved. I won't, I won't I won't," I say drolly as he shakes his head.

"Try it with a little more enthusiasm next time," he says.

"Noted. Thanks."

He nods and puts his head back down, letting me know the discussion is over. "Advertising, Malone. Make sure you mention where you work when you do whatever it is for this cockamamie contest you're in. That might win you some favor as well."

Fucking great.

Twenty-Eight

Sidney

"What's up with you? I'd think you'd be dancing on the ceiling with how well this round of voting is bringing in page visits."

"Huh?" I drag my attention away from the window I've been staring out of for the last I-don't-know-how-long and turn to Rissa. "Sorry. I was just thinking."

"About?" Her smile is wide and her eyebrows are raised as she looks toward the screen of my computer and then back at me.

"Oh. No. Not him," I stumble over the words as I alt-tab out of my screen, which was open to Grayson's picture.

"I'm sure you weren't. Why daydream about him when you can have him whenever you want, right?" she teases and has me catching my breath momentarily. Does she know? Does anyone know? It isn't as if our water fight couldn't be fodder for Sunnyville gossip, but he left under the cover of night. After I put his clothes through the drier, he jogged right out the front door in time to get Luke from the movie Grayson's mom took him to.

Rissa's words still give me pause. They make me question whether anything has been said. Instead, I laugh and decide to go with my assumption that no one knows. "You're going to start more rumors, Rissa."

"If it's in the *Sunnyville Gazette*, it must be true." She winks.

"What's in the *Sunnyville Gazette*?"

"That you and Grayson were seen out at dinner at McClintock's the other night."

This time, I laugh for real. "Is McClintock's the restaurant that overlooks the Hoskins' vineyards?" I swallow over the bitter taste in my mouth at the mention of one of the many businesses Claire's family owns.

"The one and only."

"Well, I, for one, have never been there. Not even when I was a kid . . . so rumor away."

"Shush!" She waves a hand my way. "Let me pretend you were there so I can live vicariously through you and that fine specimen of a hot man."

If she only knew.

I think back to the other night. To Grayson and everything he was more than capable of handling when it came to me.

"Get your own man, Rissa. Better yet, let me spread rumors about you being with Grayson. That would be more believable since you're a resident here. Since your kids are around the same age as Luke. I mean, you're a match made in Heaven."

"First off, you're the only one who could get away with sleeping with a contestant and not get fired." I choke out a cough. "Your dad would can me in a second if our positions were flipped."

"Nice try, but the warning has already been not so subtly issued. Any fraternizing with the contestants could be perceived as bias as it relates to the voting," I say, using my best impersonation of Frank Thorton all the while remembering my and Grayson's discussion about bias and the sexy smile that was on his lips. "Didn't you know? Life is never allowed to interfere with business when you're a Thorton."

"We're talking hypothetical here." She lifts her eyebrows and holds a finger up to stop me from interrupting her. "Unless you have some juicy details you're withholding."

"Yeah, right," I say through a nervous laugh.

"You better not be; besides, I think the town would turn against me if I went after him. They love the idea of you two together. Hometown hero who was wronged by his ex and the popular prom queen who returns to reunite with her long-lost crush."

"Oh Jesus."

"That's what's being said on the streets."

"You mean on Main Street." I glance back out of the window and shake my head before looking back at her. "And I'm sure you have absolutely no part in the spreading of these new rumors."

"Who me? Never." I can't tell if she's being serious or not. "All I did was get the ball rolling. You're the one who pushed it downhill with that kiss. But I will tell you that the gossip hens in this town are already secretly planning your wedding."

"Yeah, well, that is *not* going to happen," I say as that unsettled feeling hits me again. The same one that hit me when he left my house. The same one that got stronger each time my phone rang and it wasn't him. I know that isn't what she means. I know Rissa is playing in her pretend world, so I go along with it.

"Oh my God! Could you imagine the story we could do if that happened? *Modern Family's* hot dad contest nets him a wife." She holds her hands up like she's reading the words off a billboard.

"You need help."

"Nope. It's you who's going to need help if he ever acts on the look he gets in his eye when he watches you. Pure lusty sexiness." She wiggles her shoulders for emphasis, and I roll my eyes at her.

"I'm going back to work now." I turn to my social media account to check my ad statistics where click-through rates and impressions and organic reach figures litter the page.

"And I want to know why you aren't acting on it."

I sigh in exasperation and lean back in my chair, turning my head her way. "Didn't we just talk about why? My father. His rules. Bias?"

"So, you do want a little something from Malone."

I just walked right into that one.

"It's complicated." Great answer, Sidney. Way to shoot her down.

"Everything good is."

Don't I know it? Grayson's groan fills my ears. The way he bit into his bottom lip as he came owns my mind. "Leave it be, Rissa."

"You've seen him, right? Six feet plus. Nice ass. Great smile. Sexy as sin. Hell, you're the one who wrote his bio. You know all about that fine package." *Package.* I gulp down the laugh that bubbles up and will the flush on my cheeks to go away. "So, why don't you want to act on it when he's there for the taking?"

"Uh-huh."

Leave.

It.

Be.

I've been on cloud nine since he left my house. Cloud fricking nine. Regardless of how many times I've told myself it's just because the sex was incredible, I still don't buy it. I'm obsessing. Over him. Over wanting him again. Over telling myself it was just sex.

One time.

Well, technically two times . . . but that was all it was.

Sex.

Not love.

"Sometimes rules need to be broken. Sometimes that's the answer you're looking for," she says after a few moments and has me freezing mid-motion as a myriad of consequences flicker through my mind, one more than all others. "What is it you're afraid to lose if you act on it and sleep with him? Dreaming about that big job at *Haute,* were you?"

I do a double take. Did I accidentally say that aloud? "How did you know about that?"

"I figured it out." She shrugs. "There's no reason you'd accept a job here at a parenting magazine unless there was a serious upside to it for you. A week before you showed up, I heard rumors about the editor-in-chief position at *Haute* possibly coming up for grabs next year and figured that was what you were aiming for."

"How did you hear that?"

"I keep tabs on positions within the company . . . I never know when I might want to live the high-journalism life again," she says and winks.

"Keeping your options open is always a good idea."

She looks outside at the kids who are getting off the bus and falls silent for a moment, her voice quiet when she speaks again. "Do you miss it?"

"Miss what?"

"Your old life. Your high heels that are meant for fancy nightclubs instead of the Main Street sidewalks of Sunnyville. The city life. The smells and the sounds of it." She laughs, but it's small and almost wistful. "That's what I miss the most about working for *The Post*. How the city would come to life. The galas and the functions and the hobnobbing, even though none of them trusted me not to put their words on the record."

"My life isn't as glamorous as everyone thinks it is." I say the words but, sometimes, it actually was. They all acted as if that part of my life was something I couldn't be without. Yes, I loved the galas and the functions and the social parts of my job, but I could take them or leave them most nights.

"Oh, shush, and let this divorced mother pretend that it's everything I think it is."

"Okay." I smile when I look at her. Her hair might be pulled back in a clip, and her lipstick may have faded with the hours of the day, but I can see how she once fit into that life. "In the meantime, I'll be over here, trying to figure out how to make the next round of voting that much more spectacular."

"Well, if you look out that window right there, you might just get some inspiration."

I turn to look where she points, and my breath hitches when I see Grayson walking by with Luke sitting atop his shoulders. Luke has a cone of cotton candy from the farmers' market in one hand while the other is resting on Grayson's hat. Grayson has a hold of Luke's feet so that his biceps flex with each step he takes.

"Oh."

"Uh-huh," Rissa says in that knowing tone that tells me that, if I were to look at her, she would see right through me to the fact that I've already slept with him. "Maybe you should start by getting a better picture of that man of yours for the site."

I sigh dramatically. "He isn't my man."

"I know, but maybe if you do a photo shoot, you'll get to spread oil all over that chest of his so those muscles of his shine better in the pictures, and then that would lead to some horizontal hallelujah with him."

Rissa is just as bad as Zoey is.

I laugh. "You are seriously messed up."

"You're telling me you don't want to see him shirtless and wet?"

I have.

"He doesn't have to be shirtless to win the contest. Some women look for other attributes."

"You just keep telling yourself that, and my Braden is going to win."

"You and your Braden." I roll my eyes.

"Then get a photo," she says as she stands and moves toward her desk. "You could always put him into a sex coma and then snap a picture of him barely covered by the sheet. That would get him votes right quick."

I start to refute her and then stop. "I know, I know. You're just living vicariously through your fantasies of me."

"You got it, girl." She gives a glance out the window to where Grayson is no longer in view. "If you want to live vicariously through me—because let's face it, everyone is jealous of my life—I can show you how to wear sweatpants and cook frozen freezer meals." I snort. "See? I told you my life was glorious."

"Divinely glorious."

Twenty-Nine

Sidney

I DRUM MY PEN ON MY DESK.

Why am I nervous about texting him?

Maybe it's because he hasn't taken the first step to call me? I've tried telling myself it is because Luke is always present. I can tell myself it's because it was a one-off thing and he doesn't want to talk to me.

I can't deny it stings a little that I thought we had a great time and now we're at radio silence.

As much as I want to overanalyze the situation, I do have a job to do. One that I told Rissa was already done. One that is more important than being worried about my hurt feelings after sleeping with the self-proclaimed pussy ninja.

Even that makes me smile. Being mopey and having a smile on my lips don't go together well.

Why am I being such a chicken about this?

Type the text. Do my job. Think of Haute. Think of Dad. Think of greasing oil all over Grayson's chest during a shoot.

I pick up my phone.

Me: Hi, Grayson. Voting is going well. For the next round, we'll need to get some new photos, though. We are having them

done for all the contestants.

I add that last part in response to his comment the last time we went through the picture conversation. But I don't hit send. I stare at the screen, wanting to say so much more.

Thanks for the other night.

I want it to happen again.

Jesus, you're incredible.

After staring at the blinking cursor a bit longer, obsessing, I type none of that and hit send. I'm surprised when he responds immediately.

Grayson: You'll have to work around my schedule with Luke.

Professionally, this is a good thing. He's agreeing to the photo shoot without a fight. Personally, I can't help but feel a little twinge in my gut that there are no niceties, no "how are you," no nothing.

Then again, I didn't offer any, either.

Me: Great! We can include Luke in the photos if you want. Some of the other men are including their children in their shoots.

I twist my lips while I wait impatiently.

Grayson: I told you before when I agreed to do this for you—no Luke.

Me: Why not? It might make him feel like he's a part of the whole contest with you. It'll be cool for him.

Grayson: I said no Luke. The Hoskins cast him aside without a second thought. There's no way in hell I'm giving them a glimpse of my son. Non-negotiable.

I sit and stare at the words for longer than I should as I try to understand the kind of hurt that must have caused him. To love someone so much while other family members discarded him without a second thought.

I think of the fight Luke got into and can only imagine the quiet rage he doesn't quite understand that fueled it.

I think of Grayson and how he pushes his wants and needs aside to make sure his son is okay.

Respect.

That's what that text conversation just earned him. A respect that overshadowed my own insecurities and made me want to be with the man that much more.

Me: Understood. Send me your schedule, and I'll set up the photographer for whenever works for you.

I put the phone down, thinking that will be the end of the conversation, and a second later, it vibrates again.

Grayson: We can use the helicopter for pictures if you want.

And just like that, he hands me the little extra Rissa was talking about. I'm still smiling as his next text comes in.

Grayson: The other night was incredible. When can I see you again?

I fight a little yelp of pleasure as well as the beginnings of flutters in my belly.

How about now? I want to ask but know that sounds a little too eager.

I'll make him wait a bit before I answer. That way, he won't read into it, and I won't look so desperate.

I'm being pathetic. The man just wants more sex.

Incredibly good sex, that is.

And, of course, I'm slowly coming to the realization that I'm a bit more involved on my end of the stick.

Slowly? That's a lie.

I know I want more . . . I'm just not sure what that more exactly is.

More lust? More sex? More friendship? More of a little bit of everything?

I'm leaving in a few months. That's one thing I know for sure . . . so I guess that's my answer. More lust and sex, please.

So why does knowing the answer feel less satisfying than I'd expect it to?

Reel it in, Thorton. Don't be a giddy girl. Be a grown woman who can have sex without strings.

Thirty

Sidney

"**I** SHOULD'VE FIGURED."

"Should've figured what?" I ask to the door at which I'm currently staring, the one thing that is separating me from seeing Grayson. It's been a long week since the last time we saw each other. A long week since his lips were on mine and the heat of his body was in my bed. And on top of me.

I've seen four other very sexy men up close and personal during my travels to the other finalists' photo shoots over the past week. I've seen chiseled chests and flawless smiles and have been charmed to death by one after another. I've been taken to dinner, been wined by their wives, and dined with their children, and yet, the one man I can't wait to see is standing behind the door in front of me.

Needless to say, I'm kind of anxious about it. Even if it's in this setting: at his station with his crew sitting around and waiting for a call, all of them anxious to harass the hell out of him.

I'll take him any way I can get him at this point.

"I should've figured that you'd finagle a way to see me." His laugh is muffled.

"Finagle? Who me?"

"Says the queen of manipulation. Tell me, did you plant any

stories in the *Gazette* telling people we're getting engagement photos done today or something?"

I stare at the door with wide eyes, trying to say no and that it was all Rissa before, but before I can get the words formed and out of my mouth, the door opens, and I lose any and all ability to speak.

I may have seen other perfect men this week, but none of them stole my breath like Grayson does in this moment.

There is a teasing grin on that cocksure face of his and humor in his stunning blue eyes. Those two things together I may have been able to handle, but he's in his flight suit, which makes it all too much. He's just too damn sexy.

I allow myself a quick moment to appreciate the sight of every inch of him.

Just lust.

It's even better knowing exactly what he looks like beneath it, too.

Just sex.

I feared he was too good to be true. That I'd relived the sex we had over and over in my mind—I mean, c'mon, that's a normal thing to do—and worried that I made *it* better than it was. That I made *him* better than he was.

That's all, I remind myself.

Now that we're face to face, now that every part of me sighs at the sight of him, I know I didn't make a damn thing up.

And I know I'm so very screwed.

"I did not finagle you. Not then. Not now." I stand my ground, despite the smile playing at the corners of my lips. "Even if we are engaged."

Our eyes meet. Hold. His smile turns salacious, and just as I hear voices down the hall, Grayson yanks me into the room where he was changing. Before I can even yelp in surprise, his mouth is on mine in a mind-numbing, lip-bruising, thigh-clenching type of kiss that I never want to end but know needs to if I don't want to be ruined for any other guy.

When he finally tears his lips from mine, he steps back, leaving me out of breath and a little overwhelmed. The grin he flashes is one of pure arrogance.

"If we're engaged, the least I get to do is reap the rewards for putting that imaginary ring on your finger."

I look down at my ringless ring finger, raise my eyebrows, and then look back up to him. "Look who's doing the manipulating now."

He shakes his head and chuckles quietly before putting his hand on the back of my neck and pulling me in for one more mesmerizing kiss.

Thankfully, we don't get caught as we are sneaking out of the room like a pair of hormonal teenagers. In fact, we never even meet each other's eyes as the photographer and I speak about staging and various ideas while Grayson gets teased by his crew about the photo shoot in general.

But I hear the taunting comments. I see the raising of eyebrows and lifting of chins in my direction, and I know the engagement photo rumor is in full swing and will most likely be perpetuated by these guys.

Knowing that my every move is being watched makes me heed caution every time I look Grayson's way. Don't stare too long. Don't smile shyly at him. Don't act like I'm familiar with him. Don't drool at how sexy he looks.

I'm more than aware that one questionable cell phone shot snapped and sent to the *Gazette* would piss my dad off and jeopardize everything I've been working for.

But it's extremely hard to watch Grayson in all his uniformed glory without giving any tells. With his hand on the door of the chopper and a serious look on his face. With his flight suit unzipped to his abdomen with a sneak peak of his delicious abs. With him sitting in the cockpit and a grin on his lips. Every picture is an aphrodisiac until the next one is clicked.

"What is it with these Malone boys? I mean . . . whew," Marcy, the photographer says with a low hum of a whistle.

"What's that supposed to mean?" I look over to her. She's tall and lean and has her auburn hair piled on top of her head.

"I photographed his brother a while back. They both have the same good looks, but his brother Grady was cockier with his smolder, while this one here is more intense. But damn, I'd let him smolder on me," she says and lifts her chin to where Grayson stands and waits for her assistant to shift the reflector and check the lighting.

"Don't I know it?" My laugh is soft, and for the first time, I allow my eyes to remain glued to Grayson.

"You're the one responsible for him being in the contest?"

"I'm the one who set up the contest, but his brothers are the ones who entered him. If you listen to the Sunnyville rumor mill, he and I are sleeping together, engaged, and maybe already have three children."

This time, she laughs, drawing Grayson's attention. He meets my eyes and smiles that smile I know will get me in trouble. Grady really isn't the only one who can smolder. Damn. "I wouldn't be complaining if I were you, but I'd definitely check my rearview mirror for angry women mad you took a great catch."

"Let's not be so loud. We don't want his ego to get big," I tease as Grayson angles his head to the side and tries to figure out what we're talking about.

"I doubt he has one. Isn't he rumored to have saved those people in the High Sierras but won't let anyone credit him with doing it?"

"So they say," I murmur as I watch him. It's beyond me that a man so hell-bent on protecting his son would be so willing to risk his own life to save others, yet, Grayson does it all the time.

Just another mystery that makes me want to get to know him that much more.

"When I was setting up, one of the crew was telling me he had been grounded for disobeying orders. Something about flying in a thunderstorm when command tried to ground him, and then flying to a different hospital or something despite the dangerous weather. Pretty damn noble." She looks through her lens at him for a beat and then looks at me with a laugh. "He can save me, any day."

"No doubt."

"So, Sidney, since you've seen what photos the other contestants have submitted, is there anything else you want me to shoot? Any special poses you want me to take that I haven't already taken?"

"Let me talk to Grayson for a second to see what he's comfortable with. The flight suit hanging around the waist is always a good look, but I'm not sure it's one he'll be willing to do."

"Convince him," she says as she looks down at her camera's digital screen. "The camera loves him . . . and it would be a shame to hide that perfection underneath clothing."

I walk toward him and the massive helicopter behind him. It's white with red graphics, and I'm taken aback by its sheer size, maybe because it isn't every day I get up close and personal with a helicopter.

Or, maybe it's because of the man in front of it. Sexy. Endearing. He makes every part of me come to life in the few short feet I hold his eyes.

"Quit looking at me like that, Princess, or else someone is going to figure out we've slept together." His eyes light up when he smiles.

"You're in a flight suit looking sexy, but I'm not looking at you in any way," I feign innocence when I'm anything but.

"But I'm looking at you that way." He lowers his voice as his eyes track my movement until I stop right in front of him.

"You are, are you?"

His gaze follows my hands as I reach out and unzip his flight suit, wondering just how low he'll let me go with it.

"Mm-hmm. I'm wondering what you taste like. I'm picturing that heart-shaped birthmark on the inside of your thigh. I'm thinking about the sounds you'll make the next time I get to make you come."

"Oh." My hands falter. My thoughts liquefy into a heat between my thighs. But I don't look at him. Can't. Because if I meet his eyes, I'm going to want to kiss that sweet mouth of his that is saying such wicked things.

"You wore those heels and that skirt."

"I wear them every day. So?" My voice breaks.

"And I wear a flight suit most days."

I know that, if I don't look up at him, the people standing around and his crew inside will read between the lines and there will be no denying that there is more going on here than just magazine editor and contestant.

So, in a bid to keep our secret, I look at him. There's so much suggestion mixed with amusement in his eyes that my breath catches.

"Turnabout's fair play, Sidney."

"No one said anything about playing fair."

He lowers his voice. "I'll remember that the next time I have you."

I glance over toward the building where I'm sure his crew is watching us from behind the tinted windows. "Aren't there beds in this place?"

His laugh echoes off the concrete around us as he zips his suit up. "Beds. *Plural.* As in all in one room." His smile is crooked when he shakes his head. "We won't be using any beds here. I don't like to share."

I open my mouth to speak and then close it. "Who knew you were so dominant?" I tease.

"You know what they say . . ." he says as he takes a few steps back from me.

"No, what?"

"It's always the quiet ones you have to worry about."

It's my turn to laugh. "I'll keep that in mind." I take a few steps toward Marcy, who quickly averts her eyes to pretend as if she hadn't been watching us, and then I turn back to Grayson. "Hey, Malone?"

"Yeah?"

"Keep the suit unzipped. Let the sleeves hang."

"You're undressing me in public now?" he asks, and laughs ring out around us. "What will I get in return?"

"Votes."

Thirty-One

Sidney

"WHAT DID YOU FORGET?" I ASK RISSA AS THE FRONT door of the office opens and closes. I stare at the proofs of Grayson. The ones I can't seem to take my eyes away from. The ones that tell me I'm in too deep when I'm not supposed to even have a toe in the water. When I realize I haven't received a response yet, I ask again. "Rissa?"

I rise from my seat, startled to see Luke standing in my doorway. "Luke? Is everything okay?" I hate that my immediate reaction is to be worried about Grayson. "Where is your da—"

"Dad's not here," he says with a sheepish look on his face while I panic over what he is doing here. And then, before I make it around my desk, he holds out a bunch of handpicked daisies. Every hard part of me softens in a way I never could have expected. "I'd like to know if you'd go on a date with me."

"What?" My chuckle is one of disbelief as I look over his shoulder and spot a woman standing in the lobby. She has shoulder-length silvery-blond hair and a soft smile on her face. "Hello."

"That's my nana. She brought me here."

"Oh." I blink a couple of times as I look from his nana then to him and then back to her. "Please come in."

"Stay there, Nana. I need to do this on my own," Luke says, looking back at her. She holds her hands up and gives him the most adoring grin before she nods.

He clears his throat as he meets my eyes again. "Miss Sidney, I wanted to know if you'd go on a date with me."

How this little boy melts my heart every single time I see him is beyond me, but he does. I drop down to one knee in front of him. "A date, huh?" I accept the flowers and sniff them. "Thank you, they're beautiful."

"Nana says you're supposed to bring a lady flowers. I'm not sure why. They smell pretty, but then they die, and you have to throw them in the trash, but she said you have to, so I did."

"Well," I say through a laugh, "they do die, but they also make the lady feel awfully special." I cup the side of his face. "Where exactly would you like to take me on this date of yours?"

"I was wondering if you'd go to a picnic with me."

"A picnic, huh?"

His teeth sink into his lower lip as he rocks on his heels. "There's a picnic that we have here in Sunnyville, and I was wondering . . ." His eyes are innocent and full of hope.

"If I would go with you?"

He nods and then straightens his spine as if he realizes that he needs to act like a grown-up. "We were on our way there, and I asked Nana if it would be okay if we stopped by here and asked you to come with us. We already have a lunch made. There are sandwiches and sodas—I only get to have soda on special occasions—and chocolate chip cookies. Nana makes the best chocolate chip cookies because she puts extra chips in them and—"

"Chocolate chip cookies?" My mouth waters at just the thought of them.

He nods enthusiastically, and I notice how the fingers on his right hand are crossed for luck. This kid is killing me in the best kind of way.

"You're on your way there right now?"

"Yep."

"We didn't mean to interrupt your day," his nana says as she steps forward and puts a protective hand on Luke's shoulder. "I'm Betsy Malone, Grayson's mom." She extends her hand, and I stand to shake it.

"Nice to meet you."

She's striking. There's a graceful fluidity to her when she moves, her smile is welcoming in every sense of the word, and her eyes—so similar to Grayson's—are the sort that see way more than you want them to see.

"Like I said, we didn't mean to just barge on in here, but it's a beautiful afternoon and we thought you might like to get out and enjoy Sunnyville instead of being cooped up in this office."

"Thank you for thinking of me," I say with caution because I know how sensitive Grayson is to Luke being around women he is seeing.

Seeing? Is that what we're doing? Seeing each other?

But if no one knows that's what is going on, would it bug him if I went to the picnic with them?

I really don't want to turn Luke down, but how exactly do I ask to call Grayson to find out if this is okay and not offend Betsy or Luke?

"I think I . . ." I look from Betsy to Luke and then back to Betsy. "Does Grayson know you're here?"

"Nope," Luke says and laughs. "Nana is all about spontaneity. She says it's the best kind of adventure." He looks back her way as if he's so proud that she's taught him this.

"Grayson will be fine with it," Betsy says with a nod. "But you're more than welcome to give him a call and ask. Although, while he's at the dispatch desk, he typically doesn't carry his cell. It's a department protocol thing." She waves a hand in indifference. "If he gets mad, I'll take the heat."

Stuck in indecision with a pair of puppy-dog eyes loaded with hope staring at me, I put my hands on my knees and bend over so Luke and I are face to face.

"So, this is like a friend date? Food and fun and friends?"

"And nanas." He bounces on his toes.

"Okay," I say with a definitive nod.

Luke's eyes widen, and his smile does even more so. "You mean you want to go with us?"

"Of course, buddy. I just need a few minutes to sort some things."

"Okay, we'll wait out here."

He shuffles his way out to the reception area with Betsy in tow. I have a task list a million miles long and yet I can't help but wonder why I'm walking to a picnic when a few weeks ago I would have laughed at the idea of doing it.

My desk is loaded with Post-It notes of things I have to do, but I shut my laptop with a click and walk out of the office without any qualms about leaving it until tomorrow. I'm actually kind of looking forward to sinking my heels into the grass—there has to be grass at a picnic, right? And getting to hang out with Luke.

The small-town air is affecting me.

That has to be what it is.

But I let it affect me even more, along with Luke's giggles, as we play chocolate chip cookie warfare—a game we made up as we sit under the shady elm on the outskirts of the playground at his school. My cheeks hurt from laughing, and I know for a fact a little piece of my heart has been lost to Luke.

"Luke. Man. Come play."

Luke angles his head over to his friend—a cute little guy with red hair and the most adorable freckles across his nose and cheeks. "Sorry, Jim, I'm busy with my friend."

"You sure? We're in an epic battle over here." He points to the handball court.

Luke nods and smiles. "Yep."

"You don't have to entertain me, buddy. I'm just enjoying the sunshine. Go. Play. I want to watch."

"You want to watch?" His eyes light up just like his smile.

"Of course, I do." He gives me one last look for reassurance before he runs off, and I call out to him, "Good luck."

So I watch. Battle after battle of handball with rules I don't know. I'm cognizant of some of the other moms peering at me from behind their sunglasses. Betsy does her best to introduce me to everyone who comes over. I know most of them are here to satiate their curiosity as they ask me benign questions that seem simple on the surface but are really searching for more.

But it's okay.

The sunshine and laughter and a huge grin on Luke's face make the chocolate chip cookies I'm going to have to exercise off and the dirt I have to clean off my heels worth it ten times over.

Thirty-Two

Sidney

A FIST BANGING ON THE DOOR SHATTERS THE QUIET OF THE house and scares the hell out of me. At first, I freeze, but the sound is so threatening that it has me quickly back-stepping into my kitchen and out of the line of sight from the front windows.

"Open up, Sidney."

Grayson?

My heart leaps into my throat and then lands with a confused thud over being excited to see him and at the same time knowing something is wrong.

"What's wrong?" I ask as I open the door. The minute I catch sight of his expression—a mask of fury—I wish I had pretended I wasn't home.

Without a word, he barrels past me. "Shut the door."

"Grayson? What is—?"

"You!" he shouts as he turns around and jabs a finger in my direction. "You are what's wrong."

"I—uh . . . what?"

"What in the hell do you think you're doing?"

"Letting you into my house so you can yell at me when I obviously shouldn't have. Can we back up here, so you can tell me what's going on?"

The muscle in his jaw ticks as he stares at me. "You went to the *mother-son* picnic with Luke. Are you out of your mind?"

I stare at him—his fury unmasked—and know without a doubt I made a huge mistake. It takes a few seconds for my thoughts to line up so I sound coherent. "It isn't what you think."

"What I think?" His laugh is cold and unwelcome. "What exactly is it that you think I'm thinking?"

A million things flash through my mind and unfortunately, all of them spill out in a tangled mess. "I didn't mean anything by it. I didn't even know it was a mother-son picnic. I wasn't trying to manipulate the situation to fuel more rumors. I wasn't trying to get in good with Luke. I wasn't trying to . . ." My words fade off as he just stands there and stares at me with hard eyes and mouth a straight line. "They stopped by the office and asked me to come. He was so sweet asking me on a date. I told him I'd go with him as a friend. That's it. I met your mom," I ramble as I twist my fingers together. "She was sweet, too. I didn't think it was a big deal."

"Of course, you didn't think it was a big deal." His voice escalates in pitch with each word. "After everything I've said to you. How could you go with him without asking me first—"

"Your mom said it wasn't a big deal. That you were at work and—"

"And my mom isn't raising my son. I am."

"Grayson—"

"Just stop. Your excuses. Your reasons. You're proving me right."

"What the hell is that supposed to mean? Proving you right?"

"Nothing. Just . . ." He holds his hands up in front of him as if saying this is too much and not worth it as he takes a step toward the door.

"You know what? Screw you, Grayson. You don't have a right to come here and chew me out. Your mom and Luke showed up, they asked me to go get some fresh air. If you think your concerns about Luke and his attachment to women didn't cross my mind, then you're an ass and don't know me very well. They asked. I went. Big freaking deal. Now get out." I point to the door, my emotions a tumultuous eddy inside me.

I've thought about him for days. Relived every water-soaked moment and what happened with him after. Looked forward to my date tomorrow night with him. So, to have him come here and treat me as if I did something horrible when it was completely innocent is a crock of shit.

"Sidney." His fists clench and unclench. His eyes fire with anger and uncertainty about what to do next.

"It seems that, no matter what I do, I'm wrong. Luke's a great kid, Grayson. Incredible, even, and that means a lot when it comes from a woman like me who has a hard time relating to kids." I look at my hands for a moment before looking back up to his eyes. "There were no ulterior motives today. He was so adorable with his flowers that I couldn't say no. Your mom was teaching him what a gentleman does, and I realize now that it wasn't my place to help her . . . but I did, and I'm sorry you're upset because of it. Like I said before, I was conscious of what he was asking, of how he'd perceive things. I figured since your mother stopped by . . . I don't know."

He scrubs a hand over his face and mutters, "My goddamn mother. Her and her search for a wife."

"Search for a what?" I ask, not sure if I heard him right.

"Nothing." He walks to the window that overlooks the backyard and the mesmerizing rows of vines on the hills beyond. When he speaks again, his voice is more serious, resigned. "You know Luke has a major crush on you, right? You know he had been worried about this picnic for the past few months because he thought he was going to be left out. I offered to take him. I offered to dress up as any superhero he wanted so I could prove to him that I could hang with the moms here, too. That he wasn't so different. When, in reality, I would have stood out like a sore thumb. I would have been the talk of the damn town, but it doesn't matter because he's my son. He's my job to take care of and protect."

"Grayson . . ."

"He asked my mom to take him, so I went to work, thinking my mom was going alone. When they came home, he wouldn't stop talking about how much fun he had, about how you were there, too, stepping in to be *his mom*."

Well, that explains his anger.

"I didn't step in to be his mom." He's blowing this out of proportion, but I don't dare say that to him. I'm not a parent, so I have zero legs to stand on when it comes to any opinion I may have.

"Christ." He paces the short distance of the room and runs a hand through his hair and exhales. "How am I going to tell him otherwise?"

"What do you mean? He's old enough to know that he can't expect every woman he sees you with or who is nice to him to be his mom."

Grayson laughs, but it holds no humor. "Easy to say when it's coming from a twenty-eight-year-old woman. He's an eight-year-old kid with the pressure to be like everyone else when he knows he isn't. All he wants to do is fit in. All he wants is for kids not to ask him why he doesn't have a mom, or why his mom doesn't love him, when I pretend day in and day out that she does for his sake. So, don't tell me he should look at it like you do, because it's nowhere near the same."

"I know it isn't. And I know you try your best—he's an incredible kid, and it shows. But Grayson, at some point, you have to take a harder line or he's only going to end up being hurt more by it."

When he turns to face me, he looks like a man lost in No Man's Land. Torn between protecting his son from life's harsh realities and admitting that he needs to gently break them to him. His sigh fills the small room, and when he meets my eyes I know his temper has faded enough for him to really hear me. "You're right." He shrugs in resignation. "I know it, and it fucking kills me to admit it because that means I've failed him as a parent."

"Gray—"

"No. I'm doing the best I can, and it isn't enough. It's such a hard thing as a parent to recognize that fine line where protecting your child turns into hurting your child." I step forward and put a hand on his arm and squeeze, his sudden vulnerability coming on the heels of his fiery temper is almost unnerving. "He's had a rough couple of weeks. Nightmares. The fight . . . I don't know what's bringing all this on, but I know it's on me."

"My mom used to tell me there are no instructions to having a kid, and being a parent is one huge learning mistake after another."

He gives a measured nod but keeps his eyes focused out the window to the front yard. I hate that he won't look at me. "You shouldn't have gone today without talking to me first."

I open my mouth to speak and then close it, my inability to read his body language giving me pause. So I say the only thing I can. "I'm sorry."

He nods but doesn't look my way. "I've gotta get back to Luke. To home." And without waiting to see if I respond at all, he opens the door and exits completely different than he was when he entered.

Resigned and silent.

I stand at the window and watch him—those broad shoulders of his as he walks toward his truck, the way he slides behind the wheel, rests his elbow on the sill of the open window, and runs a finger over his lip.

He sits there for some time, seemingly lost in thought. The sight is heartbreaking. A man so strong otherwise, conflicted over teaching his son truths he knows will hurt him.

When he pulls away from the curb a few minutes later, I pick up my cell and call my father just to say hi.

Watching Grayson struggle with this has made me understand my father a little bit more now, and how hard making his decision to send me here must have been on him.

Thirty-Three

Sidney

THE MORNING COFFEE RUSH IS IN FULL SWING AS I SIT IN THE back of Better Buzz with a cup of my own and work on my laptop. It's louder and more chaotic than the office, but it makes me feel like I'm back in the city. It makes me not feel so homesick when, after last night and everything with Grayson, I am desperately so.

He may not have walked away in the fit of rage he stormed into my house with, but his silent resignation almost feels worse.

Is he still mad at me? I don't know.

What I do know is that every part of me wanted to drive over to his house and talk to him . . . but I took a step back and told myself that he was dealing with Luke. That Luke comes first. That my showing up would only have proved to him that I think of myself first, when I've been fighting against that preconception since we first met.

Zoey. I miss her, and if she were here, she'd calm my crazy—her warm hugs, knowing looks, and the effortless way she seems to just *get me*. I miss the fresh flowers at the corner florist stand that I used to pass every day on the way to Thorton Publishing's main office. I miss Stink, the homeless man parked on Greer and 4th who I brought some kind of food to a few days a week. I even miss my own place, with its seemingly endless supply of hot water and its pillow-loaded bed.

Funny how I didn't realize how homesick I was until Grayson got mad at me, and how alone I was here until Rissa didn't pick up her phone. That is probably for the better, though, since I can't tell her about what happened.

"Sidney, is that you?"

When I look up from my laptop, I find Betsy Malone standing at the coffee doctoring station with a cautious smile on her lips.

"Hi." We eye each other with a wariness that says we both know what this conversation is going to be about but are uncertain if we want to go there.

"May I have a minute of your time?" she asks, but before I answer, she has already crossed the short distance and is lowering herself into the empty chair across from me.

"Uh, yeah, sure." I laugh the words out, my sudden uneasiness showing. "What can I do for you?"

She stares at her hands, which are wrapped around her paper to-go cup, and it's a long minute before she meets my gaze. She looks nervous. Nervous, when yesterday I found her to be not only quite funny and inquisitive but also carefree and open.

"I need to apologize for a couple of things."

"If this is about yesterday," I say and shake my head, "you don't need to apologize for anything."

"Yes, I do. I told you it would be okay and that I'd take the heat for it and . . ."

"And I'm a grown woman who can make her own decisions." I smile warmly at her. "Let me guess, he overreacted and unleashed his temper on you, too?"

Her eyes well with tears briefly before she blinks them away. "He may have overreacted . . . but I deserved it." Her silence as she stares at the steam coming from her coffee quiets the protest on my lips. My reassurance won't matter. It's her son's rebukes that will hit her the hardest. She shrugs and looks up at me. "I was curious about you. All I know is what Luke has told me and the gossip from town, but not a single word from Grayson. That in and of itself says a lot, so maybe I bypassed asking Gray if it was okay to let Luke invite you . . . maybe I told you he would be okay with it when I wasn't one hundred percent certain. I only wanted to see if it was all true."

"You wanted to see if I was good enough for Grayson?"

Betsy clears her throat. "That isn't what I said."

"You don't have to. He's your son. Luke's your grandson. Just like I'm sure you've heard rumors about me—then and now—I've heard them about you." Her lips purse and eyes narrow. "Like how fiercely protective you are of your family. How you want all your boys settled down and happy. I get it. I do . . ." But I was the one who got his wrath because of it.

"I know Grayson's wishes for Luke come first. They always should. I overstepped, and because of it, I landed us both in hot water—irrational, overreacted, or not. I'm sorry. I . . ." The sincerity swimming in Betsy's eyes, and the disappointment in herself over her actions, is clear as day. As much as I want to be mad at her, I can't. She didn't do this alone. Knowing how Grayson felt about women around Luke, I should have known better. I should have made an excuse and not gone to the picnic. Luke would have been disappointed, but at least then I would have been respecting Grayson's wishes. "Please forgive me," she says.

"Thank you for your apology, but like I said, it isn't needed."

Her shoulders heave with her sigh of relief. "Grayson was also upset about what the gossip column might print . . . I didn't think of that when we invited you, so I called a friend and made sure that nothing about the picnic and your attendance would be reported in the upcoming gossip column."

I hadn't thought of that, either, or the repercussions it would have on Luke. After the last photo landed him in a fight at school, I should have considered it. I should have considered a lot of things I hadn't. Christ, this is so much more complicated than it needs to be. So much more everything. "Thank you, Betsy. I never would have thought about that and how it would affect Luke."

"Luke would be able to handle it just fine; it's my son who would go through the roof," she says and winks playfully. "I was actually on my way to your office when I saw you. I couldn't stand thinking that you and Gray had gotten into a fight because of something I'd allowed."

"It's fine."

"Okay, then," she says as she sits up some, "I'll let you get back to it. I'm sure you have a ton of work to do with the magazine and the contest and all that."

I smile and nod, completely stunned by how the woman I should be mad at has kind of won me over.

This small-town air is definitely messing with my vibe.

"Have a good day," I add.

"You, too." Betsy takes a few steps away, and then just before I look down to my laptop, she turns back to me. "Sidney?"

"Mm-hmm?" I'm more than aware that some of the eyes in the coffee shop have turned our way.

"My son is a good man. Don't let anything I've done deter you from, let's say, taking a chance on him."

My eyebrows lift. "Oh."

"I mean, the fact that he's never really mentioned you to me says more than anything. That means he wants me to steer clear and not mess things up for him. Maybe you're the one who'll change his mind about not wanting to take a chance on marriage and the like again."

This time, I choke on my breath—not because of what she said but because of the sudden interest our conversation is getting. I figure I'll swallow the shock value and use this attention to my advantage. "I'm flattered you think that, but honestly, my main focus right now is *Modern Family*. Besides the fact that I'm not looking for a relationship, I don't think it'd be very fair if I were to run the contest and be involved with Grayson at the same time. That might come off a little biased to the general public." I take a sip of coffee. "Anything you've read in the *Gazette* is plain rumor."

"Okay." Betsy draws the words out as I glance around at all the people who are listening but trying to make it seem as if they aren't.

Her smile widens when she steps beside me and pats me on the shoulder as she whispers. "Good thinking. We'll keep this our little secret. A woman knows when another woman is smitten with a man, and I can tell you're smitten."

The sigh of awe she gives before she walks away has me shaking my head and questioning whether I adore her more for that last statement or if I think she's crazy.

Thirty-Four

Sidney

THE CRICKETS SING THROUGH THE NIGHT AIR AS I WATCH Grayson from where I stand midway down the street.

I couldn't resist. I tried. I reminded myself it's just sex, it's just lust, it's nothing serious. Yet, here I am after the debacle of yesterday and the canceling of our planned date via text.

He's sitting on the porch swing, holding a beer in one hand and music playing softly somewhere near him. He's deep in thought—that much I can tell, but I can only imagine over what.

There's a sadness to him, an air of a man in conflict, which twists my insides in ways that tell me I care about him when I'm not sure if it's a good idea.

This is why I've never gotten involved with someone who had kids. Too much baggage. Too much drama. Too much stress, when a relationship is hard enough as it is.

As much as I tell myself that I should turn around and quietly walk the miles back to my house, I move forward, down the sidewalk and up his front walk. I know he knows I'm there—I can tell by the slight pause of the beer to his lips before continuing—but he doesn't speak, and he doesn't turn my way.

I take a seat in the swing beside him, the seat creaking under the added weight, and just sit there for a bit, listening to the night around us and a song by Florida Georgia Line on the radio.

"Where's Luke?" I ask.

"Asleep."

"Oh." I take a deep breath, suddenly nervous to be out here with him. I know we need to address some issues, and that if we don't, there is really no need for me to be here. "Your mom came to see me today."

"I know." He takes a sip of his beer, still not looking at me.

"She told me she was upset that you got mad at her."

"The two of you seem to be getting cozy the last few days."

"Don't be a jerk, Grayson."

"It seems to me it's the only thing I'm good at these days." He sighs and shoves up out of the swing, leaving me to rock on it by myself as he moves to the other side of the patio. "Fucking Christ. Should I presume that makes two of you?"

"Two of us?" What in the hell is he talking about?

"Mad at me." When he turns to face me, he looks like a little boy who'd just been scolded, unsure whether he's in trouble or not.

"I'm not mad at you. And I don't think she is, either. I think she was hurt, more than anything."

"Yeah, well . . ." The song changes. Something a bit softer. "No one tells me what to do or how to do it when it comes to my life or Luke's. Unless you've walked in my shoes, you don't get to judge."

I chew on my bottom lip as I try to figure out what he means. Does he know what my conversation with his mom was about today?

Or is he referring to something else altogether? I decide to bite the bullet and get it out in the open. If I'm going to be held to some unobtainable standard, I might as well know what it is.

"What happened with Claire?"

I catch the subtle hitch in his breath, but when he doesn't respond right away, I assume he isn't going to answer. When he finally speaks, it takes me by surprise. "We started dating after I got back from flight school. I fell fast and hard and she was my everything. She got pregnant. I thought we had forever. And she left. *The end.*"

Trying to digest the understandable hurt and derision that edges his voice, I clear my throat and prepare for his temper. "Why did she leave?"

"Why did she leave?"

The scrub of his hand over his shadowed stubble fills the night around us as I sit and wait.

"She left because her precious parents on the hill couldn't handle her dirtying her hands with a public servant like me."

Public servant? The man flies a helicopter and saves people for a living. That is hardly digging ditches, but even if it were, what would it matter? Then again, the Hoskins were always rooted in their money and status.

So are the Thortons.

I must blink ten times as I try to comprehend what he's telling me. What he's implying. What I don't want to believe.

That someone would choose their status over love. That someone would choose abandonment instead of parenthood to maintain their societal prestige.

My mom came from a blue-collar family, and it never stopped my father from loving or marrying or having a life with her. Love is love.

"But there was Luke," I say, still trying to process.

"Yes, there was Luke." He grabs a fresh beer from the cooler tucked in the corner. The crack of its top coming off reverberates around the uncomfortable silence. He braces his hands on the railing of the porch and looks out into the darkness. His shoulders are broad but defeated, and I can't seem to look away from them as he continues. "When Mommy and Daddy Warbucks threaten to yank your trust fund if you decide to disgrace your family by having a child at age twenty, and with a commoner, well then, you realize that money talks, and love gets shit-canned—and your kid does, too—without a goddamn second thought."

It was horrible to even think it was possible to be so shallow, but hearing Grayson confirm it, listening to the pain owning every syllable he spoke, shows me only a sliver of what he endured.

Of what he still lives with.

"But there was Luke," I repeat.

"Yep, there was Luke. And her family made sure to offer a nice cash settlement when she signed the paperwork giving up all rights to him. A little something to grease my palm so I wouldn't spread harmful rumors about their beloved princess." He finally turns my way, and there is pain and anger etched in every line of his face. My heart hurts for him and what I can only imagine he went through. "Needless to say, I tore the check up. Watched it burn in the fireplace. There was no way I was going to take their guilt money and live on it—no matter how much I needed it at the time. No fucking way."

He angles his head and meets my eyes, and there is so much inexplicable emotion in his that I just want to crawl into his arms and hold on . . . but I know that's crossing some invisible line we've drawn.

"Grayson, I can't imagine what that must have been like for you."

"Yeah, well, rock-bottom about sums it up." He takes a long pull on his beer. "What about you, Sidney? How come you aren't married with two-point-five kids sitting pretty in your high-rise in the city?"

"Because that isn't what I expected out of my life."

"What *do* you want out of your life?"

I shrug, knowing it's going to sound so very different from the life he leads. "I wanted a career and the freedom to move about as I please."

"You mean head off to St. Tropez on a whim?"

I glare at him. "That's not fair."

"Yeah, well . . . it's the life you're used to, right?"

"Does it look like that's the life I'm used to?" I hold my hands out, knowing that it's the only defense I have when he's right. Packing my bags and leaving at the drop of a hat is what I sometimes do . . . because I can.

"Yes. It does. So that begs the question, what in the hell are you doing here in Sunnyville? You told me you were here to help save the magazine. Fine. But there's more there you aren't telling me." He's ready to pounce on any response that I give, so I give him the truth.

"I screwed up." I think I'm startled by the admission as much as he is. "I was working for the main office of Thorton Publishing. We had a big interview with Wendy Whitaker."

"You mean the fashion lady who's on all the shows? The one who just blew the whistle on the fashion designer and his abusive behavior?"

"She's the one, and that was *our* exclusive . . . until I botched it." I can still feel the crushing panic I felt when I realized what time it was and that I'd missed our appointment. "She had contacted my father and said she wanted to speak to me personally. We had met at industry events because fashion is where my passion lies, and she knew enough about me to know I would keep her name quiet. Anyway, she told my father he could have the exclusive for our weekly news magazine. It was all set up. Then Zoey, my best friend, called me because she needed me—like *needed me, needed me*," I say, not wanting to spill her secrets. "I was so busy helping her that time flew, and I missed the meeting."

"And the story broke elsewhere."

"Yep. And her name with it, when she wanted it to be kept secret." I stare at the streetlight a little way down the road before I respond. "I screwed up big time."

"Choices always have a chain reaction. How did that chain reaction lead you to Sunnyville?"

"My dad was pissed, which is putting it mildly, since it wasn't the first time I had done something to let him down—"

"Impossible expectations? It's always hard working for a family member."

"Perhaps, but I really did screw up. Not only did I let him down, but also, I let myself down." I glance his way, expecting judgment but finding compassion instead. "My dad said I was acting like Richie Rich. Wanting everything without having to work for it." I say the words knowing full well how they are going to hit his ears after everything he went through with Claire.

"And what is the everything that you want?" He angles his head to the side and holds my gaze. I hate that I almost tell him that it's *him* I want.

Then I get a grip and come to my senses.

"My two loves are fashion and writing about fashion," I explain as his eyes narrow some as he tries to follow me. "That's the job I want someday, to be an editor-in-chief of a fashion magazine, so I can do something that has to do with both. For now though, it's proving myself to my father and boosting the circulation of *Modern Family* somehow and increasing the online constituency."

"So, the contest was your idea?" he asks. I nod, feeling rather shy about it all of a sudden. "And how are you managing living in small-town USA when it isn't your thing?"

"There's nothing wrong with small-town USA, but—"

"Those red-soled shoes of yours don't quite fit the town image for you." Irritation edges his voice.

"That isn't fair, Grayson."

His chuckle fills the air as he looks at me over the edge of his bottle as he tips it up. "It doesn't seem that life is fair much at all."

When I rise from my seat, I have no idea what my intentions are, but I make my way across the short distance and stop right in front of him. We stare at each other for a moment as the crickets continue to sing and the moths fly in front of the porch light, casting shadows that shift and dance around us.

"And when you tire of Sunnyville like you did before . . . what then? Where to then?"

I stare at him and am thankful for the shadow over my face because I realize that I never told him I was leaving. I never explained to him that after this contest, I was moving on.

For the life of me, I can't bring myself to say the words. I can't make myself tell him that I'll be leaving in a few months. Telling him about my dream job was my subtle way of letting him know that I'm not here long term . . . and yet I fumble with what to say because the thought of not being near him is suddenly unwelcome. When I finally speak, my words are soft and my voice breaks. "Just because I like my red soles, doesn't mean I wouldn't fit in here if I wanted to. I did once."

"You did once because you were born here, but from what I remember, you were always itching for more of the limelight. You'd sit in that diner and talk about all the places you wanted to go, while some of your friends talked about the next party, the next whatever that wouldn't mean shit once you graduated."

I stare at him, a little shocked, a lot moved. "You really paid attention, didn't you?"

We spent so many nights in that diner. So many nights filling space and being obnoxious—throwing our napkins and straws on the floor and not caring that he was going to have to clean them up. So many hours of mindless chatter after the diner had closed, none of us caring about the boy named Gray behind the counter who probably wanted to go home.

"It was hard to ignore you when your crew would take over Lulu's for hours on end." He lifts his eyebrows as if to say he didn't have a choice.

"Speaking of that . . ." I take a deep breath. "I owe you an apology for how I acted back then. I was immature, and you were always nice regardless of how rude we were or how late we kept you when I'm sure you wanted to clock out. I'm not that girl anymore. The one who was so wrapped up in herself she'd rather ignore someone else than risk looking uncool to her friends."

He just stares at me with a nod that's meaning I can't discern. Our gazes hold, his blue eyes to my brown, as we try to wade through this conversation that is bringing up things people talk about when they are in a relationship. Things people talk about when they are trying to understand each other better.

"We all change." He takes a long sip of his beer. "So, when you left here, did you find what you were looking for, Sidney? Is your sterile glass tower warm at night? I might not live the high-life, but my house is warm and full of laughter and love and little-boy cooties."

I hesitate to respond. I hate that his words make me realize how many nights I go to bed alone, and even though I tell myself that's what I want, I remember how I felt a few weeks back when Luke was chatting and Grayson was on his iPad and everything felt so very different from what I'm used to.

"Maybe I was itching for the limelight, Grayson, but you can't fault someone for wanting to spread their wings. Like you said, people change. People try things and see if they like them. If they don't, then they adjust and try again. You changed. You used to be shy and unassertive, and you're neither anymore. Should I fault you for being that way?"

"No. I learned from my mistakes."

He stares at me, that muscle pulsing in his jaw and his subtle scent of shampoo and soap filling my nose. There are so many things he wants to say written in those eyes of his.

"We've done enough talking, Malone," I murmur as I take the initiative for the first time since we've met. I lean forward and kiss him. Gently. Slowly. Teasingly. His body jolts in surprise. "You canceled our date."

Another kiss. A slide of his hand up my back to pull me into the V of his thighs where he's sitting on the railing. Another soft sigh into the night.

"I figured you'd had enough of my crazy life." He chuckles and then meets my lips again.

"Not crazy. Just protective." Our lips brush over each other's as we speak. His hand cups the back of my neck. His thighs squeeze gently against mine. "I'm sorry about yesterday. I didn't mean to upset you, and I didn't look at the situation through your eyes or Luke's."

"I'm sorry I went off the deep end."

"Not that I'm any judge of it, but you really are a good father. You just need to remember that it's okay to be a man, too."

He guides my hand to rest atop where his dick is hard and presses against the fabric of his shorts. "Is that man enough for you?" I chuckle against his lips.

Just the feel of him hard for me sends a hit of desire straight to the delta of my thighs.

"Is this the part where we kiss and make up?" I ask as every sense goes on high alert at the mere promise of another kiss. Of another touch. Of him.

Our lips meet. Our tongues dance. Our bodies react.

"I like this part," he murmurs as one hand slides under the back of my shirt so that his fingers skim along the skin just above my waistband. He drugs me with his mouth. He entices me with his touch. He makes me anticipate with that groan in the back of his throat. "Luke's inside," he murmurs against my lips and rests his forehead against mine.

"And?"

"And what if he wakes up?"

"It seems you have eyes in the back of your head when it comes to him, so I think it would be perfectly fine if you kissed me."

"Like this?"

His lips possess mine. Thoroughly. Intoxicatingly.

"Just like that."

Thirty-Five

Sidney

THE BED IS HOT DESPITE THE COOL SHEETS AGAINST MY BARE skin.

The sun is bright through my eyelids.

When I stretch my arms overhead, I feel the tug of Grayson's hand against my side, pulling me in against his body, and the tempting hardness of him against my ass.

Good God, the man is like a drug. He can piss me off, cancel a date on me, test me on more levels than I'm used to, and yet, I still want more of him.

That's a scary thought.

I wiggle my ass against his crotch, which earns me a sleep-drugged groan and has his hand pulling me tighter into him.

Then there's the knock.

"*Dad?*"

The thought of sleepy morning sex goes out the damn window as Grayson jumps out of bed as if I've just poured a bucket of ice water on him.

"Oh fuck. Fuck. Fuck. Fuck," he says in a harsh whisper as his eyes widen and plead with me for what to do. "Just a second, buddy."

"Daddy? Why is the door locked?" The handle jiggles, and

Grayson walks over to open it and then realizes what he was just about to do and stops. He's gloriously naked and completely flustered.

"You can't be here," he whispers to me, his hand in his hair, his lips pressing into a stunned smile, and his dick flying at half-mast.

"But I am here—" He covers my mouth with his hand as we both try not to laugh as the handle jiggles again.

"Give me one second, Luke. I was uh—uh—just getting out of the shower."

"Yeah. So? I've seen you naked before."

I lick my tongue out between my lips against his hand, which is still firmly pressed over my mouth, and his eyes warn me to stop as his own chuckle falls from his mouth.

"I know, but, uh—" He moves the hand from my mouth and starts to pick up my clothes, which are strewn all over his floor, and throws them onto the bed beside me. "I'm all wet and don't want to get it on the floor."

"Are you talking to someone in there?" The jostling of the handle. "Is someone in there with you?"

"No. Of course not," he says in all seriousness while he fights the laughter before leaning forward and whispering in my ear. "Stay here. Be still. He'll leave for school in fifteen minutes then you can go. Be a good girl."

"But I'm not a good girl."

"Dad?"

"I know you aren't," he says, the heat of his breath making chills run down my spine. "But you're going to be for me." Then he presses a chaste kiss onto my lips that has my body begging for more. "If you are, then I'll reward you for it."

"So much for being a ninja," I say.

"Shush," he warns but snickers.

And with that, Grayson pulls on a pair of gym shorts before yanking the comforter over my head and patting me on the ass.

I hear the door to the bedroom open. "Good morning. Let's go downstairs and get some breakfast."

"I thought you were in the shower?" I can picture the curious look that Luke is giving Grayson, and that makes my having to remain still even harder. All I want to do is laugh.

"I was."

"Then how come your hair isn't wet?"

"I, uh, didn't wash my hair. You interrupted me."

I hear the click of the bedroom door closing and then Luke's muffled voice. "Why are you shutting the door? You never shut your door."

"I left my window open, and I don't want it to make the hall cold."

"But it wasn't cold in there."

"Luke . . ." Their voices fade down the hall, and after a few seconds, I throw the comforter off my head, stare at the ceiling, and use the pillow beside me to muffle my laugh.

I lie there for some time before I decide to get dressed. Should Luke venture back upstairs without Grayson or me realizing it, the last thing he needs to see is me naked in his dad's bed.

Once I'm dressed and cleaned up, I sit on the edge of the bed, staring at the locked door and listening to the sounds of normalcy down below. The scrape of plates. The teasing laughter. The responsible reminders about behaving at school.

This was what he was talking about last night when he said he lived in a well-loved home. I can feel the difference between here and my own apartment back in the city, which makes me wonder what waking up to this every day would be like.

The thought scares the shit out of me. I don't think this way. Grayson and I aren't that way. We're just sex. We're just lust.

And even I know I'm beyond feeling that way, but I repeat the mantra to myself anyway, so at least I can pretend I don't feel more for him than that.

Because I do.

When the door handle moves against the lock, I jump. "He's gone. I got him to walk with the neighbor and her son to school today. It's safe to come out now."

I open the door to see Grayson standing there. His hair is

disheveled, his shorts are slung low on his hips, and he has the most adorable smile on his lips.

"Oh. My. Fuck," he says as he walks past me and falls on his back onto the bed with a definite thump. "That was horrid and hilarious."

He looks up, and when our eyes meet, the laughter comes. Uncontrollable laughter that makes my sides ache and my cheeks hurt. We are both still grinning when he yanks my hand and pulls me on top of him, wraps his arms around me, and presses a kiss to the top of my head.

"Adventures of the pussy ninja," I say, and we erupt into another fit of laughter. When it subsides, I close my eyes and enjoy the feel of his body against mine. "I take it that doesn't happen that often."

"It never happens. No one ever gets to spend the night in my bed."

This has me laughing again, but it's a bit more forced as I freak out a little bit. I'm not certain if it's because I want to be the first person who he's let sleep in his bed, or if the fact it happened at all means I'm not alone in what I'm feeling. That things between us are a little more serious than I'm allowing myself to acknowledge.

My thoughts turn elsewhere when Grayson's hands begin to wander, and his lips begin to possess.

"I was a good girl."

"Mm-hmm," he says as he lifts my shirt up and traces a line down my lower belly as his other hand tugs down my shorts and panties. My legs spread. His tongue licks. My hands grip. "And now I'll reward you."

Thirty-Six

Grayson

THE THREE MEN IN SUITS SIT BEFORE ME WHILE I STAND. I HATE the way they stare at me in judgment, as if they haven't known me my whole life. I hate the way they handle this whole thing as if it's my fault, when they're the ones risking lives by grounding me.

"You're pretty sure of yourself, thinking you can take a five-million-dollar helicopter out during a thunderstorm on a call when you were advised against it. On top of that, you went and switched hospitals on your own accord when you'd been ordered otherwise," Mike says as he peers at me over the top of his bifocals with his bushy black hair moving as he nods his head.

I clear my throat. "I have to be sure of myself to do what I do, sir."

"Being sure of yourself and putting lives at risk are two completely different things." This time, it's the red-haired one who speaks. He was my little league coach once, but I don't think that piece of history will sway his vote either way.

"If it were your loved one I was trying to save, would it matter?"

He glares, my point more than made, and he doesn't like being shown up. "I'd like to think that it doesn't matter who the patient is. You put the lives of your crew and the patient at risk."

"I did. I left for the patient against Cochran's orders, but I didn't force anyone to go with me. My crew chose to fly with me, sir. Some opted not to. Others opted to assist. The patient was critical to begin with."

"And the helicopter? How would you cover the cost if it had crashed from a lightning strike?"

I'd be dead so I wouldn't be able to pay for shit. I reign in the words I want to spew and lower my eyes for a second and take a deep breath, knowing I need to eat a bit of humble pie to get my wings back. When I look back up, I meet the eyes of each of the three gentlemen before I speak. "Gentlemen, I realize I made an error. My months at dispatch have taught me there are rules and protocol for a reason. I understand that I took unnecessary risks. I also understand that the reason you have me as your pilot is because you know I'm good at what I do. You know that when it comes to our patients, they are who matter. I was monitoring the weather on a second-by-second basis and reevaluating our situation as needed. The air pressure was within acceptable parameters, and the helicopter's performance was not hindered during the flight."

The three of them look at one another, and there are a few whispers between them before they look back at me and the black-haired one speaks. "If you had the chance to do it all over again, would you still defy orders and take the helo on the call?"

Yes. Without a doubt.

"I've had an awful lot of time to think about this during my grounding, while I waited for the investigation to conclude, and I'd like to think that answer would be no." *Fuck you for telling me I shouldn't save a life.* "That I'd put the best interest of the company, its crew, and its property first and obey the order." *Smile big, Grayson.*

"That's good to hear, son," my old little league coach says.

I'm not your son.

"You have quite an impressive history with the company," the blond man, who hasn't spoken yet, says as he thumbs through a file in front of him. My file, no doubt. The one full of commendations and positive performance reviews.

"Thank you, sir."

"I'd like to see that history continue."

"Yes, sir."

I sound like a goddamn kiss-up, but I can't pay my bills with hopes and prayers. I need to get back up in the air.

"All of your crew speaks very highly of you."

I save my dignity and forgo speaking, so I just nod.

"Is there anything else you'd like to say?" the black haired one says.

"Flying. Saving lives. That is my passion. It's what I'm meant to do. I chose Mercy-Life because you are the best of the best. Just as I still am. None of that has changed. I'm anxious to get back to work again."

"We'll take that into consideration. If you'll give us some time and step out of the room, we need to confer, and then we'll call you back in once we have a decision."

"Thank you, Mom."

"Any particular reason why you want Luke to have a sleepover tonight?" Hope is in her voice, and I just chuckle. I know she thinks it's because of Sidney—and it is—she just doesn't need to know. "Because I'm going to have some drinks and celebrate that in two weeks' time, I get my wings back."

"You know this is a small town, right?"

"I'm painfully aware of that."

"It's just that if your truck were to be left out front of, say, someone in particular's house, people would know it's yours and would likely talk."

"No shit."

"I was just giving a friendly reminder of that. You told me that you were concerned about the appearance of impropriety when I brought Sidney to the mother-son picnic, so I was just—"

"No one said my truck was going to be parked in front of Sidney's place," I say just to rile her up. "And I was upset about you trying to orchestrate another Malone marriage."

"Oh shush, I know better than to start that with you," she dodges when I know damn well that was what she was attempting. "All I was saying is that it seems to me you're in a top position in this contest, so you wouldn't want anyone to think you won because you were . . . uh . . ."

"Sleeping with Sidney?" I throw it out there and grin like a little boy as I hear her cough to cover her tracks.

"Well, that's none of my business."

Like that has ever stopped her before. "No, but you were implying that I might just be headed over to Sidney's house to be a grown man and do whatever the hell I please without my mother sticking her nose in my business and fishing for information, correct?" I shake my head, love and irritation playing equal parts in my tone.

"Grayson." It's all she says, and I know I've got her flustered.

"Mom, I love you. Madly. I couldn't do this parenting thing without you . . . but my sex life is off-limits." I laugh when she stutters a response. "Good night, Mom. I'll grab Luke in the morning."

"Take your time."

When I end the call, I stare at the old Kraft house across the street. My words repeat in my head. *My sex life is off-limits.* Is that all this is? Because fuck if it doesn't feel different this go around. Fuck if the minute I got my clearance to return to work in two weeks, the first person I wanted to go tell was Sidney.

But why?

Why do I feel this way when, normally, a thought like that would cause a panic attack of epic proportions?

I glance at the white daisies in my hand and shake my head.

There is no going out with the crew tonight. There is no getting drunk to celebrate.

She's the one I want to celebrate with.

Thirty-Seven

Sidney

"GRAYSON!"

I'm thoroughly shocked to see him standing in my doorway. And I'm more than fully aware what an absolute train wreck I look like—no makeup, hair piled on top of my head, and definitely no red-soled shoes making me taller.

"Hey." It's all he says before he shoves a handful of white daisies at me and lifts his brows. "Miss Sidney, will you go out on a date with me?"

I laugh. I can't help it. He's giving me the same hopeful look that Luke had given me. "A date, huh?"

"It worked for Luke," he says as he steps into the foyer and I shut the door behind him. "I figured it might work for me, too."

"Oh really?" I murmur, letting him pull me close so he can brush a tender kiss on my lips.

"Yep. Is it working?" His smile is mischievous when he leans back.

"I'm not sure," I tease, prompting him to lean in for one more kiss. This one is longer, softer, toe-curling. "Yes, now that worked. A date, huh?"

"A date on my terms."

And there it is. The little reminder that as much as this *is*, it will never really *be*.

"Where are we going?"

"That's for me to know and for you to find out." Another tempting and tender kiss. "And completely off anyone's radar."

"Okay . . ." Excitement bubbles up. "What should I wear?"

"Dressier than what you're wearing, but not as formal as you normally wear." He shrugs as I take the daisies and bury my nose in them. Other than Luke, I can't remember the last time a man brought me flowers. It seems as if the Malones are just a bunch of charmers.

"That isn't a lot of help."

"Jeans, but it's a shame to cover up those legs of yours," he murmurs as his eyes darken and run the length of my body in pure male appreciation that make this female feel desired. "Shirt, unless you want to walk around without one. I mean, I have absolutely no problem with that one." He winks.

"Funny."

"Always. And a jacket."

"A jacket? It's hot out tonight."

"Not where we're going, it isn't."

The past hour has gone by in a blur.

Sneaking out to Grayson's truck under the cover of night. The unexplained trek across town and out to Miner's Airfield. The shock that bled to nervousness when he pulled next to an airport hangar and explained to me he was flying me to our date in his friend's helicopter.

Flying me.

Not a driving me through the country, not a walking me through a park, but a flying me . . . in a helicopter date.

Despite the nerves edging my laugh when he told me, I find myself calming some as Grayson straps my belts and adjusts my headset so I can hear him. Once we're in the air and he's maneuvering us through the dark night, I find myself completely at ease as I look out over the small towns with their glimmering lights.

"Off the radar, huh?" I ask as my stomach flops back into place when the landing skids touch down to the ground.

"You caught that?" he says, flashing me a grin before turning back to all of the instruments he's flipping and switching as the rotors overhead begin to wind down.

"Very clever."

He removes his headset and then mine before leaning forward and pressing a kiss to my lips. "You ain't seen nothing yet," he murmurs.

He's right. I haven't. Because when the rotors stop and he helps me from the helicopter and to the place he found, strictly by the light of the moon, my breath catches. We're standing on a huge plateau on a mountaintop that overlooks the whole of Napa Valley below us.

He leaves me for a moment to enjoy the utterly astonishing view while he collects a few things from the helicopter. And within no time at all, we are relaxing with a blanket beneath us, a bottle of wine breathing next to us, and a comfortable silence between us.

"Napa, huh? You fly away from *our* own Sunnyville wine country to the one that rivals ours?" I tease as his fingertips draw feather-light lines up and down the length of my spine.

"Well, I'm not a fan of the people who own the majority of our vineyards. Since the Hoskins are that majority, they kind of took its beauty away when everything happened with Claire."

He falls silent, and I instantly regret my question and the grief it brings him. The unimaginable heartbreak he must have endured raising a baby and losing the woman he loved. Learning that it's, in fact, money that makes the world go 'round and not love.

"It must have been hard in those early days. Figuring out fatherhood. Dealing with it all."

"You have no idea. It felt like I was cemented to the bottom of a well that was filling with water. Work saved me, while at the same time, it also terrified me. Every second I was away from Luke, I worried that he thought he'd been abandoned by his other parent, too."

"He knows you love him and would never leave him."

"He does, but knowing that never stopped me from worrying."

"Speaking of worrying, do you ever fear that Claire will realize what a huge mistake she made and change her mind? That she'll come back and want to see Luke?"

"I fear that every single goddamn day . . . but even if she did, she signed away her rights—forever, without recourse, so she can ask all she wants but there's not a chance in hell I'd let her see him."

"So that's why you're so quiet about it."

"I'm quiet about it because it almost broke me in every way imaginable, and I had to make a conscious effort to let it go and move on. If not, it would have slowly killed me."

"You're a better person than I am. I would have told everybody in town so they knew her true colors."

"I wanted to . . . but what good would that do me other than hurt Luke when he's older? You know this town. You know how people like to talk. He'd find out somehow. Besides, I agreed to sign an NDA—protect their precious reputation—which allowed me to make a clean break and have a new start without any of their strings attached."

"You know, I still can't wrap my head around how you've managed to work your ass off to provide for Luke—make a life for the two of you—and still seem so positive about everything. It has to be hard, living in the town in which they own at least some part of everything you look at."

"We're doing just fine." I can see pride war across his face. "I could have left town, but that would have meant leaving my family. Having them be a part of Luke's life is more important than my wounded ego."

I keep my eyes focused on the valley below but reach over and link my fingers with his in a show of silent support.

"Hey, Sid?"

"Mm-hmm?"

"I appreciate you caring and wanting to know about how this all affected me, but this is our date night. What do you say we stop talking about Claire and what happened? I have Luke. He's a good kid. We'll be fine. Besides, men aren't too keen on talking about their shortcomings."

"Grayson, you did nothing wrong—"

My words are cut off when he leans over and kisses me. "Stop talking."

"Only if you'll keep kissing me."

"Now that? That I can do." He extends the kiss a little longer, a little deeper, a lot more satisfying. "Life is good right now. I'm getting my wings back shortly. Luke had a great report card. And I'm up here on a moonlit mountain with a beautiful woman. There are definitely no complaints here," he murmurs before pressing his lips to mine again.

When he stops, I rest my head on his shoulder, and we fall silent as we stare at the view and wonder what in the hell this is between us.

Or at least, I do.

"We were sidetracked."

"That's putting it mildly," he says through a chuckle. "I can sidetrack you some more if you'd like."

"Definitely, but first, tell me how you know about this place. And how do you know they're cool with you landing here?"

He takes our linked hands and presses a kiss to the top of mine as if it were a normal thing. Something about the action steals my breath and makes me take pause. So much so that I miss the first part of what he's saying.

"The guy is a family friend and this is his family's land. They use it for corporate functions, weddings, and stuff like that. They own a helicopter company that takes tourists around, and they also shuttle corporate executives between here and San Francisco or Los Angeles."

"It feels like we're on top of the world up here."

"It does. I'm surprised you weren't scared about me taking you up."

"I hid it well," I say with a laugh. "But you seem very competent."

"Just competent? Not incredible or mind blowing?" He chuckles.

"We are talking about flying, right?" I ask and squirm out of the way when he reaches out to tickle me. Unfortunately, in my scramble to get away from him, I knock over the bottle of wine, which he saves before too much spills. "My hero. Grayson Malone is my hero!" I shout to the hundreds of lights twinkling in the valley below.

"Don't even start that hero crap again," he says, but he's laughing right along with me.

"Oh, Mr. Malone, you are such a hero," I continue.

"Says the defiant damsel." He hands me a glass and begins to fill it with the almost spilled wine. "Scratch that—says the queen manipulator."

"It was all Rissa," I refute as I take a sip.

"Uh-huh. I'm not buying that for a second."

"It was, I swear. I told her you were the one who was going to win the contest. She has her sights on another guy. She decided to plant a few stories in the *Gazette*—against my knowledge, I might add—to make sure it was a 'fair fight.'"

"She doesn't think I can win?"

"Not against her man," I say, realizing I'm spurring on the competitive side of the man next to me.

"Bullshit," he snorts, and it makes me laugh. "*Rissa*? It was seriously Rissa who set all this shit up?"

"The article. The hero party. Not my idea." His eyes find mine through the moonlit darkness. "Now you have no reason to be mad at me, right? Your brothers signed you up, and she egged it on."

"You're far from innocent, Thorton."

"Only in all the right ways." That earns me a pinch on my side. "For a man who takes risks for a living, though, you should learn to be a little more comfortable being called a hero."

"Whatever." He takes a drink of his Coke and leans back on one hand.

"Tell me about the High Sierras."

"They're a mountain range in California," he says drolly.

"No shit." A part of me loves that he helps without wanting the attention, but I want to hear this story for me, not because I want to use it for votes. "What about the hikers you rescued?"

He looks over to me with an angle to his head and a sudden shyness in his expression. "Who said I rescued any hikers?"

"C'mon. Everyone knows it was you, why are you too shy to talk about it?"

"I don't rescue people to get accolades."

"No one said you did." I can't figure out why he's so cagey about responding.

"Anything I tell you is off the record, right? No telling Rissa so she can call the *Gazette*."

"This whole date is off the record."

His smile spreads across his lips and warms so many parts of me. "I don't talk about it because it was stupid on my part." His voice lowers, his eyes soften.

"I would hardly say that saving a whole family is stupid."

"Yeah, but I could have ruined lives, too. I took off, thinking only about Luke. Thinking about how, if that were my son, I'd move heaven and earth to find him and save him. It wasn't until I was in the air and the chopper pitched and swayed that I realized how goddamn stupid I was. That I was risking my life and could very well end up leaving Luke fatherless. It was a stupid move. Just too risky."

"And, yet, you did it again, and it got you grounded."

He falls silent and shifts to meet my eyes. "If someone needs help, I have a hard time turning my back."

"And that's why you're good at your job."

"Like I said, I take too many risks."

"Not all risks are bad things."

Thirty-Eight

Grayson

IT HAS TO BE THE DAMN MOONLIGHT IN HER HAIR.

Or the high altitude.

But every time I look at her, I think that this is too perfect. That this feels too real. That she makes me feel way too comfortable.

Then I tell myself to step back from the ledge. That I'm only allowing myself to think shit like that because of the night and the moon and I'm fucking thrilled to be getting back in the air.

Good things.

Positive things.

Things that make me wonder if the woman sitting next to me is too good to be true.

"Thank you for bringing me up here," she murmurs, her lips pressed against my bare chest. Her tits are warm against my body, her thigh hooked over mine as if we are casually lying in a bed instead of on a mountaintop in a field of wispy grass.

Who knew uptown Sidney would have been okay with that?

Maybe I was testing her to see her reaction. Could she handle my flying? Would she trust me? Would she be okay coming to one of my favorite spots in the world?

She passed with flying colors, but now what? What other tests could I possibly ply her with to prove she isn't Claire? When do I stop and just trust that she isn't?

Sabotage is never pretty when you're trying to do it to something good.

"Earth to Grayson?"

"Sorry. I was just thinking." I shake my head and meet her eyes.

"I thought I just sexed you up so good that you couldn't think."

"Ah, you're right. Maybe I should call you the dick ninja."

She bursts out laughing, and the sound of it shakes the negative thoughts from my mind. Christ. I can't even enjoy an evening without throwing my past in my own face to screw it up.

"The dick ninja. I like that."

"Those words sound so funny coming from you, the prim and proper Sidney Thorton."

"I don't think anything that I just did to you was very prim or proper."

"Mm." It's all I can say as my mind relives every lick of her tongue and suck of her mouth over my cock. The way my hand held on to the back of her head, silently begging for her to let me shoot down the back of her throat. But, of course, she had other plans.

Like riding me into oblivion, her tits on perfect display as she ground back and forth on my cock. The way her lips parted. The way her hands ran over her nipples and she pinched them between her fingers. The way she screamed as she came, her pussy pulsing around my dick and milking my own orgasm out of me.

Prim and proper. Definitely not what comes to mind with the sex spell she just drugged me with.

"Mmm?" she asks.

"Shh. Quiet," I say as I pat her on the ass. "I was just remembering it play by play."

"I guess I didn't do a good enough job knocking you into a sex coma, then."

"Either that or it was so good that I can't stop thinking about it."

"Nice recovery."

"Not quite yet, but I'll be good to go in a bit."

"Aren't you the cheeky one?" she says as I squeeze her ass cheek, which is centered in the palm of my hand.

"Thank you for coming with me, Sidney."

"Ha, that is one thing I *definitely* just did." The husky sound to her voice makes my dick want to stir to life, but it's spent. She just worked me every which way, and I want to save my energy for round two once we get back down from here.

I'm not ready to move yet. There's something comforting about the way she has her head on my chest and traces lines over my skin. About the way I'm so damn at ease with her I could fall asleep with her in my arms. About how we can be here like this, enjoy the moment, each other, and she doesn't feel the need to fill the silence with endless chatter.

It takes a few minutes for those thoughts to really sink in. When they do, when I realize I'm wondering if this is how things would be between us if we did this on a more regular basis—if people were allowed to know we were seeing each other . . . if I let Luke know we were seeing each other—I tell myself we need to get going. We need to get up so the feel of her body against mine stops filling my head with shit that can't be.

That isn't possible.

But I don't move. I just press a kiss to her head and breathe her in as I run my fingers through her hair. I tell myself to enjoy not having to worry about picking up Luke or not skipping out after sex to get home so Luke doesn't know.

"Are you sure we have to go back?" she groans.

"Only after you drink the rest of this wine."

"You sure you don't want any? I feel like a lush drinking this whole bottle myself."

"No drinking and flying for me, but"—I sit up and slide out from under her—"we could always continue this back at one of our places if you'd like."

"Really?" She draws the word out, and even though I don't look back at her, I can picture the suggestive smile that's toying at the corners of those gorgeous lips of hers.

"Really. Luke's with my parents until tomorrow."

"So maybe you should bring me back down to earth," she says through a laugh, "so you can take me back to heaven again."

My laugh echoes in the empty space around us as her lips press a kiss onto my shoulder.

It seems as if that simple action allows Sidney Thorton to slip into my life in a way I never saw coming. In a way I never wanted. In a way I'm not sure I'll be able to give up.

Nor do I even want to think about it.

Christ.

I'm in deep, aren't I?

Thirty-Nine

Sidney

Grayson: I've been thinking about you all day.

I look down at the text and smile before turning my attention back to Rissa and our plans for how we're going to end this round of voting and move on to the top five.

"So, I think we close it out and then maybe take the next week and announce one of the finalists each day. Give little tidbits about each of them, make readers like them more, just have fun with it."

My phone beeps again with another text, and I bite back the new grin trying to form on my lips. Rissa only huffs, eyeing my phone with annoyance. "Sorry, let me turn my ringer off."

And then I have to feign nonchalance when I look down at my phone and find another text.

Grayson: My dick is rock hard, and it's you I'm imagining. It's in my hand when I'd rather it be in your mouth with my fingers in your pussy, working you into a frenzy.

"Is everything okay?" Rissa asks, making me realize I must have made a noise when I read the text. "You look startled."

I glance back at the text again and shake my head while every part of my body comes to life. "Yeah, it's, uh, fine."

"Your ringer." Her brows are lifted as she glances to my phone and then back to me.

"*My finger*?" I squeak, thinking she saw the phone screen.

"Ringer. Sound on your phone."

"Oh, yes . . . sorry." Flustered, I fumble with my cell, and before I can even switch it off, another text alert pings.

Grayson: I want to bend you over and watch as my cock slides in and out of you.

"So back to next week . . ."

"Yes," I swallow over the desire lodged in every place it should be and try not to glance at my phone as it vibrates again.

"Are you good with that plan?" Rissa asks as I shift in my seat to abate the sudden ache burning brighter than bright.

"Yes. Sure. I think that sounds like a great plan."

Grayson: I want my cock buried so deep that you feel every damn inch of me.

"Are you sure you're okay?"

"Yeah, why?" My voice breaks like a prepubescent teenager.

Grayson: I want you to come so hard you have to bite the pillow.

"You look a little flushed. Are you coming down with something?"

Grayson: You always have a choice. Isn't that what you said to me once? Make a choice, Sidney. Isn't it time to head to lunch?

"I mean, yeah, maybe." I pull at my collar some. "Maybe that's why I feel so flushed all of a sudden."

Grayson: Meet me on the backside of The Cottages. Room Six. Fifteen minutes.

"Either that," she says as she stands and heads to the door, only turning back to give me a wink, "or you're guilty as hell. Maybe you should go take care of that itch texting you . . . or take some Tylenol. Whichever one it is, I think you should take the afternoon off."

Grayson: Choose me.

"Oh." It's the only thing I can think to say because my brain is otherwise occupied imagining Grayson following through on his promises.

"And, Sid?"

"Yeah?"

"I sure hope he's every bit worth breaking the rules." She winks. "It's about damn time. Your secret is safe with me."

I rush out of the office, embarrassed but horny as hell, and park in the central lot that sits squarely in town. Trying to be as inconspicuous as possible, I walk around the block a few times before I figure the best way to get to the back side of The Cottages, which is a local bed and breakfast.

For some stupid reason, I'm nervous when I see the number six on the door of the only cottage that seems to have complete privacy. Is it because going to a hotel room in the middle of the day for sex is weird, or is it because it's hotter than hell?

Judging by how damp my panties are, I'm betting on the latter.

I take a deep breath and knock on the door. When it opens, Grayson is standing there buck naked in all his glory. His dick is rock-hard and is more than demanding my attention.

"Nice choice." He lifts his eyebrows and a ghost of a smile is on his lips.

"It's always the quiet ones you have to worry about," I murmur when our eyes meet and speak a million greetings as I step into the darkened room without any hesitation.

The minute the door is shut, he says, "Take your clothes off."

Unable to speak, I do exactly as he demands. I remove every single item of clothing, one by one, as our eyes hold and his hand strokes ever so gently over the shaft of his cock.

When I'm done, our lips meet in a kiss that is so contradictory to the moment it's staggering. It's soft and tender while our hands are greedy and desperate as they roam over each other's bodies.

"You distracted me at work," I murmur between kisses.

"That was my plan." Another kiss. A nip to my lip. "And I'm about to distract you again." He turns me around and laces a row of open mouth kisses over the slopes of my shoulders before using his hand to push my back forward. "Bend over."

I obey without a fight—probably the only time I ever have in this casual sort of relationship we have. I tell myself that the only reason I do so is because I know just how well Grayson Malone can give it.

I bend over the edge of the bed and prop myself up on my elbows. There is silence for a brief second, which has my every nerve high on anticipation. The texts were foreplay enough. I already want him. I'm already more than wet for him, but I startle when his hands rest on my ass and squeeze.

That action is followed by him burying his nose into my slit and taking one long slide of his tongue from my entrance back up. My breath catches. Every muscle affected by the lick of his tongue tightens in anticipation. *Every part of me wants.*

"I'm going to fuck you, Sidney." Another lick. "I'm going to bury my cock in this tight pussy of yours." His breath hot against my tender flesh. "Then I'm going to slip my finger into your ass." The soft press of his thumb against my rim of muscles. "I'm going to fuck you with both so that when you come, every single damn part of you does." The slide of his tongue into my pussy so that every part of his face is buried against me. "Do you understand?"

I nod, the dark promise of his words an aphrodisiac poured on top of the seduction he's already plied me with.

"Uh-uh-uh," he murmurs as he fists my hair in his hand and gently pulls my head back as he runs the tip of his nose up the length of my spine. His finger slips into me just as his mouth reaches my ear and his dick presses against my thigh. "No nods." He works his fingers in and out of me, the sound of how wet I am filling the room. "No easy way out." They slide back out and the trace of his coated fingertip travels up the crease of my ass and then down. "I want you to make a noise, Princess." The tug of his teeth on my ear as his fingers tuck back in and curve against my G-spot. "I want you to scream." A soft tug of my hair. "And I want to know you know who's making you scream."

Jesus. I could come from the dominance in his voice alone.

"Yes, Grayson," I say as I push my ass back toward him and prepare myself for the pleasure.

"Good." The heat of his breath hits my ear as his fingers slip out of me. "Mmm, you taste so fucking good." My breath picks up, and the only part of him touching me is the promise of his cock between my thighs, just at my entrance. Another gentle pull of my hair, this time he turns my face some so he can slip his fingers between my lips. "Suck."

I taste myself on him. I wrap my tongue around him and suck as hard as I can. His groan fills the room as I do so, and then it takes everything I have not to bite his fingers when he leaves them there as he thrusts his hips forward and fills me completely.

"Take it," he murmurs as he grinds his hips against my ass so that I buck and writhe and beg for him to move again. To manipulate those nerves again. To make me come like he promised.

"God, yes," I finally say when he slips his fingers from my lips and slowly pulls out before slamming back into me again. My hands grip the sheets as his hands grab the globes of my ass and spread them apart so he can watch as he fucks me.

Thrust after pleasure-inducing thrust, and with each one, my breasts jolt forward and brush against the comforter beneath me. It teases my nipples, which are, aroused to the point of being painful, but the sensation only seems to add to the whole of it.

"Sid," he moans as he bottoms out and grinds into me at the same time I feel pressure on the rim of muscles.

"Yes," I pant as I grow even wetter at the thought of sharing this with him. Of giving this to him.

He holds still as his finger presses ever so slowly into me. There's resistance at first. A slight burn of pain. When the moment passes, and he begins to move his cock as his finger moves ever so gently in and out of my ass, my pleasure center is stretched to maximum capacity.

I want him to stop. I want him to never stop. I want him to take every ounce of bliss he's giving me and somehow get it in return . . . but I can't speak. I can only feel. I can only react. I can only let him take whatever it is he needs from me.

And I know when he does. I know when he's done being the considerate lover and the strings of his restraint have snapped.

The current in the room shifts.

Grayson picks up the pace.

There is nothing gentle about him anymore. There is no sweet touch or tender affirmations. There is pure dominance. A side to him he's hinted at but has never really shown me before.

This woman is definitely not going to complain.

While he is relentless in the pursuit of our orgasms, bringing me to the brink and then edging me down so I don't come before he wants me to, there is something different about today.

Something shifts between us.

I can't quite put my finger on it, but I can feel it when he kisses me goodbye.

I can hear it in the tone of his voice when he says he'll call me later.

I can see it in the look in his eyes as he shuts the door behind me.

I think about it all the way home and still can't figure it out. Maybe I don't want to.

All I know is that Grayson Malone just pulled the most classic display of "this is casual sex," I'd ever seen.

It was just a display, though.

Because what we just did was so much more than casual. It was intimate and tender and demanding and so many things, and I'm not sure what the hell to think about that other than wanting more.

Forty

Sidney

"SO, LET ME GET THIS STRAIGHT. THE MALONE GUY—THE contestant from your hometown who you kind of remember from high school but don't—is the one you've been sleeping with?" Zoey asks. We are at a small table in the back of the Greer Vineyard's tasting room, and even though there aren't many people around, I'm tempted to shush her.

"For the fifth time, yes, yes, and more yes." I take another sip of wine, hoping this will be the end of it but knowing this is only the beginning.

"But you neglected to tell me the man you were sleeping with and hot pilot boy were one and the same. Why?"

"It slipped my mind."

"Ha." She laughs. "More like he slipped into you and you forgot your mind."

"Well . . . can you blame me?"

"But you're sneaking around doing the whole clandestine lovers thing why?"

My mind goes back to last week. To the naughty texts and the sexcapade at The Cottage. And then I realize how much I've missed him since he started back to working his twenty-four-hour shifts.

Texting is fun, but it definitely isn't the real thing.

"Work. My dad. The appearance of impropriety that I'm sleeping with the contestant who is currently winning the contest," I finally say when I realize I haven't responded.

She gives me a sour look and lifts her brows. "So, the small-town gossip you told people was a total lie really wasn't?"

"No. Some of it is a lie. Do you see a ring on this finger? Do you see me engaged?"

"You know I'd kick your ass if you were hiding that from me, right?" she asks as I avert my eyes and look around again. "Wait. You don't want that, do you?" The expression on her face—raised brows, lax jaw, wide eyes—looks just like the shock in her tone.

"No! Of course not," I say and shake my head like she's crazy. "We've only been seeing each other a couple of months and—"

"And your parents dated for what? Three months before they got married and are now going on forty years of wedded bliss."

"You're crazy." I laugh and take a sip of wine to quell the mini panic attack her words just brought on as I envisioned Grayson in a tuxedo, standing at the end of an aisle, waiting for me to walk to him.

"Okay, so then why are you being so secretive about him with me? Why did I not even know there was a thing? And more importantly, why are you overthinking this? If he's a wham-bam, oh-hot-damn type of guy, then enjoy the bam and the wham and scream hot *damn* before walking away when it's done."

"God, it's good to see you, Zoey." I missed her hard-hitting, no-nonsense, I'm-going-to-call-you-on-your-bullshit attitude.

I need it to clear the fog in my mind and stop the things in my heart that I don't want to feel but do.

"I know. I've missed the hell out of you. I feel like I've lost my left arm without you near, and being one handed is kind of hard, which is why I came here to surprise you. I'm also the one who keeps you honest, so give me answers or else I'll ply you with more wine to get you drunk so you'll talk."

"Funny."

"It isn't like I haven't done it before," she says and takes a sip of her merlot.

I know she's serious, so I sigh, take a sip of my wine, and then glance around to see who's nearby.

She angles her head to the side and stares at me. "Your hesitation speaks volumes here, Sid."

"I'm not hesitating on shit."

She clears her throat. "And I'm the Virgin Mary."

"You didn't ask me anything to answer."

"Exactly. Normally, you talk a million miles a minute, and right now, you're zipped up tighter than a whore in church. What is it? Talk to me."

"Nothing," I murmur, when it's actually everything. She knows me well enough to read my mind and ask the questions that need to be asked when I don't want her asking any of them. I just might have to face the truth if I answer them.

"You really like this guy, don't you?"

"Yeah, I do." There's no shame in admitting that, right?

"*But?*"

I pinch the bridge of my nose and wonder how this conversation, which was supposed to be light and fun because we were celebrating my friend being in town, turned real and serious.

"Where do I start? He has commitment issues, and that bothers me even though I don't want a commitment. He has a kid, and I've never been good with children. He lives here, and I'm leaving as soon as the contest is over. The list goes on and on . . ."

"Everyone has commitment issues until they don't. That's just a fact of life. Sometimes it takes the right person to make you see through your fear. He has a kid." She shrugs. "Lots of people have kids."

"You know me. I'm unstable. I like to flit around from place to place on my time off. I never really have a steady guy because that comes with strings and strings tie you down."

"And sometimes strings are meant to hold you back from running in the wrong direction." She takes another sip of her wine and eyes me above the rim. "And the fact that you'll be leaving town soon . . . I can't help you with that one. What does he say about it?" I just stare at her. "You haven't told him, have you?"

I hesitate. "It didn't really matter because we weren't really any-thing . . . and then, all the sudden, it feels like we are something, but now that it does, I don't know how to say it."

Her eyes warm with compassion as she shakes her head. "You need to tell him."

"I know."

We both fall silent as she angles her head and studies me. "He makes you happy. It's written all over your face."

"How do you know it's because of him?" I play devil's advocate, never wanting my happiness to be solely dependent upon a man.

"Fine. I'll rephrase. You're different—in a good way—and I know it isn't this Podunk town doing it to you, so it has to be him *doing you* in this Podunk town."

I know I'm beet-red by the time she finally shuts up, and I wave a hand at her. "Will you please stop being so loud? The natives will chase you with pitchforks if you talk ill of their beloved town like that."

"It isn't San Francisco, but is it really that terrible?"

I twist my lips as I stare at her, and then smile as I realize that it isn't. With as much as I've complained to myself about the lack of nightlife, this town has grown on me. More than I expected it to. "You know what? It really isn't. It's quaint and other than the gossip column that I can't seem to keep my name out of, the people are nice, the at-mosphere is laid back—"

"And there is wine. Lots and lots of wine." She laughs and then drains her glass as my own lips pull into a small frown. We're talking about this—about me—as if I'm staying here, which isn't an option. What's worse is that we are talking about it and I'm not freaking out about it. "The upside is you're still you in every other sense. Still as fashion-forward as ever in your Louboutins. I was a little afraid I was going to find you in mom jeans and Crocs."

"What?" I laugh, drawing some attention from those around us. No doubt, some of those people are actually wearing mom jeans and Crocs.

"I'm happy to report that we are both the most stylish people in this joint," she says with a dismissive wave of her hand.

"Well, you don't have to worry about it rubbing off on me, because this? My being here? Is not a long-term thing."

And why does saying that cause my chest to constrict?

I think of the lunch delivered to my office anonymously. The unexpected knock on my door one night when Luke stayed over at a friend's house. A surprise invite to go hunt for tadpoles with them for Luke's school project that I swore was gross but ended up laughing until my sides hurt. Late nights on the phone until we fell asleep with the connection still open. The two bouquets of dried daisies that each of the Malones gave me, which are well past dead but I can't bring myself to throw out.

"Uh-huh." She draws the word out as if she doesn't believe it. "You just keep telling yourself that, and maybe you'll start to believe it."

Forty-One

Grayson

"GOD, I MISSED THIS," I SAY INTO THE MICROPHONE angled in front of my mouth.

"The adrenaline is like a drug."

"Damn straight." I look over at Devon and nod as the rotors reach speed, then I pull back the collective and the chopper lifts off the ground.

"It's as if everyone was waiting for you to come back to have an accident or something," he says with a laugh as he runs over the switches to check their positions.

"No shit. It's one call after another today," I say as the heaviness of the sleepless night is swept away by the adrenaline coursing through my veins as I clear the landing zone.

"MVC. Drunk driver in a truck head-on with a mini-van. Patient is a two-year-old female thrown from vehicle. Ambulance ETA to landing site ten minutes."

"Christ," I mutter.

This is what I don't miss.

The frailty of life.

The fear that in the few extra seconds it takes me to make sure there are no power lines, make sure I can land safely, might be the difference between life and death.

"This is Mercy 445. Ten-four. Our ETA is eight minutes and counting," I say.

God, please let the little girl hold on.

☙❧

Exhaustion takes hold.

I can barely keep my eyes open as other patrons drone on around us in the Better Buzz, but I'm doing everything I can to be present for Luke.

"Did you have a lot of calls last night, Dad?" he asks as I pour creamer into my coffee and shake the exhaustion from my brain.

"A lot," I say, realizing how hard it is to get back into the swing of things after being off for so long.

"Did you save them all?" he asks as if we hadn't missed a step in our routine.

"Not sure yet, buddy." I wrap an arm around his shoulders and squeeze. "Some are still getting help from doctors." My mind pulls to the little girl who was ejected from a car seat, which had been strapped in wrong. To the faces of her parents as they stood outside the helicopter and watched their world being taken away, trusting in me to get her to General so she had a chance.

"Okay. I'll say prayers for them tonight to help them get better."

"I'm sure they'd appreciate that, bud."

"Looking good, Malone," a voice rings out across the shop, and I turn to her with a tired smile.

"Hey, Desi." I pull my sister-in-law's best friend, now turned family friend, in for a hug.

"Are you trying to make every woman in here salivate at your hotness? You really should ditch the flight suit before you leave work if you hope to have a chance of making it home. You'll end up having to resuscitate all the women fainting over you."

"Good to see you, too." I laugh.

"Hey, Luke." She ruffles his hair and talks with him for a moment. I look up and am startled to see Sidney on the other side of the street. I shouldn't be. I see her in passing all the time. Usually, we just wave to each other and pretend not to be together, and yet something about seeing her now pulls at me.

"Give me a sec," I say absently as I walk toward the window and watch.

Yep, that's her, all right. She's with another woman with jet-black hair that is pulled back in some kind of fancy knot. They are both dressed alike—heels, skirts, button-up blouses. They both are carrying shopping bags galore from some of the boutique shops in town.

They also both look like they don't belong anywhere near Sunnyville. They stand out like an anomaly. Sidney, with her dirty blonde colored hair and brown eyes and legs for days, looks like the picture of California, but one where there are stars on the avenue instead of vines on the hills.

It's a stark reminder of how different our lives are. She's more like Claire than either of us wants to admit, and I'll always be me. A Malone.

I've been coasting along with this . . . whatever this is . . . telling myself that we could make this work, that she could be content here. Seeing her like this—looking so out of her element, has the realization that I've been lying to myself fall like an anvil onto my chest.

The pressure from it is debilitating.

I stand squarely in the picture window of Better Buzz and just stare. Somehow, some way, she senses me. Her feet falter. Her head turns. Our eyes meet.

She smiles.

Waves.

I may be staring at her, but I don't acknowledge her in the least. I can't. I've already gotten too close, when I've been convincing myself that I've kept her at arm's length.

So I don't nod. I don't smile. I don't react at all. Instead, I turn my back and walk deeper into the coffee shop, to where Desi and Luke are laughing. To where I can bury my thoughts. To where I can get mad at myself for even thinking I could let anything more happen between us.

Over the last few weeks, I'd allowed those thoughts—those ideas, possibilities, *emotions*—to creep in.

Seeing her on the street was a solid one-two punch to the gut, reminding me why shit like that can't be.

Fuck this. Fuck Sidney. Fuck her looking just like Claire with that air about her that screams money and privilege and everything that doesn't want someone like me.

In the back of my mind, I know I'm being a dick. I know she can't help but be herself . . . the woman who has invaded my life without warning. But the sting of my past, the feeling of déjà vu, is real and raw and tattooed in invisible ink. It's a scar on my heart I can't fucking get rid of.

One she doesn't deserve to have to deal with.

One I'm hiding behind instead of facing the truth.

I'm fucking falling for her.

Desi looks up and smiles at me as I sit across from them, but her smile freezes and her eyes narrow when she looks closer.

"You okay?"

"Yep."

I'm perfectly fucking fine.

Wait. Actually, I'm far from it.

She stares at me a bit longer, not believing me, and then saves my ass from having to pretend with Luke by turning her attention back to him.

I watch them joke, build a castle out of sugar packets, and have a staring contest. I've never been more grateful for her and her quirky sense of humor.

Because seeing Sidney like that—looking so much like Claire— brought me right back to that time, to the night Claire came home.

Luke was four months old—crying any time you set him down or moved the wrong way or God for-fucking-bid breathed the wrong way. She walked in the door drunk. I'll never forget that. The look on her face. The smear of her mascara down her cheeks. The shame in her eyes.

Our fights had been more frequent. I chalked it up to having a newborn—a colicky one at that. It was why I wasn't upset that she had gone out. She needed space, time to think and decompress.

"I have something I need to tell you." Her words were slurred, her eyes averted.

"I don't care that you went out. I know he gets to be overwhelming with the crying, but it's a phase. It's all just a phase." I reiterated the same calming words my mom had told me when I had called her out of desperation.

"It isn't a phase," she said softly. "It's a life sentence."

"How can you say that?" I looked down at Luke, the life we'd created. He was a little bit of perfection in such a fucked-up world, and I was unable to comprehend how she couldn't see it.

"I can't do this, Gray. This isn't me."

My laugh must have sounded so ridiculous to her, but it was all I could give above Luke's crying. "I know we're young and don't have much, Claire, but—"

"That's exactly it. We don't have anything!" she shouted, and I paused in the bounce, bounce, shift rhythm that usually calmed Luke.

"Your parents got to you again, didn't they?" I shake my head and try to move toward her without upsetting Luke, but she won't look at me. "This is all we need, Claire. Us. Luke."

"I need more than that." Her voice was barely a whisper, but every single syllable was like a nail being driven into my heart. It was then that I knew . . . I knew they had won. I knew she had gotten drunk so she'd have the courage to tell me. I knew she was leaving.

I knew, in her mind, she'd already left.

Luke started crying again. I wanted to put him down so I could beg and plead with her, but I couldn't do that to him. I couldn't abandon him when I already knew one parent was going to.

"Claire-bear—"

"Don't." Her hand came up as she squeezed her eyes closed for a second. "Fuck. Don't call me that."

"Don't you love me? Don't you love us?" Fear was all I could hear in my own voice. Fear rioted in my veins. "Don't you love *him*?"

"I just don't know anymore."

"Yes, you do!" My shout was loud enough that the windows in our tiny apartment rattled as my chest constricted. I couldn't seem to breathe.

"I'll have my attorney draft up something—"

"You mean your parents' attorney."

"Yes." Still no eye contact. Still absolutely zero acknowledgment of our son.

"You've told them to fuck off a million times. Rebelled when you dated me because I wasn't part of your cotillion bullshit. What's so different now? What changed?" Confusion owned every part of me.

"There's a way to give up all my rights. It's called voluntary relinquishment of rights."

"You know the term?" I shout. "You've already done it, haven't you?"

"I'll sign the paperwork so you don't ever have to worry about me coming back for him." Her voice . . . God, her fucking voice was so devoid of emotion it made me want to scream and give up at the same time. The Hoskins' brainwashing had finally worked.

"How can you do this? Look at him! Look. At. Him." She lifted her eyes and took him in, her bottom lip quivering before she stared me dead in the eyes.

"It's the money, isn't it?"

"It's a lot of things, Gray."

"They finally threatened your trust fund?" Her lack of an answer was the only answer I needed. Fear turned to anger. Anger to rage. Rage to hysteria. "Get the fuck out! Our son—*MY SON* is worth more than any goddamn bank account."

The first tear leaked over her eyelashes and slid along the mascara track that was already on her cheek. She had cried for someone else but could barely muster a fucking tear for us. She didn't bother to brush it away. She just stared at me with regret and a sadness that to this day, I have never been able to fathom. How could money be more important than your own flesh and blood?

"One of these days, Claire, you're going to look in the mirror and realize you're a selfish piece of shit. You're going to want to know *my* son. Don't bother knocking on that door because I'd rather die than let you see what an incredible person he's going to be. I'll make damn sure of it."

She didn't react. Didn't fucking care.

All I know is that when she turned her back and left without so much as a second glance at her son, I cried more than he did that night. And for more nights than I cared to remember, I fell asleep in a bed she bought, under a comforter she selected, beside a son who had eyes shaped just like hers.

When I look away from where I'd zoned out staring at my coffee, Desi is making faces and Luke is falling backward giggling like a loon, clutching his sides and gasping for breath. I know we're better off without Claire's selfishness. I know she would not have stayed trapped in this life of runny noses and little league games. She wouldn't have given up a single piece of herself to make someone better. I know I would be worrying every single day that she was going to give in to the temptation of her parents and their house high up on the hill above the vineyards.

I know we're better off for it, but fuck if it still doesn't sting.

Fuck you, Claire.

"You sure you're okay?" Desi asks with a soft smile and a pat on my knee.

"Yeah. I'm sure. Thanks for this. With Luke. I needed a minute to figure shit out."

"Did you get it figured out?"

"Nah. It's a work in progress."

"Isn't everything?"

Forty-Two

Sidney

I DON'T KNOW WHY I HESITATE BEFORE KNOCKING ON THE FRONT door. Maybe it's the ten or so texts I've sent Grayson that have gone unanswered.

Maybe it's my overthinking everything about us since Zoey left yesterday.

Maybe it's my not wanting to admit I miss him after only six days of being apart.

He's canceled on me every time we've set to meet because Luke has been sick, so I've attempted to do something nice and bring them some dinner.

Okay, so I have ulterior motives for doing it. I wanted to talk to him. To see him. To just be with him even if it's only to drop the food off at the door for five minutes.

Just as I go to knock, the front door opens. The man facing me freezes at the same time I do. The bag of food rattles in my hand.

"Hello there, young lady, what can I do for you?" He's Grayson in thirty years. That's my first thought when I see the kind but hardened eyes and the smile that turns up just like his.

"I was coming to see Grayson?"

"You say that like it's a question." He laughs, and the rumble of it makes me smile. "I'm Grayson's dad. Everyone calls me Chief."

"Nice to meet you. I'm Sidney Thorton." I reach out and shake the hand he offers.

"I knew your dad well before he left town. How is he doing? Well, I hope."

"Yes. He is."

"I'm ready, Poppy!" Luke's voice screeches as he skids to a halt right behind Chief, and then his eyes widen when he sees me. Maybe not as much as mine, though. "Miss Sidney!"

"Wow, you look like you're feeling better! That's so good to hear."

Luke's little brow furrows as he brushes his hair off his forehead. "What do you mean? I wasn't sick." He shakes his head as if I'm being silly, but I catch the confused look on Chief's face. "Did you come to play Creepers with me?" And before I can even respond, Luke's arms are around my waist.

My body wars with emotions, and I do my best to hide them. I just don't understand how my heart can swell for this little boy and feel broken in half by his father at the same time.

"Hey, Luke. I'm sorry, maybe later. I stopped by to talk to your dad about the contest." It's a little white lie, but at least it allows me to save face.

"What's in the bag?" he asks.

Chicken noodle soup. Oyster crackers. Brownies. "Nothing. I just stopped by the store and didn't want the food to spoil in my car."

"Cool. Did my dad win?"

"Not yet. We're almost ready to announce the top five," I say and give him a wink. "Then the voting for that round will start soon after . . . and then we'll be done. We'll have a winner."

"He's gonna win," Luke says right before his hand finds mine as if it were the most natural thing in the world. Chief takes notice of the action but doesn't say anything about it.

"I think he's gonna win, too," I whisper. "But I'm not allowed to say things like that."

Chief and I hold each other's gazes for a brief but awkward

moment as questions flicker through his eyes but don't manifest on his lips.

"Are you ready to head out, Luke-ster?" Chief asks.

"Poppy is taking me to the car races in Millville."

"Car races, huh?" My voice breaks. He definitely is not sick.

"They even have a demolition derby." There is so much excitement in Luke's voice that I manage a halfway genuine smile in response.

"It's something we do once a month," Chief says.

"It's our thing." Luke gives a nonchalant shrug and drops my hand.

"It's very cool." I hold the smile as I look from Luke to Chief. "It was very nice to meet you."

"Likewise. Tell your father hi for me."

"I will."

"Gray's out back. I'll assume you know where to go." He points through the house to the back door and then walks down the pathway, Luke following on his heels. I enter and shut the door behind me.

I stand there and take in a deep breath.

I will not cry.

I repeat the words to myself as I walk through the familiar living room. Past the signs of a life well lived—photos of the two of them here and there, a half-built tower of Legos on the floor. Past dishes drying in the rack beside the sink—a coffee cup half-filled, an apple half-eaten.

After setting the bag of food on the counter, I stand there for the briefest of seconds to gather my scattered thoughts currently tinged by hurt.

I should just leave.

Grayson's made it clear he's done with me—the lies say that.

I should stay.

I want to go out there and confront him because he has no right to make me . . . *want* something, only to slam the door in my face.

The sound of the lawnmower pulls me to the back door when every part of my pride tells me I shouldn't be where I'm not wanted.

When I open it, my breath catches. There is Grayson, shirtless, sweaty, and pushing the lawnmower from one side of the yard to the other. He moves slowly over the small patch of grass, his biceps flexing with each turn of the corner.

Domesticity has never been sexier.

The sight of him has never been more painful.

Eventually, he notices me, but even after he does, he keeps going until he's finished with the yard.

"Hi."

"Hey." Head down, eyes focused on cleaning the mower.

"You aren't working at the station," I finally say, when he doesn't say anything more.

"Nope."

Okay. What's going on here?

"You haven't answered my texts, so I thought maybe you were on shift."

"Nope. Just busy."

I hate the dread that slowly trickles into my belly. He isn't looking at me. He's not really talking to me.

"Looks like Luke made a full recovery." Now that? That puts a hitch in his step, but he still doesn't say anything more. "You lied to me, Grayson. Luke said he hasn't been sick."

He grunts in response but still refuses to look my way as he fiddles with this and that on the lawnmower.

"Have I done something wrong?"

"Nothing you can help."

He hoses off the mower and moves it to a shed in the far corner of the yard, then rolls the trashcans to the side of the house without another word.

I try not to take it personally. I try not to overthink what exactly has caused this shift in him—that he's done with me and has moved on to the next person in line. When he finally walks my way, I try to engage him again.

Things just aren't adding up, and every single one of them is making my stomach churn and chest constrict.

"I saw you the other day."

His steps falter. "I see you a lot of days."

"But you saw me and acted like you didn't." It's stupid to be hurt by it, but I am. I had spent all afternoon talking to Zoey about him, acknowledged out loud for the first time that I had feelings for him. Then when I waved to him, hoping he would come out so I could introduce him to Zoey, he looked at me as if I had done something to him or, even worse, as if he didn't even know me, and damn it if it didn't really hurt my feelings.

His only response is to grunt again.

"Did I do something wrong, Grayson?"

"Nope."

Sick of being ignored, I walk over to where he is busying himself snapping cushions onto the chairs of the patio furniture. "What's your problem?"

For the first time, he straightens and turns to look at me. I see confusion. Hurt. Uncertainty. And when he speaks, his voice is a low, even tone. "You just reminded me of someone I used to know."

Past tense? *Reminded*?

"We're back to this again?" I throw my hands up in frustration.

"You don't know the half of it, Princess." His derisive chuckle forewarning of a storm waging beneath the surface.

"Grayson, what in the ever-loving hell are you talking about?"

"You don't fit in here." Confused, I reach out to touch his arm, and he steps back so I can't. He can spew any words at me—I have tough skin—but that action hurts more than I want to admit. "You and your friend in your designer clothes and loaded shopping bags . . . you don't fit in here. Isn't there some fancy party you need to attend or something?"

"You aren't making any sense." But he is. He's making perfect sense. He saw me with Zoey last week, and instead of seeing two ladies having fun, he saw Claire. He saw what he thinks is my getting bored of Sunnyville and preparing to move on. I know exactly what he saw, but that doesn't mean I have to like it.

"Sid." He hangs his head for the briefest of seconds and sighs, defeat in every part of his posture. "It's probably best if you just go. I'm in a shitty mood, and I'm dealing with crap that makes no sense to you and . . ." His words fade as he turns from me, laces his hands on the back of his head, and paces to the end of the yard.

"I'm not Claire."

"Uh-huh."

"Goddammit, Grayson! I'm not Claire!"

"Aren't you, though?"

"Fuck. You." Every part of me screams the words that my lips speak in such an even tone.

When he turns to face me, his expression is stoic, at best, emotionless at worst, and I scramble for how to fight with someone who looks like the fight has already been taken out of them.

Then my thoughts click into place. The lie. The lack of communication after we'd been talking daily. Nightly. Every moment in between. It all makes sense. *He wasn't? Was he?*

"You were testing me, weren't you?"

"What's that supposed to mean?"

"You lied about Luke being sick and canceled our dates to see how I'd react."

His chuckle is condescending. "Well, your little tantrum right now pretty much proves my theory right."

"Your theory?" I yell as rage riots within. It all makes sense. The sudden disappearance of Grayson and him blaming it on Luke. His accusations that I'm like Claire. He wanted to see if I'd bail on him like she did.

When he was the reason he couldn't see me.

"Yeah. Your little tantrum because I haven't been at your beck and call proves me right. You only think about you. You only care about you. You'll get mad if I have to cancel because something happens with Luke."

"I wasn't mad at you at all until now! Until you lied to me to try to prove I was like Claire. Until you didn't trust me." I scream. "You can take your theory and shove it up your ass. You can take the homemade soup that I made two different times because the first batch was horrible that's sitting on the counter in your house and shove it right along with your theory. I was worried about the two of you because Luke had been *sick* for so long that I tried really hard to make something for you when I don't cook."

Tears burn as they well in my eyes, but I blink them away. I will not give Grayson the satisfaction of seeing me cry over him.

It's my turn to move. To pace. To abate every ounce of anger I have vibrating within.

"This is my life, Sidney." He throws his arms out to his sides and matches me shout for shout. "Luke gets sick. I have to cancel things. Luke's needs aren't always first, but they are a lot of the goddamn time. Can you handle that? Can you handle being second place in your first-class world?"

I stare at him. He's so fucking gorgeous I don't want to look away, yet the sight of him makes me want to scream and yell and tell him to go to hell.

"Screw you."

"Apparently, that's the one thing we're good at." His nonchalance only serves to enrage me. The way he just cast aside, with those few words, how close we've become hurts more than expected.

"What the fuck is this, Grayson? What are we doing here? Because I can't figure you out. One minute, you want me, and the next minute, you don't. One minute, you're lying to me, and the next minute, you're giving me some kind of fucked-up test to see if I'm good enough to be a part of your life. Is this just sex? Is this more? Because you send so many goddamn mixed signals that I don't know which way is up anymore. Do me a favor and make up your mind and quit playing with mine." I fight the tears that threaten as he stares, the muscle in his jaw pulsing and tension radiating off him.

"Sid . . ."

"I'm fighting for you, Grayson. Is that what you want? I'm fighting for you when she wouldn't, but I sure as hell won't compete against your ghosts."

"I've never asked you for anything."

I feel like every part of my body has been wrapped as tightly as possible in barbed wire. Like I'm suffocating although I'm in the open air.

Fuck you.

I hate you.

Screw you.

I don't say any of those things because as much as I tell myself that I don't care, that this is just a fling like he says, I know I feel more from him. I know there is more between us than this.

I love you.

Oh. God.

"We never talked parameters, Sid. All I can offer you is fun and done. I never promised you more."

"I never asked for more," I whisper to save face when every part of me is reeling from those three words that never grace my lips.

"Good," he says and turns back to the cushions on the damn chairs as if we didn't just close the door on whatever this was between us.

"Good."

Without another word, I turn on my heel, walk inside, pull the brownies from the bag on the counter, and leave.

Forty-Three

Grayson

G o.

Wait.

Fuck this.

When she slams the door, it reverberates in so many more places than just the house. It's in every part of me.

Christ.

I scrub a hand through my hair and tell myself to go after her, a split second before I tell myself not to.

That I should just leave things be.

I made my point. To myself. To her.

And now, guess who feels fucking miserable? Guess who feels like a fucking asshole? Guess who just messed up the best thing he had going for him in the longest of times and doesn't know how to fix it.

Track her down. Say you're sorry. Beg if you have to.

Fuck. The past few days have been miserable without her constant presence in some way, shape, or form. I've felt it. Luke's felt it.

It isn't just the lack of sex I'm missing. If it were, I could fix that with a phone call.

It's the companionship. It's the ability to laugh over something stupid. It's the wish to tell someone something after a chaotic day and have someone care. It's the need to share and not feel so fucking alone.

But I don't chase after her.

I walk into the house, see the bag of food on the counter and cringe, the sight of it reinforcing how much of a prick I am.

Fuck, yes I tested her.

Fuck, yes I waited to see if I'd get the whiny texts complaining about how she hasn't been able to see me and how she wants me to just get a babysitter. I waited for her to send that so that I could then sit around and wait for her silence after I told her I couldn't.

But I received none of the above.

Instead, I got text after text asking me how Luke was doing. Seeing if I needed anything. Asking if I wanted her to watch him for a bit so I could get a break.

It was a great fucking test.

Great way to make me look like more of a fucking asshole than I already am.

Great way to try to mess up her feelings because I can't figure out my own.

Nah, I can figure them out all right.

They're just ones I swore I'd never let myself feel again.

Forty-Four

Grayson

"YOU'RE BEING A MISERABLE FUCK."

"Grady Malone. That is no way to talk at the dinner table," my mom says, shooting him a scowl that can make any one of us shrink.

"He kind of is, though," Grant chimes in.

I glare at both of them and then tip my Coke back and make sure my middle finger is front and center, so they get the point.

"Is there trouble in Sidney-ville?" Grady asks as he scoots back to avoid the quick kick to his shin I just missed.

And despite my mom's ears perking up like a damn jackrabbit at the sound of Sidney's name, she says, "Leave him alone."

"We fought." It comes out of my mouth without thinking, but I've been sitting on it and stewing about it for the better part of a day, and the longer I keep silent, the more I feel like a jackass for the things I said to her.

"Best part about fighting is the make-up sex," Grant says as he eyes Emerson. Her response is a swift swat to the back of the head before she presses a kiss there and takes off to make sure their girls haven't gotten into too much trouble with Luke.

"What did you fight about?"

"Drop it, Grady," I say.

"You're the one who brought it up." He shrugs and grins at me over his beer. "Did you finally tell her you want more than just slipping and sliding and she said screw you?"

We all burst out laughing at the look on our mom's face, and she just shakes her head.

"Not quite."

"Oh." The chorus rings out around the table, and Dylan twists her lips as she stares at me.

"Let me guess, you told her there was nothing there when there is."

"Not exactly—"

"Can I just call it now? He's trying to sabotage it because she's actually a keeper, and that scares the fuck out of him," Grant says with a sarcastic edge that has me clenching my fists and my mom patting my arm to calm me down.

"Hey, Grant? Stay the fuck out of my—"

"Look who I found at the store!" My dad's voice cuts me off and has everyone turning toward the patio door.

Every part of me falls at the sight of her. She looks nothing like the girl I saw the other day on the street with her friend. She has on jean shorts, a red tank top, and red Converse. Her hair is piled on top of her head, and her face is completely free of makeup.

She steals my fucking breath is what she does.

Our eyes meet. Hold. And I hate the hurt that flickers through hers. The hurt that I put there.

A chorus of greetings ring out, but I just nod, needing to say so much to her but scared to fucking death to form the words. I know that if I do, all I'll be doing is opening myself to more hurt.

To more of everything I swore I'd never allow myself to feel again.

"Shit, Gray," Grant whispers as he leans in to my ear, "beg, borrow, and steal, but don't let *that* walk away, especially when she looks at you like that."

"Fuck off," I mutter under my breath as Sidney is pushed into my family with introductions. I wait to see if she shrieks when Moose comes up and puts a wet nose against her hand.

She doesn't.

I study the looks on my sisters-in-law's faces as they meet her because women are judgmental and an approval from them goes a long way.

They approve.

"She was walking in when I was walking out, and I thought she might like to have some company."

"How noble of you," I mutter to myself, knowing damn well my mom and her matchmaking skills are starting to rub off on my old man.

I get a glare of a rebuke from my mother and then just shake my head, telling her I'm confused as fuck about what to do.

"She said she had been looking for Gray so she could give him some good news. That he must be so busy he isn't returning her calls," my dad says, and I see Grady shake his head in my periphery.

Yeah. Yeah. I'm a disgrace. I get it.

"What's the good news?" This comes from my mom, who has graciously taken a break from mapping out my and Sidney's wedding, honeymoon, and first three children together.

"You're a finalist. You made the top five." I know she's addressing me, and I let the cheer go up around the table. I grit my teeth at the pats on my back and let them distract me from meeting her eyes because . . . fuck, Grant's right. She looks goddamn gorgeous as she stands with my family. Fitting in when I don't think I want her to. *Think* being the operative word.

"Calm down, guys. It's just a popularity contest," I say and roll my eyes.

"No, it isn't," Dylan interjects. "It's a beefcake contest, and you're grade-A prime."

Grady turns his head to spit out his beer because he's laughing too hard to swallow it. "See why I married her?" he says of his wife. "She gives as good as you fuckers."

"Grady." A warning by our mom that gets completely ignored. "You'll have to excuse the manners of my boys. They seem to have reverted back to second grade for some reason."

"It's fine. I promise you I've heard the F-word before," Sidney whispers and winks, a smile warming on her lips.

"Sit. Drink," my mom says as she wraps her arms around her in a motherly welcome and then ushers her to the table. "Food will be cooked shortly."

"Thank you. I feel bad, though. This was so unexpected, I should have brought something to contribute to the meal."

"Nonsense. The more the merrier, I say." Mom is clearly in her entertaining element. "I'll grab you a chair."

And she does. She grabs a chair while Sidney stands there awkwardly and waits to see where she puts it. Of course, she positions it right next to me.

"Hey," I murmur but don't look her way. Every single one of the people sitting at this table can read how I feel about her clear as day, but that doesn't mean I want her to as well.

"Hi," Sidney says as she takes a seat and accepts the beer my dad offers her.

A beer.

Sidney drinks beer?

"I tried to get out of this," she murmurs under her breath. "The last thing I wanted to do was make you uncomfortable."

Now I feel like more of a dick.

"It's fine."

"Do you think my boy here really has a shot at winning?" my father asks.

"Jesus, Dad," I mutter as Grady and Grant begin the catcalls.

"You're the ones who signed him up," Sidney says with a shake of her head. "You don't get to talk shi—crap now." She blanches as the kids giggle down on the lawn.

"No worries," Grant says. "Sadly, they've probably heard it more times than they should have."

Small talk ensues. The weather. The kids. The influx of tourists to Sunnyville for the harvesting season.

My attention is on Sidney, even though I still refuse to look at her.

How she interacts with my family. How she slips right into the conversation as if she's always belonged. How Luke comes and sits on her lap and she wraps her hands around his waist and rests her chin on his shoulder. How, every so often, she'll say something that makes him giggle.

All the while, I sit and brood and watch and listen, trying to figure out how this all fits into my life.

If it could.

If I want it to.

It always comes back to how I've already been left once, and I refuse to put Luke or myself in the position to be left again.

And then the focus turns back to Sidney.

"So why journalism?" Emerson asks as she leans forward, hands propped under her chin, eyes kind and genuinely interested.

"Probably for the same reason you all do what you do. It's a passion. I love helping to tell stories or be part of the narrative."

"But a *parenting* magazine?"

She looks down to the label of her bottle and then back up with a smile. "Fashion is where I'd like to end up in the future. Being an editor of a fashion magazine is my dream job." She shrugs. "What can I say? The opportunity came up to help save the magazine, and I took it."

"That's wonderful, dear. And when the contest is over? Do you have other plans for the magazine? Will you be moving on to an editor position?" My mom fishes as my brothers glance at each other.

Sidney looks at me and then my mom and draws in a shaky breath.

She doesn't need this shit. The Malone inquisition.

And neither do I.

Without caring what my family thinks, I shove my chair back abruptly and stand. "Can I speak with you inside for a moment?"

Sidney's flustered by my request, that much I can tell, but she makes a quick apology to everyone at the table and follows me into the house. I head for the living room—the farthest room from where everyone sits on the patio—and wait for the squeak of her shoes on the hardwood floors to come to a stop.

Forty-Five

Sidney

H
E KNOWS.

That's my first thought when Grayson turns around. It's as if every emotion a human being can feel has been thrown in a blender, turned on high, and then blended again. His eyes swim with the words his lips can't seem to form.

He already knows I'm leaving. He found out.

I panic with what to say since he's not saying anything. I fumble for words, with how to explain, then chicken out and choose avoidance. I let him take the lead. "Congratulations, again, on making the top five. You should be ecstatic."

He grunts. "Hmm. I don't feel very *ecstatic.*"

He doesn't know?

"Grayson?" Nerves take over every single part of me as the realization hits that I have to tell him that I'm going to be leaving. I can't . . . I shouldn't put it off anymore.

He's already mad. I'm already miserable. Wouldn't it be better to just tell him right now and cut ties while I'm already a step back? "I need to tell you—"

He takes a step closer and holds his hands up to stop me. "Look, I fucked up. *Again.* I owe you an apology but . . . but those are just words, and for a man who takes a lot of pride in standing behind his every word, I sure seem to keep fucking them up when it comes to you." He takes a step closer to me. "I've picked up the phone a million times, and each time I knew I was going to fuck this up further because, honestly, you have no reason to trust that I'm not going to be an ass again."

"I need to—"

"It's been a shitty couple of days knowing I hurt you, and the only time it hasn't been was when you walked in here tonight. It seems the only way I'm good at expressing myself to you is by showing you."

And without preamble or pretext, Grayson pulls me against him and kisses me. I'm completely shocked by it at first. From the caged look he had to the restlessness he exuded, I for sure thought we were in for a huge fight but this . . . the kind of kiss that is so tender and soft that I feel like I just crawled inside him and melted . . . this is not what I expected.

I tell myself to fight it. To push him away because he doesn't just get to kiss me and make all the hurt from what he said go away. After the misery I've felt over the past few days from fighting with him—the loneliness, the sadness, the everything—it feels so damn good to have his lips on mine. It also doesn't hurt to know that he has been just as miserable as I have.

When the kiss ends. When the laughter from the backyard seeps in through the open windows. When my thoughts are so scrambled I can't remember what I was supposed to be telling him. When his hands framing my cheeks direct my face so I can look up at him . . . I know without a doubt my heart has been lost to this man.

I also know I still have to stand my ground.

"That doesn't fix everything," I murmur, still floating on air from that kiss. My body a mix of contradictions. My mind telling me to take my hands off him but my heart saying not yet. Just give me one more second of this feeling.

"I know it doesn't."

"You tested me."

"I was an ass."

"You said things."

"I was an even bigger ass."

"Grayson." I chuckle in protest, and his lips meet mine again and then he rests his forehead against mine.

"I said a lot of things," he says, "most of which I'm not proud of. They're my hang-ups, Sid. They're things I need to fix if we're going to make this work. They're things I need to fix so that I can be a better man."

It takes me a moment to swallow over the lump in my throat his words have formed. To realize what he is telling me without coming out and saying it.

"Make this work?"

He looks like a scolded little boy having to explain himself, and I hate that I want to step into him and take it all away.

"Yeah. Make this work."

That panic I felt moments before intensifies for so many reasons . . . all of them good except for one.

"There are things I need to say, too, that haven't been said."

"Not right now." A brush of lips. A soft touch of tongues. "This is my turn to apologize. This is my turn to tell you that we're good together, Sidney. That it's been a long time since I've allowed myself to feel whatever this feeling is. I know we still have to be quiet about seeing each other . . . but can we just figure out how to enjoy this right now? Can we just accept this step and take it day by day without sticking parameters on it while we feel our way through?"

My heart swells and soars, and yet I meet every word he says with a cautious trepidation. The ball is in my court when it comes to us, and I don't know how to respond.

"Gray . . . I . . ."

"I know." He chuckles. "It's a lot . . . especially coming on the heels of the other day, of the shit I accused you of. But Christ, Sid, I've been so damn miserable."

He reaches for the nape of my neck and pulls me in for a kiss that reflects the despair it seems we both felt being at odds with each other. While he might not think he can express himself with words, the ones he is speaking are saying a lot.

The kiss he's giving me is saying even more.

A throat clears, and I try to jump back, but Grayson just holds me in place.

"Gray?"

"Dad." His name is a warning. "Can't you see I'm trying to kiss a girl here?"

Chief chuckles. "As long as I'm paying for the roof over your head, there will be no kissing any girls in this house," he says in the most fatherly of tones, I can assume he's perfected over the years.

We both laugh, and the groan that Grayson emits when he steps back and gives his dad the look of death has my cheeks heating.

"Good to see that you two are getting along," Chief says with a knowing smile. "Gray, the station keeps calling your cell." He holds it out.

"Christ," Grayson mutters as he dials, but I can already see the transformation from the Grayson I know to Grayson in command.

"This is Malone," he says when whoever answers picks up. "He's what? How long will he be out for? Okay. Okay. I can cover, but I need to check about Luke."

"It's fine," Chief interjects, and Grayson nods, glancing at the clock on the wall.

"I'll be there in about fifteen, twenty at the most. Is that good?" There is another stretch of silence before he says, "Okay. Yes. Ten-four." His laugh rings out. "I know you do."

Grayson's already in motion when he ends the call. "Luke?" he calls out the open door before turning back to us. "Charlie came down with the stomach flu mid-shift. They need someone to cover."

"It's fine," Grayson's dad says. "We'll get Luke home so he sleeps in his own bed and is ready for school tomorrow." He winks at me. "It isn't the first time we've had a child."

I smile at him and then follow after Grayson.

"Grayson." He stops when I say his name, and turns to look at me.

"I'm sorry," he says. "I seem to be saying that an awful damn lot around you." But his smile is there with his words, and for a split second, I feel like all is right with this world.

"You don't need to apologize. Just be safe."

"Always."

I watch the chaos unfold. The frenzied hugs and kisses between Luke and Grayson that represent an obvious routine. Selfishly and ridiculously, a part of me is jealous of the attention that I'd have a share in, too, if I were part of the equation.

But I'm not.

That thought makes me just that much more insecure, since it comes on the heels of the revelation that I've fallen in love with Grayson Malone.

"Sidney . . . you'll get home okay?"

"Go," I say as he grabs his wallet and keys and shoves them into his pockets. "I'll be fine."

"Only if you're sure."

"Yes."

"Walk me out?"

I wasn't expecting that, but since I'm still craving that connection with him, I nod. We go out the front door, and the minute it shuts behind us, his lips meet mine in the softest of kisses. It's slow and tender and makes every part of my body vibrate with the bittersweet knowledge that this is what I'll be walking away from when the contest is over. A man whom I never expected but now I don't want to figure out how to get over.

When he pulls back, it takes me a second to get my footing because he just kissed me like he already knows when I know he doesn't.

"Sorry that I'm leaving you here with my family." He runs a hand down my arm and links his pinky with mine.

"It's okay. I kind of like them."

"I'm also sorry we didn't get to finish our conversation." He squeezes that pinky around mine.

"We said what we needed to say," I murmur.

"You're amazing." His words startle me as he presses a chaste kiss to my cheek and then heads down the pathway.

You're amazing, too.

And it's the first time he's ever walked away from me that I've felt uncertainty. He just took a huge step in opening up to me . . . and I didn't do so in return. I'm still hiding something from him because I'm scared to death of ruining this feeling.

He said we're just going to go along with whatever this is. Day by day. I'm not naïve enough to think that day by day means I don't have to tell him what's going to happen after the winner is announced.

I know I need to. I know I should have. But this all happened so fast that now I'm the one stuck being the asshole.

When I walk back into the house, Grayson's dad is standing there waiting for me.

"You okay?" he asks, eyes searching mine in a way that tells me he sees way more than I want him to.

"I'm fine."

He laughs softly. "My Grayson can be a tough one to figure out," he says without prompting. "Strong but sensitive. Stubborn but fair. He's our peacekeeper around here."

"I can see that."

"He likes you, you know? He wouldn't be pushing you away so hard if he didn't."

"Oh." It's silly that my heart swells hearing this.

Chief settles onto the arm of the couch. "Shh, don't tell Betsy I'm sitting here." He winks, and I shake my head. What is it with these Malone men and their charm? "She has a strict rule for the boys about butts anywhere but the cushions, but I earned it."

"I won't tell her. I promise."

He looks at his thumbs, fiddling together as if he's trying to figure out whether he should say something or not. "I know you two are pretending there's nothing between you." He holds up his hand when I start to talk, and out of respect, I bite my tongue. "Let me say my piece, and then, just like my sitting on this armrest here, you can pretend it never happened."

"Okay." I smile because I can't help it with him.

"I get why you have to keep things on the down low for the sake of propriety when it comes to the contest. I'm no stranger to how Grayson has conducted his affairs in the past because he wants to protect Luke. Or that's what he says, when it's clearly the only way he knows how to protect himself.

"Gray has always been the most loyal of my boys. He's always trusted fiercely. And when Claire shattered that, I swore it broke something inside him. He didn't let anyone get close to him. But since you've been around, I've seen a lot of that fight come back. That means he cares, Sidney. That means he's scared to death. And, so help me God, that means he's going to push you away to prove you aren't going to stay . . . so if you aren't going to stay, let him push you. Do him the courtesy so that he doesn't get more attached and then become equally as crushed when you walk out of Sunnyville and never look back. If you're going to stay, I hope like hell you'll fight for him, because he's worth every misspoken word and uttered curse and ounce of confusion."

I stare at him with tears in my eyes and so much conflict in my heart that I don't know what to say or do. How does he see that one of my feet is already out of the door when Grayson hasn't?

Understanding my silence, he gives me a soft smile and stands. "C'mon. Enough fatherly lectures. Let's go have a beer and some food. Poor Gray is gonna miss out."

Forty-Six

Grayson

Me: I'm just around the corner if you want to get your stuff ready to go.

I send the text to my mom when I'm stopped at the light and then turn into my neighborhood. I look at the response when I come to a stop sign, idling for longer than I should while staring at the words.

Mom: I'm not at your house with Luke. Sidney is.

Sidney is?

My initial reaction is no. Just flat out no. This is my mom's way of meddling. This is my mom's way of pushing an issue I'm not ready to broach yet.

Sure, Sidney and I made up yesterday. Sure, we agreed to try to figure out what this is between us. But this? Her being with Luke where he can become more attached than he already is? Christ, this is not what I meant by taking it day by day.

It definitely isn't something my mom should get to decide without asking me. God, I love the woman, but she's driving me crazy.

All I've thought about since I left my parents' house is Sidney.

All I did during downtime was lay in those cots and stare at the ceiling while all of my crew snored around me and wonder how in the fucking world she got to me? How did she stalk those heels up to my porch, tell me I was in a contest I didn't want to be a part of, and how did that lead to me not going ten minutes without thinking about her?

I never expected to say that shit to her. Sure, I've thought about it—especially when staring at the ceiling most nights after we talked, but I never thought I'd say it aloud. I thought the feeling would die. I'd expected to be too scared to voice it.

Once shit is out in the universe, you can't take it back.

I scrub a hand over my face. I'm so fucking screwed.

And confused.

Because I said it. And I meant it.

That leaves the one thing I have left to figure out, and, of course, my mom is trying to fucking force my hand.

I may have told Sid that I wanted to try to make this work, but I have no fucking clue how to invite her into our lives further without possibly messing with Luke's head.

Do what you've been doing, Gray. Little bits at a time.

It's the logical answer, but it's way easier said than done when it comes to a little boy desperate for a mother figure.

By the time I pull into the driveway, I'm fucking fried. The mixture of exhaustion from work, the confusion from everything with Sidney in the last couple of days, and the knowledge that I'm going to have to convince Luke that Sidney and I aren't getting married is enough to have me on edge by the time I unlock the front door.

The family room light is on, but the house is silent. Sidney's purse is sitting on the counter, but there is no sign of her anywhere. Back door's locked. Bathroom is empty. Television isn't even on. I set my stuff down and climb the stairs. When I make it to Luke's room, I swear to fucking God that every single part of my heart shatters, and I'm not sure whether it's a good or a bad thing.

Sidney is lying on the bed beside Luke. He's under the covers and she's on top of them in her shorts and tank top. A Harry Potter paperback is folded open and slightly off her lap, but he's holding her hand, and her chin is resting on top of his head.

They look like a mother and son.

The sight knocks the wind out of me.

How odd. Until right now, I hadn't realized how they could pass as related so easily.

I'm exhausted and starving, but I stand there in the doorway and watch the two people who are part of my life, day in and day out, as they sleep. How did this happen? How did I *let* this happen?

If this were a test, she just passed it with flying colors.

But it wasn't.

Or maybe it was my mom's way of testing me. Maybe it was her subtle way of saying "Test this woman any way you can and she's going to come out on top each time."

The two of them. Side by side. Asleep. At ease. Peaceful.

Things I've said I never wanted slowly stir to life inside me, and the effort is half-hearted to shove them back into the usual place I keep them hidden.

Tears burn in my eyes as the sight just reaffirms what I already know: Luke is missing so much by not having a mom. The quiet comfort. The woman's touch. A different view of everything.

But seeing Sidney here, being able to study her in her sleep with my son in her arms, makes me want to hold on tighter. This woman—with the Converse and shorts and tank top—could fit in here. Does fit in here. She'd be willing to give me the things that I want.

But the woman with the red soles and designer wardrobe who first walked into my life . . . Sunnyville doesn't have enough to keep her. At some point that editor-in-chief position of a fancy fashion magazine will call her name, and its glamour will shine brighter than the charm of this town. And just like that girl I used to listen to in the diner who couldn't wait to leave town, she'll leave again.

What are you doing, Gray?

The doubt creeps again. The questions rage. The need to protect flares.

And yet, here I am, staring at her. Wanting her. Needing her. Begging myself to let her in. Convincing myself that people change. That she's changed in the months since she's been here.

Or maybe she's always been her, and I've just been looking at her through Claire-tainted lenses.

Fuck. I scrub a hand through my hair, confused as fuck and not wanting her any less, regardless of my thoughts.

Screw the contest.

Can't I just have her as the prize?

I'm not naïve enough to think that prizes don't come at a cost.

I step forward and slowly untangle Luke's arms from Sidney's. They both stir some but neither wake fully. I slip my arms beneath her knees and under her neck and pick her up.

It takes me a second to find my balance as she slips her arms around my neck, but the moment I do, she knocks me completely off kilter when she murmurs, "I love you, Grayson."

I stand there with her cradled in my arms, my son asleep in front of us, and stagger under the weight those words hold.

It's been almost eight years since I've let a woman say those words to me. Eight years since I've allowed myself to react to them. Eight goddamn years since I've wanted to say them back.

I can't. My tongue ties and every damn thing I was just thinking comes back and hits me again. *Sunnyville doesn't have enough to keep her.* So, even if I do . . . *could* love her, even if I do ask her to stay, that would be asking her to be someone she isn't meant to be. That would only end with her leaving.

This is who we are. Changing for each other would mean compromising who we inherently are, when that isn't what a relationship is about.

So, I do the only thing I can . . . I carry Sidney into my room and lay her on my bed. I don't know how much time passes as I try to calm what those words did to my insides, but I stand there and memorize everything about her as she sleeps.

The rise of her chest. The line of her nose. The curve of her hips.

The shape of her lips. The smell of her perfume.

I wonder a thousand what-ifs before I shove them down, lock them away.

It doesn't stop me from wanting to show her how I feel about her. It doesn't stop me from testing the same three words out on my own lips as I stand in the darkness of my own room. It doesn't stop me from leaning over and kissing her with every ounce of embattled emotion that I feel.

When I do, when that soft sigh falls from her lips in response, when her lips react in turn before she fully wakes up, I know I'm a goner. I know she's the one I've waited for, even though I know she was already gone before she stepped foot back in Sunnyville.

There are no words between us. There is no rush as we touch and taste and enjoy. Hands running gently over skin. Sighs filling the room. Unspoken emotions filling our hearts. There is nothing but us as I slip into her and show her how I feel in a way I can't express with words.

As I show her I love her in the only way I'm capable of letting her know.

Forty-Seven

Sidney

"**D**O YOU HAVE AN INNIE?"

I'm startled awake by Luke's voice, by the curious face that's angled to the side, staring at me, and by the grin he's fighting a losing battle with.

In the split second it takes me to remember everything that happened last night, it's already too late to escape this situation unscathed. My hands tighten the comforter around me as his eyes glance at my bare shoulders. I cringe as I imagine what he's thinking.

Stay cool. Stay calm.

"Shh, your dad's asleep." I look next to me, where Grayson's forearm is over his eyes and his breathing is still even.

Deep breath. I'm just going to have to talk my way around this one.

"Do you have an innie?"

"You mean my belly button?" I ask, more than aware that I'm absolutely naked beneath the cool sheets sliding over my skin.

"No, silly." He laughs, and in that moment, Grayson jolts in awareness beside me. But he's good. He stays still despite his breathing telling me he's silently freaking out. "I mean a vagina. An innie. Sam told me that men love women because they have vaginas. Dad said that's not true. He also said that boys have outies and girls have innies.

So is it true?"

I cough in response as I try not to laugh at him or embarrass him when he shouldn't be, but my sleep-drugged mind is freaking out about whether his question refers more to marriage or more to sex and how exactly I should answer.

"Well, I am a girl," I say with a soft smile, remembering just how sweet he was to me last night as we talked Creepers and Justice League and then went through the PS4 games that were his. Not the ones in the top cabinet that were ones he could only play with his dad. "So, I guess that means I have an innie."

"Hmm." He puts his index finger on his chin as if he's thinking. "How come you slept in here last night instead of my bed?"

Knowing Grayson is listening makes this so much more nerve-racking because I fear I'm going to say the wrong thing. "Your bed was kind of small, so your dad offered to let me sleep in here, so I didn't have to drive home when I was tired."

That curious smile that melts my heart reappears and tells me he isn't buying my story. "Justin told me his parents sleep in the same bed. He even said that sometimes he hears weird noises coming from their room when the door is shut, but his dad told him it was just him and his mom playing their PS4. I think they're lying to him. Parents don't have PS4s in their rooms."

I choke on my breath of air. "What do you think they're doing?"

His cheeks flush, and he clears his throat before he talks. "I think they're wrestling. Or kissing. One of the two."

"Oh." I'm sure the expression on my face is priceless, but so is the one on his.

"I've gotta get ready for school. Are you going to take me, or is dad?"

I stutter momentarily at how easily Luke is accepting this situation. "Your dad is. Why don't you go get dressed, and I'll get him up? Make sure to brush your teeth and wash your face."

"Are you going to remind him to do the same?" He lifts his chin over to his dad.

"Definitely. I'll even make sure to have him wash behind his ears."

"Ewww!" Luke says as he bounds toward the door. "Hey, Sidney." He stops and turns back to face me. "Thanks for spending the night. It was fun. Hopefully Dad will let you do it again soon."

I stare at him and nod as tears fill my eyes. This—a kid, or rather, a man with a kid—used to scare me, but now, the whole situation seems so very normal.

As I watch Luke retreat down the hallway, I try not to think of last night. Of the tenderness in Grayson's touch. Of the intimacy we shared. Of what felt like making love but couldn't possibly have been.

"Thank you." Grayson's voice is gruff as he moves his arm off his forehead and turns to face me.

My God, he's breathtaking. With his hair mussed and sleep lines etched in his face. But it's his eyes full of unspoken emotion that do me in.

"I know you're cautious of what he knows . . . just tried to cover as best as I could."

"You did fine," he says as he grabs my hand and presses a kiss to the center of my palm. Every part of me swoons and wants to curl up next to him and waste the day away. "He handled that better than I expected."

"He's a good kid, Grayson. You've done a great job with him."

He nods but doesn't speak as my words hit his heart. "Thank you."

We both fall silent, our fingers intertwined, both of us staring at them instead of looking at each other.

"We should get up," he says but doesn't move. "You know, before he figures out that you're supposed to stick the outie into the innie."

I stifle my laugh, knowing damn well he could be listening down the hallway. "Maybe I could stay over again soon and play PS4 with you."

He squeezes my hand. "I'm pretty versed in which buttons to push."

"That you are."

Forty-Eight

Sidney

"I BET YOU CAN'T WAIT TO GET THAT CUTE LITTLE ASS OF yours back to San Francisco." I look up to where Rissa is standing with her shoulder against the wall as she people watches the flow of traffic outside of my window.

Her words launch a bittersweet pang to my system. "Yeah."

"Yeah?" she asks.

"Sorry, I'm just preoccupied with this," I say, pointing to the blank Word document she can't see.

"I didn't know. I'm sorry. Do you want to go over the rundown now or later?"

I roll my shoulders and lean back. It isn't as if my father hasn't grilled me over it ten times already this week. "Sure. Let's get it out of the way." And use it as a reminder that the time left on my clock in Sunnyville is ticking.

"The plus side, which I'm sure your dad has said over and over, is that the numbers look fabulous. You really improved every facet of the visibility, and for that, I owe you. Keeping my job is definitely a plus."

I nod. "To be honest, I wasn't sure the idea would take."

"What? You thought once you become a mom, your sex drive dies and you can't appreciate a good-looking man?" Rissa laughs at the look on my face. "I'm so glad we've proven you wrong."

"You definitely have." Images of a naked Grayson come to mind. Then of him bending over Luke helping him with homework. Both are sexy in different ways. I owe Zoey an apology. She was right. A man and his child can definitely be sexy.

"And to think we're almost in the homestretch. In a few weeks, a man will be crowned Hot Dad, and even if we only retain fifty percent of the new interest, it still leaves our numbers above what our target was, so there will be absolutely no complaints on our part."

A few weeks . . . hearing her say it makes it all the more real. The project I've eaten, slept, and breathed is almost over . . . and then what? I should be happy, right? I should be thrilled to be getting back to my life and hopefully moving on to my opportunity at *Haute*, so why am I not?

Grayson.

"Uh-oh. You have that look on your face."

"What look?" I force a smile, although I know she's not going to buy it.

"The one that says as sad as we are going to be with you leaving, you're going to be even sadder leaving someone else."

"You're being ridiculous," I say while silently begging to talk to someone about all of this.

Rissa gives me the motherly glance any child recognizes before they are able to stand, and shuts the door, cutting us off from the rest of the staff.

"You're horrible at hiding your emotions, Sidney."

"Emotions about what?" I feign innocence, even though I know she knows.

"Love."

"Love?" I laugh out the word. "What about it?"

"So, it's just lust then?"

I chortle a laugh. "Lust? I'm not following you." But I damn well am.

"Mm-hmm. Says the woman who took off out of here a few weeks ago like a bat out of hell to break some rules . . . and hopefully a head-board." I choke on the air I'm breathing and stare at her wide-eyed. "Girl, you wear it on your sleeve."

"What exactly am I wearing on my sleeve?"

"You're going to try to play it off like this whole thing with Grayson, the thing you can hide from everyone else but me, is just a case of lust and sex and everything in between . . . but I can see it in your eyes. I can tell by how sad you get every time we talk about this project wrapping up and you moving on. You've fallen in love with him, haven't you?"

"Love?" I repeat the word again.

"Yeah. Love. It's a wrecking ball flying through the air, and you, my friend, have been hit with it. Classic case of being in the wrong place at the wrong time."

"Rissa," I warn.

"What?" She flashes a smile. "Isn't that how you feel right now? Blindsided and overwhelmed by it all?"

"I'm not in love with anyone."

"The door is shut. The conversation is off the record. Do you care to revise your previous statement?"

I laugh. My nerves rattle, but every other part of me wants to talk. "Are you going all investigative journalist on me right now?"

"Damn straight, I am. Look," she says, and everything about her softens—expression, smile, eyes. "You've been high on Grayson Malone since that first meeting. It only got worse after the first gossip column. And every time you've tried to hide him talking to you on the phone . . . or, uh, texting you, I've seen it." She winks, and I want to die.

"Being in love with Grayson Malone . . . that's a new one."

"Nah. You've known it for a while, but you've just refused to ad-mit it to yourself." I hate that she can see right through me and love knowing I'm not alone, all at the same time. "But you have now, hav-en't you?"

I nod. My first and only indication to anyone other than Zoey that I'm in love with Grayson. And that simple gesture is such a relief.

"Okay. That's the first step." She winks before turning serious. "Now, should I guess he's the reason you look downright miserable when I mentioned *Haute*?"

I stare at her and tell myself not to talk, but my lips speak anyway. "I'm leaving soon."

"Uh-huh. And you don't want to leave?"

My smile is soft as I fight back the emotion. "I don't know how it happened." And I don't. I've tried to pinpoint when Grayson Malone became more than just a hot dad in a contest I was running and became someone I fell in love with—God, even thinking those words surprise me—and I can't.

"No one ever knows how it happens, Sidney. It kind of just creeps up on you and then subtly hits you everywhere at once." I laugh despite the tears welling in my eyes. "Did you have a fight?" she asks.

I sigh because I still don't know what we have. "Yes and no. We fought. We made up. We admitted this was more than just a thing . . . but we never went beyond that."

"And what does he say about you leaving? Are you going to try to make things work—oh. *Oh.*" The expression on my face must give everything away, because the shocked look in her eyes and her sudden epiphany tells me she gets it. "You haven't told him, have you?"

I shake my head. "I don't know how to."

"Sidney." It's a scold. It's shock. It's compassion.

"One minute we were nothing, just a little fling to have some fun—and the next minute he's telling me he wants to try to figure this out. Take each day as it comes. When I tried to tell him, he cut me off with his own apology."

"You have to tell him." The foreboding in her voice has nothing on how I feel and what I fear inside.

"I know. Communication doesn't seem to be our strong suit." I shake my head, using the cop-out, which is nothing more than a bull-shit excuse.

"Love is a bitch, ain't it?"

"You can say that again."

"Let me ask you this, if he were to ask you to stay, would you?"

"I don't know." The answer is automatic, and yet, my head and my heart don't match up on this one.

"What would it hurt to try it and stay? I can find a spot for you here. You've done a hell of a job so far, so I know you're good for it."

"But I have a life back home."

"Do you?" She angles her head and studies me for a moment. "Do you really want to go home to an empty apartment at the end of every day when you're so very used to going home to him?"

"That's the million-dollar question, isn't it?"

Forty-Nine

Sidney

"WHY DID THAT WOMAN OVER THERE TELL THE OTHER woman that you're leaving soon to go back to San Francisco?"

In an instant, Luke's words yank my attention away from Grayson and the camera crew currently interviewing him.

Panic ensues. The kind that has your body shaking and sweat beading and heart pumping.

"That's where I live," I say, trying to remain calm.

"No, silly. You live here. In Sunnyville." His brown eyes search mine in a way that makes me want to crawl into the corner and hide.

"You're right. I do live here. But I also have a home in San Francisco, which is where I lived before I came here."

"So, are you going back there or are you staying here?"

Grayson's laughter with the reporter for *E! News* filters our way. "For now, I'm staying here." I'm lying to a kid. Bold-faced lying.

"But when the contest is over?"

I can't look at his face, at the hurt that's there, when I can already feel it crashing down on him.

Two weeks. That's the answer I can't bring myself to tell him.

"I haven't figured that part out yet," I try to explain. "I work for a huge corporation, and sometimes, they send me to certain places to do certain jobs, and then when I complete them, I do the next one."

God how time has flown. The past two weeks have been a lot of working and a lot of Grayson and me taking things day by day. There has been a lot of pretending that nothing is bugging us when everything is. The me not telling him my assignment is almost up and the him not telling me whatever is preoccupying him. The kind of bugging where asking if something is wrong just prompts a million reassurances that everything is all right.

"If you leave for a different assignment, you're still coming back here after, right? You're still coming back to the Kraft house when you're done?"

I turn from where Grayson is standing and answering questions. One of his helicopters is at his back, and the reporter is interviewing him, asking the same set of questions she's asked the other top five contestants. When I meet Luke's eyes, I kneel so I'm on his level.

"Of course." The words get caught in my throat, right next to where my heart is lodged.

He eyes me, uncertain if he believes me, and the confused expression on his face only serves to tear me apart even more. "My mom left me. My dad tells me she still loves me, but she wouldn't have left me if she did. People who leave never come back, even when they promise."

Chills blanket my body as his words hit me one by one, and I take my hand and put it over his heart. "I'll prove differently, Luke Malone. I promise you if I have to leave, I'll be coming back to see you."

His skepticism slowly blurs with tears welling in his eyes. Then he nods. "I believe you . . . but don't come back just because of me. Come back because of my dad. I think he really likes you."

Oh, my heart.

"He does, does he? What makes you say that?" I feel ridiculous asking an eight-year-old to tell me why his dad likes me, but I'll own it.

"Because he doesn't need coffee in the morning to not be grumpy anymore. Because he puts cologne on before you come over. That, and he said he's going to move the PS4 into his bedroom. I think he wants you to come over and play with him some more."

I burst out laughing. I can't help it, and then I have to apologize to the camera crew for ruining their take, even though I'm not sorry at all. Luke and his comments are all I need to hear to encourage my thoughts to keep going in the direction they have been headed.

Fifty

Grayson

"IT'S TRUE ISN'T IT?"

Grayson stands in my doorway. I haven't even opened the screen door, but his words are out and now there is a whole hell of a lot more between us than the piece of wood-framed mesh.

"Is what true?" I push open the door, but he just holds it still, almost as if it's a barrier protecting him from the truth.

But I know he knows. It's in his posture. In the tension of his body. It's in the hurt in his eyes.

"You're leaving."

I stare down at my fingers twisting before looking back to meet his eyes. "I've tried telling you."

"Not hard enough." It's the first trace of anger.

I wish there was more. This would be easier if there was a ton more. Rage, I can deal with. Defeat is a whole different emotion.

"Gray . . . we were casual. We were enjoying the secret-lovers thing. You made it clear that there would be nothing more between us, so I figured that by the time I had to leave, you'd be done with me."

"Don't put words in my mouth to make this easier on you, Sidney. Don't turn this on me. I made a lot of fucking mistakes—things I did and the things I said to you . . . but when it came to how I felt—to how I feel about you, I never lied."

I shift my feet. I go to push open the door again, needing to connect with him, but his hand holds it firmly shut. *Shit.* Tears well, and I blink them away.

"You're right. I . . . I don't have an excuse. We were fun and flirty one minute, and then the next you said you wanted to try to figure this out. You wanted to try to make this work. I should have told you then. I should have—"

"You should have let me have a choice in the matter whether or not I fell in love with you. But you didn't. And now it's for nothing."

"Grayson." His name is a broken plea as every part of me absorbs the words I didn't expect but now know I don't deserve.

"I thought you were staying. I took a chance on this—on us—because I thought . . . Christ, I don't know what I thought." He runs a hand through his hair and lifts his head to the night sky above. The tendons in his neck are taut and his hands fist and unclench as he processes everything.

"I'm so sorry."

"No. You're not." He shakes his head as he lowers it back down and the gravity in his eyes tells me all I need to know. I've already lost him. "You let me fall in love with you when you knew there wasn't a future here."

"Please."

"Save it, Sid. You knew what you were doing all along."

"No. I didn't. I mean . . . I knew the project was going to end, but you, I never expected you." My voice breaks right alongside my heart. "Believe me when I tell you I know I messed up. I should have told you." The first tear slips down my cheek as that all-consuming panic takes hold. "I should have, and then we kept getting deeper into this thing, and there was no perfect time to tell you, so—"

"So you let my son tell me."

Those seven words have every thought in my head die a quick death . . . because he's right. I knew Luke would tell Grayson about our conversation. I knew he would connect the dots I didn't connect for Luke.

Is it possible to hate myself any more than I already do?

I hiccup a sob and push against the door. This time he lets it go. This time I reach forward and touch his face. The rough of his stubble scrapes against my hand. The hitch of his breath fills my ears.

This time, I use his words back on him. "I'm not very good with apologies, Grayson. I seem to keep screwing them up when it comes to you, so I'll show you in the only way I know how."

When I press a kiss to his lips, there's hesitancy there. And then there isn't. I taste anger on his tongue. I can sense the violence beneath the edge of it. I can feel it in his touch, the desperation for him to be wrong about my intentions. But there is nothing satisfying about the kiss because I know I'm trying to use it to save myself.

I love you.

And I know when I step back and look into his eyes, that it didn't do a single thing to fix this.

"I believed you were different. I thought you'd changed. I should have known better."

And with those words, Grayson turns on his heel and leaves.

I scream in my head for him not to go. Silently, I shout *I love you.*

But there is nothing I can say that will fix this. There is nothing I can say other than I'm sorry. There is nothing I can do that will take the look he just gave me out of my mind.

All I can focus on is that he didn't say he hated me.

He didn't ask me to stay.

He said he loved me.

What am I going to do now?

Fifty-One

Sidney

I TURN THE PAPER OVER IN MY HANDS. THE ONE THAT WAS SITTING on my desk when I got in this morning.

Meet me at Miner's Airfield at five p.m. Wings Out Hangar.
—Gray.

I think back to how well I held it together when I saw the note on my desk. The sob I held back. The tears I blinked away because God knows I'd shed way too many in the past few days.

I've sent what feels like a hundred texts to apologize. Left a dozen voicemails.

None of them have gotten a response, and now this.

I look at the hangar in front of me and wonder what he is doing. What this means. I try to rein in the hope that maybe he wants to try to fix things. Maybe he wants to ask me to stay.

What would I say if that were the case? Would I agree? Would I give up my life in San Francisco? Would I give up the job at *Haute*? All for a chance at love? All for a life with him, here?

I don't have the answers. I don't know.

That's a lie. I do know. And maybe that's why nerves rattle around as I get out of the car and head to the hangar with the big Wings Out sign above it.

Unsettled and excited, shock mixes in there when I pull open the hangar door to find a table sitting in the middle of the room. There is a mess of candles and a bottle of wine in the center of a red-checkered tablecloth.

It's oddly romantic in a way that wouldn't have appealed to me in my old life, but being here, meeting Grayson Malone, may have changed that . . . and many other ways I look at the world.

He's going to steal my heart, isn't he? He's going to tell me he's sorry in that way he has, he's going to tell me he wants me to stay, and I'm going to have to make a decision. Six months ago, I wouldn't have batted an eyelash before I packed my bag and hopped on the flight back home. Standing and looking at candles flicker softly, the decision seems impossible.

My heels click on the concrete floor as I make my way over to the table. Music is playing softly on speakers somewhere in the hangar. There's a bunch of wild, white daisies in a vase, and napkins folded in an attempt at something artsy that doesn't quite make it but is thoughtful nonetheless.

The door behind me opens, and my heart jumps in my throat when I turn to find Grayson there, haloed by the sun setting at his back. A tight-lipped smile spreads across those kissable lips, and confusion flickers in his eyes.

"You did all this?" he asks, surprise in his voice as he takes a few steps toward me.

"Me?" I laugh nervously. "I thought you did."

We both turn at the sound of footsteps, and if it were even possible, my heart falls further. There's Luke in a vest and slacks with a napkin over his arm and a sheepish smile on his face.

"Luke?" Grayson asks as he looks at me and then back at his son. He obviously didn't expect him to be here.

"I request your presents at the dinner table," he says loudly before glancing into the far corner of the warehouse and nodding to someone I can't see.

"Presence," Grayson corrects as if it's second nature before turning and looking at me. "Did you know anything about this?"

I shake my head. "I thought this was all you."

The look he gives me—eyes narrowed and a slight roll of his shoulders—tells me he's here out of courtesy. He came here thinking I set this up, and he wanted to see what I had to say. What he doesn't realize is that with that one revelation, he's given me a tiny bit of hope that we can right our wrongs.

"I think we've been set up," he mutters under his breath, his irritation palpable despite the smile he displays for his son.

"I think I'm okay with that," I say and give him a soft smile. Then he places his hand on the small of my back out of manners and ushers me to the table.

"What's all this, buddy?" Gray asks, struggling to be gracious to his son while still resenting me. He tries to pick Luke up but has his hands batted away.

"I am your server this evening," Luke says and tries not to giggle. When he fails, and his laughter echoes in the space around us, it's almost as if an invisible weight has been lifted. As if Luke's laughter is the encouragement we need to maybe take the first step to talking. "It isn't kind of you to touch the servers."

"It isn't, is it?" Grayson chuckles. "What's going on?"

"I wanted you and Sidney to have a nice dinner before the final vote . . . and before she has to leave." And it's out there. I swallow over the lump in my throat and hate Grayson's wince. "I thought a romantic dinner without children present was very important. And without people in town knowing so you don't mess up the vote."

"Without children present?" Grayson says and lifts his brow.

"Servers are not children." He laughs again, and another piece of my heart falls at this little boy's feet. "And this server selected every item on your menu tonight, so don't throw tomatoes if you don't like it."

"We promise not to, especially since said server doesn't like tomatoes," Grayson says and winks.

We are both given the biggest grin, which is followed by a nod. "I'll leave you two to get settled, then. Oh, and wine is there. Breathing when it doesn't have lungs." He rolls his eyes. "But I'm not old enough to touch it, so that part you have to do yourself."

"Yes, sir," Grayson says. "May I ask who's helping you?"

"Women." It's all he says and grins.

Emerson. Betsy. Dylan. My bet's on them.

"Thank you, kind sir. Tell the women thank you, too," I say and turn to look at Grayson. He quickly averts his eyes, but not before I catch the appreciative once-over he gives me.

Silence settles. Shifts. Smothers. We stand here, both more than aware of the millions of unspoken words that need to be said. We are also aware that doing so would risk disappointing a little boy with a wild imagination and a huge heart, who only wants the best for his father.

Grayson clears his throat and I jump. It's ridiculous, but I'm so nervous.

And then he speaks.

"You look stunning," he murmurs and steps in to press the softest of kisses against my cheek. My body hums from the slight touch, and before it even starts, I know that this evening might be the hardest one I've had in a long time.

Hard to pretend I don't care that I'm leaving soon. To put on a brave face for Luke while I'm slowly dying inside. To know there's so much here worth fighting for, and yet I haven't seen Grayson lace up his gloves or pull up the ropes to step foot in the ring.

"You have one hell of a son, Grayson Malone."

"I do, don't I?" Pride lights his eyes. "Shall we?" He pulls out my chair and hands me my napkin before he takes his seat across from mine and pours the cabernet.

The hangar is expansive. Its windows are a good two stories up on the corrugated steel walls, allowing the dusk to seep into the space. There is a plane in the far corner. It's small and white with blue stripes.

Behind us, there is what appears to be a set of steps that lead to a loft.

It isn't a setting I'm used to, but it's one that fits the moment and the man across from me perfectly.

"Thank you," I murmur as I take a sip of wine and meet his eyes above the rim. They hold. And search. And question. But what they search for, I have no idea.

Luke serves us his favorite gourmet salads, which are really just lettuce, balsamic dressing, and croutons, while Grayson and I make small talk. The weather. How busy he has been at work. How the voting is going and all the elevated press we never expected but are so thrilled to have.

Luke has set the stage for a romantic date, and we play the part for him, but every soft smile when he comes near, or interaction to make him laugh, is with an undercurrent of tension and longing.

Of wanting to lean across the table and press a kiss to Grayson's lips. To connect with him in a real way. Everything thus far—from conversation to eye contact to touch—has been light and impersonal, and it kills me not to tell Grayson to be mad at me. To scream at me. To call me every horrid name I know I deserve.

But then I smile when I see Luke carrying in our entrées. Slices of pizza. Grayson's laugh echoes off the concrete floors as Luke beams with pride.

"It's *your* favorite!" Grayson says and then waits until Luke has ever so carefully set the plates in front of us before he pulls him in for a huge hug.

"Not entirely," Luke says through his giggle. "I only like cheese. I made sure there was pepperoni on there for you."

"How noble of you, sir." Grayson plants a big kiss on his cheek and then tickles him some more.

"Hey, Luke?" I ask and get his attention. "Why don't you pull up a chair and have dinner with us. I don't think the three of us have ever eaten a fancy meal together."

His eyes widen, and his smile turns lopsided. And then it falls. "No, I couldn't. I'm the server."

"Servers have to eat, too." I shrug. "But if you aren't hungry or anything . . ."

"I'll get some pizza."

While we eat, we giggle over stupid things like how the bubbles of Luke's Sprite tickle his nose. They debate where they want to go if Grayson wins the contest. We talk about upcoming little league games, and Luke and Grayson give me silly ideas for articles I should write for *Modern Family*. It feels normal, the three of us in a hangar, shut away from the world so people can't gossip about us being together, and so I can savor each and every moment of this time without any interruption.

Savor my time with Grayson even though I have to be cautious of Luke's perception.

It's such a bittersweet feeling. This act we're putting on . . . but it still feels real. It still gives me a taste of what this family could be like. It still shows me exactly what I screwed up and what I might be missing out on because of it.

Even now . . . with him mad at me and the fear that I won't win this battle and he won't accept my apology, I still want him. I want Grayson any way I can get him, even if what he's willing to give me will never be enough. I'll just keep wanting more.

After the food is gone, Dylan and Emerson and Betsy take a bow, which leaves me wondering if they knew about our fight . . . our demise . . . and so they helped spearhead this little romantic dinner. They accept our thank-yous before they take Luke home and leave us alone.

We no longer have an excuse not to talk about the elephant in the room.

An awkwardness settles around us.

"That was adorable," I say.

"It was." He rocks back on his heels before nodding toward the steps. "There's a balcony of sorts upstairs if you'd like to get some fresh air."

"There is?" I ask, but I'm already following him as he climbs the stairs. Blindly and with little hope that we might be able to salvage whatever is left between us.

"Yes. This used to be where Emerson lived. When she ran the sky-diving school, before she ended up buying it, they converted the loft for her should she ever need a breather." He laughs as if her taking a break is ironic.

He opens a door into a small studio apartment. There is a bed in one corner and a kitchenette in the other. We walk through the modestly decorated space to another door. When I step out onto the deck, I'm blown away by the view. Runway lights, trees beyond the strip of asphalt, and hills covered in vines in the distance. There is a soft breeze that blows my hair across my face, but it feels good against the warm night around us.

When I turn to find Grayson, he isn't staring at the view, but rather, at me. His expression is intense. His eyes are a sea of uncertainty. I want to crawl into his arms. I want to stay right there for as long as we can, so we don't have to figure out what needs to be faced.

I'm afraid to be the first to speak.

"What are we doing here, Sidney?"

"Looking at the view?" I say to try to add some levity, but he doesn't even crack a smile.

"I'm serious." He exhales. "What are we doing here? Are we pretending that we're something we aren't? Are we simply accepting that we only have a few weeks left together before you leave and that we're just going to enjoy the time we have? Or should we call it quits now and save ourselves from the inevitable?"

"Grayson." His name is barely audible when I speak it, but only because every other part of me is dying inside. "I screwed this up."

"You did . . ." He shakes his head and takes a step toward me. "But I did too. I screwed up a lot of times and it wasn't fair for me to ask your forgiveness time and again . . . but you did. And then the first time you screw up, I didn't give you the same courtesy. But damn it to all hell, Sidney, you're leaving, and you didn't tell me?"

My sigh is loud and loaded with the mixture of emotions warring inside me. Fear. Hope. Desperation. Love. Everything I feel and am so damn scared to express. "This wasn't my intention. To come here. To find you. To fall for you."

His breath hitches and I know he heard me. "I know you have a life to get back to. Well you know what? So, do I. A life that had no room for you in it, but goddamn it, you've weaseled your way in somehow. Now what am I supposed to do? I have more than myself to protect here. I have Luke to think about. I have . . . Christ." He runs a hand through his hair and paces to the railing before bracing his hands on it and staring at the view beyond. "This will never fucking work."

The pain in his voice owns me, and I keep hearing his dad's words in my mind. *"If you're not going to stay, let him push you . . . But if you're going to stay, I hope like hell you'll fight for him, because he's worth every misspoken word and uttered curse and ounce of confusion."*

Is he pushing me, or is he making it easy for me to leave without regret?

Fuck that. There will always be regret. That much I know.

"We could try to make things work. Weekends and little trips back and forth," I say and then realize how stupid it sounds. How shallow it sounds. That's no way to have a relationship.

"I can't make you happy here. This isn't some big fancy town where trendy nightclubs pop up as quickly as they shut down, and Michael Kors isn't likely to set up shop any time soon. There isn't anything here but Luke and me and goddamn grapes on the hill. That's not enough to make someone like you stay."

"*Someone like me?*"

He groans in frustration. "That isn't what I mean."

"It's what it sounds like."

"It can sound like whatever you want. It seems in your world *I'm staying* and *I'm leaving* don't really seem to have any significance, so does it really matter?"

"Don't be a jerk."

"I'm just telling the truth."

"So are you saying you want to end this—?"

"Sid—"

"Are you pushing me away because you're too scared to say you want to make this work?"

"Dammit—"

"You think that I think I'm too good for you and Luke and this town and so it's easier if—"

"Quit putting words in my mouth, Claire!"

And right there is the dagger to my heart. Right there is the exact reason we could never work.

It's one thing to accuse me of being like her. It's another to call me by her name because deep down he just can't get over her.

I take a step back.

"Sid . . ."

I take another step.

"Sidney." He reaches for me, regret and fear and heartache playing across his features. "I'm sorry . . . I didn't mean—it was a slip of the tongue. You were thinking I was referring to her and then . . . *FUCK!*" He shouts and bangs a fist against the railing. "I didn't mean it."

He meant everything by it. My heart already knows it.

"You may not think you do, but you did. You have held me up against her pretentious pedestal since the minute you opened your front door almost six months ago. And you know what? Back then, you probably had every right to accuse me of being like her. I was. But things have changed, Grayson. Being here . . . working for Rissa . . . meeting Luke . . . being with you. That has changed me. It has changed me in ways I never saw coming. So for you to stand there and call me her name, it just proves that you don't know me at all."

I stand tall, my shoulders square, and in this moment, I realize everything I just said is true. This place has changed me. The people in this town were a huge part of that. And not only did they change me—how I look at things, how I look at other people—they also made me realize how empty my life was before. How hard it's going to be to go back to it, step into my old life, and not miss all of this.

"You're right . . ." He takes a step toward me, and all I can do is shake my head and take a step back. "You're not the same person who set foot here. And I'm not the same man you met. People change. Minds change. Sometimes it takes longer for a heart to forget what was done to it in the past. I guess it's taking mine longer than most."

I love him. It's plain as day to me as I stand here livid with him for telling me I'm just like Claire while at the same time being man enough to admit it.

"But how long is too long to wait?" I ask him, knowing that if he isn't over her in eight years' time, when will he be? "There comes a time when you have to choose whether you're going to remain rooted to your past and the things she did to you, or to take a step forward with a clean slate. You always have a choice, Grayson. What do you choose?"

Choose me.

"It isn't like that."

Choose me.

"It isn't? You tell me that I made a mistake and you've forgiven me, but with that one mistake, you've already talked yourself out of believing this could work before we ever had a chance." There is defiance and accusation and desperation in my tone. He has to see what he's doing, that he is so scared of possibly getting hurt that he's shut himself away from so much of the good in life as well.

I love you.

Don't you see that?

Why can't you see that?

"I've already asked one woman in my life to stay—the only other woman I've ever let in—and look how that turned out for me. So, I'll be damned if I ask you, too."

"I'm not looking for you to *ask* me to stay. I'm looking to hear you tell me that you *want* me to."

"Same difference."

He's so frustrating it's maddening. "That's the crux of it, isn't it? You'll never be over her, and I refuse to take second place."

"I was over her the minute she walked out my door," he says

through gritted teeth.

"You were? It doesn't seem that way from where I stand."

"Really? I told you I wanted to try for something here. For us to figure this out . . . and you lied. How does that not make you like her?"

I stare at him, sick to my stomach and more than knowing I'm in an uphill battle that I don't think I can win. When I walked into this hangar tonight, I was still one hundred percent undecided I wanted to fight for him.

But I'm fighting.

Because, with him standing in front of me, I know.

It's just that simple.

"I never lied to you! I just didn't tell you because I was scared!" I scream, frustrated at him and his fear and how he's throwing everything but the kitchen sink into this fight to push me away. To paint me in a bad light so that he can walk away with less guilt. "I was scared to tell you and lose you, but it seems like I already have. Just like you're scared to fight to keep me because you might have to open yourself up to letting someone in. Well, guess what? The possibility of getting hurt is always part of the equation. *Always.* But so is being loved and cherished and fulfilled. Those are the things you don't ever talk about or focus on. The late-night calls just to say I love you. The early morning looks over coffee. The knowing you have a friend to sit with you in silence after you've had an absolutely shitty day. Those are the things you're forgetting. Those are the things you're 'protecting' Luke from seeing. What you don't realize is that when he grows up, he will have no idea what is normal and fulfilling. So, you can keep being scared because, damn you, Grayson . . . you scare the hell out of me, too."

I pound my fist on the railing because I have so much pent-up emotion, and I'm so mad at him that it's either that or grab him and kiss him. The latter of which, I don't want to do. "You take risks every damn day in your job—you've made a name for yourself doing it—and yet, you won't take a goddamn risk on me, will you?"

"It isn't that easy, Sidney."

"The best things in life never are easy. You have to work at them and struggle with them just to make them work, but that's the best reward . . . that you didn't give up and it netted you something beautiful. We could be beautiful." I've never pleaded in my life, but I'm doing it now. I need to hear him tell me he'll try. That I'm worth the risk. That he wants me to stay. "I love you, damn it, and I don't have a fucking clue what to do about it other than to ask you to choose me. To tell me I'm worth the risk."

Every part of him freezes as every single part of me dies inside.

"I don't know that I can," he murmurs. His eyes well, and he blinks the moisture away before turning his back and walking to the edge of the space.

"I never looked for this. I never meant to fall in love with you . . . but I did, and I can't stop it, and nothing you can say to me can stop it . . ." I hiccup a huge sob.

Ask me. Choose me. Fight for me.

"Sidney . . ."

"It's okay." I shake my head as I take a step back, and he turns to face me. "It's just as shocking to me as it is to you. I have a heart. Who knew?" I say through another hysterical sob.

He takes a step forward, and as much as I tell myself to run as far away from him as possible to protect my heart because he hasn't given me an inkling of hope, I don't move.

Not when he frames the sides of my face with his hands.

Choose me.

His lips press kisses against the tracks my tears have left.

His lips meet mine in the sweetest of ways.

Choose me.

Then his hands remain on my cheeks, his forehead rests on mine, and his breath feathers over my lips.

"I'm fucked up, Sidney. And I'm going to keep fucking up. I'm man enough to admit my pride is in the way and I need to sort it out. I need to fix myself or else it isn't fair to drag you into my life more than I have. It isn't right for me to attach blame to you when you don't deserve it. I thought I'd gotten over what she'd done . . . and then your first fuck-up, I call you her name. That isn't fair to you." He kisses me oh so softly as my tears fall. "I love you. I think that's why I fought you so hard. All along, I knew I would fall, and yet, I can't ask you to stay. I can't tell you I'll be perfect. I can't give you the things that you need to thrive. I have to let you go. It's going to fucking kill me, but I can't hold you back here. I can't clip your wings."

Ask me to stay.

My shoulders shudder as I fight back the sobs. This tenderness—*his tenderness*—is too much when I feel like this is our goodbye. I thought I had two more weeks to prepare for this. I thought I'd be able to change his mind even though my mind hadn't been made up yet.

It is now.

And now he's pushing me away.

"You deserve so much more than I can give you, Princess."

For whatever reason, that term—the one he's always used as a dig but is now used as an endearment—undoes me, makes my bottom lip quiver.

But I want you.

Makes tears fall harder.

"Once you step away from here . . . once you go back to your city and your sidewalks and your nightlife, you'll see that you missed it all. You'll know that you'd be settling if you stay here. And you . . . I don't want you ever to settle."

My lips find his again. My hands need to touch him. My body needs to feel his against mine—in mine . . . one last time.

Because this is goodbye.

I know it. It's inevitable.

He knows it. I can feel it in his touch.

Choose me.

So, we make love on the balcony. We make love in the moonlight. We whisper apologies. We groan sweet nothings. But we make no promises.

And later, when he walks me to my car as I fight back the tears, and he presses yet another bittersweet kiss onto my lips, I know this is over.

I could fight. For him. For us. For more. But unless he wants to fight, too, it's useless.

Maybe he's right.

Maybe I'm so caught up in the moment I've lost sight of everything else.

Maybe he's right and I'm wrong.

And that's what hurts the most.

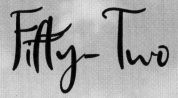

Fifty-Two

Sidney

"Hold up. What's going on here?" Rissa asks and props her hands on her hips as her eyes narrow on the half-filled cardboard box on my desk.

"Just packing up."

"You're really leaving, just like that?"

The tone of her voice has nothing on the stabbing pains I feel everywhere in my body and my tear ducts that have run dry.

"Not just like that." I fake indifference. "The contest has one week left. I'm going to head back and facilitate some final PR stuff from the main office. I'll have more help there, people with better connections, etcetera."

"The same kind of people you can pick up a phone from here and ask for the same kind of thing? Those kind of people, right?"

I don't answer her, and I don't try to pretend that I don't hear the anger in her voice. She deserves to be mad at me. I'm bailing on her because I can't handle being in this town another day knowing Grayson is somewhere close. Knowing that he's pushing me away and I don't know how else to fight.

"Yeah. That kind of people."

"I love you, honey, but I call bullshit. Are you really going to tuck that pretty little tail of yours between your legs and run away without a fight?"

"I did fight, Rissa. I tried. You can't make someone love you in return."

I love you, Sidney. I can hear his voice. I can feel his lips. I can *feel* his love.

And yet . . . he won't ask me to stay.

"He loves you, all right. He's just scared," she says, and I whip my eyes up to look at her. "Anyone who has ever been within a ten-foot radius of the two of you has seen it. Why do you think rumors still fly even though you two go through painful steps to look like you're not seeing each other? Hell, just the way he walks by here and then stands in front of that window, waiting for you to look his way for a whole five seconds' worth of eye-fucking tells me all I need to know."

"Well." I cough out the word, a little surprised by her vernacular. I'm also vaguely saddened that it's obvious to everyone else how Grayson feels about me but he can't see it himself.

Correction. He can see it. He just doesn't want to believe it.

"So, that's it? The girl who came here with the determination to do whatever it took to fulfill herself professionally and win the *Haute* job is just going to lie down without a fight and not fulfill herself personally?"

I look out the window she was just referring to and blink away tears. It's been two days since I've seen Grayson. The bittersweet last kiss still burns on my lips. The feel of his arms around me still makes me want more. Yet, he made it very clear that I wasn't fulfilling any personal wants with him.

"He thinks I only want to stay here because I'm here. That once the idea settles, then I'll want out, and if I want out—"

"Then he'll be the one in the crosshairs to get hurt again." She shrugs. "This town does have a way of being all-consuming. Everyone is everywhere, and so you kind of eat, breathe, and live it."

I'm not ready to hear her say that. I'm not ready to hear anyone tell me that Grayson might be right.

"I think I just need a bit of space, Riss. I need some clarity. I'm wondering if being here made my world that much smaller and, in turn, my feelings for him that much stronger. Did I put up with being on the down low because I wanted to be, or because I'm so removed from my real life that I compromised what I deserve?"

Even as I say it, I know it's just another excuse to soothe my bruised heart.

She chews her lip as she stares at me. "How about: this whole contest thing screwed with perspective and made you have to be incognito together, and maybe you should stick around till after it to see what happens between you then?"

"Perhaps."

"But you aren't going to stay, are you?"

"There were never plans made for me to stick around after the contest."

"There never was a Grayson in the picture either."

I sigh, hold her gaze, and see the disappointment in her eyes. "I'm going to go home for a bit. Gain that distance. Then I'll be back for the party you planned."

"How did you know about that?" She at least has the decency to look shocked that I know.

"Seriously? This is Sunnyville. Should I assume you're having a party here in Sunnyville and have invited all of the final five because you've acquiesced and know that Grayson is going to win so you want him to be in front of his hometown crowd?"

Even after all of this, I still want him to win.

She quirks a brow. "The party is for everyone and is nearby because of the office . . . and maybe to thank the townspeople for all of their support—"

"Sounds a little biased to me." I wink and smile as best as I can.

"Maybe it is, but that man . . . he's a trophy all in and of himself. Besides, why would you think he's going to win? Have you peeked at the stats?"

"I haven't had time to." It's a partial truth. I haven't looked at the numbers in a few days—since our hangar date to be exact—because I was trying to gain a bit of distance for my heart's sake. The last time I did though, Grayson was well in the lead, but things could have changed.

"Good. I'll change your password then so you can't look."

"What?" I say through a laugh.

"Then at least I know you'll be curious and still come back for the reveal."

"Sneaky bitch."

"And you still love me."

"I do." The room falls silent as I realize this is goodbye. For now. "I just want to say thank you for all of your help. You could have been a royal bitch and pegged me as a nepotism queen and made things difficult."

"You were the nepotism queen, but then you worked your ass off and proved to me and everyone else in this office that you know what you're doing. I'm proud of you, and I'll make sure to let your father know." I nod in thanks. "And, uh, remember to never forget the little people." She winks. "I'll be waiting for that phone call to be your junior editor."

She grabs me in a hug, and I just hold on tight. She's been so much more than just a coworker to me over the past few months, and I know I'm going to miss her.

⌒⌒

"Hey, buddy." Luke startles as he looks at me and then back to everyone sitting at the lunch tables and then back to me.

"Did I do something wrong? Is my dad okay? Why are you here?"

"Everything is fine," I tell him with a reassuring smile. "I just wanted to stop by and let you know I'm heading out for a while."

His expression falls, taking every part of me with it. "You're leaving, aren't you?"

"Just for a week," I enthuse. "I'll be back for the big party they are throwing for your dad, but I, uh, didn't want to leave without saying goodbye or getting a hug from you."

He stares at me, chin quivering, and I realize what a mistake this was. There is so much I don't know about parenting. Maybe Grayson was right . . . this would never work. I should have waited until after school and told him when he didn't have friends around. When he didn't have to pretend to be cool while I told him I was leaving him. When I could hug him and not embarrass him in front of his classmates.

"Yeah, sure," he says. Simple words but both of them waver when he says them.

"I brought you something, but you have to promise not to open it until you get home."

"You brought me something? Like a present?"

More like something to remember me by.

"Yes, like a present." I pick up the bag sitting beside me on the bench and slide it across the table. His eyes widen with each inch closer that it gets, and the other boys at the table turn to watch. "But you can't open it now. The last thing you want is for your teacher to take it away from you before you even get a chance to see it."

"I promise, Miss Sidney, I won't."

He holds my gaze and nods, so much in his little eyes that I hate to add to it by leaving.

By leaving him, the one Malone who I know has fought for me.

I fight back the tears that threaten, and wave him over to my side. "I have to get going and you have to eat your lunch. Is it too uncool for you to give me a hug?" I ask, praying that he's okay with it because I can't go without getting one.

Even if it's to assuage my own guilt.

"Of course not," he says and winks. "I'll just tell them all you're my girlfriend."

This kid. I tell you . . . he really is everything.

I hug Luke Malone as if I'm never going to see him again. I know I promised him I would, and I will . . . but who knows whether his resentment over my leaving will have kicked in and he won't like me anymore.

I breathe him in. The little boy smell. The shampoo in his hair. The feel of his tiny arms as they squeeze me tight.

Then I force myself to leave before I make a blubbering idiot out of myself. As it is, I have to sit in the parking lot for several minutes, waiting for the tears to subside so I can see well enough to drive.

When I pull out of the school's parking lot, it's almost as if Grayson knows I'm stealing away in the light of the day without saying goodbye—a helicopter flies overhead. It's white with blue graphics, and the numbers 4-4-5 are on the underside.

"Goodbye, Grayson."

I can barely get the words out as I hiccup over the sob. He's going to save someone. He's taking a risk.

Just not on me.

I force myself to drive. I turn south to head out of Sunnyville, a woman so very different from the one who drove into the town a little over five months ago.

Fifty-Three

Grayson

"WHAT'S THIS?" I PULL A WHITE BAG OUT OF LUKE'S backpack as I empty out his stuff. Luke's grin grows as he runs over to me and snatches the bag from my hands. "Whoa, dude, where's the fire?" I laugh before falling onto the couch with a sigh.

It's been a long ass day. First the shift. Then getting Luke from my parents' place. And now the whole bedtime routine.

Oh, yeah, and trying to avoid thinking about Sidney when all I want to do is drive over there and see her. But . . . clean break. It's best this way. For both of us.

Maybe if I keep saying it, I'll start to believe it.

"Miss Sidney brought this to me today at school."

"She what?" Now that got my attention.

"She came to say goodbye."

I rise from my seat as if in protest. "She what?" I repeat, not wanting to believe my ears but definitely hearing the sudden rush of my pulse in them.

Luke gives me a funny look. "She said she'll be back for the party but that she had to go for now."

I stare at my son and wonder how he's taking this news better than I am.

She left? For like good, left?

"Oh. My. God. Holy. Cow."

"What?" His utter astonishment pulls me from my confused thoughts as I look over to him and see his eyes wide and jaw lax. "What is it?"

"She . . . she had a Block made just like me."

I feel like I'm walking through a fog.

She left.

"*A what*? Luke, what are you talking about?"

"She had a Minecraft figure made to look just like me. A Steve Block, but I guess it's a Luke Block." His laughter makes me hurt even more. "It even has a shirt like my favorite one."

She left me.

"There's something in here with your name on it, Dad. Do you want it?"

She left us.

I grab the letter from Luke more forcefully than I should have, but I don't think twice before tearing it open to find her handwriting.

Grayson,

I wasn't sure how else to leave, but I knew I couldn't go without saying goodbye. I figured this might be the best way since we all but said goodbye the other night at the hangar.

Walking away is probably one of the hardest things I've ever had to do, but I know it's probably for the best. You aren't ready to forget your past, and I'm not willing to give up my future on the chance that you might. You aren't ready to make that choice and choose me. We were good together, though, weren't we?

I learned so many things about myself in the time I spent with you, and I've left a changed person. For that, I owe you.

Thank you for the time we shared. For the memories we made. For the friendship you gave me even though I know sometimes you looked at me and saw someone else.

And thank you for Luke. He's one hell of a kid and deserves the world, just like his dad does.

I meant what I said the other night. All of it. You are worthy of love. You are worthy of a life with a woman who can make you laugh every day and who never reminds you of her. She'll be a lucky woman when you find her. Make sure to take the risk.

Please take care of yourself.

Love,

Sidney

I stare at the letter. At her penmanship, which is curvy and perfect just like her. I read it over again and have to turn my back to Luke so he doesn't see what it looks like for a woman to bring a man to his knees like Sidney just did.

Holy shit. She really left.

Fifty-Four

Sidney

MY FIRST NIGHT BACK IN MY PENTHOUSE, AND IT FEELS nothing like when I left it.

It's cold.

It's empty.

I curl my knees up into Grayson's shirt that I took with me, and I cry myself to sleep.

Fifty-Five

H IM TEXTING ME WAS INEVITABLE, BUT WHEN HE FINALLY
does three days later, it's crippling.

Grayson: You left without saying goodbye.

I stare at his text for the longest time, trying to figure out how to
take it. Is he angry? Is he surprised? Is he disbelieving?

Me: I thought we had already said goodbye.

**Grayson: You didn't even tell me you were leaving early . . . but
you told Luke?**

**Me: I didn't want him to think I abandoned him. That was very
important to me. And you? It was just easier this way.**

Grayson: Easier for who?

Me: You. Me. I don't really know anymore.

Grayson: Neither do I.

I stare at my phone—so many words I need to say, his voice the one thing I desperately want to hear—and I close my eyes as I remember everything about him.

Me: I'm sorry.

Grayson: So am I.

Clutching my phone to my chest, I squeeze my eyes shut and don't even bother to fight the tears.

Distance doesn't make the heart grow fonder.

Distance makes you want the person more.

Distance makes you realize just what the hell you are missing.

That wrecking ball didn't do me any damn favors.

Deep breath. This will get easier in time.

It has to because, right now, this sucks.

Fifty-Six

Grayson

MY CHEST BURNS.

I focus on my breathing. On the cadence of my steps. But it doesn't matter how fast I run or how much distance I cover because her goddamn letter is on repeat in my mind.

Just like it was last night. And the night before that. And on and on.

Fuck.

She'll be back in a week, my ass.

The Kraft house is empty. All her stuff is gone. The vase where she kept the dead flowers she didn't realize I'd noticed has been emptied. The hose she'd always leave stretched across the drive is rolled up on its hook. The blinds on the house are pulled closed.

She's gone for good.

And I'm running. I run. Because I'm being a dick to everyone around me, taking this out on Luke with a short temper when it's no one's fault but my own. When I'm the only one who can fix this. But I can't until I make sure my head's as straight as it can be.

I run until I can't run anymore. Until the lactic acid makes my muscles seize and my lungs can't catch air fast enough. It's only then that I collapse on the side of the track of Sunnyville High School and just lie there with my arm hooked over my eyes and my body exhausted in every way possible.

"I haven't seen you run in years." I should have known he'd find me here. I should have known he'd be the one to notice. "Not since before . . ."

Not since Claire left me, he means.

"Leave it, Dad," I huff, but I don't uncover my eyes, even though I know he's leaning over me, blocking the sun for me.

"Nah. Not this time. I've left it for too damn long."

"I'm not in the mood."

"Yeah, well, neither am I. I'm not in the mood to watch my son suffer any more than he's already suffered when the answer's right in front of his damn nose."

"Christ."

"You're going to need a lot more than Christ, son, if you don't straighten up and listen when I tell you you're being a total dumbass for letting that woman walk out without a fight."

"It's none of your business, Dad."

"Like hell it isn't. You're my business. Luke's my business."

"She left. Can't fight for someone who didn't stay."

He mutters something under his breath, and I'm pretty sure he was calling me something. "Of course she left. I didn't see you fighting for her. Did you ask her to stay?"

"No."

"Why not?"

"It's complicated." I move my arm just enough that I can peek up at him. He's standing over me, hands on his hips, and that look that says, "I'm the chief of police, you'll do as I say," written all over him.

"That's a bullshit excuse. Most of the time, life is complicated. Life is putting yourself on the line and taking your chances."

I snort. "Been there. Done that. Been burned."

"That was eight years ago. Don't you think you've changed? Matured? Grown into a better man? Don't you think you deserve a second shot at happiness? I think you do." He sighs and shakes his head. "Look, it's honorable that you try to be all Luke needs, but some-day, he's going to grow up, move out, have a life of his own . . . then where will you be? Alone."

"Dad . . ."

"Stop wasting your chances. We're all afraid of things. Hell, after all these years, I'm still afraid of your mom's cooking some nights," he says and smiles. "I still brave it because she's worth the risk."

Worth the risk. There's that damn phrase again.

"That was supposed to make you smile, Grayson."

"Thanks for the pep talk, Dad, but I'm just trying to figure things out."

"You've already figured them out. Now you need to act on them."

"Easier said than done."

He holds a hand out to me. We hook thumbs, and he helps pull me up.

"Remember this—someone who really loves you sees what a mess you are and understands that you can be a moody son of a bitch but wants you anyway."

"What's your point?"

"I believe Sidney saw all that in you and still wants you. She just isn't sure how to fight for someone when they refuse to see the same in themselves."

Christ.

"It isn't that easy."

"A long time ago, someone once told me to find what I love and let it kill me." He lowers his head for a moment before looking back up and meeting my eyes. "It's okay if Sidney ruins you, Gray. Don't be afraid of it, because she may also be the one to help bring you back to life. She may just be the air you need to breathe, the one you can't live without."

My dad holds my gaze and nods ever so slightly before he turns and walks back to wherever he came from.

I run a hand through my hair and know he's right. About all of it. I've felt like shit the past few days. It's more than just my missing her.

It's knowing I want her and somehow let her slip through my fingers.

It's knowing she is the one risk I want to take, consequences be damned.

It's knowing I was too damn scared to ask her to stay . . . and now that she's gone, the answers are all clear as fucking day.

Fifty-Seven

Sidney

"**I** '**M PROUD OF YOU, SID. YOUR WORK AND DEDICATION REALLY** had a chance to shine in this contest."

"Thank you." My words are muted, my mind elsewhere as I meet my dad's gaze. He can probably see the confession of everything I did wrong.

Like fall in love with a contestant.

I clear my throat. "Numbers have definitely improved, and not just for the contest pages. The click-through to other articles has had a significant increase as well."

"So the numbers show." He flips through more pages of statistics and then looks back up at me, a proud smile on his lips. "Zoey came to see me a few months back."

I whip my head up to look at him, utter shock blanketing my face. "You mean my friend Zoey, Zoey?"

He gives a measured nod. "Yes."

"Okay." I draw the word out, mentally scrambling to come up with a reason why she would do that and coming up with nothing.

"Why didn't you tell me you missed the interview because you were helping her?"

Completely blindsided by this conversation, I open my mouth

and then close it more than a time or two before I finally speak. "Because it didn't matter. She asked me not to tell anyone and seeing as how it was her personal business, I didn't. Even if I had told you, it wouldn't have changed the fact that I screwed up. I needed to own up to it. I should have kept track of the time or called someone to let them know . . . and I didn't."

"So you took the punishment without saying a word."

"Yeah. I guess. I just did what I felt was right."

For a second, I swear I see tears well in his eyes, but I know that's not possible. Frank Thorton never shows emotion. Ever.

"Your work at *Modern Family* was incredible, Sidney . . . but I'm more proud of you for what you did with Zoey. For not making excuses and taking the assignment in Sunnyville with dignity. And for making the most of it." He smiles as I fight back my own tears, his praise has always been hard won. "You earned it, kid. The spot at *Haute* is yours. You'll have to learn some of the particulars here at headquarters, but after that, I'll be more than happy to recommend you for the editor-in-chief position without any hesitation."

He says the words I've waited to hear. Not just about the position at *Haute*, but that I'd done a good job. And yet, I don't feel a single ounce of elation.

None. Sure, I love that I made him proud . . . but I feel like shit. I feel like I've betrayed myself by being here, fighting for this when I didn't stay and fight harder for Grayson.

Maybe I am more like Claire than I'd like to admit.

Words are hard to come by and not because I'm ungrateful but rather because I didn't stay and fight *harder*. "Thank you."

"You say that as if you're reluctant. C'mon—" He throws his hands up. "Get excited. You just worked your tail off and are going to reap the rewards." His eyes narrow as he looks more closely at me. "It's the party you have to go back for, isn't it? Don't go if you don't want to. You've done your job; you aren't required to be there."

The thought of not going, of not seeing Grayson again, has me choking on air. "No, I want to go back."

"That surprises me."

"In fact . . . in fact, Dad, I don't think I deserve the position at *Haute*."

What am I doing?

He snaps his head up, stunned. "You what?"

"I, uh, I took a lot of credit that wasn't mine to take. Your editor-in-chief of *Modern Family*, Rissa Patel is the one who helped me a lot."

Did I really just say that?

"So, you didn't do the work then?" Confusion etches in the lines of his face.

"No, I did. I did all the work . . . but I think someone else is more deserving of the position than I am. I think with her background and originality, she'd be a better fit."

"I'm not following you, Sid."

Fight for him.

"I want to stay in Sunnyville. I want to work on *Modern Family*. If Rissa wants the position at *Haute*—only if she wants it—then I would love a shot at her job at the magazine."

"You're telling me you want to *stay* in Sunnyville?"

I want to prove to him that he is what I want.

"Yes."

He pinches the bridge of his nose as he tries to process what I'm telling him. That his daughter wants to leave her beloved city and stay in the suburbs. Willingly. The same place she stomped her feet at when she was told she had to go there.

"May I ask why?"

Because he's worth the risk.

"Because I learned a lot about myself when I worked there, and I think there's a lot more for me to improve."

"I see."

And because I like the woman Grayson makes me want to be when I'm with him.

Fifty-Eight

Grayson

Me: Text me when you get to town. We need to talk.

I hit send and then realize what a dick I sound like, but I can't take it back.

Fuck. Can I do anything right?

All I have to do is tell her that she's my choice. That I choose her.

It's only been seven days, and I'm going fucking crazy without her. Seven days of waking up and repeating the steps without any color in my life.

I scrub a hand over my face as I stare at the screen and wait for a response. Any response. Something to let me know that she knows that her leaving was a mistake. Something to let me know she'll be at the party tonight and that this—*she and I*—is somehow still on her mind. Is something she still wants.

Only, she doesn't respond.

She doesn't text back.

I end up sitting with my phone in my hand while Luke plays on the PS4, and I try to figure out how to fix something I broke.

How to prove to her that it won't happen again.

"Dad! Someone's at the door!"

"Who is it?" I ask as I jog down the stairs, less than thrilled at the high school and its never-ending fundraisers these days. We've already had two teenagers today selling mixed bags (whatever those are) and candy.

"Some old guy," Luke says, and I stop in my tracks.

"That's not nice." The reprimand is instantaneous, but fear flickers through me just as quickly.

It's the attention from the contest. He's come back as a representative for Claire. He wants to see Luke.

"Dad? You okay?" Luke's face is a mask of confusion as he stares at me.

"Yeah. I'm fine. I need you to go upstairs and play for a minute."

"Dad?" Brown eyes narrow and question.

"Just do what I say," I grit out and jab my finger to the stairs.

Feelings hurt, Luke eyes me again and trudges toward the stairs as every part of me wars against opening the door. It's finally happening.

They finally came back for him.

My pulse rages in my ears.

Over my dead body.

Once Luke clears the landing so I can't see him, I take a deep breath and steel myself for what I've always known I'd have to face someday, despite everyone telling me it would never happen.

Fuck you, Claire.

I yank open the door.

"What do you . . ." My words fade as I finish with a weak, "*want?*"

It isn't Claire's dad standing on my porch. Far fucking from it. It takes a second for that to register and then another for it to hit. The resemblance is there. He may have silver hair at his temples and a hulking figure that makes the porch seem tiny, but his eyes are brown and the same almond shape as Sidney's.

Relief flickers momentarily and then falls flat as memories come back. Claire's dad at the door. His threatening words. His condescending voice. The way he wouldn't even look at his own goddamn grandson.

"Can I help you?"

Why are you here?

He's going to ask me to leave Sidney alone.

He's going to tell me to go to hell.

"Grayson Malone?"

His voice. Aristocracy lilts in his tone, and I square my shoulders.

"Can I help you?" I repeat. We stare at each other. Measure each other. Judge.

"Frank Thorton. Nice to meet you."

I stare at the hand he extends and hear my father say, "Never look a gift horse in the mouth." Yet, all I want to do is look. All I want to do is stare.

All I want to do is question.

Reluctantly, I shake his hand, leery and cautious as I wait for whatever shoe might drop.

"Likewise, Mr. Thorton," I murmur.

"Call me Frank," he says with a definitive nod.

The expensive suit is something Claire's dad always wore, but the warm smile that slowly spreads across Frank's face is anything but.

"Frank," I say.

"I'm sure you're curious as to my sudden appearance on your doorstep."

"You could say that." I should invite him in, but I hesitate.

"It seems to me you've made quite an impression on the readers of *Modern Family* . . . and on my daughter."

Every part of me tenses as I wait for the words. She's too good for you. You're not the type of man we have picked out for her. And on and on. The Hoskins' comments ring in my ears all this time later.

"I assure you it was unintentional." I laugh, nerves suddenly running side by side with my caution. Is he going to tell me I can't see his daughter? Is he going to warn me away from her just when I've realized I don't want to live without her?

"May I ask you what your intentions are?" He shifts his feet, but his eyes hold mine.

"My intentions?" I sound like an idiot, but fuck if I don't feel like I've been brought back to ten years ago. This time, though, I know just how brutal the fallout is. I know just how devastating the woman you love leaving is.

"Yes. How are you going to win the contest and end up with Sidney without it looking as if the contest was rigged?"

I stare at him for a beat, blinking and trying to work out what he's saying. He has the look of a father who wants answers, not a businessman wondering about the integrity of his business, so I know where this conversation is headed.

"I already dropped out of the contest."

"*You what*?" He's a man used to being in the know, and that little tidbit just knocked him off his stride.

"Yes, sir. I dropped out of the contest earlier today." I think of the shocked look on Rissa's face when I told her and then the knowing grin that followed.

"Why's that?"

"Because your daughter is more important to me than any prize I ever could win. That's why." The words are a challenge thrown out, daring him to question me and tell me I'm wrong.

His eyes harden. His lips purse. And then they slowly spread into a smile. "Is that so?"

"Yes, sir. That's so." I cross my arms and lean my back against the door, more than aware that I still haven't invited him in. I'm ready for the fight. "If I stay in and win, then it taints the contest she worked so hard on. The last thing I want is questions about her dedication or accusations of a rigged contest to be angled her way. I made a deal with her that I'd participate to help make the contest a success. I fulfilled my end of the bargain, but now her success may be questioned if I stay in . . ."

"So, you'd give up the money and prizes?"

"It was never about the money or the prizes." I take a step toward him. "Like I said, Sidney means more to me than that . . ."

He purses his lips again. "You are talking about my Sidney, right?" And when that smile breaks on his face, I feel like I can breathe for the first time. His laugh echoes around the porch as he cuffs the side of my shoulder while I stare, trying to absorb all of this. "Stubborn? Always right? Fiery temper?"

It takes me a second to believe that this is real. That Frank isn't here to tell me I can't see Sidney. That he is nothing like the Hoskins.

"That's the one," I murmur.

His laugh is a bit louder this time. "God help you. You're going to need it." Then he winks. "But she's worth every argument and compromise you'll have to make."

I nod, hating the emotion in my throat. Hating that I never realized how much I needed this, but now that Frank is here and has expressed his approval, I know that I did.

"That she is," I say, wondering how exactly I'm going to prove to her that I know that. How I'm going to prove to her I love her after letting her walk away. How I'm going to prove to her that I know she isn't Claire and that I'll never make that mistake again.

Because I won't. This time spent without her and how goddamn horrible I've felt is enough of a reminder of what life without Sidney is like . . . and I don't want to live like this.

I want her.

Plain. Simple. Complicated. Her.

"And how do you plan on making this work?" he asks in a way that should have my back up, but as a father, I recognize a parent only wanting the best for their child.

"We'll figure it out," I say. When I sent her the text this morning, I knew I was going to fight for her, but how much so just became so very apparent. "I know she needs her city, so we'll have to make long distance work for the time being."

"Do you think that will work?"

"It will have to. All I know is that my life is better with her in it . . . that much has become obvious since she left here . . . so making it work is the only option we have. It's the only outcome I'll accept."

"That's a big compromise, son."

I shrug. "She's worth the risk."

Fifty-Nine

Sidney

I'T'S LIKE DÉJÀ VU, STANDING IN THE BACK OF HOOLIGAN'S.

So many faces are the same as last time, but the buzz is a lot bigger this go 'round. Sunnyville is anxious to make one of their own *Modern Family's* Hot Dad of the Year.

There's a live band playing. Someone from *Modern Family* has placed signage in optimal spots for photographs, and there are red and white balloons tied to the ends of the booths to add a splash of color.

From where I stand in the back, I've managed to catch a glimpse of four of the five contestants. All but the one I crave to see—Grayson.

For the first time since I stepped foot back in Sunnyville months ago, I feel completely out of place. Strangely enough, my place has kind of been beside Grayson, and to be so uncertain of how he's going to react to seeing me again is nerve-racking.

"Look at you! It's only been a week, and I already miss the hell out of you." Rissa grabs me in the tightest of hugs, which makes me wants to cry.

"It does feel like forever, doesn't it?"

"See? It's all that clean air talking and messing up your thinking." She laughs and squeezes my hand.

"Not hardly."

"When you didn't respond to any of my texts, I didn't think you were coming."

"You texted?" I ask. "My damn phone is acting up. I did that update, and I'm not getting any of them. It's been frustrating as hell."

And, of course, that says nothing about how it feels wondering if Grayson has been trying to text to me too.

I doubt he has, though. My hoping that he has, and I just haven't been getting them, is nothing but wishful thinking.

"Have you seen him yet?" Her voice lowers, and her eyes soften as the bar buzzes around us.

I don't trust my voice, so I just shake my head.

"Hmm. Neither have I."

"But I saw Braden . . . and while he's more than gifted in the looks department, he isn't my Gray—he isn't Grayson." It's easier to slip into this banter between us than to think about the nerves rattling around inside me.

"Girl, don't be dissing my Braden. He's fine as fuck."

"He is, but he's no Grayson." I wink. "I'm sure the people of Sunnyville would agree with me."

"Of course they would. That's who they're all here to see." She looks around and gauges the crowd. "Speaking of Grayson . . ."

I follow her gaze, and everything about me freezes, melts, wants, and needs at the sight of him. I'm sure my breath catches. I know my hands tighten. I know I rise onto my toes to get a better view.

Grayson is flanked by his brothers. Both Grant and Grady have smiles on their lips that seem to widen with each and every person who greets them, but it's Grayson who owns my attention. He's wearing a button-up dress shirt and jeans, which makes him look impossibly more handsome, and yet the smile on his face is more cautious than anything. The look in his eyes as he scans the crowd more pensive than at ease.

And for the briefest of moments, our eyes meet. His feet falter. My breath hitches. Hurt. Longing. Need. Want. Desperation. It's everything I tell him in the simple glance. Everything I can think to say with a look, since when I say it with words, it doesn't seem to matter.

"*Lawd have mercy.* What I wouldn't give for a man to look at me like that."

He's looking at me, all right. But he looked at me the exact same way the last time I saw him . . . right before I climbed into my car and drove away after Luke's date night for us at the hangar. Looking at me that way didn't make him chase after me, and it definitely didn't make him fight for me.

Will he now?

"Now that he's here, we can get this show on the road," Rissa says and pushes my back so that I move toward the front of the room. I want to stop her and tell her that I have no business even being a part of this anymore, but she doesn't let me.

I suddenly have the sinking feeling that my conversation with my dad was a huge mistake. Each step I take toward Grayson—toward the front of the bar—only serves to solidify it.

It isn't as if I was envisioning that he'd walk into the bar, stride over to me, and kiss the breath out of me. Well . . . maybe I was. But he could at least make a move toward me instead of standing there, frozen in place, stoic as can be.

Before I can steer his way or catch his eye again, Rissa is pulling me with her onto the makeshift stage where the band's gear is set up. She holds a microphone out to me, and I stare at it without taking it.

I can't do this.

I can't announce Grayson as the winner.

I can't stand here and smile and congratulate him without breaking down and crying. It would make me look like a complete fool and call even more attention to our rumored relationship.

"No. You do it," I murmur, hating the feeling of so many eyes leveled on me.

"This is your baby."

"No, you're the one who got the ball rolling . . . you should see it through."

Rissa gives me a curious look and then shrugs. "Ladies and

gentlemen, on behalf of *Modern Family*, I'd like to thank you all for coming out tonight to celebrate the culmination of a joint effort between Sidney here and myself. We wanted to find a way to celebrate fathers. To give them the praise they deserve for being hard-working and good-loving. What better way than to have a contest and involve America in helping us find someone to celebrate? So Sidney thought up this contest, which I normally would have said didn't fit our model, but when people started applying, I realized it could work. And it did. After four rounds and millions of votes, we have our top four contestants!"

Four? I look at her. How much has she had to drink?

"Tonight, we will crown the first ever winner of *Modern Family's* Hot Dad contest." The crowd cheers, and no matter how hard I try to see through the stage lights blinding me, I can't find Grayson. "So, without further ado, let's announce the winner. Coming in fourth place, we have our dad of adorable twin girls! He is an executive by day but doesn't hesitate to pull diaper duty at night. Give a round of applause to Gideon McMaster!"

A cheer goes up, and everyone claps as a strikingly handsome African American man makes his way to the stage, smile wide and fist pumping to the cheers calling out his name.

"And in third place, we have Christian Oliver. Christian is the father of five—FIVE, people. He's a navy officer, helping to protect and serve as well as being a devoted dance dad." Another round of applause erupts as Christian makes his way through the crowd, giving high fives as he goes.

"The runner-up, folks . . . what can I say? He is a man who I have a little crush on," Rissa says, and I nod subtly, knowing that she's talking about Braden and that Grayson won. "He's a high school teacher, educating minds and I'm sure causing a few crushes among his students. He's a father of one super adorable little boy and a triathlete on the side. Congratulations, Ethan Elliot! You are the esteemed runner-up of the Hot Dad contest."

Ethan makes his way through the crowd. His hair is a little long around the ears, his glasses are slightly askew, and the blush on his cheeks is damn adorable. It makes me like him on the spot.

While I'm watching him, it dawns on me that he isn't Braden. And Braden should be second place since I know Grayson was solidly in first the last time I checked the numbers.

Rissa meets my eyes ever so fleetingly, and there is something there I can't register before she turns back to the crowd. "Now . . . for the moment you've all been waiting for—the Hot Dad of the Year! The winner of the ten-thousand-dollar cash prize, a trip to anywhere in the continental United States, and the man who will grace the cover of next month's issue of *Modern Family*. He isn't only fit and sexy, but also, he's one hell of a dad. And by day—and sometimes night—he saves lives for a living. Let's welcome your *Modern Family* Hot Dad of the Year, Braden Johnson."

There is a cheer across the room, but I'm too stunned and more than a little confused to participate.

Something is going on.

The next few minutes are a blur—Braden gives a cute little speech, Rissa thanks everyone for their support and then tells them to stay tuned for the next contest coming soon. My mind spins as I try to figure out what the hell just happened. How did my go-to guy not win? How did the face of my contest not even place?

How is Grayson going to face Luke and tell him there is no vacation?

I look for Grayson in the crowd at the same time the crowd breaks out in a chant of his name.

"Gray-son. Gray-son. Gray-son."

In much the same unassuming fashion he used the night of the other party at Hooligan's, Grayson ambles to the stage, not wanting the attention but getting it nonetheless. When he steps up, our eyes meet, and he gives me that shy smile of his that curls up at one corner and makes every part of me need privacy. To talk to him. To tell him I'm here to stay. To beg him to choose me.

He waves a hand up to everyone and shouts out a thank you

without bothering to take the microphone. And the whole time, all I can focus on is him. The scent of his cologne. The curl of his hair over the collar of his shirt. The strength in his hands. Simple things I've missed.

The crowd cheers, they take a drink to toast their hometown boy. How can they all look so relaxed while my confusion over the contest and my want to connect with him surmount everything?

"Speech. Speech. Speech."

Oh my God. Leave him alone because I want him. I need him.

I don't have to hide it anymore. He's mine.

Rissa holds out the microphone again, and Grayson gives an exaggerated sigh before accepting it.

"You should've won!" I think it's Grady who yells it, but all the patrons echo his sentiment.

"Nah. None of that," Grayson says into the microphone. "Congratulations to all the men who were a part of this contest. It was so nice to be a part of something that paints fatherhood as sexy instead of the down-and-dirty job it can be most of the time." He looks at his feet for a moment and twists his lips in a way that tells me something is on his mind. He looks out into the crowd, and I'm thrown for an even bigger loop when I see him meet my father's eyes and nod. My dad nods back before looking at me, smiling softly, and then stepping back into the crowd like he isn't even here. I don't have time to process his presence or his exchange with Grayson because when Grayson speaks, his words knock all thought process from my mind. "I didn't place in the contest because I pulled myself from it this morning."

"What?" My response is just as loud as the rest of the crowd's.

"Yep." He nods through the ocean of boos. "I did."

"Why would you do that?" another person yells. I think it's one of his crew from work, but I can't tell.

"I did it because there's this girl . . ." he says, and then laughs softly. The sound weaves its way into my body and wraps around my heart. "There's this girl I met, who, uh . . . well, she blindsided me. Point blank. She walked her heels up to my front door a few months back to let me know I was one of the top twenty of this contest, and even though I slammed the door in her face, she persisted."

He looks back at me, and the emotions swimming in his eyes unlock every single part of me that I didn't know was still guarded. He reaches back and takes my hand, linking our fingers together and squeezing gently. It's that gesture that tells me this is going to work.

I just know.

"I dropped out of the contest because I wanted this on my terms. I wanted *her* on my terms. We've tried to pretend like something wasn't going on between us. We denied the ridiculous rumors in the *Gazette*. We did everything we could so no one would think she rigged the contest if I won . . . and even with all that, I went and fell in love with her. *Love.* Scary shit for me . . . but it's true." His nerves are more than adorable as my heart riots against my rib cage. He meets my eyes again. "I love her."

The bar erupts in a symphony of cheers that I don't hear because all that's on repeat in my ears is: *I love her.*

His lips meet mine in the sweetest of ways, warming me all the way to my toes and back up. I'm so lost in the moment, so caught up in Grayson that when he ends the kiss, he's all I see. He's all I know.

"You chose me." His words are barely audible but filled with wonderment as his eyes well with tears before he blinks them away.

I nod. "I chose you."

"I'm sorry it took me so long to see."

"See what?"

"That you're worth the risk, Princess."

If my smile could light up a room, everyone in here would be shielding their eyes from the brightness.

"So are you," I whisper as he lifts our clasped hands to his lips and presses a kiss to the back of my knuckles. And then it hits me. "How did you know?"

"Know what?" The startled look on his face worries me.

"That I was coming back to stay for good. That I told my dad to give the editor-in-chief job at *Haute* to Rissa. That—"

"*You what?*" I'm not sure whose voice rings out the loudest—Rissa's or Grayson's—but they are both chock-full of astonishment.

I turn to Rissa, whose jaw is slack and eyes blink rapidly as if she's trying to comprehend what I just said. "Only if you want it, Riss." I smile. "I'd never uproot your family or take your place unless you wanted to do it . . . but you deserve that position. You deserve to have your chance again."

"You aren't kidding, are you?"

"I wouldn't kid about a thing like this. I told my father that you were the right person for the job, and he agreed. The promotion is yours if you want it."

"Oh my God!" And before I can prepare for it, she launches herself at me and pulls me into a tight hug. "You really did this for me?"

"Yes."

Her gratitude feels better than anything I've felt in the longest of times.

Nah. I take that back. When Rissa steps back and Grayson steps forward, pulls me into his arms, and presses a kiss to my lips, that's the best thing I've felt in the longest of times.

"That was incredible," he murmurs against my lips.

"Not as incredible as getting to wake up next to you every day."

"But you gave up your dream?" His hands never stop framing my face as his eyes search mine. I can see the fear flicker there, the worry that being here won't be enough to keep me. How can he not know that he's all I need?

"You pushed me away. You expected me to leave. I'm here proving to you I intend to stay. I want you to know that dreams can change . . . and this—you, Luke, Sunnyville—is my dream now."

"All of this even before you knew if I had my shit together?"

"Do you have your shit together, Grayson?"

His smile is quick. "Yes."

"Are you sure?"

"Damn sure."

"I have to warn you," I say, giving him a teasing smile and making sure that every ounce of love I feel for him is reflected in my eyes. "I'm not an easy girl to please."

"Oh, I know . . . but I'd rather argue with you any day of the week than kiss someone else."

And there he goes, sweeping me off my feet.

"I guess now's the perfect time to tell you I put an offer on the old Kraft house."

"You what?" His laugh sounds so damn good to my ears that I want to make him do it again.

"I did."

"Cold showers and all?"

"Cold showers and all. Who knew I could live among the little people," I say to give him grief and follow it with a wink.

"I have an even better idea."

"What's that?"

"Move in with me."

"Would we get to play PS4 in your bedroom?"

He throws his head back and laughs, the vibration going from his chest into mine before he meets my eyes again. "God, I love you."

And then he kisses me.

It's sweet. It's sexy. It's nothing I came to Sunnyville looking for, but it's everything I need.

It's everything I ever wanted.

Epilogue

Sidney

"**A**RE YOU FRICKING KIDDING ME?"

"What?" he murmurs quietly. Smart man. He's learned over the past two years and is treading lightly.

I look over at Grayson, who's sitting in the chair across from my desk, with his feet crossed at the ankles and his phone in his hand, and I want to strangle him. Not just strangle him, but him and everyone else in this office. Especially with that blank look on that gorgeous face of his that tells me he has not a care in his world while mine seems to be slowly falling down around me.

"This!" I point to my computer screen and then jab a finger to the office beyond mine. My staff is milling about as if there's nothing wrong when the draft of the next issue of *Modern Family* on my screen says anything but. "We're getting close to the deadline for print, and nothing's right. Not the layout. Not the . . ." I scroll through the pages and growl—yes, growl—in frustration when, in an article about winter break activities for your kids has the word "you" randomly slapped on the page. "This stupid program. Stupid glitches."

I sound like a petulant child, but everything with this issue has gone wrong. Everything. Including the fact that the window at Grayson's back says it's already dark outside and the computer screen in front of me tells me that I'm going to be missing our dinner date, which I'd been looking forward to.

"I take it there's a problem?" His casual demeanor turns stiff. He knows what's coming. He knows I have to cancel and is pissed. He has every right to be upset, and yet, my hands are tied . . . I have to meet my deadline.

"Yeah. A huge one." I glance at the screen again, and the mess that seems to be on every page as I scroll through the issue. "It's like someone took a bunch of crappy clip art and just erratically placed it all over the articles."

Grayson takes his time standing, and it only irks me further. I get he's off for the week. I get it isn't a big deal to him. But, *gah*, this is huge to me. This is what my success is measured on. This is how I keep everyone happy who needs to be happy.

"So, you won't be able to go to dinner, then?"

If looks could kill, the one I'm sending his cute ass right now would land him in the morgue.

"No. I won't," I snap, and the minute the words are out, I hang my head and sigh because I'm being a certifiable bitch and he doesn't deserve it. "Look, I'm sorry. I didn't mean that. I just . . . I'm frustrated is all. I was really looking forward to our date tonight. I mean *really* looking forward to it and . . ."

"And things happen." He shrugs, but I can tell he's not too thrilled with it. "We can always reschedule . . . or I can ask the restaurant to make it to go, and I can either bring it here or we can make our own date at home in the backyard."

I do not deserve this man.

Not in a million years.

"I just need to . . . maybe we can salvage . . ." But I know that we can't.

"What's this issue about?" he asks.

"This is the issue where I let the staff vote on what the theme should be."

"I thought that was a big hit last year."

At least he pays attention. "It was," I say and pinch the bridge of my nose. "Except for this one, they wanted to pick weddings. Winter weddings. Why not winter wonderland activities? Ways to keep the Christmas spirit alive. *But weddings?* We're a family magazine. Not *Bride to Be.*"

"Is that a real magazine?" Grayson asks, looking confused.

I rise from my seat and love that even though I'm stressed to the gills, he can stand here and make me love him and smile all at the same time. "Yes, it's a real magazine. But not this one. Not the one I run."

"So, you have something against marriage?"

"No," I say through a chuckle. I have nothing against marriage, but it's a topic we've never broached. One I never thought he wanted again after everything with Claire.

"If you're not happy with the topic, why did you let them have a choice, then?"

"Because I'm learning . . . and I learned last year that letting them feel like they get to help with the decisions makes them more invested than the times when I make the decisions."

"I always knew you were smart. That's why you love me."

And just like that—with a flash of his smile and a dash of his charm—he can erase my stress.

For a moment.

I lean forward and press a kiss to his lips. Just a hint of everything I love, fully aware that my staff is within viewing distance, before tapping him on the butt.

"Thank you. I love you. But I need you to go before you see me cry tears of frustration that I then take out on you."

His chuckle fills the space, but the squeeze of my hand makes up for it. "We wouldn't want that."

"We wouldn't."

"That would mean no sex when you get home."

"Oh, there was a promise of sex?" I ask, batting my eyelashes coyly.

"Mmm. Mind-blowing sex."

"Better go home and charge the PS4 remotes so Luke thinks we're preparing for an epic battle."

His laugh sounds off and eases a bit more of my tension momentarily. "Does that mean you were planning on screaming my name later?"

I roll my eyes. "You're such a guy."

"Thank God for that." He brushes a kiss to my lips. "You'll get it fixed. It's probably nothing major." Another kiss. "And we'll do epic sex later."

It's my turn to laugh. And then sigh. The last time there was a program glitch like this was my first Harvest Festival back. I think of him here in the office. Taunting me. Seducing me without me even realizing it. And then, of course, my jealousy and assumptions.

The softening in Grayson's eyes tells me he's remembering the same night. The same emotions. The same building block that helped make us what we are today.

"Promise?"

"Promise." He leans in and kisses my cheek. "Good luck."

"Thanks," I say as I take a seat. "I'm going to need it."

And I don't look up again as the door shuts, because I'm already pouring over the layout. The errors. The misplaced words sitting erroneously in the middle of articles, looking almost like a ransom note gone wrong.

Like this one here. It's an article on flowers and arrangements. Haphazardly plopped on top of the article is the word "me." Or this one here about perfect venues, where there is a bold-faced type more than a hundred times larger than the regular font spelling the word "will." And then, of course, there is the image of the gorgeous cover couple all fancied up in their wedding attire in the middle of the vineyard—the shoot we had done that hit every note perfectly—with a comic book type of POW over it, but instead of the word "pow," it says "marry."

So frustrating.

I begin trying to manipulate the program that I've learned inside out over the past year. I click, I refresh, I do everything I know to do and nothing—I mean absolutely nothing—is working.

With my focus on the computer, I reach over and click on the phone intercom. "Jamie?"

No answer.

All of these pages. I line the erred ones up on the screen.

"Jamie?"

Not even a sound.

Wait a minute.

When I look up, the office is dark. The staff is gone. Just the front light is on.

The clock tells me I've been working a while, but for them to leave without saying anything?

Another page I found. The perfect wedding cake and there is a huge question mark covering the tiers of it.

What the hell is going on?

I drag that page over to my desktop as I rise from my seat, suddenly unsettled and a whole lot confused.

"Hello?" I call out as I step back from my desk with one last look at my screen.

And then my heart stops.

And starts.

A laugh escapes my lips as my fingers go up to touch them, and I stare at the screen. In disbelief. In shock. In *holy shit*.

I can't be right. Can I?

The screen. The messed-up pages. When they're all together, I see what they say, but my eyes don't want to believe it to be true.

Will. You. Marry. Me?

My heart pounds as I stare at the screen and then look out to the office beyond. "Grayson?" I walk out of my door, the click of my heels the only sound I hear. "Gray?"

When I turn the corner to the front waiting room, my breath catches as I lock eyes with Grayson. He's standing in the lobby, looking exactly as he had hours ago in my office—shorts, polo shirt—and yet, the man just stole my heart all over again. His eyes are all I see as I stand there, because, in them, I see so many things I never thought possible. So many things I used to scoff at but now want for myself.

Lining the wall behind him are all of the pages I was trying to fix—in poster size—but this time, they are spread out and in the right order. Will you marry me?

"Grayson." Part hope. Part shock. All love.

It's all I have to say to have that nervous smile spreading on his lips. "Want to skip dinner and do this instead?"

Unable to get the words out, I nod emphatically as he takes a step toward me.

"So, there's this girl," he says and chills race over my skin as my heart melts and pulse races.

"And there's this boy . . ."

He nods as his hands find mine, trembling ever so slightly. "There's this girl who walked into my life a few years back, took everything I knew, took everything I thought about what I wanted for my life, and she tossed it upside down." He chuckles, and the shy smile on his lips makes me want to kiss him. "She challenged me in ways I never expected. She told me that she was not a kid person, even though time and again, she stole both my and my son's hearts. She said she hated this small-town life despite walking proudly through it in her high heels and slowly letting them sink into the grass without a single complaint. I told her I was ruined. I accused her of being just like the person that ruined me. I told her never again . . . but nevertheless, she persisted. She wore her way into my heart, into my life, until a day was not complete without her smile, her laugh, the scent of her perfume. You knocked me on my ass, Sidney Thorton . . . knocked me down when I didn't even know you were coming . . . but then you picked me back up. You made me whole. You made me hope. You made me love." His eyes well with tears and mine follow as my pulse thunders in my ears. "And I don't want to spend another day without you knowing that you are the one I want. You are the risk I chose to take. You are the one I choose."

"Grayson." My chest aches from all of the love.

"Will you marry me, Sid?" He lowers himself to one knee, smiling up at me. "Well, me and Luke, but he and your parents and my family and your staff—who helped me frustrate you by choosing this topic—are all waiting for us at Hooligan's to celebrate if you say yes."

My laugh echoes around the empty space. "That's a lot of pressure, Mr. Malone."

"You have no idea." His chuckle is laced with nerves. He produces a ring box with a very delicate infinity band of pale yellow diamonds that is stunningly gorgeous and simple and everything I could have ever asked for. Just like him. "I wouldn't have asked if I didn't know without a doubt that you're the one I've waited for. All the pain, every bit of the heartache led me to you. Led me to fighting against you . . . and then fighting for you. Will you marry me, Sidney?"

I lower myself to my knees as my head nods and my hands reach for his hands and my lips find his lips. "Yes. Yes. A thousand times yes." We kiss. It's soft and delicate and packed full of every emotion I could ever imagine. "On one condition," I say against his lips.

"You're giving me a heart attack here, Thorton."

"No, it's going to be Malone soon. You have to get used to that." Another press of a kiss. "I want to adopt Luke. I want him to be mine, too."

When Grayson leans back and looks into my eyes, there is so much love and shock and surprise in his that it's enough to last me a lifetime. He swallows over the lump in his throat as he nods until he can find his voice. "Deal."

"Whew," I say and laugh. "It was going to be hard to adopt him and not marry you if you had said no."

"I'll never say no to you." Another kiss as he slips the ring onto my finger. "Never."

And so starts our life.

Together.

The three of us.

It was definitely worth the risk.

The End

Did you love meeting Grayson Malone?

If you loved meeting Grayson Malone and would love to meet his brothers, Grant and Grady, you can find them in their own standalone novels. Cuffed (Grant) and Combust (Grady) are out now and each book is a complete standalone. You can find them HERE and HERE

And in November of 2018, you'll learn a little bit more about the ever quirky and equally loved best friend in the Everyday Heroes series, Desi Whitman in *Control*.

Control is something Desi Whitman abhors. Why live life in black and white perfection when you can messily color outside the lines? But when she comes face to face with SWAT officer Reznor Mayne, he's about to show her just how good control can feel.

About the Author

New York Times Bestselling author K. Bromberg writes contemporary novels that contain a mixture of sweet, emotional, a whole lot of sexy, and a little bit of real. She likes to write strong heroines, and damaged heroes who we love to hate but can't help to love.

A mom of three, she plots her novels in between school runs and soccer practices, more often than not with her laptop in tow.

Since publishing her first book on a whim in 2013, Kristy has sold over one and a half million copies of her books across sixteen different countries and has landed on the *New York Times, USA Today,* and *Wall Street Journal* Bestsellers lists over thirty times. Her Driven trilogy (*Driven, Fueled,* and *Crashed*) is currently being adapted for film by Passionflix with the first movie slated to release in 2018.

With her imagination always in overdrive, she is currently scheming, plotting, and swooning over her latest hero. You can find out more about him or chat with Kristy on any of her social media accounts. The easiest way to stay up to date on new releases and upcoming novels is to sign up for her newsletter (http://bit.ly/254MWtI) or text KBromberg to 77948 to receive text alerts when a new book releases.

Connect with K. Bromberg

Website: www.kbromberg.com

Facebook: www.facebook.com/AuthorKBromberg

Instagram: www.instagram.com/kbromberg13

Twitter: www.twitter.com/KBrombergDriven

Goodreads: bit.ly/1koZIkL

Printed in Great Britain
by Amazon